# VANITY

Lucy Lord is a journalist and columnist who has written for *The Times*, *Guardian*, *Independent*, *Evening Standard*, *Time Out* and *Arena*. Her favourite pastimes are reading, writing, lying in hammocks, lunching on beaches and throwing parties. She lives in London with her musician husband.

Also by Lucy Lord

*Party Night (Short Story)*
*Revelry*

LUCY LORD

*Vanity*

HARPER

*Harper*
An imprint of HarperCollins*Publishers*
77–85 Fulham Palace Road,
Hammersmith, London W6 8JB

www.harpercollins.co.uk

A Paperback Original 2013
1

A catalogue record for this book
is available from the British Library

ISBN: 9780007441747

Set in Meridien by Palimpsest Book Production Limited,
Falkirk, Stirlingshire

Printed and bound in Great Britain by
Clays Ltd, St Ives plc

*To my wonderful parents, Elizabeth and Christopher,*
*with all my love.*

# PART 1

# Chapter 1

'Bollocks,' said the blushing bride, scrutinizing her crotch through her wedding dress in the floor-to-ceiling mirror. 'It's too see-through in daylight, isn't it? I'm going to have to wear those bloody remedial granny pants.'

The pants in question were an exorbitantly expensive pair of sheer nude silk Myla boy shorts, hardly the passion-killing girdle the comment implied. But Poppy Wallace had set her heart on going commando on her Big Day.

'Never mind,' said her best friend Bella, topping up their glasses with Veuve Clicquot. 'Damian can rip them off with his teeth later.'

They both looked at Poppy's reflection. Transparency problem aside, she looked more beautiful than Bella had ever seen her, and that was saying something. The sheer white cotton voile dress, suspended from spaghetti straps and embroidered with daisies at the hem and strategically across what there was of her chest, skimmed her tiny body and floated to her delicate ankles. Her streaky white/

3

gold hair flowed loose, halfway down her bare brown back, crowned with a sweet-smelling garland of white and yellow spring flowers. Her only jewellery was her vintage diamond-and-emerald engagement ring and an anklet fashioned out of silver daisies. She was barefoot, and her lovely little face, all wide green eyes, small nose and perfect teeth, was glowing.

Bella's eyes filled with tears.

'Oh, Pops, you look gorgeous. Can I hug you without ruining anything?'

'Course you can, you silly arse. Come here.' She flung her little arms around Bella. When she released her, Bella could see that her eyes were suspiciously shiny too. Poppy only cried on the rarest of occasions (unlike Bella, who found herself gently weeping like George Harrison's guitar with embarrassing frequency now she was in her thirties. Sad news stories, soppy song lyrics, old episodes of *Friends* she'd seen a million times before – it didn't take a lot these days).

'If it wasn't for you, Belles, I wouldn't be standing here today. So thanks, lovely. For everything.'

They downed their champagne and Poppy added, 'Looking pretty gorgeous yourself, if I may congratulate myself on my exquisite taste. In friends *and* clothes.'

'Such a pretty dress.' Bella dabbed at her eyes with her fingers, then licked them, trying not to get any watery black residue on her cotton voile halterneck bridesmaid's frock (she'd predictably forgotten to pack waterproof mascara). She and Poppy had spent ages choosing the exact shade of coral pink that most flattered Bella's dark hair and eyes.

'Thanks for not putting me in lilac frills.'

'It was touch and go, especially when you kept going on about having my hen do at School Disco.'

They both laughed.

'Shit, look at the time!' said Bella. It wasn't hard to miss, a fluorescent LCD display projected against one of the whitewashed walls of the ultra-glamorous, ultra-modern villa. 'Take one last look at yourself as a single woman, babe. No last-minute regrets?'

Poppy shook her golden head. 'No last-minute regrets.' They both looked at her reflection again, different memories racing through each of their minds.

'Let's go then. But you'd better put your knickers on first.'

Mark looked around the crowded beach and smiled broadly. What a way to get hitched, man. Playa des'Estanyol, a little sandy cove halfway up the east coast of Ibiza, was a bugger to get to, located at the bottom of a long and bumpy pine-tree-shaded track, but that hadn't fazed Mark. He'd relished bombing down in his hired jeep, sending up clouds of white dust, fucking up the tyres and making his girlfriend Sam squeal. And even his unromantic heart had thrilled at the beauty of the beach, nestled into warm yellow rocks and backed by the lush green forest. The scent of pine groves mingled with the sea air, and clear tourmaline water lapped the pale shore. Further out, where the ocean changed to navy, pristine white sails breezed across the horizon.

Nudists habitually basked on the rocks and in the crystal waters at the southernmost end of the beach, but today they'd kept away out of deference to the nuptials.

Spoilsports. In Mark's experience, the more a nudist wanted to flaunt their bits in your face, the older and saggier they were (Scandinavians aside), but sometimes a young chick with a hot bod slipped through the net and he wasn't above a sneaky peek. Still, it was early season, only May, and, although it was a beautiful day, in the high 20s already, the sea was probably still cold enough to freeze your nuts off.

Arctic camouflage material fluttered above the stone-clad bar/restaurant area, giving a dappled shade to the tables that had been laid for the wedding feast. Sam had said it looked like crochet from a distance. Now she was ordering a drink at the bar, possibly unaware of the fact that every male eye on the beach was currently feasting on her.

That's my girl, thought Mark proudly, taking in her pretty little body in its short yellow dress, huge knockers threatening to burst through the thin floral fabric. Her long, straightened, henna-red hair was caught by the breeze as she noticed him watching her. A genuine smile lit up her sweet young face and she waved, tottering over the sand on foolish heels. Mark could have fucked her right there, in front of everybody.

'Isn't this wicked?' she breathed in her husky voice as she reached him. 'I can't wait to see Poppy's dress. And Bella's. I bet Poppy's got her something really nice to wear – they're such good mates. Not like when Karen made me wear puke-green satin.' She made a face to illustrate and Mark laughed.

'You'd look gorgeous in anything, babe.'

Much as Mark couldn't believe his luck about Sam, he had long harboured threesome fantasies about Poppy and

6

Bella: Poppy so fair, Bella so dark, both of them so fit. And he'd nearly had his wicked way with Bella a couple of times last year. But that was before she got together with Andy. And before he met Sam, of course.

Damian was doing the rounds, sweating slightly in his cream linen suit. He'd be glad when he could take the bloody jacket off. It was great seeing all their friends and family gathered on the beautiful beach, the result of months of excited planning. The planning had been amazing, without doubt the best nine months of his life. He'd nearly lost Poppy last year, in more ways than one, and the joy he'd felt when she'd surprised him with a proposal had been overwhelming. Relief had turned to magical excitement as they planned every last detail of what they hoped would be the best day of their lives, and he'd never felt closer to anyone. But by God was he nervous now. He was almost 100 per cent sure he was doing the right thing.

'Not getting cold feet are you, darling?' asked Simon, his best man and fellow journalist on the men's style magazine *Stadium*. 'Here, have some of this.' He passed him his drink, an ice-cold White Russian.

'Thanks, mate.' Damian took a swig. 'And no, I'm not. Well – maybe a bit.' He laughed. 'But only stage fright, not the till-death-us-do-part bit, I'm absolutely convinced about that.' He looked at Simon through his wraparound rock-star shades, fully aware of what most of his friends had made of Poppy's behaviour the previous year. 'And I'm bloody hot in this suit.'

'*Il faut souffrir être beau.*' Simon's affected campery could be misleading sometimes. 'Anyway, you're lookin' mighty fine, dude.' And Damian was. The cream linen set off his half-Indian, half-Welsh complexion beautifully, and the sharp cut emphasized his lean build. The shades, which he planned to take off during the ceremony, concealed soulful dark eyes that slanted down at the corners.

'But maybe you should have taken a leaf out of that couple's book.' Simon was now laughing in the direction of an ageing pair of ravers in matching purple sarongs. The man was bare-chested, the woman improbably pert-breasted in a gold-and-lilac paisley bandeau bikini top. They were boogying barefoot in the sand to Moby, half pissed already by the look of it.

'That's Bella's dad and his latest,' said Damian, laughing too now and waving over at them. 'Hey, Justin, hey, Jilly.' They waved back, blowing kisses.

'You don't mind them not making more of an effort?' Simon was very conscious of his own and others' sartorial standards. Today he was impeccably dressed in a white open-necked shirt under a similar suit to Damian's (only in a muted *café au lait* shade, so as not to upstage the groom).

'Why do you think we're getting married on a beach, you twat?'

He just wished Poppy would hurry up so they could get this over with.

Natalia Evanovitch sipped her Cristal and surveyed the scene coolly from her hillside vantage spot. She would descend in her own time. She had only known Poppy and Damian since they'd been engaged, and in that time she had grown very fond of them; they were a good-looking, intelligent, fun-loving couple who were a great addition to her little black book. Hence the generous offer of her extraordinarily glamorous clifftop villa as both the reception after-party venue and somewhere for the wedding party to stay for the week.

Natalia was seriously loaded. As she looked down at the hipsters milling around the beach in their Alice Temperley frocks and designer shades, she reflected on the contrast between her new sunny, carefree world and her cold, dark past in Kiev. And they say that money cannot buy you happiness, she thought scornfully. *Ерунда!*

But if it wasn't for her past, the money almost certainly wouldn't exist. For a moment she gazed out over the sea, lost in thought. With an effort she snapped herself out of it. Across the pass, the wedding jeep was making its juddering way down the hill. Natalia adjusted her multicoloured silk minidress, checked her smooth platinum-blonde ponytail in the rear-view window of her state-of-the-art silver Ferrari and made a leisurely descent to the beach.

Justin and Jilly were having a whale of a time. They'd been nearly the oldest swingers in town at Pacha last night and snorted much of Colombia's finest. The Viagra-assisted screwing had lasted till dawn, so they'd only had around three hours' sleep.

She's not bad for an old bird, thought Justin, checking out Jilly's childless flat stomach and lifted tits. Even though he was at least ten years older than her, he was used to much younger totty, and his forty-five-odd years of experience as a fashion photographer generally guaranteed him access to it. But he was still smarting from the hideous events of the previous year. A young model he'd screwed had accused him of rape after he'd failed to get her picture on the cover of Italian *Vogue*. Justin's moral boundaries were pretty vague, but rape? No way, José. He'd assumed she fancied him; he was still pretty buff, if he did say so himself. He thought he'd taken her to heaven and back.

So, for the time being, Jilly was as good a compromise as any. She wasn't what you'd call a babe (too old), or a beauty, like his ex-wife Olivia (also too old, but her eyes made up for it), but she was fun, with a body that could pass for a much younger one if he closed his eyes. Which he found himself doing with increasing frequency.

'Another tequila, you naughty old wretch?' Jilly brandished the bottle she'd hidden in her purple, suede-tasselled handbag.

'Thanks, angel tits.' Justin took a hearty swig then belched slightly. Heartburn. How the fuck did Ronnie Wood do it?

'Justin! Jilly!'

They both looked around guiltily.

Olivia regarded them with affectionate amusement. Some things never changed, and by God was she glad she wasn't married to the silly old 'See You Next Tuesday' any more. She and Jilly were good friends, and knowing Jilly's disastrous track record she thought the stupid buggers probably deserved one another. Olivia was looking beautiful in one of her Ossie Clark original maxidresses. Her chocolate-brown hair was piled into a messy up-do, her expressive dark eyes lined with kohl. The resemblance to her daughter Bella was startling.

'Isn't this absolutely beautiful?' she said to Jilly, ignoring Justin, who was trying to hide the tequila bottle down the front of his sarong. 'I must say I think we're honoured to be invited. As far as I can make out, the only other aged Ps belong to the bride and groom.'

'We *are* parents of the bridesmaid, Liv,' said Justin pompously, giving up with the tequila bottle and chucking it on the sand. He started rolling a spliff. 'And we've known Poppy since she was a little girl. She must have been about . . . seven?' After the excesses of the years, details could get a little hazy.

'Ah, yes, I remember it well,' said Olivia drily. 'Bella first brought her home from school when they were both ten. God, they were sweet.' Always maternal, she smiled fondly at the memory of the two little girls in bunches and ankle socks, holding hands.

'Here's your vino, Princess.' A gargantuan man in a lurid tropical-print shirt appeared at the edge of the group and thrust a glass of white wine into Olivia's slender hand. His own fingers were fat and bedecked with signet rings.

'Thanks, Bernie, darling.' Olivia smiled at him.

'Bernie, mate!' Justin was effusive in his greeting, even though the four of them had lunched together at Las Salinas beach only the previous day. He had a lot of time for his ex-wife's partner (horrible word, but what else could he call him? Boyfriend was ridiculous, at their age, and he drew the line at lover when talking about his ex-wife).

'Fancy a toke on this?'

'Not my bag, me old china, but cheers anyway.' Bernie's beady little eyes were as amused as Olivia's large brown ones. 'So did you two find anywhere to carry on partying last night?'

'On this island? With this body?' Jilly thrust her hips in

a manner that even Justin found faintly embarrassing and hard to respond to.

'Pacha,' he said quickly. And because he was a nice man, despite everything, added, 'You were the most gorgeous babe in there. Just check out those abs!'

'Oh, do shut up, you ridiculous old man. They're coming! Don't you want to see our daughter in her moment of glory?' Olivia put a finger to her lips with one hand and smacked her ex-husband's wrist with the other.

They watched in silence as Poppy floated down the beach on her mother's arm, Bella a few paces behind. An aisle leading down to the water's edge had been fashioned out of terracotta tubs of miniature orange trees, in full bridal blossom. Damian, now without his shades, was waiting where the sea lapped the shore. Even from where they were standing near the bar, Olivia could see how nervous he was.

'Doesn't our little girl look beautiful?' said Justin, wondering if he really could make out Poppy's nipples underneath the embroidery on her dress.

'You may now kiss the bride,' said the be-garlanded, white-suited registrar. '*Un beso, por favor!*'

Damian clasped Poppy to his linen breast and Bella felt her eyes misting up again at the sight of them, so perfect against the gradated blue of the horizon. She looked around for her boyfriend, Andy, who smiled at her. She smiled back. He looked very handsome and very tall in an olive-green linen jacket over faded Levis. The bright spring sunshine bounced off his oblong specs, which (by luck, rather than design; Andy was not a vain man) emphasized high cheekbones and a strong jaw.

'I declare this sea well and truly open!' shouted Poppy, chucking her bouquet over her shoulder and dragging Damian into the water with her. Bella ran to catch the bouquet but just missed it. She picked it up, trying to shake the sand off the pretty yellow and white flowers, and turned to see Andy looking at her again. He wasn't smiling now. She ran over, slightly embarrassed.

'Think I'd better ask them to put these lovely flowers in some water.'

Andy nodded. Bella knew he was wary of marriage, but he needn't be quite so fucking obvious about it.

Soon everybody was dancing in the sea to Groove Armada – singing about sand dunes and salty air – some more careless of their costly garb than others.

Mark had been right about the temperature of the sea, but the mood was infectious and it was ages before they all sat down to lunch.

The meal was typically Ibicenco and utterly delicious. Local ham with rustic bread, aïoli and olives, followed by huge paellas bursting with fresh seafood, peppers, rabbit and chorizo, served from big, hot pans at the tables. Bella squeezed a wedge of lemon over her steaming rice and wiped her fingers on a linen napkin.

She was sitting in the dappled shade of the Arctic camouflage net with Andy, Simon, Natalia, Mark and Sam. The bride and groom were sharing a table with Damian's parents and Poppy's mother. Poppy had been heartbroken that her father, in the advanced stages of Alzheimer's, was too ill to be at her wedding – whether it had been held in the UK or not. He wasn't even aware she was getting married,

13

poor old love, despite the happy couple's repeated and increasingly desolate announcements, complete with ring flashing, at his care home.

The two hundred-odd guests sounded pretty happy with their lot as decibel levels rose with the rosé consumption. At the next table, Bella's mother, father, Bernie and Jilly were already on their fourth bottle.

'What a lovely day,' she said, full of tipsy sunshiny happiness. 'I just knew Poppy would get it right.'

'I think she had a lot of help from her devoted friend, no?' said Natalia, turning her slanting grey-blue gaze on Bella. The diamonds in her ears and scraped-back hair emphasized the height and acute angle of her cheekbones.

'I guess so.' Bella grinned, recalling the hours she and Poppy had spent poring over fabric swatches, menus and playlists. 'But I enjoyed every minute of it.' She glanced over at the bridal table.

Poppy was throwing her head back in peals of laughter at something Damian had just said. Bella was so happy they were back together. This time for real. Last year, she'd caught Poppy in flagrante with Ben Jones, Bella's then boyfriend, an up-and-coming actor. At the time, Bella had hated them both with every fibre of her being, and, were she honest, wished them both dead. But Ben went on to cheat on Poppy, who subsequently OD'd on a cocktail of drugs, both recreational and prescription. Despite the Balearic sun, Bella went cold as she recalled finding Poppy unconscious in her flat, surrounded by narcotic parapher-nalia. Thank God she'd found her when she had.

Everything's worked out for the best, she thought

contentedly, gulping back her delicious chilled rosé and turning her face up to the sun. She was happier with Andy than she'd ever been in her life. Eight months on, she was still waking every day with an idiotic grin on her face.

Impulsively she leant over and kissed him on the cheek.

'What was that for?' He smiled at her.

'Nothing really. Just thinking how happy I am that everything's worked out like it has.'

With the *crema catalana* came balloon glasses half filled with ice and *hierbas*, the potent local hooch made, as its name might suggest, from mountain herbs.

'So how are things in the men's magazine world?' Andy asked Mark and Simon, who worked alongside Damian on *Stadium*, the men's 'style' magazine that liked to think it had more substance than the rest. Simon and Damian were columnists, which involved churning out variations on a superiorly misogynist theme, month after month. Mark was the art director, which gave him so much opportunity to ogle naked female flesh you'd think (erroneously) that he could take it or leave it by now.

Andy's career – he was an investigative reporter for one of the better respected broadsheets – earned him grudging respect from Simon and slight resentment from Damian, who had always harboured ambitions in that direction himself. Still, as Simon said, the perks and parties at *Stadium* more than made up for a little professional jealousy. Or at least they used to.

'Not great, to be honest,' said Simon. 'It's a bloody drag. Sales have been hit badly by the recession. The downmarket rags – *Nuts* and *Zoo* and now *Front*; did they really need another one? How many boobs does the Great British Public need? – are cornering the market.'

Bella nudged Andy. *Stadium* was not exactly what you'd call a boob-free zone, though the boobs it showcased tended, with the odd honourable exception, to be smaller. Classier, you see.

'Well that whole bespoke ethos is a bit anachronistic at the moment, isn't it?' said Sam, one of the honourable exceptions, in her husky voice, earning a look of surprise from Simon. 'You should see your face! I'm not that thick, you know, and I've been reading *Stadium* cover-to-cover ever since I first appeared in it. I like to keep up on Marky's job.'

Sam had taken up glamour modelling to pay her way through London University, where she was studying philosophy and psychology. She and Mark had met on a shoot. Fond though Bella was of Mark, she reckoned Sam was streets ahead of him intellectually. But she was young and easily impressed and Mark was seriously sexy, in a brawny, doltish sort of way. Today he was wearing tight white jeans and a scarlet racer-back vest top, revealing rippling biceps, triceps, pecs and lats in all their worked-out glory. To say nothing of the vast packet. His head was shaved, his smile crooked. When Bella first met him (long before she experienced the full – ahem – thrust of his lust), she'd had her doubts as to whether he was Arthur or Martha.

As if to prove the point, he laughed and kissed Sam way more explicitly than manners dictated, groping her left tit and shoving his tongue down her throat. Bella remembered what it was like kissing him and reached for Andy's hand, flushing suddenly.

16

'Ugh, get a rrrrrooooom, please,' said Natalia, shuddering. Sam pulled away from Mark and laughed.

'Sorry,' she said. 'He does get carried away sometimes. Anyway, where were we? Oh, yes, surely all that handmade suit and expensive trainers stuff just doesn't cut it when people can't even pay their mortgages?'

'It's aspirational luxury though.' Simon stuck stubbornly to his guns. 'People need things to cheer them up when times are tough. Just look at the Busby Berkeley movies of the thirties.'

'Are you comparing *Stadium* to Busby Berkeley movies?' Bella laughed. 'Not sure what your emphatically *not gay* metrosexual readership would make of that.'

Simon laughed too. 'Oh, I don't know. It's too depressing to discuss on such a lovely day, anyway. Are you working on anything interesting at the moment, Andy?'

'Interesting, yes, but not what you'd call uplifting.' He smiled briefly at Simon and squeezed Bella's hand, trying to reassure her.

'Try me,' said Simon.

'Do you remember that piece I did on the Albanian people-traffickers last year?' As Simon nodded, Andy muttered, 'People-traffickers . . . fucking euphemism for what these animals do . . . Anyway, one of them has tipped me off about another, bigger gang, which controls half the underage brothels in London.'

'Wow,' said Simon. 'That's heavy stuff. Why didn't he go to the police though?'

'He's seriously scared of the retributions if it got back to the big boss, who has his spies, even within the police force. He seems to think he can trust me though.' Andy's clever eyes were serious behind their glasses. 'I suppose he can. Even though I still think he's lower than scum, if we get this lot, hundreds of girls might be saved.'

'Eees the big gang Russian?' asked Natalia, who was watching and listening intently.

Andy smiled at her apologetically. ''Fraid so.'

'I really wish you could investigate slightly less horrible and dangerous people,' said Bella, trying to keep her tone light, though the thought of her beloved Andy in danger was tearing her guts to shreds. 'Or start working for a tabloid, where the extent of your investigative journalism would be rummaging through minor celebs' dustbins, or even a spot of phone hacking . . .'

Andy laughed and kissed her on the forehead.

'Don't worry about me, my love. You know I'm always careful.'

# Chapter 2

The newlyweds stood at the edge of the cliff, looking over at the lights in the Old Town.

'Shall we just fuck off to Space and get off our tits instead?' asked Damian. The after-party was raging colourfully behind them. He was sure he could hear Bella's dad shouting something inappropriate.

'And leave behind the people we love, who've come a long way to be with us, to meet a whole load of strangers we don't, and who haven't?' Poppy laughed and kissed him on the nose, standing on tiptoes to reach.

'I know, I know, it's just . . . if we were with a whole load of strangers, it would feel like it was just us, alone, amongst – well, strangers . . . But now we're with people who know everything about us, and I want to feel alone with you, Mrs Evans-Wallace.' He started to kiss her so hard that they both fell onto the scrubby grass, inches away from the cliff-face.

'Well, Mr Wallace-Evans . . .' Poppy panted, fumbling

at the crotch of his linen trousers, 'I don't know about you, but I think we're pretty alone here.'

She started licking the top of his cock, and as he moaned, she murmured, 'Move away from the edge you silly sod, I don't want to be widowed on my wedding night.'

They both laughed and rolled backwards together away from the edge. Poppy started licking his cock again and he moaned some more, then stopped. He gently pulled her head back by her silky long blonde hair.

'What's wrong?' Nobody turned down Poppy's blowjobs, let alone her husband on their wedding night.

Damian pulled her up so they were eye to eye.

'Nothing's wrong, my dearest Poppydoodle. I just don't want to consummate our marriage like this. I want to be inside you, like . . .'

'Like this?' Poppy grinned wickedly and, in an impressive display of agility, manoeuvred herself on top of him, pulling her flimsy wedding dress up and equally flimsy Myla boy shorts to one side. Soon she was groaning too, biting her lip to stop shouting so loudly they'd be heard by all the guests. Just as she was about to come, Damian withdrew, threw her over, whipped the pants off altogether, then lunged back into her with such force she thought she might explode. Then she did cry out, but he shoved his hand over her mouth.

'Shhhh, Mrs Evans-Wallace. You're all mine now.'

As Poppy came to her senses she grinned again. 'Well, Mr Wallace-Evans, if this is what being married is all about, I think I could get used to it. Shall we gaze up at the stars like lovestruck teenagers for a bit now?'

Damian smiled and kissed her again but she pulled away

and forced him to look at the stellar landscape above their heads. 'I always thought that Ursa Minor sounded like a poor little boy being bullied by someone like Flashman at a horrible Victorian public school . . .'

The villa was like nothing Sam had ever seen in her life. The vast, modernist, starkly white edifice seemed to grow organically from the hillside. How could that be possible? How could something potentially so incongruous, definitely so gratuitous, look so at one with the landscape? Sam, who'd read up on Ibiza thoroughly before coming to the wedding, assumed it was because the lines followed those of the hill and that the white building, while modelled on a far larger and more glamorous scale than those traditional cuboid cottages, kept the Ibicenco essence.

There had to be at least five levels of asymmetrical terraces, all of which were occupied with Poppy and Damian's guests, whose laughter and chatter filled the air. Or perhaps not quite filled, thought Sam, ever precise. She'd surprised and delighted her parents by getting 12 A*s at GCSE and 4 A*s – Maths, Biology, Chemistry and English – at A Level. She'd always been clever, but her mum and dad worked so hard keeping their small catering business afloat there had never been a huge amount of time for things like parents' evenings and helping her with her homework. And looking after her little brother Ryan was a full-time job in itself, of course.

The reason the guests' chatter and laughter didn't quite fill the air was the insistent hum of cicadas that served as constant background noise, and the deep thudding bass line of some classic house that emanated from whichever balcony one of the island's numerous obnoxious DJs was playing. Every other plant, from pines to palms and bougainvillea, was lit up with fairy lights, and candles in jewel-hued Moroccan glasses illuminated every path.

It was all breathtaking, but what really made it, in Sam's eyes at least, was the pool. It actually went all the way around the house, like an enormous turquoise moat, with waterfalls gushing down in stages from the back, where it was higher up the hill – and according to Bella, the coolest place to escape the fierce midday heat. At the front, the infinity pool seemed to stretch right to the edge of the cliff. Sam, who'd come up from the beach with the others after dark, imagined that in daylight it would be difficult to know where the pool stopped and the sky or sea began. In the middle of the pool was an island with a bar on it, and three palm trees, now silhouetted gracefully against the horizon.

The view, even at night-time, was phenomenal. Bella had told her you could see Formentera from here too. She was looking forward to taking the ferry to Formentera with Mark. She'd read that the water was unbelievable there and that there were loads of nudists. She was happy baring her body, as she'd done it for the cameras enough times, and thought it would be really sexy to be skinny-dipping with her gorgeous hunk in the beautiful sea. She felt happiest with him when they were both naked – that was when she knew he loved her. Even though she thought she was probably as clever as he was, he and his friends seemed so sophisticated that she always felt a bit out of her depth in their company.

His friends at lunch today had been lovely, of course.

Bella had always been particularly kind to her, and even that weird Natalia didn't treat her like some kind of tart.

But loads of the guests today, just like other friends Mark had introduced her to, looked her up and down in two very distinct, and very obvious ways. The blokes looked as if they just wanted to shag her, and she could deal with that, really, because blokes had wanted to shag her ever since she hit puberty. What peed her off was the way they nudged Marky and came out with their not-so-subtle innuendos, just as if, because she had big tits, she wouldn't understand a bloody word they said.

It was the women who were the worst though. Sam was savvy enough to realize that women in their thirties felt a bit threatened by her young, nubile body, but all she wanted to do was scream at them, 'I don't want your bloody boyfriends! If it wasn't for Marky, I wouldn't be here anyway and he's more than enough for me.' But she just had to smile politely at their bitchy comments and get the odd bit of satisfaction at their looks of surprise when Mark boasted about her philosophy and psychology studies. Though one particularly hatchet-faced old bag did mutter something about 'dumbed-down Britain' and 'of course, *everybody* has a degree these days.'

She wished Mark would hurry up with her drink. Three blokes had already tried to get her into the pool, saying she'd win any wet T-shirt contest going, and she felt a bit of a pillock, really, standing around on her own in her uncomfortable glittery platforms.

Andy and Bella were floating on blow-up armchairs towards the infinity edge of the pool, which was so brightly lit that the people swimming naked underneath could be seen in all their glory. Sadly for Bella, her father was one of them, but she'd seen it all before; for as long as she could remember, he'd been partial to swimming and sunbathing in the altogether.

'Daddy, can't you put your willy away?'

'What's that, sweetheart? Sorry, water in my ears, can't hear you.' And he went back down to ogle a bit more.

'Don't worry about him, darling,' drawled Jilly from the bar on the island, wiping white powder from her nose. 'He'll never change.'

'But it's so rude to you, Jilly. He makes me so cross – why do you put up with it?'

'Your father is what he is, sweetheart. We have a damn good giggle, he's kind to me, unlike some of the arseholes I've known, and he's never promised me anything. Besides, Jorge here is far more handsome, don't you think?' She guffawed and, as Bella refocused her eyes, she realized that Jilly was fondling the barman's tanned and muscular naked buttocks. All the barmen were wearing g-strings and little white aprons.

Natalia, who was perched on one of the island's white linen upholstered bar stools, long legs elegantly crossed, winked at Bella. She had changed out of her Pucci minidress into a Schiaparelli pink high-cut swimsuit and a crystal-embossed, rainbow-hued sarong.

'You want some naughty dust?'

Finding Poppy nearly dead from a cocktail of coke, ecstasy, Temazepam and vodka last year had put something of a dampener on Bella's enthusiasm for the hard stuff.

But in such a ridiculously bacchanalian setting, who could say no, really?

'Yes, please.' She suddenly sounded embarrassingly jolly-hockey-sticks, as though Joyce Grenfell had been her favourite teacher at Malory Towers or St Clare's. She looked at Andy. 'Darling?'

'Well, I have never been in a pool with an island and a bar before, so I think, yes, please, too!'

Taking advantage of one of her beloved's rare moments of frivolity, Bella manoeuvred her floating armchair towards his to kiss him. As she reached out she accidentally launched herself into the water, knocking Andy out of his chair too. They were both laughing as they re-emerged and hauled themselves up onto the island.

'What an amazing place you have here, Natalia,' said Andy, handing her back the silver-plated coke straw. She put it onto the mirrored bar top, next to the absurdly over-the-top silver coke urn, and Andy went to the edge of the island to look out at the view, shaking the water out of his short black hair.

'Yes, it's just fabulous,' said Bella, following his lovely tall body with her eyes. He wasn't excessively muscular (Andy had far more important things to do than waste time in the gym), but he still made her weak at the knees with his long legs and broad shoulders. All at one with the world, she tried to focus on the view too. 'Isn't that Formentera over there?' She pointed in the direction of the Old Town.

'No, no, sweet Bella, that is Old Eivissa,' said Natalia.

'Bugger, I've never been any good at directions.' Bella

laughed. 'But this really is out of this world, and it's so great of you to do this for Poppy and Damian.'

Natalia waved her bejewelled hands around impatiently.

'Pouf, I haf money and small villa! What use is it for me on my own?' Then she looked at Bella curiously. 'Anyway, do you not think it is great for *you* to do this for Poppy?'

'What?' For a moment, Bella hadn't a clue what she was on about. 'Oh, you mean the Ben stuff. Well, he was an absolute wanker anyway, and I'm happy with Andy now, so . . .'

'So . . .' Natalia patted her on the shoulder. 'You are a good and strong woman, like my old *mamushka*.' She looked sad, and Bella was torn between sympathy, curiosity and an unedifying desire to be compared to something more glamorous.

Mark, Sam and a load of people she didn't know, but who all seemed to know Marky, were lounging in Natalia's rainbow chill-out room, which wasn't as awful as it sounded. An enormous, circular area, half open to the sea a long way beneath, with every bit of floor covered in cushions of all colours, fabrics and sizes, at least three layers deep, it gave new meaning to the concept of chilling out.

The only pieces of furniture were several low white stone tables, essential for the balancing of ashtrays and glasses. The expanse of semi-circular whitewashed wall was hung with around fifteen vividly coloured, apparently abstract paintings. Once you got closer, you could see that they were more impressionist than abstract, all depicting the same view at different times of day, night and year.

Individually, each painting would have been nice to have on your wall, thought Sam, but all bunched together like this they were incredible.

'Bella really got lucky when she met old Nat.' Mark laughed, drawing on a badly rolled spliff.

'Don't be nasty, Marky!' said Sam, then snuggled up to him again, not wanting to put him off her. 'Bella's a brilliant artist.'

'Oh, I know she is, babe. Who's the one who keeps giving her freelance illustration work?' Mark puffed up his huge chest and pointed at it, making Sam giggle.

'I asked you a question, babe! Who?' He started tickling her and, even though she thought she might die from lust, she eventually managed,

'You are, Marky!'

He kissed her, using his tongue.

'That's better. Remember who's boss around here, gorgeous.' He took another draw on the spliff. 'But you gotta admit Bella's fucking lucky – finding someone as cunting loaded as Natalia, who's fucking obsessed with mad colours, to buy them all at her first exhibition? That's what I call bollock-busting luck.'

'Are you talking about my daughter?' asked an amused and very posh voice.

Mark looked over lazily in the direction of a beautiful older woman whose kaftan suited the surroundings so much he thought she'd be just perfect for a *Stadium* shoot, if they ever had a granny-fanciers' edition.

'Oh, hi, Olivia. Yeah, just saying how great for Belles that old Nat bought all her paintings.'

'Yes, that was certainly a lucky break. Well, I just came

in to see how they looked in here, and I must say I think Natalia's done her proud.'

'Hi,' said Sam. 'I'm Sam.'

'Oh, how lovely, Bella's told me all about you. I'm Olivia,' said Olivia, extending an elegant hand. 'Do you mind if I join you?'

Sam got up and fussed around with some cushions, trying to make it comfortable for her, but Olivia brushed her off.

'Thank you, darling, but don't be silly. It's absolutely fine as it is.' And she sat down, cross-legged in her kaftan, opposite them. Catching sight of the spliff burning itself out in the ashtray, she added, 'You young things nowadays seem to have no idea how to roll joints. Give that to me, please – I can hardly bear to look at it.'

Momentarily terrified with dope fear, Mark passed Olivia the ashtray.

'D'you have any more skins?' she asked, and he reached into his pocket for a packet of Rizlas. Deftly, she tapped off the burning end and tore the silly thing open.

'That's better, isn't it?' She beamed around at them, having re-rolled a perfect, tight little spliff with her right hand. Her left was holding a large glass of white wine. 'I do hate waste.'

'Bugger me, where'd you learn to do that?' Mark laughed.

'I was a teenager in the sixties, darling, was married to Justin Brown, and spent an awful lot of the seventies in Morocco. May I?'

Mark nodded and she lit it and toked, inhaling deeply.

'Gosh, that really makes Bella's colours look cool,' she

said, gazing at her daughter's paintings on the wall, and Mark and Sam both laughed.

'Sam, darling, you're awfully pretty. Oh, of course, you're the one who dabbles in modelling. I did that donkey's years ago, though I was slimmer then . . .'

'You're still beautiful,' said Mark and Sam simultaneously, and Olivia laughed.

'Past my prime, I'm afraid.' She turned her hypnotic gaze on Sam again. 'I imagine modelling's very different these days. We used to make up our own faces, and sometimes we even wore our own clothes, you know.'

'Yes, I've heard about that,' said Sam, wondering exactly how much Bella had told her mum about the nature of her modelling, and trying to ignore the smirk on Marky's face.

'I don't have any of that old shit,' said Big Sean, the obnoxious DJ that Poppy had poached from Pacha for a small fortune, rolling his eyes. As he was about five foot seven, the name was presumably meant to be ironic – unless his Napoleon complex was seriously out of control.

'Find it then. It's my wedding and I'm paying you enough,' Poppy said steelily. 'And I'd like you to dedicate it to Natalia. If that's not *too* much trouble.' The little cunt looked as if he wanted to throw himself off the cliff, then looked once more at the opulence of the villa and Poppy's intransigence and took out his BlackBerry.

'José, mate, I'm dealin' with people who want old shit.'

He rolled his eyes again and Poppy whispered to Bella,

'Once he's played the music for Natalia, we can all chuck him in, fucking CrackBerry and all.'

Bella giggled and jumped back into the pool, feeling as wonderfully mad as good mad can feel. Poppy joined her and they swam over to the island for another line. The entire party was rocking now, the best (or worst) of London's media twats splashing about in the water, smoking dope in hammocks or just ecstatic at the sounds of their own voices as they pontificated. Poppy worked in TV production, Damian in the men's magazine world; it was hardly surprising that a large proportion of the guest list was very pleased with itself indeed. Most of them had started believing their own publicity years ago.

'Oh, Pops, I love you.' The girls exchanged soggy and effusive hugs on the island. 'HAPPY WEDDING!'

'Yay! Happy my wedding too!' Poppy lay back on the deck in her virginal white bikini and said, with all the seriousness that a drunk and coked-up bride could muster, 'But also, babes, I'm so happy you're so happy with Andy. He's a wonderful man.'

'Yes, he is,' said Bella dreamily. Then she laughed. 'Just listen to us. It's your wedding. Damian's a wonderful man too, and I've never seen you look so beautiful.'

Poppy shrugged it off, as only somebody who's been told she's beautiful every day of her life can.

'No, Andy's better.'

'No, Damian's better.'

'Andy's better.'

'Damian's better.'

'Andy!'

'Damian!'

And on and on they went until Poppy pushed Bella into the water. Bella pulled Poppy in after her by a slender ankle and they laughed and laughed, looking up at the Balearic stars as they floated on extraordinary buoyant fake water lilies that glittered in the myriad lights of the pool.

After a bit, Poppy said, 'Let's go and find our wonderful men and see if Pig Sean has managed to find the Beatles track for Natalia yet.'

'Pig Sean!' Bella spluttered, nearly falling off her fake lily. 'That's brilliant, Pops!'

'I know. Just call me Oscar Wilde,' retorted Poppy solemnly. And arm-in-arm, they walked up the pool's wide, mosaic-tiled steps, happy as pigs in shit.

Natalia wasn't used to letting her defences drop. In fact she couldn't remember the last time she had danced with such abandon, but Poppy and Bella had told Pig Sean to play 'Back in the USSR' for her, and insisted that everybody – even the guests enjoying themselves on other terraces – danced around her main pool to it. She loved the song, of course she did, especially the bit about the Ukraine girls knocking the Beatles out. She could remember her *mamushka* playing black-market Beatles LPs when she was a little girl back in Kiev. But for all her apparently insouciant glamour, she would never have insisted on it herself; she wanted everything cool by DJ standards. They were so lucky, these English kids, with their automatic assumption that people wouldn't call them tacky. They could be 'retro' or 'ironic' and still considered cool. For Natalia (aged 39 forever) the line was too narrow.

Bella's ridiculous father was shouting along to the chorus, thrusting his skinny hips at her.

*Ha! You would be so lucky*, Natalia thought. *Men like you used to pay me five grand a night.*

Something snapped inside her, and for the first time in years she allowed herself to let her hair down in public. Literally. She unleashed the painfully tight ponytail and shook her platinum-blonde hair around her face as she gyrated round the fabulous property that she had worked so long and hard for.

The crowd whooped and cheered. Quite staggeringly, not a single person was talking about him- or herself, all mesmerized by the ice queen apparently melting. Poppy and Bella, both still in their bikinis, were dancing around her, swishing their wet hair madly.

Once it had finished, Poppy took the mike from Pig Sean.

'Can we all now raise our glasses to our fabulous hostess, Natalia Evanovitch! Hostess with the mostest!'

'Hostess with the mostest!' people hollered drunkenly, though some of them were now starting to lose interest and wanted to talk about themselves again.

'Natalia, we love you. Thank you so much for everything,' said Poppy, as Damian approached with an enormous bouquet of lilies. He kissed Natalia, and the less self-absorbed people still watching cheered some more.

'Natalia, we can never thank you enough for your generosity, so . . . I'll spare your blushes. Enough's enough, but one more toast, please, ladies and gentlemen . . . NATALIA!'

'NATALIA!'

Pig Sean put his shades on.

'Can I go now?' he said petulantly. 'I'm starting my set at Space in two hours.'

'Feel free,' said Poppy, winking at Bella. 'And I'd like to thank you for being so gracious and accommodating. It's really made my wedding special.'

As Pig Sean walked along the edge of the pool to collect his DJ stuff, Poppy gave him a little shove. Caught off guard, he went flying into the water. The look of indignation on his arrogant face was priceless, and although (or perhaps because) Poppy's gesture was so childish, all the people who generally considered themselves sophisticated pissed themselves laughing.

Natalia's white-blonde hair was wavy about her face, her slanty, wide-apart eyes almost invisible with laughter.

'Oh, you guys,' she eventually spluttered. 'I cannot recall more fun ever. Thank you!'

She reclined on one of her incredibly expensive sun loungers and looked up at the stars, laughing happily.

She was still smiling to herself as she sat on her terrace, at the top of her tower – the one above the semicircular chill-out room. She had just risen and the party was still going strong somewhere in her massive villa, but she, Natalia, had had enough by about six a.m. and had taken herself up to her own private sanctum.

She had a baby hangover, but that was OK. It had been worth it. Natalia only took two, maybe three lines of cocaine on special occasions, and she paced herself with the champagne. She had always had to keep her wits about her. For a moment, she felt envious of Poppy and Bella, so stupidly wasted in the pool, and having so much fun – the worst they could ever have from a hangover was embarrassment. Natalia knew differently.

She could hear some music. Aha – that's where they all were – around the back, singing along to some ridiculous song about being in the mood for dancing. Then multiple splashes. The deep thud thud thud of a very different kind of dance music had been reverberating, almost lulling her to sleep, yet now they put on this? Again, she envied their total confidence that whatever rubbish (and this music *was* rubbish) they played, nobody would sneer. She loved the fact that people were enjoying her hospitality, but it was bittersweet. She could never really be one of them, not with her past.

She heard Bella trying to whisper, but actually shrieking quite loudly, 'Shhh, maybe we should turn it down a bit? Natalia's probably still trying to sleep.'

Sweet girl. Sweet life.

But she was a little bit hungry now. Natalia needed her pineapple, mango and green tea in the morning. She laughed to herself as she recalled what hunger used to be, when she would devour bread because there was nothing else. These idiots with their intolerances. Bread and milk were the staff of life when you had that perpetual gnawing hunger pain. The self-indulgence of pampered Western women, claiming they were intolerant to wheat or 'dairy' made her quite sick. However, she had adapted, and realized that by cutting them out, she could keep the remarkably slender frame she'd had since her teens. Her stomach was as flat as it had ever been.

Natalia caught sight of her reflection in one of the shiny glass doors leading out from her bedroom. With her white-blonde hair tied back loosely, her skin nearly baby-soft, wiped clean of make-up with Eve Lom cleanser, she looked much younger than she normally did, with the tight ponytail and diamonds. Comfortable in her pistachio-green silk chiffon French knickers and camisole, she stretched her legs out on the marble-topped table, admiring their length.

Natalia was almost entirely without vanity. Her body had served its purpose and she regarded it with fond objectivity. Without it, none of this would have been possible. Even though they were no longer necessary, old habits died hard, and she was scrupulous in her body's maintenance, even enduring painful Brazilian waxes when she couldn't remember the last time anybody had seen her *влагалище*. For Natalia, love, or even sex for pleasure, was not an option. She had a vibrator to cater for such needs and had never had any reason to view men with anything but fear, suspicion, and a very canny eye for the main chance.

Thinking again about the old days, she rang the bell and asked for a croissant. What the hell. Wheat intolerances be damned – she could afford to indulge herself once in a while. She looked out at the wonderful view. Several yachts were floating on the deep-blue sea, their sails whiter than white against the horizon. Maybe she should buy a yacht? They were very expensive, of course, but her finances were in pretty good order now. She threw back her head and laughed with sheer joy. Not only had she escaped, but now she had this!

'Señora?'

Natalia turned around to accept her breakfast platter.

The dark-eyed waiter grinned, exposing three gold teeth, and suddenly she knew that this happiness was not here to stay.

'Georgiou? Is it really you? What you want? You want money? I haf plenty money,' she said in slightly broken

English – it happened when she was thrown off kilter, which wasn't often these days.

'I know,' he said in Russian.

Trying to stay cool, Natalia walked slowly inside to find her Chanel handbag, where she always kept 2,000 US dollars, in case of emergencies. This was one emergency that, after the initial years, she had prayed would never occur. As she took the notes out, several fluttered from her trembling hands. The dark-eyed waiter watched as she bent to retrieve them. She knew he was loving every minute of her cowed subservience.

'Please, take them, Georgie, and never come back.'

He smiled again. Never had gold teeth looked so repulsive.

'Talia, I thank you. But I'll be back.'

# Chapter 3

Ben Jones walked naked to his large American fridge and cracked open a Bud. It tasted like piss, but he was prepared to put up with weak beer when he considered the compensations.

He'd just been for a run along the beach at Malibu Colony. He'd been in LA for two months now and still couldn't get over the babes and endless sunshine. Today (like yesterday, and the day before, and the day before that) would have been the best day of summer back home; any one of the girls he'd met during his run would have been the best-looking babe in London. Wales wasn't comparable, on either count.

He was used to hanging out with models and actresses, but they were a completely different breed here in California. The edginess/quirkiness/kookiness (take your pick) so prized by the coolest London model agencies would be greeted here with absolute bemusement. If anything fell short of cookie-cutter perfection, the little darlings just went and got it fixed.

Without even trying, he'd picked up a fistful of colourful business cards during his run. He picked a few off the breakfast bar and laughed.

*I'm Carrie* (heart drawn above the i). *Actress, model, spiritual healer. Call me!*

*Melissa – I do pedicures and aura cleansing. Let me make you beautiful, inside AND out! Sole and soul!*

*Jennifer Jackson. Nutritionist and personal trainer.*

He turned over the last one to see the photo (they all had photos on the back) and recalled the mixed-race girl with a wide smile, dreadlocks and body to die for. He'd actually stopped for a few seconds to watch her arse as she sauntered off in the sand. Then he'd jogged back to the rented clapboard beach house his agent had found for him. He put Jennifer Jackson's card to one side – she might be worth a booty call.

Beautiful, and vain as hell, Ben walked over to the floor-to-ceiling mirror that lined the far wall of his open-plan living space. His floppy gold-streaked light brown fringe, still a little damp from the shower, grazed his long black eyelashes. His pink pouty lips, delicious blue eyes and high cheekbones had made him such a hit back home that he had managed to acquire an LA agent almost without trying.

*People Like Us*, the UK sitcom whose first series he had starred in, had been a runaway success and attracted the interest of Belinda Hyman, one of the most notoriously hard-bitten agents in Hollywood. He was contracted to star in three series of *People Like Us*, and due to start filming the next in a few months' time, but if he landed a movie role – well. Belinda wasn't known as the Bitch of Beverly Hills for nothing.

Ben flexed a muscle or two and smiled in satisfaction.

*Looking good, boyo.* Occasionally, the Welsh accent resurfaced, though only in his head.

'Benny, honey? Baby's getting lonely,' called a very young voice from his bedroom.

He smiled again, focusing on his newly whitened teeth, as he recalled the cheerleader he'd picked up at the game last night. Sweet seventeen and definitely been fucked. He'd been to watch the LA Lakers with a couple of fellow ex-pats and this fantastic specimen of perky blonde near-jailbait had – well – just thrown herself at him. No other way of putting it. He did love California, despite the weak beer.

But during his run, his mind had been on Bella, Poppy and Damian, all of whom he'd comprehensively shafted the previous year. Ben wasn't one for an enormous amount of introspection, but even he felt bad about what he'd done.

Bella had been great to start with – fun and sexy, with a healthy appetite for all the good things in life. But once they had that horrible intimacy thing going, she got so bloody needy, and the way she gazed at him with those huge hurt brown eyes made him feel guilty as fuck, especially when he'd shagged the odd model on the odd shoot (a man's prerogative, he'd always felt – or at least an accepted perk of the job). As an angelic-looking only child, Ben had been spoilt rotten his entire life and wasn't used to being denied what he wanted.

Fucking Poppy hadn't been his best move, but Poppy was the antithesis of Bella – tiny, blonde and fiery – and the contrast (and, to be scrupulously honest, the illicitness) had turned him on. He'd tired of Poppy pretty quickly, after the initial thrill, not least as she had been so evidently off her pretty face on coke all the time, going on about her guilt about Bella, boring the pants off him. Still, he shouldn't have moved in on his best mate's bird; that was unforgivable. Ben and Damian had grown up together and he still missed Damian's easy good nature and laid-back sense of humour; he'd yet to meet a comparable buddy in the States. All things considered, if he could have done last summer differently, he would. It had been a mad time for all concerned.

But now wasn't the time to be crying over spilt milk.

'Ben, honey, where ARE you? Are going to come and show me how to do it again? I was a virgin until last night, but you've given me a real taste for it. I'm only seventeen . . .'

The Laker Girl was clearly lying and up to every trick in the book but, nevertheless, Ben felt his cock getting hard.

'I love America,' he sang as he made his way to the bedroom. The cheerleader was on her hands and knees, arse aloft. Her skin was golden brown, soft and peachy.

'Does that feel good?' asked Ben, loving the feeling of her tight, young body.

'Oh . . . Yeeees . . . Oh, Benny . . . I've never done this before . . . Ohhhh . . .'

If she was telling the truth, she was half his age, and just for a split second he felt ever so slightly like a dirty old man. Then he refocused. Christ, she was hot.

And so was he.

\* \* \*

Driving up the freeway en route to meet Belinda at Chateau Marmont (it was difficult to express how much he loved the LA cliché), Ben turned up the radio, which was playing the Red Hot Chili Peppers.

*Californication.*

He laughed, and for the second time that day thought of Damian, thinking how much he'd have enjoyed the serendipity. He put the idea firmly out of his mind and dwelt instead on nubile nymphets, fame, fortune, blue skies and palm trees. A pretty brunette in a white convertible lifted her shades to get a better look at him. She kissed her fingers and clutched her heart, feigning undying love. He clocked the rings on her fingers and blew a kiss back. Then he put his foot on the gas.

Modelled in the 1920s on a chateau in the Loire Valley, the Chateau Marmont was still the ultimate byword for hedonistic glamour. As Ben walked out of the lobby towards the pool, he could feel the cloisters themselves oozing their Tinseltown, rock'n'roll heritage. The stars who had stayed under this roof included Judy Garland, John Belushi (who had OD'd here, poor bugger), Vivien Leigh, Jim Morrison, Jean Harlow, Led Zep . . . The roll call was as bibulous as it was illustrious. He continued through beautifully fragrant and lush gardens until he'd reached the pool, which was surrounded by even lusher plants, and tables shaded by black-and-white stripy parasols.

'Ben! My handsomest client, looking sexier than ever. If I didn't know you better, I'd think you'd just had a pretty piece of LA ass!'

Belinda winked and Ben laughed. Was it really so obvious?

His agent didn't look like the hard-nosed bitch whose reputation preceded her, even the other side of the Atlantic. In fact, when he'd first met her, he'd wondered if he'd walked into the wrong office. Belinda, who was probably in her mid-forties, though it was hard to tell, contrived an air of luxe hippy softness, in the Rachel Zoe/ Nicole Richie mode. Her golden hair was loose and tousled around her shoulders – a casual California style that cost at least $1,000 a month to maintain. She wore a simple spaghetti-strapped maxidress in a splashy floral silk, flat tan leather sandals, wooden bangles stacked up her sinewy, Bikram-yoga'd arms, dangly vintage silver-and-turquoise earrings and the most enormous pair of shades Ben had ever seen.

'Looking pretty bloody gorgeous yourself, darling.' Playing up the posh-Brit thing hadn't done Hugh Grant or Rupert Everett any harm, after all.

The pool wasn't as big as he'd imagined, but Lindsay Lohan was swigging from a bottle of tequila on a black-and-white-striped sun lounger, bitching into her BlackBerry about 'that asshole who calls himself my dad', and one of Keith Richards' daughters was having her photo taken for a magazine shoot. Belinda had wanted to meet him at Café M on Melrose, the hottest new health-food café, insisting that Chateau Marmont was for wannabes, but Ben wanted to live the full LA dream. Besides, he wanted a real drink, somewhere he wouldn't be accused of being an 'alcoholic Brit'.

He sat down opposite his agent.

'I guess you want something alcoholic?' she sighed.

'Well, a cocktail would be nice.' He gave her his most winning smile. 'What're you drinking?'

'Iced green tea with ginseng. You should try it sometime.' He did his little-boy-lost look and she laughed. Belinda was just as susceptible to his charms as every other female on the planet.

'Hey, I'll let you off this time.' She put a hand weighed down with cocktail rings on his arm. 'And I'll have whatever you're having. We may have something to celebrate.'

'What?' Ben felt an enormous jolt of excitement. 'Why, what's happened?'

'Don't get your hopes up too quickly, handsome boy,' said Belinda, loving the power she had over him. 'Let's wait for the drinks.'

It was agonizing waiting until the waiter (a 'resting actor', good looking but not nearly as fit as Ben – which was presumably why he was resting) came back with their Margaritas. But Ben feigned nonchalance, complimenting Belinda on her body and business acumen.

'Well,' she eventually drawled. 'Paramount are casting a new movie. It's gonna be huge, they say, but they always say that . . .'

'What's it about?'

'The South of France in the 1950s. Saint-Tropez, Bardot, you know.'

'Oh, cool. And I love that part of the world. I went backpacking along the Riviera with all my drama-school mates in the college holidays ten years ago.' It was more like fifteen, but Belinda didn't need to know that. 'Nice,

Antibes, Juan Les Pins, just so we could get a glimpse of the stars at Cannes.' He remembered them all smoking dope and drinking cheap wine out of their rucksacks on the beach, assuring one another that they'd be up there one day. *If they could see me now, that little gang of mine . . .*

'You European kids,' said Belinda, slightly wistfully. 'So much culture at your fingertips. Anyway, Cannes is the cynical premise behind this venture. The producers think that a movie based on its doorstep might get those uptight bastards to sit up and take some notice of something produced by a MAJOR studio, for once, instead of one of those fall-asleep-in-your-popcorn subtitled crapolas where everybody, like, dies.' She made a gesture that combined an extravagant yawn with slitting her throat.

Ben laughed easily. He was amazed by his own patience.

'And? Do they want to see me, or what?'

'Oh, honey, of course they want to see you. I wouldn't be telling you all this now would I, if they didn't? What kind of a woman do you think I am?'

She pouted and Ben refrained from telling her.

'It's a period romcom, along the lines of *To Catch A Thief.*'

Ben wasn't sure how Hitchcock would have reacted to one of his classics being referred to as a period romcom, but he let it pass.

'So you mean, I'm up for the Cary Grant character?' It was difficult to keep the excitement out of his voice.

'Get real, handsome. They'll only go with a proper, American star for the good guy.' Wasn't Belinda aware

44

that Cary Grant was originally from Bristol? 'No, you're the bastard Brit who messes with our heroine's heart.'

'Silly me.' Ben laughed again. 'We Englishmen are always the villains. But, bloody hell, Belinda, that is amazing! When do they want me to read for it? And who are they thinking of for the lead roles?'

'They haven't decided yet for the lead, but maybe Scarlett Johansson or Amanda Seyfried for the girl. Somebody suggested Gwynnie, but she's way too old of course.'

As Gwyneth Paltrow was about the same age as him, Ben nodded solemnly.

'And they want to see you in two days' time, so brush up on your French.'

'Mate, that's amazing news,' said Tom, one of Ben's new ex-pat buddies, a trust-fund twat who had moved to LA to write a screenplay, thinking that anyone could do it. As he could neither spell nor string two sentences together, Ben thought it unlikely Tom's masterpiece would ever see the light of day. But he did mean well.

They were at Soho House LA, with all the other Brits who liked to stick together.

'But promise us you won't turn native!' bellowed Julia, an actress who'd been very successful in London three years ago but had yet to hit the big time Stateside. Possibly on account of a weak chin and a slightly-too-large nose that she'd refused to get fixed, vainly (and stupidly) thinking her work as a 'serious actress' rendered such measures unnecessary. 'We don't want you to start saying "Lie-sesster Square"!'

Everyone cracked up, and Ben pretended to too, but

inside he was thinking, *If you don't like it here, then why don't you fuck off back to London?* He was growing a little tired of his fellow ex-pats, with their twee insistence on tea parties, and Sunday roasts, when it was far too hot to eat anything other than the innovatively healthy (and surprisingly delicious) fresh produce on offer locally. These people would have been the first to sneer at Brits in Benidorm demanding the full English breakfast, so why the fuck did they think it was OK in LA?

They were sitting on the roof terrace, underneath a silvery olive tree, drinking vodkatinis. Ben swivelled his head to take in the 360-degree view. LA at night sprawled, glittering and full of promise, beneath and all around him. Somewhere to his right, the gated mansions of Beverly Hills beckoned, in all their opulent splendour. *One day . . .*

'Two nations, divided by a common language!' Julia guffawed, and tried to sit on his lap, but even though she'd lost the Brit blubber and was now the requisite size two, she represented the weight of his past, and he wanted her off him. He got up, nearly sending her flying, and said, 'I've got to get an early night. Big day the day after tomorrow. 'Bye guys! Don't do anything I wouldn't do!'

Julia looked offended, as well she might. She had been his first contact in LA (they'd been at RADA together), and he'd shagged her to get in with the ex-pat crowd.

As he walked out into the jasmine-scented summer night air, he heard Julia saying, 'I do hope he's not going to get too big for his boots now.'

Outside, he lit an illicit fag. He still wasn't quite sure

why fags and booze were so frowned upon in California when dope was legal, but he was willing to toe the line most of the time when so much was at stake. As he put his lighter back in his jeans pocket, he felt a piece of card and took it out.

*Jennifer Jackson. Nutritionist and personal trainer.*

He recalled the girl with the dreadlocks, smile and fantastic arse. Now, she would be a way forward. He'd had enough of his previous life and the no-hoper Brits weighing him down. He thought for a second, then took out his phone and dialled the number on the card.

'Who is it?' A very cross-sounding voice eventually answered.

'Hi, Jenny, it's Ben. We met on the beach today—'

'Oh, for God's sakes. Don't you know what time it is? If you want to talk about training, call me in the morning.'

And she put the phone down on him. Ben wasn't sure that any woman had done that to him in his life before. He rather liked it.

'Jenny, hi, it's Ben. We met on the beach yesterday.' He put on his poshest RADA accent.

'Oh my. The Brit who woke me up at midnight?'

Ben chuckled in what he hoped was an endearing manner.

'Mea culpa, I'm afraid.'

'Well, I hope you'll make it worth my while.' She sounded crosser than ever. 'I only had four hours' sleep because of you. I was training Tom Hanks at five a.m.'

'Oh, fuck, I'm so sorry,' said Ben. 'Tom Hanks, really?'

'Of course I wasn't training Tom Hanks, you British idiot.

47

Do ya think I'd be handing out my card on the beach if I was Tom Hanks's trainer?'

Ben laughed sheepishly.

'No, I suppose not.'

'So, d'ya want me to train you, or are you just gonna annoy me with late-night calls? Your abs could do with some work. But it'll cost ya. And *nobody* calls me Jenny. My name is Jennifer.'

Bitch. My abs are fine, thought Ben, stroking his washboard stomach. But he definitely wanted to see her again.

'I thank you.'

Natalia smiled graciously as she accepted her champagne and caviar from the BA stewardess. She was flying from Heathrow to Kiev on her annual June trip to check up on the two charities to which she had been contributing generously for years. After her *mamushka* had died, there had been no real reason to go back home, but she had to make sure her money was being put to good use.

At least she had the luxury of being able to choose which time of year to return, she thought, pulling her cashmere blanket a little more tightly around her shoulders to keep out the chill of the air conditioning. Despite its soft warmth, she shivered as the memories of Ukraine in the depths of winter came flooding back . . .

'Madam? Can I get you something else?' asked the stewardess, looking at Natalia oddly.

'Excuse me?' Natalia was snapped back into the present, into the softness of her White Company cashmere blanket, so different to the itchy wool she had wrapped herself up in all those years ago. 'No, no, I thank you, I am fine.'

Once the stewardess had left her alone once more, she stared out of the window for some time, unwelcome tears blurring her view of the pillowy white clouds below.

# Chapter 4

*Poppy Wallace's bite of the Big Apple is somewhat larger than she'd initially anticipated.*

Bella looked at Poppy's Facebook update with love and irritation. It wasn't Poppy per se who bugged the shit out of her, but all her old London media friends who fell on her every word and tried to outdo themselves with how well they knew her and how cool they could prove themselves to everyone else online. Some of the fawning acolytes responded to Poppy's Facebook update with such stomach-churning stuff as *miss u loads, baby girl* (from a female journalist – there was loads of faux-dykey bollocks) and *hoxton's not the same without you, sweet poppy lops. remember OBESE-gate?*

Bella was tempted to add, *remember OVERDOSE-gate?* She wasn't able to be cool on Facebook, as some of her old friends and family members actually used exclamation marks and plenty of xxxxs at the end of their messages. It seemed rude not to respond in kind. Also, as Andy worked late so many evenings, she found herself drinking wine on her own and writing things she thought hilarious at the time, then waking in a cold sweaty panic, wondering what the fuck she had thought essential to share with absolutely everyone who knew her. The computer needed a Breathalyser.

She clicked onto Poppy's latest photos: rollerblading in Central Park, gorgeous in old-skool grey marl shorts and Yankees T-shirt; drinking at the round table at the Algonquin Hotel in a flapper dress (cue comment from fawning female journo: *you are Dorothy Parker, but a million times prettier* – nineteen other equally sycophantic comments followed); sunbathing by the pool on Soho House NY's roof terrace in a green bikini that matched her eyes and showed off her exquisitely lithe body (*wowser! looking hot babe, hubba hubba*, etc., etc., ad nauseam); sitting on the stoop of some lovely old brownstone house in rolled-up jeans and sneakers, her hair in an insouciant ponytail, reading the *Herald Tribune* (her comment on her own photo was clever, cool and abstruse).

Bella looked out of the window. At nearly half-past eight the sun hadn't yet set, but it wouldn't have made any difference if it had, she thought morosely. The English summer, which, by some freakish Act of God, had been so wonderful last year, had reverted to its usual depressing, drizzly self. She reminded herself to snap out of it. Her day had started with some great sex and she still loved Andy so much she barely even looked at other men any more. Well, she looked, but she wasn't tempted. She didn't have to go to vile offices, was paid pretty handsomely for her painting, and her life was, just about, perfect.

Yet . . . It was just the bloody weather, she told herself, and a niggling loneliness. One of the reasons she loved Andy so much was his innate goodness, which manifested itself in his dedication to his work, but sometimes she wished more of that dedication could be sent her way. Like coming home in time for dinner.

She clicked onto Poppy's next photo, in which she was giggling with loads of people Bella didn't know, in a club that was probably the Studio 54 du jour. Damian was conspicuous by his absence. Bella hoped that all was well with them. She opened another bottle of wine and started to think about all the fun she'd had in the past. She used to be that clubbing chick, the one with the cool photos and funny stories.

Then her phone beeped.

*Bella my love, I'm outside. So sorry I've been neglecting you. Bloody job. I love you! Come down. Anything you want to eat and drink is on me, wherever you want to go. And everything you want me to do to you, I'll do double. Triple. Xxxxxx*

Bella looked out of the window and saw Andy, arms outstretched, smiling up at her. Her heart soared as she ran down the rickety steps of her flat and realized she wouldn't trade any of her hedonistic, uncertain past for what she had with him, right now.

'I mean, I love her, you know I do, but it's just so fucking annoying!' Bella looked over her glass of Pouilly-Fumé at Andy. They were in her favourite restaurant, The Wolseley. Enormous iron chandeliers glowed overhead, the excited hum of chatter buzzed around her, she was with her favourite person in the whole world. Yet her second favourite dish in the whole world (moules marinières; spaghetti vongole was her first, but they didn't do it here) lay practically untouched in front of her.

'Poppy's life is just so bloody exciting, and EVERYONE loves her!'

'I don't love her.' Andy leant across the white linen'd table and held both Bella's hands in his. 'In fact, I think she's a self-centred pain in the arse, but I do love you.'

Bella smiled and kissed both his hands.

'Thanks and sorry. I love you too.'

'Not bored with me already, are you?' He said it lightly, but Bella could tell he meant it.

'I'll never be bored with you, my love. I just sometimes get a bit bored with life in grey old London, with its endless depressing news, when everybody else seems to be having so much fun, in such exotic places. Bloody Facebook.'

'You spend far more time on that site than is healthy, my darling. And let's look at it mathematically: you have – what? – 350-odd Facebook "friends"?' Andy did the inverted commas fingers signal and Bella nodded, slightly shamefaced.

'Most of us go on holiday at least once a year, so let's divide that by twelve.'

'Um – nearly thirty people on holiday every month?'

'Exactly! It may look as if everyone is having the times of their lives on beaches or mountains, while we're stuck in dreary old London, but it's a snare and a delusion. We were in Ibiza only a couple of months ago, after all.'

'Oh, I know, I know, I'm being horribly spoilt.' Bella sighed and took another swig of her wine. 'But Poppy IS getting her huge bite of the Big Apple, even during this horrid recession. I don't know why I can't be more pleased for her.' In the old days she'd have been happy, unreservedly, for Poppy, but ever since the Ben thing, something sour had crept in. She had loved helping her plan the wedding, and the nuptials themselves had been wonderful, of course, but this new, extra level of success was a little galling.

Six weeks earlier, three weeks after Poppy and Damian had returned from their honeymoon in Cuba, *Stadium* had folded, the latest victim of the recession. Simon Snell had immediately found another job on *Esquire*, but Poppy had put a spanner in Damian's job-seeking by simultaneously being offered a promotion in New York. And it wasn't just any old promotion. One of her company's proper big shots had been visiting from New York, taken one look at Poppy and decided that she was wasted behind the camera. With her gamine beauty, quick-wittedness and sarcastic London cool, the Big Shot was hoping Poppy would be the new Alexa Chung, presenting a quirky magazine/documentary-type show – an English girl's take on the Big Apple.

Damian, not wanting to be apart from his new wife so early in their marriage (and, Bella thought, probably still not entirely trusting her, left to her own devices in an exciting new city), had bravely decided to take his chances at freelancing in New York. *Stadium* had left him with plenty of contacts, after all.

'I hope Damian's getting on OK,' said Andy, and Bella grimaced.

'Not much good for his ego if he's not.'

'No,' said Andy. 'And we both know what his professional ego can be like when wounded. So enough of the Poppy jealousy, OK? Would you want to be in her shoes, constantly reassuring Damian that he's cleverer than her, while he mopes about, sulking all day, in what I imagine is their vast warehouse apartment?'

Bella laughed. 'That's such a vivid image! S'pose not.' She was smiling broadly now, as Andy's foot, which had been rubbing her leg all night, had made its way up to her knickers.

'Aren't you going to finish your mussels?' Andy smiled into her eyes, increasing the pressure of his foot.

'I'd rather you finished my muscles at home.'

The next morning, Bella woke around nine a.m. and stretched contentedly. She still loved the fact she would never again be rudely awoken by a shrill alarm signalling another dreary day in another dreary office. She felt much happier today. The sun was shining through muslin curtains, Andy was wonderful, her life was wonderful, everything was wonderful. She pottered about at a leisurely pace, putting the radio on and making herself a cup of tea. She filled her pretty eau-de-nil watering can and went out onto her balcony to water her window boxes. This little daily act gave her a disproportionate amount of pleasure. Her mint and chives were coming along a treat. She kissed her fingers and patted the plants.

'Grow, my babies, grow.' She was glad nobody could see her and wondered if this might be a sign of broodiness. She certainly didn't yearn for a baby right now. She was perfectly happy with things just as they were, and although she knew she wanted one eventually, and reckoned Andy would make a great father, she had no intention of rocking the boat.

Though her flat was really much too small for two, and she and Andy had talked about selling it and buying somewhere bigger, she loved it too much to leave quite yet. The crappy property market was as good an excuse as any, and Andy was still paying off the enormous loan he'd taken out to pay for his wedding to Alison last year, which had been called off at the last minute. The fact that Alison had been shagging her boss, so it should have been her financial responsibility, still rankled with Bella, but Andy was a slave to his tiresome principles.

By the time she'd showered, dressed, made the bed (arranging and plumping up all the artfully mismatched cushions exactly to her satisfaction) and read a chapter or two of her book over a boiled egg and thickly buttered toast, it was nearly midday. Guiltily, Bella shut the book. There wouldn't be time for her run now – she'd booked her jointly rented studio for 12.30. She couldn't imagine how she'd ever managed to get up in time to arrive, bad-tempered and dishevelled, at whichever horrible office she'd been temping at for a nine-a.m.-prompt start. Actually, the promptness had happened rarely, if ever. She felt another surge of happiness that those days were over.

As she walked towards the door and automatically checked herself out in the mirror next to it, she stopped and shook her head in dissatisfaction. Something was wrong. Bella had longish legs and a larger than average bust for her 5 foot 7, size 10/12 frame (despite slender ankles, wrists and shoulders, she always felt like a bloody carthorse next to Poppy). She'd had vague hopes of channelling Audrey Hepburn today in high ponytail, black Capri pants and a boat-necked, horizontally striped T-shirt. From her shoulders up she looked great, the ponytail and boat neck setting off her collarbones, high cheekbones and big brown eyes a treat. Audrey was not an entirely preposterous idea. Her legs were fine in the Capri pants.

But in between – oh, dear. The horizontal stripes made her bust look vast (and not in a good way – matronly was the word that sprang to mind). And for fuck's sake, was she starting to develop a paunch? She supposed it was possible, with the ongoing eating and drinking of happy coupledom, and her increasing laziness when it came to exercise. She promised herself that she would hit the procrastinating on the head as she went back into her bedroom to change. Tomorrow she would definitely get up in time for her run.

Bella eventually arrived at Westbourne Studios at 1.30 p.m.

'Yah, Daddy's just given me and Jazz a mil each to buy a flat, but you can't get anything decent round here for that sort of money,' Sienna was saying into her iPhone as Bella walked into her time-share studio. 'Oh, hi, Bella.' She smiled and waved a thin, wafty hand.

Ludicrously overprivileged and good-looking, Sienna Sax-Hoffmann was studying History of Art at London University. She had told Bella that her father wanted her to have a bolthole for her studies, when 'the Uni library gets too much. Dear Daddy, he can be so overprotective, but it's rather fun having one's own studio three mornings a week, don't you think?' Sienna only actually managed to get up in time to play on the Internet in her studio once a week, at most, but Bella didn't hold that against her (well, how could she?). She found Sienna rather sweet. Perhaps it was because she was so pretty. Bella knew that with her artistic eye, she always gave people who were easy on it less of a hard time than those who repulsed her physically – male or female. She wasn't particularly proud of this.

Sienna was about 5 foot 10, skinny as a catwalk model with an eating disorder, and pale as milk. Her naturally white-blonde hair cascaded in long waves around a coolly patrician face, all angular bones and huge, bruised, dark blue eyes. She played up her delicate appearance with fey, floaty, vintage garments, today looking breathtakingly fragile in a cream lacy maxidress, pearl choker (probably real) and jewelled flip-flops that showed off her narrow pedicured feet. Bella imagined that your average man's unimaginative, testosterone-driven protective instincts would go into overdrive at the sight of her.

'Hi, Bella.' Sienna smiled as she put her phone down. 'You're late.'

'I know. Never been much good at punctuality.' Bella smiled back as she started setting up her easel.

'I should be off then. D'you want me to pay you back for the extra hour? Not really fair for you to cough up for when you're not here. Daddy can easily afford it . . .' Sienna started and Bella laughed.

'My lateness isn't your dad's fault, sweetie. Nope, this is my punishment for being the past-mistress of pissing about.'

Sienna laughed too. 'Well, you'd better make the most of what time you've got left then.' She looked out of the window and groaned. 'Oh, Goooood. Bloody Josh is out there *again*. I swear that boy is stalking me.'

Bella followed her gaze. Sitting at the wheel of a convertible red Porsche was a baby-faced boy of immeasurably arrogant demeanour. If the car wasn't clue enough, everything about his appearance screamed money – from the slicked-back dark brown hair and ruddy pink cheeks to the immaculately faded jeans and butter-soft leather jacket. While this might conceivably have had some allure on an older man, on a boy of barely 21 it was both loathsome and faintly ludicrous.

'He is sooooo uncool.' Sienna rolled her eyes at Bella as she picked up her vintage lace parasol. 'He hangs out at places like Whisky Mist and Mahiki, trying to suck up to Harry Wales. He's thick as pigshit too – God knows how he got into King's. But he's so loaded he's got half the boring wannabe Sloanes at college eating out of his hand.'

If Sienna thought he was loaded, reflected Bella, the baby-faced Josh must be rich as Croesus. Certain sectors of society had yet to be hit by the recession, it seemed.

'Toby, shut up, you fucker! You're such a fucking loser!'

'Cretin! Thunder thighs! Fatso!'

'Loser! Wankstain! Fuckwit! Toby's a fuckwit, Toby's a fuckwit!'

Alison put her fingers in her ears and tried to ignore the screaming bickering of her teenage almost stepchildren as she concentrated on the details of the latest horrible case she was working on. You'd think the classically (some might say boringly) wood-panelled, leather-upholstered study would be soundproof, but no. Their spoilt, public-school, brattish voices, an entire floor up, would probably pierce the thick concrete walls of a torture cell (the like of which the creeps she was defending would doubtless end up in, if she didn't sufficiently deploy the Human Rights Act).

Alison was meant to have married Andy last year. They'd been together for thirteen years, ever since Cambridge, and it had seemed like a logical progression. But she'd become so caught up in the minutiae of organizing the perfect wedding, and keeping her bloody parents happy, that she'd lost sight of the fact that, somewhere along the line, they had fallen out of love with one another. When her older boss Philip, senior partner in her law firm, came on to her one night they were both working late, she'd felt properly alive again for the first time in years. They'd actually fucked on his desk. The age gap suited them both – it made Philip feel virile and Alison desired – something Andy hadn't managed at all in the last few years of their relationship, though he'd done his best to pretend. And the Eaton Square house was the pinnacle of her grandiose domestic aspirations.

She hadn't reckoned with the bloody teenagers though.

'LOSER, LOSER, LOSER, LOSER, LOSER!' Now they were stamping, banging on the floor above, to the extent she was worried the ceiling might fall in. Something sounded like gunshot. Little sods. She took a deep breath and ventured upstairs, to the room directly above her study – their *playroom*. For God's sake, at their age.

Toby was shooting an air rifle out of the window, trying to kill pigeons, while Imogen and one of her horrible little friends bounced around the room on state-of-the-art pogo sticks. They were all so bloody spoilt that neither of her parents had the nerve to tell Imogen that cropped leggings weren't the best option for her chunky little legs.

'Children.' Alison tried to smile.

Toby turned around, pointing the air rifle right at her.

'Children,' he drawled sarcastically. 'Yes, what is it, *wicked step-mummy*?'

Both girls cracked up. Alison flinched away from the gun and tried to keep her temper.

'Could you just keep the noise down a bit, please? I'm trying to work . . .'

'Trying?' brayed Imogen, tossing her dyed-yellow hair. 'Well, you probably need to try a bit harder then, don't you?'

'Hahahaha! Oh, Imo, you're so funny!' spluttered her equally obnoxious (though not so blubbery) friend.

Never the most patient of women at the best of times, Alison snapped, 'Just shut up, you little bastards . . .'

'Really, Alison,' came a mild voice from behind her. 'I'm sure it's not necessary to speak to my children like that.'

'Daddddddeeeee!' shouted Imogen, running as fast as her fat little legs would carry her. She launched herself into her father's arms, as though she were 4, not 14.

'Darling!' Philip swung her up and round in the air. Alison was amazed he didn't rupture himself. He put Imogen down and saluted his son, who had hidden the air rifle behind his bespoke pool table.

'All shipshape, captain?'

'All shipshape, sir.' Toby saluted back, grinning.

'Righty-ho. Well, as it's half-term, who's up for Pizza Express?'

'Oh, Daddy, you're the best!' Imogen snuggled up to him.

'I was going to cook coq au vin,' started Alison, even though she hated cooking.

'Darling, I thought I'd give you a break from the kitchen. It's not exactly your forte, is it?' Philip winked at Imogen, who giggled.

As Alison walked wearily downstairs after them all, Toby turned round and gave her the finger, glee written all over his smug, spotty little face.

# Chapter 5

'Owwww!' screamed Poppy as Fabrice pulled the first strip of wax from her nose. She scowled at him in the mirror. 'Surely this isn't necessary? Of all the things I've ever been accused of, having a hairy nose isn't one of them.'

'Welcome to Manhattan grooming, Blondie.'

As the pain ebbed away, Poppy tried to smile, aware that it was important to keep the people behind the scenes on your side in this business. And it wasn't actually Fabrice's fault – he was only doing his job, after all.

'Sorry – just haven't got used to it yet. *And* these ridiculously early starts. How on earth do you do it?' This week they were shooting the coolest places for power breakfasts and weekend brunches, a deliciously New York concept. That said, it was six a.m., Poppy had already been up for an hour and she *still* had Hair and Make-up to go. She was looking forward to the week they did cocktail bars.

Poppy's bosses had taken a huge punt in giving her, a complete unknown, such an enormous slice of airtime. Half an hour, Monday to Thursday nights at ten p.m., for twelve weeks. The later time meant that Poppy could be a little more risqué and attract younger, cooler viewers. Every week there was a different theme on *Poppy Takes Manhattan*. This week, breakfasts and brunches; last week, vintage clothes stores; the week before, hotels with roof terraces. To stay bang on trend, the programmes were broadcast the week after they'd been shot (so this week they were showing the vintage clothes store episodes, Poppy's favourites so far).

Already the show was gathering a loyal following. Poppy was proving to be a natural in front of the camera, chatty and conspiratorial without ever patronizing the viewer. She'd wondered how Americans would take to an English girl telling them what was cool on their territory, so she played up the fact that she was an outsider, acting delighted and awestruck with every new gem she discovered (most of the time she didn't have to act much). It worked. The natives lapped it up. The show was due to be broadcast in the UK later in the year, and Poppy hoped she'd go down equally well with British audiences.

'Haven't been to bed yet.' Fabrice tapped the side of his own ink-black, perfectly waxed nose. He probably should have paid a little more attention to his nostrils though, both of which were ever so slightly crusty.

'Ooooh – where've you been?' Poppy was always eager to hear about others' debauchery, but now she could actually indulge in her passion for gossip in the name of research. This job really, really couldn't be better. She knew how lucky she was and was working like a trouper to show her gratitude.

'Where haven't I been?' Fabrice winked, and Poppy

giggled at him in the mirror. She did like the way she looked, even with a smarting red nose.

'Oh, my screaming Andy Warhols, you are just sooooo cute. If I had even an *atomo* of hetero hormones, I would be up your tiny tight pussy faster than HIV in a seventies 'Frisco sauna!'

'Wow, thanks . . . I think. So, Fab, take me through your night. I want to hear it all – bars, restaurants, clubs, the lot!'

By the time Fabrice had hilariously and indiscreetly told all, Poppy felt they might be friends for life. The final wax strip barely stung.

Make-up passed without a hitch – New Yorkers didn't want to look like footballers' wives, after all – and she emerged looking like an even better version of herself (if that were possible). But ensconced in Hair, Poppy had a battle on her hands.

'Um . . . I'm sure you know your job far better than I do . . .' She smiled winningly at the latest addition to her hairdressing team.

'I do.' Jojo, a terrifyingly well-groomed middle-aged redhead, didn't smile back.

'It's just that, if I'm meant to be the cool Anglo chick around town, I wouldn't be all blow-dried to within an inch of my life like this. I mean, my hair's always been a bit messy . . .'

'U-huh.' Only New Yorkers could imbue so few syllables with such disdain. Jojo pulled a golden lock even harder around the round brush. Poppy tried to stay friendly.

'. . . and I think that's kind of what they wanted – you know, for me to keep my – erm – unkempt London essence?'

'If you think I am letting you out in front of those cameras looking how you looked before, then you are mistaken, Brit chick,' said Jojo grimly. 'It's my reputation on the line here.'

Poppy smiled back sweetly, knowing she'd mess up the Stepford blow-dry as soon as she was out of the Nazi bitch's hands. It was her hair, and she'd wear it as she bloody well pleased.

Damian stared at his laptop morosely. Still no new messages, unless you counted the endless press releases and PR guff that flooded his inbox daily, as an ex-important journo (he was amazed they didn't update their files more frequently and put him in the box marked useless). It wouldn't hurt any of the editors he'd approached to at least acknowledge receipt of his features' ideas. A 'thanks but no thanks' would be preferable to the interminable silence. Apart from anything else it was bloody bad manners. He wasn't some unknown hack, he was a former *Stadium* columnist, for fuck's sake. And he knew most of the editors personally – they had all drunk and snorted together at many a press hooley.

Oh, well. He tried not to let it get to him as he got up off his sun lounger. Wandering over to the bar, he marvelled at the number of New Yorkers able to hang out on Soho House's roof terrace in the middle of the day, in the middle of the week. He imagined that a lot of them were, like him, newly unemployed. Recent victims of the recession. He laughed at himself. Victim wasn't quite the right word, not when you still had enough dosh for Soho House membership. And he wasn't the only one grabbing the opportunity to go freelance, which definitely had its perks. Networking in the sunshine over a cocktail or two wasn't such a bad way to spend your days.

Damian ordered another Manhattan. It seemed appropriate.

'I've got a tab. Um. It's in my wife's name. She's the member.'

Was the bartender ostentatiously hiding a smirk?

'And your wife's name, sir?'

'Poppy Evans-Wallace.'

He knew he was being childish. Poppy had insisted on keeping her maiden name for anything professional, which he was fine with really. That was how she was known in the TV world, after all. As it happened, the barman didn't even seem to notice the insertion of Evans, as he gave a little yelp.

'Poppy Wallace? Omigod, I just love her, she's so cute. They were filming here just a couple weeks back. That show's gonna be a cult classic, y'know. Have the drink with the compliments of the house, sir.'

'Thank you.' Damian smiled, his heart swelling with pride. Even he, who probably loved and admired Poppy more than anybody in the world, hadn't foreseen her new show being quite such a success. All he had to do was emulate some of that success himself and they'd be sorted. He took his drink from the bartender, thanking him again, and walked back to his sun lounger, fired up and full of fresh resolve to crack New York.

Opening his emails again, he saw there was a new one from Simon Snell, from his *Esquire* address. His heart quickened as he opened it. Surely, Simon, of all people, would respond positively to at least one of the pitches Damian had sent him?

I'm really sorry mate, but with this bloody recession we're just not commissioning from freelancers at the minute. Of course we've got to fill the mag somehow, so everybody with a salary is working twice as hard for their filthy lucre – I haven't left the office before 9 since I started here. Not that that's much comfort to you, I imagine. They were fucking good ideas though. Have you tried *GQ*? Their budget is massive compared to ours. Hope you're having fun in NY – I see it's 90 in the shade today. It's raining here. Plus ça change. BTW I've heard Poppy's show's going down a storm – please give her my congratulations. Sorry about the feature ideas, but I'm sure something will come up soon. Courage, mon ami and au revoir x

Damian took a large swig of his Manhattan, mulling everything over. Of course he'd tried *GQ* – UK *and* US versions. Simon must have realized that. Also, since Poppy's fling with Ben last year, it was very unlike Simon to say anything nice about her – though his Best Man's speech, delivered through gritted teeth, Damian suspected, had been charm itself. His professional situation had to be bad, he concluded. So what to do? If even Simon couldn't pull any freelancing strings for him, he needed another project to get his teeth into. Hmmm. Maybe he could write a screenplay?

Excited now as much by his new idea as the two Manhattans and blazing sunshine, Damian opened a new document in Word and saved it as SCREENPLAY. Then he stared at the empty page for a few minutes. Hmmm, he thought again. He probably needed another drink for inspiration. He drained the dregs of his Manhattan and made his way back to the bar for the third time that hour.

'Same again, sir?' The bartender was positively effusive this time, flashing Damian a cheeky grin as he started preparing another Manhattan. 'Hey,' he added, to an enormous blond man standing next to Damian, 'this lucky guy is married to that cute Brit chick with the new TV show. Y'know, Poppy Wallace? The one they were all raving about last night?'

'Dude, that is cool,' said the Viking in a clearly Scandinavian accent, turning to pump Damian by the hand so hard his teeth rattled. 'She is one hot chick. I'm Larsh.'

'Damian.' He shook back enthusiastically. 'And thanks for the comments, both of you. Poppy's even more gorgeous in the flesh. She's really clever too.' He was starting to feel a tad sentimental. This bartender mixed his drinks strong.

'I'm sure she ish, man, sure she ish.' Lars was slurring a little and Damian realized he was in the company of a fellow boozer. Excellent. Damian himself wasn't generally a lunchtime drinker, but with so much time on his hands he was finding it very easy to slip into, and curiously enjoyable. He looked properly at his new companion for the first time.

Everything about Lars was huge, from his head to his hands to his feet, but he wasn't fat. Just . . . HUGE. Piercing blue eyes looked out from a good-natured, square face, with a beaming smile that revealed big, square teeth.

'Let me get you a drink,' said Damian. 'What are you having?'

'Thank you, man.' Lars slapped Damian on the back, nearly propelling him over the bar. 'I am drinking schnapps.'

'Sounds great. I think I'll join you. Two very large schnapps, please, and have one for yourself, mate,' Damian added to the barman. 'It's on my wife's tab.' All three men roared with laughter at this. The barman gave Damian the Manhattan he'd just mixed (which Damian proceeded to down in one, belching slightly), then swiftly poured three absurdly large tumblers of neat schnapps.

Lars raised his glass and bellowed, 'SKOL!'

'SKOL!' shouted Damian and the barman. They poured the drinks down their throats and the barman happily started to prepare another round.

'So if you want your eggs sunny-side up in east Manhattan, I couldn't recommend a better place.' Poppy winked at the camera. 'And I have to say this *sunny-side* East Side is an awful lot more sunny – and, dare I say it – *up* than the grey old East End I left behind me in London. They have *jellied eels* in the East End of London, you know, and they are just as revolting as they sound!'

She felt a bit guilty about her disloyalty to her beloved 'hood, but hey. Business was business. And jellied eels *were* revolting. She'd tried them once, for a bet, pissed as a fart as she staggered home from Dalston to Hoxton, clad only in a shocking-pink leotard and laddered purple tights; she'd managed somehow to lose her boots, hat and skirt en route. Poppy had, with an effort, kept the eels down; her fellow reveller, a minor rock star used to three grams of coke and a bottle of JD a night, had puked his guts up.

'It's a wrap!' said Marty, the director.

'Really?' Poppy beamed at him. This was only her second take.

'You're a natural, honey. Go have some fun now. And don't forget – eight p.m. at L'Ambassadeur tonight.'

'How could I forget?'

As it was Thursday and they'd finished for the week, Marty had suggested that Poppy and Damian join him and his wife for drinks and dinner that evening at the hottest new restaurant in town. The assistant director and his boyfriend were going to be there too. 'Thanks for this morning, Marty, you're a star.' Poppy kissed him on the cheek and Marty blushed, unable to know how to take this gorgeous yet apparently unaffected English girl, their new star in the making. She was a breath of fresh air, of that he was certain.

Once Poppy had wiped her face clean of the make-up (it might have looked natural on screen, but it felt beyond disgusting in this heat), she decided to go to Greenwich Village and hit all the vintage shops she'd been filming in last week. It was about time she bought some presents for her loved ones, and unless she was very much mistaken, the shops would be falling over themselves to give her a discount.

'Poppy Wallace!' Sandra, a 65-year-old ex-rock chick with madly teased peroxide hair, a ton of black eyeliner and a treasure trove of a clothes shop, greeted her warmly. She was wearing an original Biba minidress, turquoise tights and purple PVC over-the-knee boots. She looked rather wonderful. 'Welcome back, doll! Since your show aired on Monday, I've quadrupled my takings!'

'Really?' Poppy's delight was genuine. All she had done,

after all, was get some cameramen in there, while Sandra had been building up this Aladdin's cave for the last twenty years or so. 'Oh, I'm so pleased for you. You deserve it. This place is to die for.'

The shop's interior was a fabulous juxtaposition of rock chick and over-the-top girly. The walls were painted a grungy matte black and hung with framed album covers from the sixties and seventies – the Stones, Led Zep, Velvet Underground, New York Dolls. ('It only goes on the wall if I screwed one of the band,' Sandra had confided to camera last week, much to the entire production team's delight.) Mingling with the album covers were beautifully stylized *Vogue* fashion illustrations from the twenties to the fifties.

The matte-black walls were offset by floorboards painted a glossy white and strewn with thick, fluffy sheepskin rugs. Either side of the shop window, sumptuously thick pale pink velvet curtains pooled luxuriously to the floor. Two ornate antique chandeliers glittered overhead, their light refracted against the black ceiling in ever-changing swirls by the disco glitter-ball rotating slowly over the pale pink painted Louis XVI escritoire that acted as the cash desk. Faux-French armchairs and chaises longues had been upholstered in animal print (leopard, zebra and cow), and the two longest walls were lined with rail upon rail of exquisite vintage clothes, ranging from Victoriana to the nineties – almost a century's worth.

Overgrown exotic plants lurked in every corner, except for the one that housed the single, very comfortably sized changing room, curtained off in the same sumptuous pale pink velvet. Inside, a huge Venetian mirror was propped against one black wall and a leopard-print upholstered chaise longue lounged alluringly against the other.

'Thanks, honey. Ya want some pot?' Sandra offered Poppy the spliff she held between age-spotted, scarlet-tipped fingers.

'Thanks, but I think I'll pass today. I'm on a mission to shop! And not even for myself, which makes it so much better. Guilt free!'

'I get where you're coming from, baby doll. But surely you'll want a couple pieces for yourself too?' Sandra looked at Poppy in an almost coquettish manner and Poppy laughed.

'Oh, go on, twist my arm then. Seriously though, I really want to get something nice for my best friend Bella. I put her through hell last year and she didn't deserve it.'

Sandra knew better than to enquire further, except to ask about Bella's size, shape and colouring. She rummaged amongst the rails and after some deliberation emerged with a Halston silk empire-line maxidress, circa 1977. It was a deep emerald green, with jewelled peacock feathers creeping up both the floor-sweeping hem and the thick halterneck ties.

'Oh, my bloody God, you are a genius, Sandra! Really! I didn't even tell you that all Bella's favourite dresses have halternecks! She's got lovely shoulders. She'll absolutely love it!' Poppy flung her arms around Sandra's neck, and it had the same effect as it always did, on everybody. Sandra would be a little bit in love with Poppy for the rest of her life from now on.

\* \* \*

'Yesssssshhhh, that is right, David.' Lars tried to focus on his new best mate, his blue eyes substantially more glassy than piercing now.

'Damian.' Damian tried to pronounce his own name correctly.

It transpired that Lars had been living in the Big Apple for five years, ever since he'd been headhunted from Merrill Lynch in Stockholm at the age of 29. The previous year, along with about half of his fellow emerging market traders, he'd been unceremoniously dumped by the bank. And even less ceremoniously dumped by his girlfriend, a stunning 21-year-old Romanian, who, in retrospect, he realized, 'loved the banker, not the man'. He repeated this phrase several times to Damian and the bartender.

'She sounds like a complete bitch, dude,' said Damian. 'What you need is a proper woman with her own mind, and her own job, like my wife.' He went all misty eyed for a second.

'Wow, man, you are one lucky guy,' said Lars. He put his enormous arms around Damian in the biggest, strangest (but somehow loveliest) man hug Damian had ever experienced.

'More schnapps!' shouted Damian, aware that there was something he was meant to be doing today, but not till an awful lot later. It was still broad daylight, so he had plenty of time . . .

'Schnapps! *Skol alcohol fer dom som tol!*' shouted Lars.

'*Skol alcohol . . . der molisotito . . . fom!*' shouted Damian and the barman.

After a moment's thought, 'Hey, dude?' the bartender asked mildly. 'What does that mean?'

At that the enormous Swede started to laugh so much he was crying, wiping his eyes with his oversized fingers. 'It means . . . it means . . . cheers, alcohol . . . for those who can take it!'

Damian and the barman also started to laugh so much that great salty tears were pouring down their cheeks. Another macho group hug was in order.

After a bit, Lars said decisively, 'And now we must shing. Ssshurely, you shing, my brotherssh?'

'Karaoke? Hey, man, why not? I've finished my shift and probably lost my job anyway!' said the good-natured barman, who Damian thought was called Tom or Tim (or possibly Jim). So they all piled into a great big limo ordered by the equally great big Swede, Damian and the Swede singing 'New York, New York' at the tops of their voices. Soon they drew up at a seedy-looking place with blacked-out windows and KARAOKE in neon letters above the door. The sun was still blazing overhead.

'It's not the toniest joint in town, but it's the only one in the neighbourhood where you can sing karaoke in daytime. Most of them don't open till seven,' said the omniscient barman. But Damian and Lars weren't listening, as they shouted the final chorus of 'New York, New York' into the bouncer's face.

'It's OK, dude, they're with me,' said the barman. Lars, still singing, shoved some 100-dollar bills into his hand.

The karaoke bar gave new meaning to the word dingy, but that bothered none of them. There were only a few other punters, and although it was hard to tell in the gloom, it was fair to say that they were probably in a similar condition to Damian and his new chums.

'Born to be wild, man,' said Damian, not really aware of what he was saying.

'YEEEEESSSSSHHHH!!!' shouted the mad Swede, like a blond Brian Blessed on acid, and soon the three of them were up there on the stage with their air gee-tars, shaking their heads and belting out the theme tune to *Easy Rider*.

Poppy sat in the sun outside the second-hand bookshop and sipped her freshly squeezed orange juice in total contentment. Her shopping trip had been an unmitigated success, partly thanks to Sandra's recommendation of this bookshop, which had been run by a lovely old gent called Louis for the past forty-five years. Dapper in pink shirt and chinos, he had smilingly told her that 'books are my life', before helping her find exactly what she was looking for.

Inside, the shop was comfortable and welcoming, all polished wood bookshelves and slouchy armchairs, in one of which resided a very sleepy and affectionate tabby cat. Outside, a few rickety tables and chairs had been set out on the pavement under the trees. Louis' daughter baked a couple of cakes every evening and brought them around the next morning for Louis to serve to his customers (today's selection was carrot or lemon drizzle). Louis himself squeezed the oranges and brewed the coffee in a little kitchen round the back. It was just heavenly, thought Poppy.

She took a bite of the scrumptious carrot cake and turned her attention to her purchases. Aside from the Halston dress for Bella, she'd also found her a beautifully bound 1920s edition of *The Collected Short Stories of Dorothy Parker*, which she knew her friend would love. She was aware she was being excessively generous, but her new job paid obscenely well and she still hadn't got over her guilt over her fling with Ben. For her mother (who had been a proper, bra-burning seventies feminist), a first edition of *Fear of Flying* and a pair of Art Deco jet-and-emerald earrings, with a necklace to match.

Poppy had had to stop herself buying a first edition of *The Grapes of Wrath*, which her father, a lifelong lover of Steinbeck, would have treasured were he still in his right mind. He would have no idea what it was now, and it was seriously expensive. Just for a second her gaze misted over, then she shook herself and turned back to her bags of goodies.

For herself, Poppy had picked out a 1930s eau-de-nil silk slip edged with coffee-coloured lace, which she planned to wear as a dress, and an original hardback version of *To Kill A Mockingbird*, though that might just be on loan to herself. It would be a lovely thing to give her daughter, were she ever to have one; she remembered devouring the book when she was about 12.

*The Collected Works of Hemingway*, published in 1961 (the year the great man died, as Louis had helpfully pointed out), was a perfect present for her scrivener husband. Poppy savoured the word *husband*, still loving the sound of it. She'd pop into Macy's on the way home for a few more bits and pieces for him. Damian was a joy to buy clothes for, his lean build and dark colouring lending themselves well to most styles. It was like having her own life-sized Ken doll, she thought fondly. She was looking forward to introducing him to her boss tonight.

Poppy wiped her fingers on a paper napkin and took

another peek in the bag containing the fabulous Halston dress. She hoped Bella would take it in the spirit it was meant, that it wouldn't scream *guilt gift* too loudly. She and Bella had been inseparable best friends since they first met as new girls at school, aged 10. Shagging Bella's boyfriend would have been unforgivable under any circumstances, but when you considered that Ben had been the first person Bella had really thought herself in love with, it was just too awful to contemplate.

When Bella and Ben had first got together, Poppy had been unreservedly delighted for both of them. So when Ben had started flirting with her (very subtly at first – the odd text or Facebook message), she thought she must have been imagining it. After all, he was her boyfriend's best friend and her best friend's boyfriend. All very neat and symmetrical. But by the time Ben upped the ante and started coming on to her in person, Poppy was already out of her mind with grief about her father's illness, and using coke heavily to numb her feelings. Unfortunately, it also numbed her finer feelings.

It all came to a head after the first occasion on which her father didn't recognize her. Poppy had dealt with it (not very maturely, she knew) by going on a massive bender. It was during this bender that Ben had called her, suggesting they meet one night he knew Damian was going to be away; he had told Bella he was flying to New York for a modelling shoot. Scheming fucker.

If Bella hadn't walked in on them, maybe nothing more would have happened, maybe . . . well – who knew what would have happened? But Poppy still couldn't bear to think about how much she'd hurt Damian and Bella, and was still amazed that either of them had ever spoken to her again (they weren't so forgiving towards Ben). It was only once she'd shacked up with the vain bastard that she'd realized how incompatible they were, how much she missed Damian. Both Poppy and Ben needed an audience, someone to adore them unconditionally. They'd ended up irritating the shit out of each other, two massive egos both clamouring to be heard loudest.

Whereas, Damian . . . Poppy smiled fondly again as she thought of Damian. Dear Damian, so cool and laid-back about most things. How she'd missed his dry sense of humour and (OK, she admitted it) pretty much unconditional adoration. They had a great relationship, complemented one another perfectly.

Though it was funny that somebody so laid-back in most areas of his life could be so sensitive professionally. Despite his success in the men's magazine world (until now), Poppy knew that Damian was highly ambitious and wanted greater recognition. He was a damned good writer, after all, she thought proudly. Probably the best of the lot of them on *Stadium*, which had showcased his wit and left-field humour perfectly. She sincerely hoped that this recession would prove an ill wind that blew him some good. Who knew what opportunities New York would throw up?

She took her iPhone out of her new Marc Jacobs handbag and called him, just to hear his voice. It rang for ages but there was no reply. Strange. Damian always answered his phone swiftly, just in case it was a commissioning editor (or Poppy herself). She tried again. Still nothing. Oh, well. Instead, she sent a text.

*Hope you've had a great day darling husband. Looking forward to seeing you at L'Ambassadeur at 8. Wifey x*

She finished her cake and orange juice and went inside to say goodbye to Louis. She'd better go home and get changed. She wanted to make a good impression tonight.

Damian was having the time of his life. Ever since he'd hit London in the late nineties he'd been obsessed with obscure dance and indie music, keeping up with the hippest DJs and latest bands, always to be found backstage at gigs and festivals. None of his friends or men's magazine cronies would believe it if they could see him now, singing along to cheesy Queen hits with the wild abandon of an alcoholic uncle at a wedding. 'Don't Stop Me Now' was going down particularly well.

He and Lars were cheered along by the motley crew of fellow daytime karaoke aficionados that made up their audience. Actually, it was no longer daytime, but most of them had been there since lunchtime. Once the song was over, they prepared to descend from the stage, despite cries of 'More!' and 'Encore!'. The time had come for another drink.

'Thanks, guys,' said Damian modestly, taking a bow. 'But now I think it's time for somebody else to . . . to . . . to . . . RRRRRRRIP UP THE FLOOR!' By the time he got to the end of his sentence, he was shouting and waving his mike in the air, to rapturous applause.

'Darren, my friend,' slurred Lars. Damian couldn't be bothered to correct him. 'Am I glad to have met you, man.' And without further ado, he slung Damian over his shoulder in a fireman's lift and carried him to the bar.

Through tears of laughter, Damian started to sing 'New

York, New York' again, the words muffled against Lars's huge back.

Lars joined in from somewhere around Damian's knees, and the rest of the room happily shouted out the chorus. Then there was much shushing as the next singers had mounted the stage, about to give their performance of a lifetime.

'What you drinkin thish time, man?' Lars asked Damian, putting him back to his feet like a dishevelled half-Indian rag doll in designer jeans.

'No no no, it's my round,' said Damian, reaching into the wrong pocket for his wallet, and pulling out his phone instead. 'Ooooh, look, messssage . . . oh, *fuck!* Shit, Lars, what's the time?'

'Wasssshamatter, old buddy?' Lars furrowed his blond brow, putting a heavy hand on Damian's shoulder.

'Lars, mate, *what's the time*?' Damian had forgotten he could check the time perfectly well himself on his phone. Not to mention his watch.

Lars looked at his enormous Rolex.

'It'sh twenty hundred hoursh. But why, my friend?'

'Because I've just been reminded where I'm supposed to be, *right now*. D'you know a place called L'Ambassadeur?'

'Do I know L'Ambasshadeur?' Lars smiled broadly. 'Man, I have sharesh in that place.'

'Is it far from here?'

'I'll take you there, my friend. Who ya meeting there?'

'Oh, only my wife. And her boss. And his wife.'

Both men stared at each other for a second, then started roaring with laughter again, slapping backs and thighs in total male harmony.

\*   \*   \*

'So you see, Poppy, it is vitally important that we don't feed our kids dairy. Cows' milk is for kiddy cows. We don't express *our* milk and feed it to those kiddy cows, now do we?' Eleanor, Marty's wife, gave a nervous laugh and Poppy tried to make her own laughter sound sincere. She had to admit Eleanor had a point (if not a vocabulary that included the word *calves*), which might, at a pinch, be interesting, but all she had talked about since they'd arrived at L'Ambassadeur had been child-rearing. And not the fun stuff that Poppy's few friends with children back in the UK talked about – the very sweet things they sometimes said or did, or the anecdotes of embarrassing swearwords coming from little mouths in public. Oh, no.

Eleanor's party chitchat ran the gamut from children's nutrition to pre-school education to 'downtime'. Her only son, Hammond (Why did so many Americans have names that should be surnames?) was 18 months old. Poor little bugger. Poppy didn't think Eleanor was a bad woman, but she was just so bloody earnest, so desperate not to get things wrong. She had a face that hovered between plain and pretty. Her smile was sweet, her jawline delicate and her pale skin flawless, but her forehead was just too narrow, her eyes just too small, her lips just too thin for her to be a proper beauty. Her light brown shoulder-length hair was side parted, very straight and very shiny. A beautifully cut Narciso Rodriguez beige silk shift dress, a few shades lighter than her hair, skimmed a slender body that bore no visible signs of childbirth. Apparently, she'd been a trader on Wall Street, pre-Hammond. Poppy found this very hard to believe.

Marco, the assistant director, who was short, swarthy and good-looking, with several piercings, was wearing skinny black jeans with a corduroy biker's jacket and a vintage Alexander McQueen skull-printed scarf around his stubbly throat. His partner, Chase, a model for Ralph Lauren, was dressed entirely in Ralph Lauren and as ludicrously handsome as you'd expect a Ralph Lauren model to be, with a broad jaw, high cheekbones and golden-blond hair swept back from a magnificent brow. He appeared to have about as much personality as the shop dummy he resembled.

The conversation had not, so far, been what you'd call sparkling. For the first time since she'd been in NY, Poppy was missing grey old London enormously.

A waiter came to the table.

'Can I take your order?'

'We're still waiting for one of our guests,' said Marty, who was wearing a black T-shirt under a black Armani jacket and heavy-rimmed glasses that he thought made him look intellectual.

'It's OK, Marty, order without him,' said Poppy. 'I'm so sorry Damian's so late. It's very unlike him.' Inside, she was seething. *Where the fuck was he?*

'No, we'll wait for your husband,' said Marty, smiling at his latest protégée, who was looking gorgeous in a sage-green suede sleeveless minidress that matched her eyes and showed off her coltish brown limbs. With her streaky blonde hair loose around her shoulders, he thought she was just delicious. 'In the meantime, why don't we get some wine?'

'Sounds great. A white and a red as some of us are

having meat, and some having fish?' Poppy looked around the table.

'Two bottles?' Eleanor looked horrified.

'Hey, it's only a couple glasses each,' said Marco, kicking Poppy under the table. Poppy remembered Fabrice's tales of Martinis, crystal meth and amyl nitrate with Marco the night before and hid a smile.

'My nutritionist says there's so much sugar in wine. And sugar is *poison*.'

Marty laughed heartily and patted his wife's hand.

'Eleanor's been a lot more aware of her mortality since we had Hammond. Kids do need their moms to be alive, after all.'

Everyone laughed weakly.

'What about their dads, Marty?' Poppy couldn't help it, even though he was her boss.

Marty looked taken aback.

'Sheesh, well, of course they need their dads too! But their dads can handle their poison as they *bring home the bacon* –' he did an excruciating Cockney accent – 'while their mommies stay home and look after them. And you don't want a poisoned mommie in charge of the kiddies now, do ya?'

He actually wished Eleanor would lighten up a bit. He was glad his wife was such a great mom, but after two miscarriages that had nearly destroyed their marriage, Ellie's overwhelming joy when Hammy had been born perfect was rendered almost maniacal by the relief. Her subsequent quest for perfect motherhood was both laudable and intensely wearing.

Poppy looked at Marty askance. She had thought that

84

only the Americans in the middle of the States thought that way. The ones on the East and West coasts were meant to be a tad more liberal.

'I've never been more fulfilled than I am now, staying home and looking after Hammy.' Poppy couldn't tell whether Eleanor sounded smug or pleading, as she turned to her with that earnest, slightly scared expression in her pale blue eyes.

'It must be wonderful,' she started, trying to be nice, but her words were drowned out by two very drunken male voices. One was singing something that sounded like a Scandinavian folk song. The other – oh, good God, it was Damian – was trying to whisper, very unsubtly, 'Shhhh, mate, they must be here somewhere.'

'You musssht not worry, my friend, I have shhooo many shhhhares here, I practically OWN THIS PLACE!'

Poppy was just wondering whether hiding under the table or doing a runner would be the better option, when Eleanor leapt to her feet.

'Omigod! Lars!'

The enormous blond man took a moment or so to register, then swept Poppy's boss's wife off her feet in a huge bear hug.

'ELLIE!'

Once the Viking had put her down, Eleanor turned to Marty, eyes shining, cheeks flushed, and said, 'Hey, honey, remember Lars, who used to work with me at Merrill Lynch?'

Marty stood up and held out his hand. 'I believe we did have the pleasure once.'

'Oh, Lars, all those hours you kept us going on the

trading floor with your smorgasbord and schnapps!'
Eleanor's mouth was running away with her. 'Such fun
times!'

Damian took advantage of this fortuitous new development to sneak up behind Poppy and kiss the back of
her neck. She turned round, glaring at him, and
whispered,

'You are pissed as a fucking fart.'

'I know. Sorry. I'll do anything to make it up to you.'

Poppy turned her back on him, only to see that Marco
and Chase (who clearly was not made of wood after all)
were pissing themselves laughing, giving her the thumbs-
up and pulling up a chair for Damian.

Eleanor, Lars and Marty were still standing up, talking,
when Lars boomed, in his enormous voice, 'ASH IT ISH
MY BIRTHDAY, I WANT TO BUY SCHNAPPS! FOR ALL!'
He turned to Damian and gave him an almost imperceptible
wink. Damian, sitting in a chair between Poppy and Marco,
smiled nervously.

'Oh, honey, don't you think that sounds grand?' Eleanor
said to her husband. Lars's arrival seemed to have relaxed
her attitude to poisons somewhat. 'It is his birthday, after
all! And – oh, jeez, you cannot be Poppy's husband? My,
what a coincidence. So how did you meet my old friend
and colleague Lars then?'

Poppy pinched the tiny bit of flesh on the back of
Damian's ribcage to tell him to think of something cool.
To her relief, he came up trumps.

'Hello. Eleanor, isn't it? I'm so sorry, we haven't been
introduced properly. Yes, I am Poppy's husband. Damian
. . .' He gave a repulsively insincere grin and stood up,

holding out his hand. 'I'm a journalist. I was interviewing Lars about the Scandinavian markets earlier. What a wonderful coincidence.'

Chase said to Poppy, with the first proper bit of animation she'd seen all evening, 'Man, your husband is *hot.*'

'My bloody husband is a useless bloody drunk,' she started, quietly, only to be hushed by the gay couple.

'Babe, he is *hot,*' they said in unison.

And despite herself, Poppy started to giggle. Who was she actually trying to impress anyway? Marty was an unreconstructed sexist that she could wrap around her little finger, and the rest of them seemed quite fun now.

The waiter brought the bottle of schnapps to the table and they all drank their shots as one.

'SKOL!'

Eleanor was dancing on the table, singing 'All That Jazz' from *Chicago*. Everybody else cheered her on, and joined in with all the words they knew (basically, the song's title!). The food, which nobody had touched, had been taken away about half an hour ago by the waiting staff after Lars had thrust several more hundred-dollar bills into their hands.

Now, Eleanor was getting quite raunchy as she sang about 'rouging her knees and pulling her stockings down' – raising her skirt and giving a little shimmy as she twirled inexpertly amongst the glasses and bottles.

Poppy, sitting next to Marty, was feeling a tad uncomfortable despite the neat liquor. Her boss had said earlier that mommies shouldn't be ingesting poisons, after all. She turned to him and saw that he was roaring with laughter and applauding.

'Sorry about Lars ordering the schnapps,' she whispered to him.

'Are you kidding? This is great! THIS is the woman I married.' And, stumbling slightly, Marty got up to join his wife on the table. Alas, his greater weight was too much and the table collapsed beneath them. Husband and wife lay, roaring with happy laughter, amongst the absolute chaos of broken glass and no-longer starched linen.

'I love you, Martypoos!'

'Oh, Elliekins, I love you too!'

And they had a very unseemly public smooch. Poppy thanked God that neither of them seemed to be hurt by the scary-looking green shards of ex-wine bottles that surrounded them.

Poppy was dreaming that Ben was going down on her, his tongue expertly flicking her clitoris, his long-lashed blue eyes looking up at her mischievously. Even in her dream, she hated him, so she bashed his head, hard.

'Owww,' said Damian, who was the actual cunnilinguist. 'I thought I was doing quite well.'

Awake now, Poppy said, 'Sorry, darling. Bad dream. Please, don't stop.'

Damian didn't stop. He continued to lick Poppy's waxed cunt until he could taste her arousal. She moaned, and Damian opened her up with his fingers, feasting his eyes and keeping her waiting for a couple of seconds, before sliding the first two fingers of his other hand inside her.

He bent his head again and resumed sucking, licking, nibbling. Poppy bucked against him, moaning more and more loudly until, with a sharp cry, she came.

He waited a second or two, then started moving his fingers in and out again, ever so slowly, sucking again to milk the very last drops of pleasure from her. Only when he felt her throbbing finally begin to subside did he withdraw his hand, then move up the bed to kiss her on the lips. Poppy kissed him back, liking the taste of herself on him.

'Mmmm, thank you, darling,' she said dreamily. 'That was soooo good.'

Damian leapt to his feet.

'And now for the second course!'

He walked to the kitchen of their apartment, which was pretty much the interior brickwork urban cool ex-warehouse in the Meatpacking District that Andy had envisaged. He returned bearing a tray heaped with eggs, bacon and mushrooms, waffles and maple syrup, freshly squeezed orange juice, bagels and smoked salmon.

'Blimey,' said Poppy, laughing. 'Are we having guests or something?'

'Just wanted to say sorry for last night.' Damian looked up at her from underneath his lashes and she laughed even more. 'Am I forgiven?'

'Oh, you totally lovable thing. Thank you – it all looks completely yummy. Yes, of course you're forgiven – *this time*. But you're bloody lucky that Lars and Eleanor go way back. It could have been a fucking disaster.' She tried to look stern but Damian looked so contrite, and she was feeling so blissfully post-orgasmic, that it was impossible.

'Right, let's dig in. Hmmm, waffles or bagels to start . . . sooo tricky . . .' When Poppy remembered to eat, she had the appetite of a horse, yet never gained a pound. It was one of the many things that Bella envied about her.

# Chapter 6

Sam tried to ignore the whispering and muffled giggles as she walked into the college canteen. She had dressed as unobtrusively as she could, in jeans and an enormous black jumper that she hoped disguised her boobs. Contrary to what everybody thought, the boobs were natural, a result of her catching glandular fever when she was 14, just as she was starting to develop. Sam would no sooner have taken a knife to her young body than she'd have taken a knife to anybody else's body, but she'd grown tired of trying to explain. Practically everybody else in the glamour-modelling world had had 'something done', and she'd learned quite soon that protesting her chest was natural just got her the reputation of being a stuck-up bitch.

At uni, she tried to disguise them, just as she played down the prettiness of her young face by half covering it in heavy-rimmed specs, and hiding her long dark red hair under unflattering baseball caps. She had an adorable face, peachy-skinned with enormous dark brown eyes and what

Mark referred to as blowjob lips. Sam had got into glamour modelling by being discovered while walking the dog in a park near her parents' home in Romford when she was 17, two years earlier.

She had always wanted to go to uni, but now the fees were so high, it had seemed an impossibility until the seedy photographer accosted her in the park. Her mum and dad's small catering business was barely afloat with this horrible recession and her little brother Ryan was severely autistic. Much though Sam loved him, she realized what a nightmare (and expense) he was to look after. There was no way she could burden her parents with anything else, and if there was a way for her to fund her own education, then she'd grab it with both hands.

After the initial horror of taking her clothes off in front of men old enough to be her dad, she'd got used to it. Only a couple of them were lechy old pervs, anyway, and Sam was made of pretty stern stuff, rationalizing what she was doing in a clear-headed, logical manner. If this was what she had to do to get the proper education she craved, it wasn't such a big deal. It wasn't as if she cared what any of the people in the glamour-modelling world thought of her, after all.

But she did care what her fellow students thought of her. Sam had always been very careful to keep her assets under wraps at uni, as she wanted to be admired for her mind (although she'd come to appreciate her body, which she had thought was freakish, now that Marky seemed to love it so much). Sometimes, in seminars, the tutor would actually say, 'Could somebody other than Sam please answer this question?', which made her secretly proud. She was only a girl from an Essex comprehensive, after all, and more than half of her peers had been to posh schools.

But yesterday, horribly, one of the really posh ones, a smug wanker called Josh, had walked into the Union bar brandishing a copy of *Nuts*.

'Look what we have here,' he'd said, in his loathsome, drawling voice. 'I think that somebody in our vicinity takes their clothes off for a living! Sammi-Jo, everyone! What's the matter, Sam, can't make it with that enormous brain of yours, after all? You have to rely on your enormous tits instead! Hahahahahaaaa – hardly the next Nietzsche after all, more like a little two-bit whore!'

Josh was on the same course as Sam and clearly hated the fact that she was a million times cleverer than he was. He had the enormous sense of entitlement of the seriously rich and terminally stupid.

Everybody in the bar had been jostling to see the pictures, and a couple of pissed third-year students had actually tried to lift up her jumper to 'see what you're hiding, Sammi-Jo'. It was just horrific, worse than anything she'd ever imagined happening to her. She'd only ever worked hard and been nice to people. Her parents, while distracted, loved her unconditionally, and her schoolmates had pretty much left her to her own devices as she beavered away at her Maths and Science classes. She was completely unprepared for the humiliation of being jeered at by the community she had so wanted to join.

But she had to eat, and now she skulked into the canteen, feeling like the lowest bit of dog shit on the earth.

'Tart,' giggled a couple of girls who'd been at Heathfield together, as she walked past, head down. Sienna

Sax-Hoffmann was sitting next to them. God, she hated Sienna, with her wafty ways and her bloody lace parasol. How fucking affected was that?

Just as she thought she'd made it unscathed to the food counter, Josh, who she'd fervently hoped wouldn't be in the canteen today, stood up and shouted,

'Oh, look! It's our resident glamour model! Not looking very glam today, is she? She might look better if she got her kit off though! What d'you think, guys? Kit off, kit off, kit off!'

The entire canteen started chanting, 'KIT OFF, KIT OFF, KIT OFF!', and Sam dropped her tray, fleeing the canteen in tears. When she got back to her room she picked up every bit of crockery and started throwing it at the walls, sobbing so hard her heart thought it might burst. She couldn't understand why people could be so nasty. What had she ever done to them, after all? On balance, she found the glamour-modelling world preferable to the academia that she had so longed for all her short life. Thank God she had Marky.

She picked up the card her parents had given her and looked inside.

'Were so proud of you Sam,' it said. 'Your going to have the bestest time at Uni.' She cried a bit more as she read her mother's sweetly meant and ungrammatical message. 'Loads of love from Mum and Dad.' They had each signed it, with flourishes of kisses. Ryan had written on the other side, 'luv you sam hav fun' and drawn a surprisingly accomplished picture of her in a mortarboard.

Sam sat down on the floor and let herself cry until she thought she couldn't cry any more. She missed them so much. It was so tempting to give up now. What was she doing here anyway? She didn't belong with these people.

She was sobbing so hard that she didn't hear the tentative tapping at her door until it got louder and louder.

'What?' she shouted.

'Sam, are you OK?'

'What the fuck do you think?' Sam managed through her tears.

'Open the door, darling. I think they're a bunch of cunts and you probably need a hug,' said the voice.

Slowly, Sam got to her feet and opened the door, only to see Sienna Bitch-Hoffmann standing there, like some bloody aerial nymph or fairy in pale green lace. She was carrying a bottle of Dom Pérignon.

'Go away.'

'I'm not going anywhere.' Sienna waltzed in as if she owned Sam's room and put the bottle of champagne on her desk. Then she turned around and put her skinny arms around Sam. It was so nice, and so unexpected, that Sam just cried and cried and cried until Sienna said, 'OK, enough's enough. This is Lanvin and I'll have to get it dry-cleaned if you carry on crying on it like this. Let's have a drink. Though I can't see many receptacles left . . .' She indicated the broken crockery on the floor and Sam opened her cupboard to produce the mug saying STUDENT BABE that her mum had bought her.

'You have that, I'm quite happy to swig from the bottle,' said Sienna, expertly opening the Dom Pérignon with barely a pop and pouring it into the mug.

'Why are you being nice to me?' Sam sniffled.

'Because I think you've been treated horribly and Josh is

the biggest cunt on the planet. Who the fuck does he think he is? "Kit off, kit off, kit off!" indeed. Arsehole. We should try to get *his* kit off in public – apparently his cock's *tiny*.'

Sienna wiggled her little finger and Sam laughed, despite herself.

'That's better,' said Sienna. 'For what it's worth, I'm bloody jealous! I saw the photos and, good God, what wouldn't I give for tits like those! I've been bee-stung my entire life. Where *did* you get them done?'

'They're not fake,' Sam muttered miserably, feeling like a freak of nature again. 'I had glandular fever when I was 14 . . .'

Sienna laughed. 'Well, in that case, you really are bloody lucky! Every man's wet dream! And if those idiotic boys out there are threatened by a woman who's, by all accounts, highly intelligent *and* has great knockers, then it's their moronic problem. Don't you think?'

Feeling an awful lot better, Sam took a gulp of champagne out of the mug and said, 'Thanks. I thought you were so stuck up and posh before.'

'Oh, fuck, no, common as muck. Daddy's in trade, darling, talks like a barrow boy. It's only the schools that make you speak like I do.'

'But you're so confident. I'd feel like a complete dick wafting around in lace with a parasol . . .'

'You'd look one too,' drawled Sienna, and they both burst out laughing. Of course, Sienna could carry it off with her height and blonde otherworldliness. Buxom little Sam with her dyed-auburn hair would look as though she were auditioning for a period porn romp.

'But where d'you get it? The confidence? I mean, I think Josh is a . . . cunt . . . too . . .' Sam hesitated over the word as she'd always disliked it and her parents had been pretty heavy about the swear-box at home. 'But wouldn't it tear you apart if he did to you what he's just done to me?'

'I suppose I'll never know the answer to that – horrible little shit wouldn't dare – but I doubt it. The obscene amount of money Daddy's earned over the years must have given me some kind of coat of armour.' Sienna dismissed her birthright with a wave of her wafty hand and added, 'Let's have some more booze, then get tarted up and go and have some fun. I think you need cheering up.'

'That sounds brilliant,' said Sam, wiping away the vestiges of tears. 'What are you going to wear?'

Sienna laughed. 'Don't worry, I don't always dress like this. It's fun to have a certain image with these college idiots, mess with their boring heads, but when I go to Camden I like to rock it up a bit. Pints of snakebite and Lanvin are not the best bedfellows.'

'Camden? Where?' Sam was excited; she loved indie music, and that whole kind of grungy scene, but she'd been so focused on earning a living to study, so she could get somewhere in life, that she'd never really had time for that sort of fun.

'The Hawley Arms.'

'Fuckin' 'ell, I think that's Natalia,' said Mark to Justin, Bella's father. They were on their third cognacs after lunching at Club 55 on Pampelonne Beach in Saint-Tropez, where they'd just been shooting for *GQ*. 'She's not bad for an old tart.'

'Not bad at all,' said Justin appreciatively. 'Apparently, she goes like the clappers too. Hey! Nat!'

Natalia, who had just swum onto the beach from her yacht, was wearing an emerald-green high-cut swimsuit with the sides cut out, which made her 44-inch legs look endless. Always aware of keeping the façade intact, she had scraped her white-blonde hair back into a tight bun. There was no way she'd put her face or hair underwater. She felt a stab of annoyance at seeing Mark and Justin. Of all the people she'd met at Poppy and Damian's wedding, they were probably the ones she liked the least, with their wandering eyes and overt lechery. Oh, well. She sighed and approached their table.

'Hi, hi, how wonderful to see you.'

'You too, babe,' said Mark, getting up to kiss her and letting his gaze roam unnecessarily over her body. She tried not to let her internal disgust become apparent.

'Natalia!' said Justin. 'Not looking a day over twenty!'

If this drunken, arrogant old pig thought that she would be flattered by this, he was very much mistaken. She knew how great she looked. She spent enough time and money on it.

'Joining us for a drink then?' asked Justin.

'No no no. I thank you, but there are people I must see. Wonderful to see you again.' Natalia blew them both a kiss with her long, perfectly manicured fingers and walked over to the bar. Both men watched her extraordinary bottom, atop those extraordinarily long legs, as she departed. Justin gave out a low whistle.

Club 55 was the ultimate jet-set destination in St Trop, created in 1955 when Roger Vadim was filming Brigitte

Bardot frolicking on the beach in *Et Dieu . . . créa la femme*. Legend had it that when the crew mistook a local fisherman's cottage for a bistro, the owner's wife happily fed them all and Club 55 was born.

The restaurant, laid out behind the beach under tamarind trees, was stylishly understated, all white wooden tables and chairs with sun-faded blue tablecloths that echoed the blues of sky and sea in the dazzling sunlight. Seated at practically every table were girls, exquisite like butterflies in pink-and-turquoise kaftans, jewelled flip-flops and enormous designer shades. With few exceptions, the mahogany-tanned men footing the bills were several decades older than them.

Mark and Justin had moved to the bar area for their cognacs. The white stone bar and seats, white linen cushions and white sand emphasized the patrons' expensive tans. Mark was surprised they hadn't somehow managed to bleach the palm trees to match the rest of the decor.

The behaviour here was more outrageous than in the restaurant area. Even Mark and Justin cringed as they witnessed yet another gold-toothed rapper standing on a table and spurting yet another 2,000-euro bottle of Cristal over a gaggle of giggling, bikini-clad models. Wasn't the world meant to be in some kind of financial meltdown?

'I wonder what the poor people are doing today,' said Justin, and Mark barked with laughter.

A man who put the sleaze into sleazy approached their table. Of indeterminate age, he was rocking a luridly patterned Roberto Cavalli open-to-the-waist silk shirt atop obscenely tight white jeans. His obviously dyed-black hair looked as if it had been washed in industrial oil and his bling out-blang everybody else on the beach.

'Hey, Justin, my man!' He stretched out his arms in greeting and Justin rose to his bare feet.

'Stefan. Long time no see. Wotcha been up to, mate?'

Stefan winked.

'Half the girls in this bar.' His accent hovered somewhere between LA, mittel-Europe and Peckham.

All three men laughed, though Mark felt slightly uneasy. Although neither he nor Justin were by any stretch of the imagination clean-living paragons of virtue, there was something seriously unpleasant about this geezer. Though he had to admire the bastard's taste, if what he was saying were true.

'This is Mark,' said Justin. 'A friend of my daughter Bella's.'

'Bella,' said Stefan with a lascivious gleam in his eye. 'Pretty name, and I hear she's a pretty girl too. Don't think I've had the pleasure though . . . Is she with you?'

'No, she's at home in London. And don't you go getting any ideas, you old bastard; she's my little angel and I wouldn't let you within a hundred yards of her with a bargepole.' Justin took a large swig of his cognac as he mixed his metaphors, then laughed. 'She's way too old for you anyway.'

'OK, OK, man, I get it. Daughter's off-limits. But if you want to meet some hot chicks younger than your sweet little girl, come to my party tonight. The Linda Lovelace boat, moored in the *vieux port*, can't miss it. Hey, *babeeee*!' His attention was distracted by a very young Eurasian girl with shiny black hair that hung in a sleek curtain down to her waist. She was wearing an olive-green string-thong bikini bottom and matching tiny cropped T-shirt with

HOT STUFF written across the chest. As Stefan snaked a proprietorial arm around her, he was joined by another girl who made Mark catch his breath. She had to be the sexiest thing he had ever seen.

Probably in her early twenties, the girl had a cat-like face, with large, slanting, deep turquoise eyes, framed with thick dark lashes and beautifully arched brows. Her wide, mischievous smile revealed perfect white teeth that gleamed in her smooth brown face. Long, streaky light brown hair swished around her shoulders, and a short dress made entirely of gossamer-fine white crochet teasingly revealed a lithe brown body with the exquisite muscle definition of the natural athlete. Underneath the dress, she was wearing only the briefest of white bikini bottoms; her bare, tip-tilted breasts pushed alluringly against the white lace.

'Hi,' she said, smiling up at him through sooty lashes. 'I'm Karolina.'

*Down boy, down boy, think of Sam.* Mark willed his cock not to stiffen.

'Hi, Karolina. I'm Mark.'

'And I'm Justin.' Justin eagerly thrust his hand out. 'Great dress, babe.'

Stefan roared with laughter at their reactions.

'See? All my girls are HOT. Catcha later? Fun and games you won't regret.' He winked again and slimed off, dragging both girls with him.

'Fuck me,' said Mark. 'Did you *see* that girl?'

'Uh-huh.' Both men were still gazing after the threesome.

'Who's the geezer then?' asked Mark, when they'd

managed to drag their gaze away and were once more sitting nursing their cognacs.

'Stefan Rafael, the porn king. Not his real name, of course. He is *bad news*.' Justin laughed. 'But if those two chicks are anything to go by, his party might be worth a look.'

'Better count me out,' said Mark with regret. 'I'm practically married these days.' He did love Sam, and for the first time in his life had been faithful the entire time they'd been together. Her sweet nature and phenomenal body brought out his manly, protective instincts. But he wasn't sure he could trust himself at a porn party full of babes like Karolina. He took out his phone and looked at his screensaver: a photo of Sam's smiling young face. It was more to strengthen his resolve than anything else.

Justin laughed again and slapped him on the back. 'You're a better man than I am, Gunga Din.'

Natalia, who had witnessed the entire encounter from the safe distance of the bar, rolled her eyes and shuddered.

'You don't think it's a bit . . . tight?' Sam looked doubtfully at her reflection in Sienna's age-spotted antique mirror. Sienna had somehow managed to imbue her student digs with a bohemian charm that, while beguiling, was not so over-the-top as to feel completely out of place in halls of residence. Unlike the clothes she chose to wear.

'Darling, you look gorgeous. Besides, it's the biggest T-shirt I've got.' In purple skinnies that clung to her long legs like a second skin, and braless in a black American Apparel vest, Sienna was practically unrecognizable from the ethereal waif in floor-length lace Sam had known earlier. She'd teased her long blonde hair so it stood out madly around her face, piled on the black eyeliner and thrown several crucifixes and skull pendants around her slender white neck.

Sam was wearing a red-and-black-tartan mini-kilt over black opaques and biker boots, but Sienna had deemed the black polo-neck jumper she had wanted to wear with it 'boooorring' and insisted she borrow something from her own wardrobe to 'rock things up'. Hence, the NEVER MIND THE BOLLOCKS T-shirt that strained manfully over Sam's boobs. As Sam didn't wear much make-up when she wasn't working, Sienna had insisted on making up her eyes with as much kohl as she had made up her own. After much deliberation, head tilted to one side as she considered, she'd tied Sam's hair into jaunty pigtails.

Now, as, side by side, they looked in the mirror, Sam had to admit they looked quite cool together. She'd always played it pretty safe with her sartorial choices, but was starting to realize that dressing up, messing around with your image like this, could actually be fun. It was completely different to trying to make yourself look as sexy as possible for the 'readers' of men's magazines.

'You look brilliant, Sam,' said Sienna again. 'The boys won't know what's hit 'em.'

'Boys?' After the last two days' experiences with evil Josh, the last thing Sam wanted was to be meeting new boys. She'd thought this evening was about a night out with her new best friend. Sienna laughed.

'Oh, don't worry, they're perfectly harmless. Four sweet chaps from up north somewhere. They think of me as a kind of mascot for their band . . .'

\*    \*    \*

It was a typical London summer evening: cold, rainy and miserable.

'What are we doing in this godforsaken hellhole of a country?' said Sienna as they shivered at the bus stop on Euston Road. Sam wished she'd been allowed to keep her polo-necked sweater on (Sienna had shrugged on a beaten-up leather jacket just before they left halls). 'We should be soaking up the rays in Saint-Tropez right now.'

'My boyfriend's in Saint-Tropez at the moment,' said Sam shyly.

'Really?' Sienna looked at her with surprise, which she quickly tried to hide. 'Lucky him. What does he do? Not a lowly student like us, I take it?'

'He used to be the art director on *Stadium* – you know, the men's magazine, before it folded. Now he freelances. They've been shooting for *GQ* – that's why he's in the South of France, you see.'

'Is that how you met him?' Sienna asked, the penny dropping, and Sam nodded. The bus drew up and both girls flashed their Oyster cards at the driver before making a beeline for the back row of the top deck, oblivious to every male head (and a couple of female ones) swivelling in their direction. They were a couple of incredibly pretty young girls.

'So what does he look like, this boyfriend of yours?' asked Sienna. 'Got any photos?'

'Course!' Sam giggled. 'Who hasn't got photos of their boyfriend?'

She took out her phone and gave it to Sienna. As she started scrolling through, Sienna's voice got higher and higher.

'Sam! He's bloody gorgeous! He looks like Jason Statham! Oh, woweeeewow!' She clutched Sam's shoulder and Sam was reminded that, for all her sophisticated ways, Sienna was still actually only 19, just like her. She smiled at her new best friend with enormous gratitude, so glad to have a proper ally for once.

The *vieux port* at Saint-Tropez had to be seen to be believed. Mark and Justin had been there many times before, of course, but for the ogling, badly dressed day-trippers (soon about to depart, thank the Lord) it was something akin to Disneyland. This tiny bit of legendary celeb-ville was not much more than a small handful of prettily pastel-coloured nineteenth-century buildings clustered around a waterfront teeming with yachts, super-yachts and mega-yachts. The majority of these buildings now housed obscenely expensive boutiques, bars and restaurants. If you just wanted to people-watch, it was possible to sit at one and drink a coffee for 15 euros, though those in the know, and the students who'd read up on St Trop in the Lonely Planet, realized it was cheaper to get a small *pression* – or draft lager – for less.

Mark and Justin were beyond the stage of caring. After the fifth cognac at Club 55 (all paid for by *GQ*), they'd decided to repair to their shared room at the Byblos, where they'd snorted at least a gram to keep them going after the day's excessive boozing.

'Hahahahahaaaaa, Justin, mate, I now know where Bella gets it from!' Mark had chortled.

'She gets her looks from her mother and her stamina from me,' Justin had responded. 'I'm so proud of my little girl.'

'Yeah, Bella's great. And she's all right now with that Andy geezer. Good bloke.'

'Good bloke,' Justin had affirmed solemnly as he racked out another couple of chunky ones.

Now though, they were sitting at Bar Sénéquier on the corner where the main drag met the seafront, drinking Pernod and checking out the talent.

'Check out the tits on that!' said Justin to Mark, as both their eyes followed a ludicrous-platinum-blonde in a skin-tight sugar-pink catsuit trailing a horrible little dog on a bejewelled lead.

'Fake.'

'Course they're fake. Whose aren't?'

'Well, Bella's for starters . . .'

'Don't you talk about my daughter like that . . .' Justin tried to be the stern father, then started giggling again.

'And my lovely Sam's. They are au naturel, as they say in these places.'

'Yeah, you and your lovely Sam. That's a good thing, mate, that you think of her like that. The only chick I ever felt like that about was Bella's mum, Olivia.' Justin looked wistful for a second. Then he snapped himself out of it. 'But how can anybody expect a hot, red-blooded man to be faithful to one bird for the rest of his life? When there is so much beauty, wherever we look?'

'My man, my man!' said sleazeball Stefan, appearing out of nowhere with a trio of identical leggy blondes in Lycra minidresses.

'See what I mean?' said Justin to Mark, who laughed.

'Meet Fifi, Gigi and Mimi,' said Stefan, indicating the triplets, who simpered.

106

'Triplets? For real?' asked Mark.

'Why settle for one when you can have three?' winked Stefan. 'Anyway, we're on our way to the party. Join us later? The Li—'

'Linda Lovelace boat,' chorused Mark and Justin. They looked at each other and laughed.

'Wotcha think, mate?' said Justin.

Buoyed up with Pernod, cognac, cocaine and the balmy night air, Mark could feel his resolve weakening.

'Oh, fuck it, why not?'

The Hawley Arms was heaving with young people who had taken an awful lot of time to look as if they didn't care what they looked like.

'Two snakebites, please,' said Sienna to the very cute barman, who gave her and Sam an appreciative once-over. 'Oh, look, there are the boys.' She knelt down to muss her hair into an even wilder tangle, then stood back up and waved coolly in the direction of a table in the corner. A couple of lads with brushed-forward fringes waved back.

'I can only see Mikey and Dan,' Sienna said to Sam, *sotto voce*. 'They're like the lead singer and lead guitarist. I quite fancy Mikey actually, but don't let on.'

'Course not!' Sam laughed. 'What's their band called?'

'The Flaming Geysers.'

'Cool.' Actually, Sam thought the name sounded a bit silly, but she really wanted to fit in somewhere. The glamour world was only a means to an end (although she'd always thank it for introducing her to Mark); college life wasn't turning out a bit how she'd hoped; if the indie scene was to be where she found her feet, she could do worse than befriending a couple of cool blokes in a band.

Pints in hand, the girls made their way towards the table in the corner.

'Hey, Scotty,' said one of them to Sienna.

Seeing Sam's enquiring look, Sienna said, 'Short for Mascot. Hey, Dan, hey, Mikey. This is Sam, my best mate from college. She's like, *mega*-clever!'

Sam hid a smile at the change in the way Sienna spoke. Maybe she wasn't quite as confident as first impressions suggested.

'*Mega*-clever, eh?' said the pretty blond one who could easily pass for the lead singer in a manufactured boy band, had his apparel not been trying to shriek 'alternative' quite so loudly. His tone was affectionately mocking. 'Is that, like, cleverer than *super*-clever?'

'Cleverer than you, anyway, shit-for-brains,' said the other boy. 'Hi. I'm Dan.' He stood up and held out his hand, which Sam shook, looking up at him. Gosh, he was tall. 'Clever *and* pretty. Nice combination.' He smiled a charming smile and Sam felt a rush of blood to her cheeks. With his black leather jacket, floppy dark hair and high-cheekboned, almost lupine face, he was the stuff young girls' dreams were made of.

A couple of hours later, Sam had ascertained that Dan, Mikey, Ross (bassist) and Olly (drummer) had all grown up in Manchester. Mikey, Olly and Ross had formed a previous incarnation of the band at school together; Dan had been recruited later, after an impromptu jamming night at a student gig. All in their mid-twenties, they'd been doing the pub circuit for the last couple of years, touring the country in a rackety old Volkswagen van and clocking up a loyal groupie fan-base.

'But those girls are nothing, y'know?' Dan said, nonchalantly, sliding one arm along the back of the banquette so it rested atop Sam's shoulders. 'Silly little slappers. You and Scottie have a bit more *class* than that.' He pronounced it to rhyme with gas.

Sam looked over at Sienna and burst out laughing. Her new friend had had her tongue down Mikey's throat for at least the last forty-five minutes. One of the straps of her vest top had fallen off a pearly white shoulder and her long, slender, purple-clad thighs were clamped tightly around Mikey's probing left hand.

Dan followed her gaze and started to laugh too. 'Well, OK, maybe that's not the classiest I've ever seen Scotty behave, but believe me, you two are leagues above the rest of them.'

Just as Sam was starting to feel as cool as only a girl who's been told she's *with the band* can feel, Dan lunged at her. For a second she let herself succumb to his kiss, then pulled away, reluctantly.

'Sorry, Dan, I can't. Really. I mean, I really like you and everything, but I've got a boyfriend. And I really *love* him.' She looked up at him with enormous imploring eyes, begging him to understand, not to drive her back into social Siberia.

Dan turned away and shrugged, making Sam's heart sink. Then he turned back and smiled his sexy smile again.

'OK, cool, no worries. I'm not exactly short of totty anyway. Let's you and me be friends. I like you, Sam.'

'I like you too, Dan.' Sam beamed, feeling great. She'd

done the right thing, *and* made friends with an up-and-coming rock star. She couldn't wait to tell Marky (though she'd probably leave out the two or three seconds she'd let Dan kiss her).

'That makes two of us then,' said Dan, reaching for his Golden Virginia and silver Rizlas. 'Fancy a smoke outside?'

The Linda Lovelace boat was as tacky as you might imagine, multiplied by a hundred. Fur rugs, smoked glass, gold dolphin-shaped taps in the Jacuzzis – it was as if it had been perfectly preserved in a seventies porn time capsule. But the girls . . . the girls . . . They pretty much made up for every square inch of tackiness. Within the universally approved parameters of *young*, *slim* and *gorgeous*, the variety was astonishing. Black, white, light brown, dark brown; blonde, brunette, redhead; busty, leggy, short, tall; cute and giggly, sophisticated and sultry; every taste had been catered for here.

And boy, were the guests taking advantage. In every corner, Mark could make out threesomes, foursomes, girl-on-girl action, scenes of bondage and S&M, schoolgirl fantasies. You name it, Stefan had thoughtfully provided it.

But none of it, thought Mark, as he felt his resolve weakening still further, was as downright tug-at-your-bollocks-sexy as Karolina. She'd made a beeline for him as he and Justin had walked onto the boat, still in her white lace dress, her perfect little breasts still tantalizingly visible through the peek-a-boo fabric.

'Hey, sexy,' she'd purred, smiling up at him through those absurdly thick black lashes. 'Come with me for a little . . . *private* . . . party?'

Following her as if in a trance, Mark had found himself in a bedroom equipped with an enormous round waterbed dressed in black satin sheets. He tried to force himself to think of Sam but it was impossible.

Locking the door behind her, Karolina gave him that mocking, mischievous grin again and said, 'Well, now we are here, what do you think we should do?'

Her voice was heavily accented Eastern European. Czech, probably, Mark thought, though in all honesty he didn't really give a fuck where she came from.

Karolina turned away from him and bent over the bed, the short lacy skirt riding up to reveal perfect brown buttocks bisected by a virginal-looking white cotton thong. Stifling a groan, Mark took a step forward and put his hands on her hips, but she stood up again and looked over her shoulder, teasing, her streaky light brown hair cascading down her back.

'Not yet, sexy.' She took his hand and guided it to one of those amazingly pert breasts. As his fingers brushed her nipple through the white lace, she shuddered.

'Oh, *yessss*, baby . . .'

It was too much. Mark grabbed the short dress by its hem and yanked it over her head, gasping as he saw her lovely brown body revealed in all its lightly muscled glory. She turned around and laughed at him again, totally secure in her own desirability.

'No rush. OK?' She sauntered over to a hideous smoked-glass-and-chrome bedside table and opened up a wrap of coke. Positioning herself to her best advantage against the black satin sheets, legs slightly akimbo, she scattered about a quarter of the wrap's contents over both perky breasts.

'You sniff from here, baby? And then, from here?' And as Mark watched she dipped her fingers first into the rest of the wrap and then, coated in white powder, into her inviting, glistening pussy.

It was not an offer he could refuse.

# Chapter 7

Natalia sat on her yacht in the morning sunshine, surveying the *vieux port*. Saint-Tropez was quite delightful in the mornings, before the hoi polloi descended. White-aproned restaurateurs were setting up tables and chairs outside their establishments, laying the tables with gingham cloths. Others bartered with fishermen at the water's edge over their daily haul. Shopkeepers exchanged friendly greetings; a lone dog barked somewhere.

'Beautiful morning, isn't it?' said the florid-faced chap on the neighbouring yacht to Natalia's, a monstrous gin palace that went by the unfortunate moniker of *Lady Garden*.

'Beautiful,' Natalia said politely, then picked up yesterday's *Financial Times* and buried her face in it. Her neighbour, a self-made Brit, had been hitting on her the entire week she'd been there and she was thinking it might be time to move on (she'd heard Cap Ferrat was beautiful). She had nothing against the fact her neighbour was self-made, of course, but he was loud, coarse and persistent, and Natalia liked her privacy when it suited her. Though you wouldn't think it, given her sartorial choices.

Today she was wearing lilac bikini bottoms held together at the sides with the distinctive gold Chanel double C. Her boat-necked striped matelot top was a Chanel classic, made especially for her by Kaiser Karl in stripes of pink, mauve, aqua and yellow. Her platinum-blonde hair was swept up in its signature high ponytail and gold-and-diamond studs glittered at her ears. Her shades, which also bore the Chanel logo, were black and enormous.

Natalia's yacht was small by the standards of the gin palace next door, but beautiful in every respect. From the shiny polished oak of the deck to the navy-and-white linen upholstery, gleaming brass fittings and old-fashioned-looking (yet state-of-the-art) rigging, every detail pleased her enormously. It was by far the most tasteful thing she owned.

'Frigid bitch,' muttered the man on the neighbouring yacht, and Natalia hid a smile behind the pink paper. She liked to keep a close eye on her stocks and shares.

One of her crew, resplendent in his pristine white uniform, walked over with a silver platter bearing the morning post and her breakfast of fruit salad, mineral water and freshly ground black coffee.

'*Merci*, Michel.' Natalia put down the paper and smiled at him.

She opened the first item of post, a bank statement. Everything was ticking over just fine, she saw, with satisfaction. A couple of large standing orders had just left her current account, both to her charitable institutions in Ukraine: a refuge for battered women and a hospice originally set up for those suffering the after-effects of the Chernobyl nuclear disaster, all those years ago. Some were still suffering.

Next up was her property portfolio, which she perused for some time. Her rental properties in Hong Kong were still fetching top dollar; it had been a smart move to shift her investments to the Far East just before the crash hit. She flicked through a couple of letters from large corporations desperate for her money, a bill or two, a photo of Poppy and Damian at the top of the Empire State Building, arms around one another, which made her smile.

*Greetings from the Big Apple!* Poppy had written on the back, in curly turquoise ink. *Having a wonderful time so far. You must come and stay when you can spare a minute from your glamorous schedule – it's time we repaid your hospitality! Loads of love, P&D xxxxxxxxxx*

And then she saw it. Picking up the cheap white envelope, she felt the all-too-familiar fear begin to snake around her heart. There was no address, just her name, written in black felt-tip pen. In Cyrillic lettering.

Quickly she tore open the envelope with her mother-of-pearl-handled letter opener and scanned the single sheet of paper. After memorizing its contents, she screwed it into a ball, and made her way to the interior of her yacht, where she took a lighter from an Art Deco enamelled coffee table and set fire to the noxious missive, letting it fall into a cut-glass ashtray.

After pouring what was left of her breakfast mineral water onto the charred remains, she walked on until she reached her bedroom cabin, with its walk-in wardrobe. Here she changed out of her gaudy Chanel matelot gear and into a cream jersey-knit narrow maxiskirt that completely covered her stupendous legs. A nondescript navy-blue T-shirt skimmed her slender torso. Both garments were Calvin Klein and exquisitely comfortable – this was the closest Natalia got to dressing down. She didn't do jeans – even designer ones. What was the point on spending silly sums of money on what was, essentially, peasant-wear? When she'd worked so long and hard to leave that life behind? Besides, jeans were never long enough and she'd always found them fiendishly uncomfortable.

With her hair tied back into a simple plait, and a floppy wide-brimmed straw hat covering half her face, she bore little resemblance to the glamorous socialite of minutes earlier. This was her uniform on her yearly visits to the women's refuge and hospice back home. She hoped it would serve the same purpose of relative anonymity here. Natalia wasn't what you'd call famous, but she was enough of a fixture in the gossip columns and society pages to act with extreme caution where certain individuals and situations were concerned.

Her journey to the seedy bar on the edge of town would have been enjoyable, had her mission not been such a distasteful one. The food markets, with their brightly coloured array of fruit and veg, the divine-smelling patisseries and boulangeries, the pretty squares where elderly gentlemen played boules – some parts of Saint-Tropez were so vibrant at this time of day, such a feast for the senses, that Natalia reflected she should get out and explore some more. Much as she loved her new yacht, there was more to life than sitting on deck and counting one's money.

Despite herself she laughed at the thought, looking about 25. Then she steeled herself for the task that lay ahead and composed her features once more.

The bar was more like something from downtown Marseilles than anything you'd expect to find in Saint-Tropez. A couple of black-toothed men sat smoking and nursing Pernods on metal chairs at Formica tables. Some lairy youths were cursing and thumping an ancient pinball machine in the corner of the room. There was a strong stench of cat's piss.

'Talia.' Georgiou got to his feet, smiling his horrible leering smile, gold teeth very much in evidence. He was wearing a shiny grey suit with an open-necked black shirt. The stubbly flesh of his thick neck bulged against a chunky gold chain. 'I am sorry that this is not what you are used to.' He spoke in Russian. 'But in the old days this would have been the lap of luxury, yes?'

Natalia sat down and leant close to him.

'Can we just get this over, please? How much do you want this time?'

'Ten thousand dollars.'

'Ten thousand dollars? Are you out of your mind? You must know I cannot withdraw that kind of money just like that . . .' She was stalling and they both knew it.

'I think we both know, *baby*, that you can do anything you like with your money. And I would like that money to be transferred into *this* account by midnight tonight.' Georgiou thrust a piece of paper with some numbers written on it into her trembling hands.

'And if I don't?' Natalia thrust her chin at him defiantly.

'If you don't, my sweet *Natalinka*, then the whole world will know what kind of a woman you really are.'

Driving along the freeway in the direction of Venice Beach, Ben drained his organic passion-fruit and goji-berry smoothie and looked up at the palm trees against the cloudless sky, more than content with his lot. Yesterday, he'd had his second audition for *Beyond the Sea*, the romantic comedy set in 1950s Saint-Tropez that Belinda had put him up for. It had gone brilliantly, if he did say so himself. He thought he'd imbued the British-lothario supporting-actor role with just enough boyish charm to upstage the stuffed-shirt all-American hero completely. Well, he'd had plenty of practice at charming his way out of bad-boy situations of his own making, he thought, chortling to himself. The part really could have been written for him.

To improve his mood still further, he was en route, and looking forward enormously, to his third training session with Jennifer Jackson, the mixed-race girl with the incredible arse that he'd met on the beach. He smiled as he thought of Jennifer. She clearly fancied him, even though she'd been playing ridiculously hard to get. He'd probably make his move this afternoon. Instead of training on the beach, as they had been up till now, Jennifer had suggested they use 'my buddy Mel's gym. They use it for Bikram yoga sessions so we can turn up the heat and really work up a good sweat.' This would have been more than enough encouragement for him to pounce, had Ben been one to doubt his own allure.

And her 'buddy Mel' sounded intriguing too. Ben laughed. Melanie (or Melody?) was such an LA name

– another perfectly honed gym bunny, no doubt. Tanned, blonde and perky, he guessed. Maybe they'd be up for a threesome?

The boardwalk at Venice Beach was swarming with scantily clad rollerbladers, sun-bleached surfers, obnoxious skateboarders, tie-dyed hippies, hip-hop bling kings, tattoo artists, buskers, jugglers and jesters, all jostling for position under the blazing sun. Overweight tourists licking rapidly melting ice creams gawped on. Tanned and fit locals sat at cafés, sipping organic juices under palm trees.

Ben had found it incredibly easy to adapt to the LA scene. The healthy lifestyle, sunshine and 'me' culture suited him down to the ground; with his enormous narcissism, he was willing to devote whatever it took to achieve the body beautiful. Now he sauntered through the crowds, turning heads in his casual gear of Hawaiian-print board shorts and a faded blue T-shirt that matched his eyes.

'Hey, chubby,' said Jennifer, as Ben walked into the gym, and he laughed easily. He loved the fact that she wouldn't let him call her Jenny. Every woman he'd met his entire life had fallen over backwards (or forwards) for him. Jennifer, the first challenge he'd ever had, would be the ultimate conquest. Today she was looking sexy as hell in pale pink jersey hot pants and matching crop top, which showcased to perfection the long, long legs, washboard abs and – had he mentioned the perfect arse? Her shoulder-length dreadlocks were kept away from her face with a wide pale pink headband that set off her velvety milk-chocolate skin a treat. She positively glowed with youth and health.

Jennifer lifted Ben's T-shirt and ran a leisurely hand over his flat stomach.

119

'My oh my oh my, you boozy Brits. You've been drinking alcohol again, fat boy. Jeez, what did I tell you? You wanna six pack, you gotta eat clean.' She smiled, her pearly white teeth gleaming through bee-stung lips.

'I only had two Buds last night, and they're not even proper beer.' Ben was pissed off to find himself sounding defensive. 'Can we just get on with it?'

Jennifer winked and said, 'Sure. Changing rooms over there.'

There followed ninety minutes of the toughest workout Ben could ever remember. He was pouring with sweat – Jesus, this Bikram heat was unpleasant – and every muscle was pushed until it screamed for mercy. At last, Jennifer allowed him to lie down while she stretched him out. Lying on his back, he looked up into her black eyes as she pushed his right thigh against his chest, easing her hands into his long, firm muscles to deepen the stretch still further

'Ohhh God Jenny – I mean, Jennifer – that feels amazing,' he managed to gasp.

'Well, that was quite a workout for a lazy-assed son-of-a-bitch like you. I think we might be getting somewhere at last. But you are just so, like, tense? Turn over. I'll massage ya.'

Ben was relieved to do as he was told. He was starting to get a hard-on and didn't relish being in such a vulnerable position. Jennifer might have been the sexiest woman he'd met in a long time, but he still called the shots.

Prone, though, his erection got bigger. The way she was kneading his shoulders, pummelling his back. Ben allowed himself to fall into an erotic trance in the intense artificial heat. By the time Jennifer reached his buttocks, her fingers kneading and probing his aching flesh, his cock was painfully stiff against the wooden gym floor. Thoroughly overexcited, he rolled over and grabbed Jennifer by her dreadlocks, forcing his tongue into her mouth, totally confident that she was just as up for it as he was.

A resounding slap around the face stopped him in his tracks.

'What the *fuck* do you think you are doing?'

'Oh, come on, Jen, you know you want it . . .' Ben started, then stopped as he saw the look of abject contempt on her face. Oh, fuck. Oh, fuck, fuck, fuck. Just as he thought things couldn't get any worse, he felt himself being picked up by the scruff of his neck, as effortlessly as if he were a kitten. He looked up to see an enormous black man, whose arms had to be bigger than Ben's thighs. He was pure, scary beefcake. The fact that his eyes were completely obscured by wraparound shades made him even scarier.

'You OK, Jenny?' (Jenny? What the *fuck*?) asked the giant, in a voice so deep it made Barry White sound like a choirboy.

'Sure, Mel. Thanks, honey,' said Jennifer. She stood up to put her arms around the man, who was so not the Mel that Ben had envisaged, and then got on tiptoes to kiss him on the lips.

Ben's legs felt like jelly, and he stumbled.

'I think I may have read things wrong . . .' he started, trying, as ever, to charm his way out of a tricky situation. To his own ears he sounded like a pathetic imitation of Hugh Grant in bumbling-fop mode.

Mel laughed condescendingly and patted him on the head.

121

'Oh, yeah. Real wrong, boy. Tell you what, you just run along now and we'll talk no more about it. But you NEVER contact my Jenny again. OK, boy?'

Ben nodded, numbly.

'Say, "OK, Melvin".'

'OK, Melvin.'

Ben looked back once more, trying to decide whether to say something else. Then he ran out of the overheated gym as quickly as he possibly could. With every muscle on fire, and his tail firmly between his legs, it was easier said than done.

# Chapter 8

Bella looked in the mirror inside her cupboard door with satisfaction. She wasn't always pleased with her appearance, but today she knew she'd scrubbed up well. She was wearing a short, sleeveless polo dress from American Apparel in a bright sherbet-pink that complemented her light tan and dark hair perfectly. Just a touch of make-up – concealer, mascara, pink blusher and lip gloss – kept the look clean and pretty, and she'd played up the wholesome, preppy thing by tying her hair back into a loose plait.

She did a little twirl then poured herself a glass of white wine and went to sit on her balcony while she waited for Andy to come back from his chores. It was Saturday lunchtime and at last the English summer had come into its own. With a blissfully free agenda, Andy and Bella had decided to make the most of the sunshine and go for a picnic in Hyde Park, just the two of them. Bella couldn't think of a lovelier way to spend a day.

'Belles! I'm home!' As ever, Bella's heart leapt at the

sound of his dear deep voice. She put her wineglass down and raced back into the flat to give him a hug. But something in his dark, bespectacled eyes stopped her in her tracks.

'What is it?' she asked in alarm. 'Andy, what's the matter?'

'I just cannot get over how beautiful you are,' he said seriously, his eyes looking deep into hers the way they used to when they first met. He took her face in his hands and proceeded to kiss her with such exquisite tenderness that before she knew it they were tearing one another's clothes off and making love, right there on her living-room floor.

By the time they were walking hand in hand down Portobello Road, Bella's plait was considerably more dishevelled, her cheeks considerably more flushed. Neither of them could stop smiling as they negotiated the crowds in the market and decided what to buy for their picnic.

Eventually, laden with freshly baked walnut bread, a variety of cheeses and charcuterie, a crab, some duck-liver pâté, an old-fashioned round lettuce, a ripe avocado, several tomatoes on the vine, a bunch of spring onions, a bag of cherries and three bottles of Prosecco, they reached the Boris Bikes docking station on Elgin Crescent.

'D'you think we might have overcatered a tad?' asked Bella, laughing.

'Don't worry, it won't go to waste,' said Andy, kissing her again. Bella smiled. Andy ate like a horse, but his tall, rangy metabolism meant that he burnt all the calories off practically before he'd consumed them.

They set off through the back streets of Notting Hill, the

sun beating down on their exposed limbs, a soft cooling breeze blowing through their hair. Bella loved the Boris Bikes scheme, started only a couple of years ago by the eponymous and flamboyant mayor. What was not to love? You avoided the hideousness of the Tube, you got fit, you had fun (scary London traffic notwithstanding). And cycling through any of London's parks was just heavenly. Handy when she lived so close to one of the biggest and most beautiful of them.

Now they'd entered Kensington Gardens and cycled past the Round Pond, along a pleasing tree-lined path until they hit Hyde Park, then a quick circuit around the Serpentine. They parked the bikes and headed on foot to their favourite spot, close to the Peter Pan statue, back in Kensington Gardens. The lake was unpopulated by boats here, but thriving with birdlife in the overgrown reeds and bulrushes. On such a beautiful day the park was teeming with people, great parties of laughing picnickers with iPod speakers, footballs and Frisbees, but here, in their special place, Andy and Bella were afforded relative privacy.

Bella spread out their tartan rug as Andy started unpacking the food.

'First things first, though,' he said, popping open one of the bottles of Prosecco and pouring it into two plastic cups. 'Cheers!' He raised his cup and smiled, the breeze ruffling his thick black hair.

'Cheers, darling.' Bella smiled back at him, her heart overflowing at the sight of him looking so young and carefree for once. He'd been working so hard recently, there'd been a permanent tense furrow between his eyebrows that she longed to smooth out.

125

They drank copiously and gorged themselves on the various delicacies they had procured, making one another laugh by attacking the crab lasciviously, raising eyebrows at each other as they slurped the meat loudly from the claws.

'Wait till you see me tying knots in the cherry stalks with my tongue . . .' said Bella.

Andy laughed. 'Oh, God, I love you. Promise me you'll never leave me.'

'Of course I promise.' Bella leant over and kissed him. 'What's brought this on?'

'This is all just so perfect, and – well, I suppose work's getting me down a bit recently.'

'Do you want to talk about it?' Bella knew that Andy was investigating some Russian people traffickers, but generally he just wanted to switch off when he got home.

'Not in too much detail.' Andy smiled at her. 'The way those girls are treated beggars belief, and it makes you feel filthy just knowing what actually goes on. But I think I'm getting closer to finding out who the main boss is.'

'Jesus, Andy, what are you getting yourself mixed up in?'

'I'll be all right, sweetheart.'

'Hmmm . . .'

'Anyway . . .' Andy hurriedly moved on. 'He's been around for years as far as I can gather. Started off exploiting underage girls in former Soviet states – Ukraine, Georgia, Belarus. Once the Soviet Union split up he realized there was more money to be made from Western punters, so he started bringing the girls over here. Anyway, it'll all be worth it if we expose him and, with any luck, break up his disgusting empire.'

'God, you're a good man. What did I ever do to deserve you?'

'I ask myself the same thing every day.'

'Git.'

'*Git?*' Andy laughed. 'I don't think anybody's said that to me since I was twelve.'

Her new iPhone beeped. Bella was always the last person to get around to the technology everybody else had been using for years.

'Oooh, Facebook message.'

Andy rolled his eyes.

'It's from Poppy. A round robin about a party she's having tonight. Now, why do you think she'd include me in that? She knows I'm not in New York. Is she just trying to rub my nose in how bloody glamorous her life is?'

'Belles, stop it.' Andy took the phone away from her and topped up her glass. 'And listen to yourself. *Your* life's not too bad, now really, is it?' He gestured at the leafy canopy above them, at their lavish picnic spread, across to the Serpentine, where a magnificent heron was picking his long, spindly-legged way through the swampy undergrowth, staring at them beadily.

'No it's not, it's wonderful.' Bella lay back and rested her head on Andy's lap, smiling up at him. 'I love you.'

'I love you too.'

Poppy and Damian's Prohibition party (dress code: gangsters and molls) was in full swing, their interior-brickworked warehouse flat crammed to the rafters with glamorous New Yorkers. Not bad, considering they'd only been living there a few months. Although pretty much all of them were new contacts of Poppy's, thought Damian bitterly, as he poured himself a strong cocktail out of a teapot into a pretty china teacup. Another of Poppy's bright ideas, though he'd mixed the cocktails.

In one corner of the room he could see his wife holding court, a group of admirers hanging on her every word as she joshed and twinkled and giggled. She looked absolutely stunning, he had to admit, in the eau-de-nil silk slip with coffee-coloured lace trim she'd picked up at Sandra's vintage store. She'd set her blonde hair in pin curls against her head, topped off with a coffee-coloured lace headband.

*Come on*, he tried to snap himself out of it as the strong liquor warmed his veins. *Your wife is bloody gorgeous, and it's not her fault you can't get a fucking break.*

He'd finally come up with what he thought was a brilliant idea for his screenplay, but so far all his tentative enquiries had drawn blanks. *Early days, mate, early days*, he told himself.

'DAMIAN!' a huge voice bellowed in his ear. 'MY MAN!'

'Lars!' Damian looked around with relief. At last, somebody he could call a friend of his own. 'Am I glad to see you. But . . .' He started laughing now. 'What the *fuck* are you wearing?'

'Don't you fanshy me?' Lars did a little shimmy in his floor-length gold lamé bias-cut frock. 'I wash thinking I would be a gangster, and then I thought, *No, more fun to be a moll*. The chicksh have all the fun these days, my friend, do they not?' He was glassy-eyed and slurring a bit and Damian could tell he was more than a little pissed already. The Romanian girl who'd 'loved the banker more than the man' had a lot to answer for, he reflected.

'Never a truer word said. But where on earth did you find something like that to fit you?'

'Many specialist transvestite shops in NYC, my friend.'

Damian started laughing again. Lars really did look magnificent in a platinum-blonde Mae West wig, with long satin gloves, long beads and long cigarette holder. His cheeks were rouged, his lips scarlet, his eyes adorned with enormous, spider-like false lashes.

'And did they do your face at the tranny shop too?'

Lars roared with laughter. 'What do you think, my friend? That that is a shkill I learned at Merrill Lynch? Yesh, they did my fashe. And now I must drink.'

He poured himself a drink from the teapot, downed it in one, then poured himself another.

'And now I musht say hello to your beautiful wife.'

'In that case, come with me.'

They weaved their way through the crowds to where Poppy was now chatting to Marty and Eleanor.

'Lars!' Eleanor threw up her arms, beaming. She looked fabulous in a Louise Brooks black wig and scarlet dress made entirely of feathers, with a matching scarlet pout.

'Wow,' said Marty amiably. 'I don't know which of you three girls is the most gorgeous.'

Poppy smiled. Her boss was a good sort.

'So glad you could come,' she said, reaching up for a hug. 'You look fantastic!'

'You too, babe, you too,' said Lars, picking her up and twirling her round and round like a rag doll. Damian tried not to feel hurt that Lars had once picked him up like a rag doll. *Just snap out of it, you tit.*

'So,' Eleanor turned her sincere pale blue eyes on him.

'Poppy says you're writing a screenplay? My, what a creative couple you are.'

Damian looked at her suspiciously. Was she taking the piss?

'I wish I could be creative like that, but as Marty says, there's only room for one creative mind in *our* marriage. I was always the business brain, but I'm afraid that turned to mush once Hammy was born.' She laughed self-deprecatingly and Damian started to relax. She was a nice woman and he really had to get a grip.

'I'm sure that's not true,' he said, his natural good manners returning. 'And of course, being a mother is the most important job of all.'

'You're sweet,' she said, smiling and putting a hand on his forearm. 'So tell me about your screenplay.'

In the kitchen, Marco, Chase and Fabrice were sniffing poppers and dancing to Donna Summer. Poppy burst into peals of laughter as she walked through to get another bottle of champagne out of the fridge.

'Nothing like conforming to stereotype,' she giggled.

'Want some, cutie pie?' Fabrice offered her the little brown bottle.

'Oh, OK, fuck it, why not?' It was her party and she could sniff kiddy drugs if she wanted to. She took a large sniff and felt a huge rush of blood to her head, the disco music suddenly making perfect sense.

'I feel luuuuur-uuur-uuur-uuuurve,' she sang, dancing around with her arms in the air. 'I feel luuuurve!'

All three of her newish gay friends followed suit, and they pranced around the kitchen together, like – well, just like gay people on amyl.

'God, life is great when you're off your tits, isn't it?' Poppy shouted over the music.

'Hey, looks like I've found the right party,' said Sandra, the vintage-store owner, bursting through the kitchen door. 'Poppy, doll, you look fabulous!'

'You too, Sandra,' said Poppy with chemically enhanced feeling. Her new female friend was done up in her own approximation of gangster-chic, in black pin-striped shorts and waistcoat, with PVC over-the-knee boots, her peroxide-blonde hair piled up into a trilby.

'Guys, this is Sandra . . .'

'Hey, Sandra,' said Marco. 'We met when we shot *Poppy Takes Manhattan* in your *to-die-for* store, remember? I'm Marco, the assistant director. And this is my partner, Chase.'

'Oh, Gaaaaawd, I should have guessed. Way too good looking to be straight, both of ya. Way to go, laws of *what a waste*. And you!' She pointed at Fabrice, who was bare-chested in tight leather pants, his only concession to the dress code a trilby and white bow tie that stood out against his inky black, perfectly smooth chest. 'No point in asking, huh?'

'No point at all.' Fabrice grinned, sensing a fellow outrageous free spirit. 'I'm Fabrice.'

'Well, Sandra, you're in safe hands here,' said Poppy. 'Help yourself to drinks. I just have to mingle for a couple of minutes . . .' She was worried about Damian and wanted to check that he was OK. He'd been in a weird mood all night. Actually, all week, if truth be told, ever since coming up against his last brick wall, screenplay-wise. She'd been trying to boost his confidence, telling him how clever he was, that it was only a matter of time. But to no avail, it seemed.

'Not so fast, beautiful,' said Sandra. 'I brought someone with me, hope ya don't mind? I'm an old friend of his family, y'might say. I was *very* close to his dad.' She gave an extravagant wink.

'No, of course not, more the merrier,' Poppy started, then tried not to gasp at the man who stepped out of the shadows. Jack Meadows was *the* hottest actor of the moment, combining the indie-cool kudos of your Gyllenhaals and Cusacks with the big box-office draw of your Pitts and Clooneys. The son of a legendary hell-raising bass guitarist, his rock'n'roll pedigree and ludicrously good looks had given him an enormous advantage pretty much from the day he was born. The fact that he was a genuinely talented actor, with a knack for choosing quirky, clever scripts, had guaranteed worldwide, knockout success.

And he was standing here, in her kitchen, looking just as gorgeous as he did on screen. At least six foot three, taller than most film stars by about half a foot, his mop of curly black hair framed a boyishly handsome face that was lit up by a genuinely sweet smile as he held out his hand.

'Hi. Good of you to have me.' The accent was cultured, educated NY. 'I'm Jack.'

'I know.' Poppy laughed, quickly pulling herself together and marvelling at her own sang-froid. 'I'm Poppy. And these are Marco, Chase and Fabrice.' She gestured at the gay triumvirate, all of whom seemed, for once, lost for words. Chase looked as if he was about to offer Jack Meadows the poppers, but Marco grabbed the bottle and put the lid on it, hiding it in his back pocket.

'Hi, Marco, Chase and Fabrice,' said Jack, remembering all three names and shaking each of their hands in turn.

'Hi, Jack,' they chorused, wide-eyed.

'Hey, let me getcha a drink,' said Sandra, taking control of the situation, and Poppy flashed her a grateful smile, wondering what to do next. When somebody who is bona fide internationally famous turns up at your downtown apartment, do you parade them around as the guest of honour, or just casually leave them in the kitchen with your gay mates? She guessed the latter, but wanted to introduce him to Damian. Perhaps *this* would snap him out of his mood?

Jack leant down towards her, smiling that sweet smile again.

'I'm a big fan of your show.'

'*Really?*' It came out as a squawk. 'Gosh, thanks. Can I introduce you to my husband? He's next door somewhere, but maybe you want to stay here in the kitchen for a bit . . .'

'No, that's cool, I'll come with you. He's a lucky man.' He held her gaze for a second longer than necessary.

'And I'm a lucky woman.' Poppy tried to ignore the heart-thudding excitement that she was being chatted up by a totally gorgeous film star. *I must find Damian.*

Damian was telling Eleanor about his screenplay and for the first time all evening felt that somebody was paying him a gratifying bit of attention. In fact, Ellie seemed to think his idea was brilliant, and was just on the verge of giving him the name of a friend of hers in the film business that he *just must* contact, when—

'Jack, let me introduce you to my husband, Damian. Damian, I don't think Jack needs any introduction, do you?' Poppy was smiling and this bloody lanky bushy-haired twat was holding out his hand to him.

Jack Meadows? For fuck's sake. He hated rock progeny, with their automatic sense of entitlement, their easy access into worlds utterly out of the reach of anybody born to less famous stock. And what the fuck was he doing here? In his and Poppy's flat? The fact that Ellie was swooning, all interest in his screenplay lost, helped not a jot.

'You're a very lucky man,' said the twat, smiling at Poppy.

'So everybody keeps telling me,' said Damian, unsmiling.

'*Damian*,' hissed Poppy.

'I've got to get another drink. I'm sure you'll find enough people to talk to you.'

Damian walked away, this time being blatantly rude, and Lars, who had overheard the exchange, said, 'You mushn't mind my friend, thish ish hish British sensh of humour. I'm Larsh!' The six foot four Viking in a gold lamé dress held out his gloved hand, and Jack accepted it with something that looked like relief.

'Wow, Jack Meadows,' said Ellie, sweetly. 'I just love your stuff . . .' As she twittered on, Lars said to Poppy, 'I shall go to Damian.'

'You do that, I'm almost beyond caring,' said Poppy, close to tears now. 'Sometimes I wonder why I bother.'

Lars took her to one side and held her firmly by the shoulders, looking into her eyes. The platinum wig and heavy make-up made it more than a little disconcerting.

'Your hushband ish a good man. But it is not good for ush men to feel like failuresh. I know for myshelf.' He looked sad, and Poppy impulsively leant up to give him a hug, covering herself in his lipstick and rouge in the process.

'Oh, you dear thing, but neither of you are failures, you

must see that? It's just this horrid recession, and as I'm earning silly money now, I don't see why he can't just relax and enjoy it until something comes up for him. Damian's brilliant, he's not going to be unemployed forever, and his screenplay idea is soooo cool.'

'You are a clever girl, but you do not undershtand men. I shall go to him.'

'Thanks so much. I'm getting myself another drink. Tonight was *meant* to be fun.'

Poppy helped herself to a teacup of strong hooch, where she was waylaid for some time by one of the runners on her show, eager to talk shop. As soon as she could escape, she went back to the kitchen for more champagne – she really wasn't keen on whatever it was that Damian had elected to put in the cocktails.

On entering the kitchen she was confronted by the perturbing sight of Sandra on her knees, sucking Fabrice's enormous black cock. Chase and Marco were still sniffing poppers and roaring with laughter.

'What? I thought you were gay?'

'I am, babe, I am, but man, she's good,' said Fabrice, taking a hearty sniff from the poppers bottle. 'Man, just like that is goooooooood.'

'Still the best groupie, still got it,' said Sandra. 'I always give the best head.'

Poppy backed off, feeling, for the first time in her life, totally out of her depth. What was her party turning into? And why was Damian being such a dickhead?

As she stumbled away from the kitchen, Jack appeared through the crowds of people in her flat, most of whom she didn't know. He smiled his sweet smile at her.

'You OK?'

'Yeah, fine, thanks.' Her eyes were shining with unshed tears. 'Sorry about my husband.'

'No worries. Would some charlie make you feel better?'

'God, yeah. Thanks.' Poppy really did feel like crying. It was all too fucking weird, and she thought she could handle weird. 'I s'pose my bedroom is the best place, if we want a bit of privacy . . .'

But when they opened the bedroom door, they saw Marty and Ellie shagging each other's brains out on the floor the other side of Poppy and Damian's bed.

'Oh, Martypoos, fill me up!'

'Oh, Elliekins, I wanna feel your sweet pussy all around me . . .'

Poppy shut the door quickly, bending over as she was laughing so much that she could hardly breathe. It seemed that the reintroduction to Lars had perked up Marty and Ellie's sex life so much that they couldn't even wait to get home any more. When she looked up, Jack was laughing fit to bust too.

'OK, plan B. Come to the loo with me.'

'Loo? I love your accent. OK, cool Brit girl, I'll follow you to the loooooo.'

They had a line each on top of the cistern, then sat down on the floor.

'You really are the prettiest and coolest girl I've met in a long time,' said Jack, bending his curly head to kiss her.

*Is this really happening?* Poppy thought. Then she came to her senses and backed away.

'Thank you so much, I'm really, really flattered, but I've

only been married to Damian for a few months and I do love him, you know. He's just going through a bad time with work and stuff.'

Jack Meadows, man of a million women's fantasies, stared at her for nearly a minute, then started laughing.

'You know, I think that's the first time anybody's said no to me in years. I'm sorry, I don't want to come between man and wife. But he has been an asshole tonight. Friends?' He held out his hand and Poppy shook it. Then, as was her wont, she gave him a hug.

'Thanks for being one of the nicest men here tonight, groovy film star or not . . .'

'Groovy?' Jack laughed. 'They still say that in the UK?'

The door swung open.

'WHAT THE FUCK DO YOU THINK YOU'RE DOING WITH MY WIFE?' Damian's aggressive fist was restrained by Lars, who was standing right behind him. The rest of the party was looking on, agog.

Poppy got up and said, 'He's being a lot nicer to me than you have all night. Thanks, Lars.'

Jack also got to his feet.

'I'll say it again,' he said to Damian. 'You're a very lucky man. And, whatever she says, I doubt that you deserve her.' And he walked out of their apartment, off into the hot New York night.

The rest of the guests dissipated pretty quickly after that.

'So what the fuck was going on in there? I don't believe you, Poppy, falling for his lines. Fucking gobshite son-of-a-rock-star twat. We haven't even been married three months . . .'

'What do you think, Othello? We were having a line, he tried to snog me and I said no.'

'*He tried to snog you?*' Damian shouted, conveniently choosing to ignore the 'saying no' bit.

'Oh, just fuck off, you arse,' said Poppy wearily as she set about tidying up. 'You were being a cunt all night. Go and stay with Lars if he'll have you.'

Damian looked at her once more, then walked angrily out of the door, slamming it behind him so loudly she thought it might fall off its hinges.

Poppy stared at the door for a minute or so, before sitting down with a thud on the floor. Resting her head on her knees, she finally allowed the tears to come.

'Desde-fucking-mona,' she said to her perfectly pedicured feet.

# Chapter 9

'I am not drinking that goddamn French crap!' screamed Amy Lascelles, America's latest sweetheart, throwing a bottle of Badoit at the floor manager, who ducked. 'It tastes like piss! I only drink Evian.' She pronounced it Ay-vee-orn.

Ben snorted with laughter as he picked the bottle up off the floor, where it had landed at his feet, and took a swig.

'I suppose you think Evian comes from the good ol' US of A,' he drawled. 'Sweet home Alabama, perhaps?'

Amy Lascelles looked at him with confusion and dislike painted all over her pretty little features, then stalked back to her trailer, slamming the door behind her.

Shooting *Beyond the Sea*, Ben's first proper feature film, was not proving nearly as enjoyable as he'd hoped. This was largely due to the spoilt-madam antics of his co-star. Amy looked like a little doll, with large, round, china-blue eyes, a snub nose and pouty pink mouth. Today, in full costume, she was wearing a pale-blue-and-white gingham full-skirted, wasp-waisted frock, her golden-blonde hair tied up with matching ribbon into a swingy ponytail.

The scene they were shooting was the one where Ben's character, the dastardly Englishman, first encounters Amy's innocent American abroad. It was taking place in a picturesque fish restaurant, in a pretty square just off the Saint-Tropez main drag. The entire square, and several beyond it, had been taken over by the film crew. At the height of the tourist season, it was costing a fortune to pay off the restaurateurs, bar owners and shopkeepers who were losing business as a result, so the aim was to get the scene shot in as few takes as possible.

With Amy in her current mood, this was easier said than done.

'OK, lunch break over,' shouted Pavel, the director. 'Back to work, guys. Ben, see if you can coax Her Highness back out . . .?' His tone was pleading, and Ben took pity on him. Poor bastard – if it was difficult for Ben to act with Amy, it must be a bloody nightmare for Pavel having to direct her.

He strode across to Amy's trailer, drawing admiring glances from all the female members of the crew. He really did look ridiculously handsome in his 1950s cream linen suit and panama hat with a navy-blue band around it.

'Amy, sweetheart, time to get back to work.' He knocked tentatively at the door.

'Go fuck yourself.' Oh, *charming*.

'Come on, sweetheart. The sooner we finish this scene, the sooner we can get back to the hotel, and *you* can get back to Guru Mogadishu. We all know how spiritual you are, and you probably need to have your aura cleansed

140

after such an exhausting day's filming.' It took all of Ben's acting abilities not to sound as if he was smirking at this.

Amy had recently declared herself a Buddhist, and insisted on travelling everywhere with her own personal guru, with whom she meditated and practised yoga every morning and evening. The man was a flagrant charlatan, but he constantly massaged Amy's ego, telling her that she was on a higher spiritual plane than everybody else, as well as being, it went without saying, immensely more beautiful and talented.

Ben could hear footsteps inside the trailer, and, sure enough, the door slowly opened.

'Hurry up then, you asshole,' Amy snapped at him. 'I need to get this over with so I can get my chakras back in alignment. If you could *try* and get to the end of the scene without making any lame fuck-ups, I'd be grateful.' And she waltzed back to the entrance of the restaurant.

*Fuck you*, mouthed Ben, flipping the finger at her retreating back. Several crew members who had witnessed this cracked up in silent laughter, giving him the thumbs-up and high-fiving him as he walked past. Ben was proving unexpectedly popular on location. He was professional and good at his job, with natural comic timing, and the contrast between his charming bonhomie and Amy's incredibly stupid petulance was apparent to all.

In fact, Ben was still smarting from his encounter with Jennifer Jackson. *How could he have got it so wrong?* As a result, he had gained a little humility and lost just a touch of the old arrogance.

Back at the fish restaurant, Amy was sitting at an outside table, perusing the menu, Ben's cue to spot her from the street. Her face, a picture a minute ago of spite and self-regard, shone with innocence and sweetness.

'Take . . . Six!'

Ben sauntered down the street, hands in his pockets, whistling. As he caught sight of Amy outside the restaurant, he did a double take.

'I say.' He bowed slightly and doffed his panama. 'Do excuse me for the interruption, but you look awfully familiar. Don't I know you from somewhere . . .?'

The cast and crew had taken over one of the restaurants on the *vieux port*. Relieved that the long day's filming was finally over, and that Amy had finally buggered off back to the hotel for her nightly meditation and ego-massage, they were letting their hair down. The mood was drunken and raucous.

Ben and one of the make-up artists, Eloise, were having a good old bitch about Amy.

'God, she's a stupid little cow,' said Ben, a forkful of fennel-stuffed sea bass en route to his mouth. 'How the fuck does anyone put up with her?'

'You've been more patient than most,' said Eloise, who was trying not to let on what a crush she had on the outstandingly good-looking supporting actor. Dressed down this evening in jeans and a plain white T-shirt that showed off his tan and fantastic physique, Ben looked even sexier than he had earlier in the day, the casualness of the get-up only serving to emphasize his breathtaking beauty. 'It'll be interesting to see how Jack reacts. He's not known for suffering fools gladly.'

Jack Meadows, the proper Hollywood A-list leading man,

had not been needed on location yet. Ben was rather glad. It meant that, for the time being at least, he was without question Hot Actor Numero Uno.

'Ben Jones?' They were interrupted by a teenage girl with a pierced eyebrow and a Home Counties accent. 'Could I have your autograph, please?' She added shyly, 'I loved you in *People Like Us*.'

Ben flashed her his megawatt smile.

'Thanks, darling, of course you can. What would you like me to sign?'

'Um – I don't know! I hadn't thought that far,' the girl giggled nervously.

'Would this do?' Ben picked up the paper napkin next to his plate, and she nodded.

'So . . . who's it to?' he asked, trying not to show his impatience. He was longing to get back to bitching about Amy.

'To Sophie.'

*To beautiful Sophie with love and kisses from Ben Jones xxx*

Ben wrote his message with a flourish and handed the napkin to the teenager. When she saw what he'd written, she blushed to the roots of her dyed-black hair, then turned on her heel and ran, clutching the napkin to her breast.

'You're quite a piece of work,' laughed Eloise.

'Never take the fans for granted,' said Ben seriously. 'We wouldn't be anywhere without them, after all.'

Natalia, sitting reading on her yacht as she ate her dinner of salad and calamari, could hear the chatter and laughter from the large group that had taken over the restaurant just across the way, adjacent to the internationally renowned

Bar Sénéquier. That must be the film crew that her florid-faced neighbour on *Lady Garden* had excitedly told her about that morning. Maybe she'd wander ashore in a bit. For all her billions and apparent aloofness, Natalia loved the movies, especially Hollywood romcoms. She could escape for hours in a film, fantasizing about the happy ending she knew could never be hers. What harm could there be in taking a nightcap at Sénéquier, soaking up the atmosphere of the film people?

It was a beautiful, balmy night, the stars twinkling brightly in a soft purple sky. The air was fragrant with mimosa and lavender, mingling with delicious garlicky wafts from the red-awninged waterfront restaurants. Waiters in pristine white aprons weaved in and out of tables, wielding plates, bottles and corkscrews. There was a tangible buzz in the air as Natalia looked out at a sea of smiling, happy faces of myriad nationalities; people who had nothing more arduous to do than laze on the beach or by a pool the following day. The exception was the film cast and crew, of course, but even they seemed not to be giving much thought to tomorrow's duties, as they downed carafe after carafe of rosé wine, congratulating one another on a great day's work.

It was a magical night; the kind of night where anything might happen.

Her mind made up, Natalia slipped downstairs to her walk-in wardrobe to get changed. When she emerged, she was wearing a backless chiffon Lanvin minidress in shades of turquoise and mint green, her white-blonde hair swept up in an elegant chignon. She stepped off her yacht and onto dry land. Having slipped her feet into a pair of mint-green Chanel ballet pumps, she walked to the far side of Bar

144

Sénéquier, the side adjacent to the restaurant occupied by the film people, and sat down with her back to them. This way she could overhear snatches of their conversation and not be seen to be listening. She laughed at herself internally for being such a film groupie, but felt that she deserved a little light relief after the turn taken by recent events. She still didn't know how she was going to stop Georgiou bleeding her dry; it was taking her considerable internal resources not to go to pieces over her current situation.

Ben was laughing at a particularly pertinent comment Eloise had made about Amy when something made him glance over at the bar next door. There, only a few feet away from him, was the most beautiful back he had ever seen. It was long, elegant and lightly tanned, topped with an exquisitely swan-like neck supporting a graceful head of pale blonde hair.

He had read somewhere that Johnny Depp was first attracted to Vanessa Paradis by her back. At the time he had dismissed it as fanciful nonsense, but now, gazing at the goddess at the next bar, he knew exactly what Johnny had been on about. Occasionally, her perfectly shaped head would turn just a fraction and he would catch a glimpse of sensationally high cheekbones.

The waiter brought her drink and the goddess thanked him. Ben could tell she was smiling by the way the shape of her face, still less than a quarter visible to him, changed ever so slightly. Without a moment's further hesitation – well, if it was good enough for Johnny Depp, it was good enough for him – he leapt to his feet and walked over to the next bar, leaving a slightly miffed Eloise mid-sentence.

As he approached the goddess, he paused. *What the fuck was he going to say?* Before the Jenny Jackson debacle, he probably would have charged in, all charm and puppy-dog eyes, but now . . . Oh, God, he couldn't get it wrong again.

Now he was so close he could touch her. From behind at least, she was absolutely flawless. Not a blemish could he detect on that wonderful, amazing back; not a hair was out of place.

She clearly sensed him standing behind her as she turned around slowly in her chair, frowning slightly.

God, the face was even better than the back. Ben had become used to young girls with cute faces that would collapse like little pug dogs as they got older. Amy Lascelles was the ultimate case in point – round eyes, pouty lips, no bone structure to speak of. This woman, with her almost feline attributes, would look good until the day she died, he just knew it.

'Can I help you?' Oh, Jesus fucking God, the accent too. *Just pull yourself together, man.*

'Hi. I'm Ben. I'm with that crowd of reprobates over there . . .' Ben pointed at the film gang and Natalia did everything in her power to remain cool. He was *with the film*? He was *so* good looking, the most handsome man she'd ever seen in her life, with those thick, dark lashes framing startlingly blue eyes, those eminently kissable pink lips now smiling to reveal perfect white teeth. He had to be the leading man, he just had to be.

She smiled tentatively, and Ben noticed that her teeth, while lovely, were not absolutely Hollywood perfect. There was a tiny gap between one of the canines and incisors on the left that added a certain sweetness to her icy glamour.

'I was going to offer you a drink, but it looks as if you've beaten me to it,' he said, cursing himself for not coming up with anything wittier.

With a gleam in her eye, Natalia downed her Ricard in one.

'Now there is vacancy.' She looked him in the eye, challenging him, and Ben laughed, hailing a passing waiter.

*'Une bouteille de Dom Pérignon, s'il vous plaît.'*

'But you did not ask me what I wanted to drink. I was enjoying my Ricard.' Natalia looked up at him from under her eyelashes. She hadn't flirted like this since she used to do it for money, when it was second nature. She had forgotten how much fun it could be, in the right circumstances.

'Oh, fuck, I'm sorry. Would you really rather have Ricard?'

Natalia burst into peals of laughter, every angle of her face more uplifted than ever, her cat-like eyes crinkling with mirth.

'I'm sorry. I mess with you. Dom Pérignon is wonderful. Please, sit.' She patted the empty chair next to her. This man was doing something to her that she had not experienced for years. He looked a little familiar, but that was because he was a film star, she supposed.

Ben sat down, gazing at her.

'You're the most beautiful woman I've ever met in my life.'

OK, so he was more than a little drunk. But there was something else. Shooting his first film had stoked Ben's already fierce ambition, and he was buggered if he was going to remain supporting actor for long. He'd had enough of playing cads and bounders. No, Ben's next role was going to be the romantic lead and, somewhere in the recesses of his subconscious, he was aware that he had never been in love. Not properly. To play his next part convincingly, he had to fall hook, line and sinker for somebody. Whether he knew it himself or not, Ben was a sitting duck.

'Oh, pouf! I cannot believe that!' Natalia waved her elegant hands in the air, trying to ignore those delicious eyes appraising her unashamedly. It didn't work. They locked gazes, each drinking in the other's face, until the waiter plonked down the bottle of champagne between them, breaking the spell.

'*Ça va, monsieur, merci*,' said Ben, picking up the bottle and pouring it into two glasses.

'*Salut*.' He raised his glass, wondering what it was about this woman that made him feel like a gauche 15-year-old.

'*Santé*.' Natalia raised hers back, unable to stop the wide smile crossing her face.

'So . . . Come 'ere often?' Ben put on a Mockney accent and immediately felt like a twat again, but to his relief the Hitchcock blonde laughed.

'I am staying on my small boat – just there.' She pointed at an exquisite little yacht on the water across the way. Ben had noticed it earlier, right next to a monstrosity called *Lady Garden* over which the crew had been pissing themselves with laughter.

'That's yours?'

'Uh-huh.'

'Not – erm – your husband's?'

'Oh, fuck you, you sexist asshole.'

For a moment, Ben felt like the lowest, crassest piece of shit on the planet. But his heart lifted when she smiled again and said,

'I have no husband. I make my own money from property.'

'Wow. Good for you.'

'So . . .' She sounded shy all of a sudden, which moved Ben in ways he couldn't explain. 'You are big movie star, yes?'

'Not yet.' Ben laughed. 'But after this film, I hope so. It'd better be worth it.' And he started to tell her all about the nightmare that was Amy. They chatted about what it was like working on location, Natalia bursting with intelligent questions about the world that so fascinated her. She was gratifyingly amused, and amusing, and seemed to get all his movie in-jokes. They ordered more champagne, each fizzing with the other's company; the sheer, unparalleled joy of being alive on such a night.

'So you enjoy the cinema?'

'Oh, yes. It is my escape.' Did she *have to* look and sound so wistful? The unexpected vulnerability pushed him right over the edge, and, unable to stop himself, Ben took her face in both his strong hands and kissed her.

Natalia shut her eyes and let her mouth open, ever so slightly to start with. Then she kissed him back, with all the passion that she had missed for so many years. For a minute or so they were lost in one another, utterly oblivious to the drunken catcalls from what was left of the film crew at the next restaurant.

'You want see my boat?' Natalia whispered. She had no

149

idea why she was acting like this. She had been so guarded, so intent on her privacy for such a long time, and suddenly this man, this *film star*, was making her lose all her inhibitions. She just wanted to ride this magical night, to *ride this magical man* . . .

'Let's go,' Ben whispered back, chucking down several hundred-euro notes on the table. Taking Natalia by the hand, he dragged her purposefully in the direction of her yacht, until she upped her pace and they were running together, hand-in-hand, breathless and laughing. Nearly as tall as Ben in her flat shoes, Natalia had no problem keeping up.

*Good God, the legs too. How could he not have noticed the legs before?*

'What has happened to us?' Ben asked. 'Half an hour ago, I was a different person.'

'My life will never be the same,' said Natalia simply. While she meant it with all her heart, none of this really felt as if it were happening to *her*, Natalia Evanovitch. It was a magical dream, a dream from which she never wanted to wake.

They kissed some more, under the palm trees and the stars and the warm French sky.

'I don't even know your name,' said Ben, pushing a stray strand of blonde hair away from her face as he gazed into her slanty, wide-apart eyes.

'I'm Natalia. Natalia Evanovitch.' She kissed him again, feeling young and skittish, like the teenager she'd never been allowed to become.

'I'm Ben. Ben Jones.'

And suddenly Natalia realized why she recognized him.

Ben Jones. He was the bastard who had fucked things up between Poppy and Damian and Bella last year. The bastard who had broken Bella's heart, been responsible for Poppy's near-demise and nearly ruined Damian's life. The bastard who cared for nobody but himself. She had seen him once before, at Bella's exhibition last year. *That* was where she knew him from.

She pulled away abruptly.

'What's the matter?'

'You must go.'

'Natalia.' Ben reached out and ran his finger down her cheek, smiling. 'You don't need to get cold feet. This is real. It's happening, and it's real.'

'It was real before I knew who you were.' Natalia grabbed his hand and shoved it away from her cheek. 'Do the names Poppy, Damian and Bella mean anything to you?'

And before he could answer, she had disappeared onto her yacht.

Ben was dancing with a couple of supermodels at Les Caves du Roy, the ultimate St Trop club, located in the basement of the legendary Byblos hotel. Any man on the planet would be happy to be in his shoes, but his heart wasn't in it. All he could think of was *Natalia*. What fucking bad luck it was that she knew the people he had shafted so badly last year, his erstwhile friends. Having seen her look of contempt as she pushed him away, Ben had done a lot of soul searching, and not come to any pleasing conclusions.

The memory of last night simply wouldn't leave him, despite the ludicrous beauty of the women gyrating around

151

him. That kiss. Those kisses. That back. The balmy air. For the first time in his life he had actually felt a connection with somebody, rather than just the thrill of the chase, which was starting to get a little dull. For most of his life, the sexual encounters he'd had had been a reflection of his own gorgeousness, affirmation that he was what all women wanted.

But last night had been different. He had actually *cared* about Natalia.

All the crew were having the time of their lives in the club, which, if you were into Eurotrash clubbing, was pretty unbeatable. The opulently kitsch decor hadn't been changed since the seventies, the women were beyond beautiful, and thousands of euros were changing hands with every round of drinks bought. Everybody was now dancing with hands in the air to an early nineties house anthem, several well-oiled girls clambering onto tables to draw attention to their lithe young bodies.

Ben could bear it no longer, so he kissed the nearest supermodel on the cheek, telling her he had to go for a pee. As he walked outside he felt enormous relief that he was free again. Everybody seemed to want a piece of him, now he was on the verge of proper fame. He lit a fag and started to walk back in the direction of the port, still thinking about Natalia; her back, her legs, the way her soft lips felt as she kissed him back with such unexpected passion.

He walked towards Sénéquier, remembering the events of the previous night all too vividly. The waiters were closing up now, stacking tables and chairs, all looking forward to a well-deserved night's sleep. But Ben could do with one more drink. Just the one, a strong one, to ease

himself into oblivion. He walked inside to the bar, and saw
. . . Oh, God, he would recognize that back anywhere, and
it was convulsed with sobs, her lovely slender shoulders
heaving as she blew her nose into a paper napkin.

'Natalia? Oh, my darling, oh, Jesus, what's wrong,
sweetheart, tell me, please.'

Natalia didn't respond, just sank gratefully into his strong
arms as he kissed the top of her head and stroked her hair.

Ben sat down in the chair next to her.

'OK, you probably think I'm a complete bastard. And
you're right, I have no excuses for my behaviour last year.
But last night was magical and I can't bear to see you like
this. Would you like a drink? Ricard?' His beautiful face
was disconcertingly close, one arm around her shoulder.

Natalia laughed through her tears.

'You remembered.'

'I will never forget anything about last night.'

Ben hailed a waiter and asked for two Ricards.

'Sorry,' he said to the garçon. 'I know you want to go
home. But I think this lady needs a bit of liquid comfort.'

'*Oui oui, bien sûr.*'

Once their drinks were on the table, Ben looked
once more at Natalia and said, 'Do you want to tell me?
Surely worse things have happened at sea . . .'

Natalia had no idea why she told him, why she felt she
could trust him. With some of the information, anyway.

'I am being blackmailed.'

'Fucking hell. What for?' As he clocked her terrified look
again, he forced himself to shut up, dying though he was
with curiosity.

'You mind if I don't tell you?'

'Of course not. But I think I need to escort you back to your yacht, at the very least.'

Natalia smiled at him again and Ben felt his heart melt. That little gap between her teeth, the chink in the ice-queen armour, would get him every time.

'Thank you.'

They drank their drinks, which seemed to perk Natalia up a bit, then walked, hand-in-hand, towards her yacht.

'I . . .' She looked all shy again, her eyes red from crying. 'I thank you.'

'Do you want me to come in with you? Nothing dodgy, I promise. I just want to look after you.'

And for some reason, again, she trusted him.

'Maybe you just hug me tonight?'

Ben could do that. Shagging women who were crying their eyes out didn't really turn him on. Even if they did look like Natalia.

When Natalia woke up, she was still being cuddled from behind. Ben, the handsome movie actor, was snoring slightly. He had been as good as his word, and not even removed his clothes. She had had the best night's sleep for years, protected from all the horrors out there by his strong, masculine arms. She looked at him as he slept, just trying to absorb the man's amazing beauty.

*Make the most of it while you can, Talia. Your life has no happy endings.*

As though he could feel her gaze, Ben's eyes started to open, and he sat up straight, yawning. Rubbing his eyes, he looked around.

'Fab boat, Nat. You feeling a bit better today?'

He sensed he had to play it a bit cool.

'Yes, thank you. But don't you have to go to work? For the *film*?' All her favourite movies were floating around in her head, and now she had a proper film star on her boat, seemingly in no hurry whatsoever to get back to filming.

'Nope, day off,' said Ben. 'Tell you what, why don't we just have a day out of time? Get to know each other a bit better?'

Natalia looked out of one of the portholes and saw that it was yet another incredible day. The deep blue sea was glistening, the sky almost as deep a hue. She felt happy, despite Georgiou and his blackmail. *Fuck him.*

'That sounds wonderful.'

'Oh, I love this so so much!' Natalia shouted over the air, as the speedboat galloped over waves, splashing water in their faces. Her legs, in a tiny pink miniskirt, went on forever; her smile seemed to light up Ben's world.

'D'you like fairgrounds too?' he shouted.

'Oh, my God, yes, rollercoasters, valtzers, all of them! All those things make you feel alive, don't you think? Speed and being turned upside down and round and round! I love it all!' Her blonde hair was taken by the wind, her face aglow.

'Me too! I love all that stuff – never understood people who say it makes them feel sick.'

'Oh, not me, I am never sick.'

Natalia smiled again and Ben realized that whatever he thought he had felt for anybody in his previous life was utterly meaningless.

Once Natalia had agreed to spend the day with him, Ben had decided to take control. He remembered a beautiful island, the Île du Levant, that he and his drama-school mates had picnicked on, all those years ago, and reckoned it would be a lovely, romantic place to take his Hitchcock blonde. They had gone to the covered market in Saint-Tropez to buy lettuce, tomatoes so ripe they looked as if they might burst, some ham and a baguette, still warm from the boulangerie's oven. Neither of them needed more food than this. In fact, most of the baguette would probably remain untouched, but it smelled amazing and looked appropriately Gallic (or possibly phallic) sticking out of its paper bag.

Pavel, Ben's director, had a speedboat that he was happy to lend his supporting actor on his day off, and here they were, racing across the sparkling sea, which gradually, as they approached the island, started to change from deep navy to a vivid clear turquoise.

'Beautiful,' said Natalia, as the island rose from the water to greet them, all rocky coves, powdery white beaches and lush, pine-covered hills. They drew up at the jetty, moored the speedboat and stepped onto land.

NUDISME OBLIGATOIRE proclaimed an enormous sign.

'Ah,' said Ben. 'I promise it wasn't *obligatoire* when I came here before.' Oh, for fuck's sake, how could he have forgotten the nudists? He was almost convinced that he and his RADA mates hadn't been sitting around in the altogether as they discussed Beckett, Stoppard and Pinter with the earnest pretension of the young, making one another laugh with Pinteresque pauses. But they had been very stoned a lot of the time back then. Hence the Pinteresque pauses, he supposed. In retrospect.

Natalia was going to think this was a really ghastly ploy of his to persuade her to get her kit off.

But when he looked at her again, she was laughing and pulling her top over her head.

'I'll do it if you will.'

'OK.'

He took his shorts off, trying not to gawp at her amazingly long, lean body. Natalia, meanwhile, was trying not to look at Ben's cock, which was just as staggeringly perfect as the rest of him.

Two families that were clearly English – two mothers, two fathers and several burnt, freckly children – walked past, laden with beach bags, towels, hats, buckets and spades, trying to hide their bodies behind lilos. They looked hideously embarrassed to have ended up on an island where nudism was *obligatoire*, but, Blitz spirit intact, were not going to head back to their villa with their tails between their legs. So to speak.

'Can I still wear my armbands, Mummy?' asked a little boy.

Natalia looked at Ben and started laughing so much, utterly uninhibited by her exquisite nakedness, that it took every bit of strength he had, naked himself, not to get the most enormous hard-on.

As they walked to the nearest beach, Natalia and Ben simply couldn't take their eyes off one another. They were, without a doubt, the most beautiful people on the island; they looked exactly how everybody else wished they could look naked.

The beach was crystalline white, the sky a darker blue than it had any right to be in the middle of the day. A yoga class was taking place next to some rocks, its humourless downward-dog-performing participants seeming to care little for the fact that their dangly and not so private bits were way more visible than was considerate to others. Even for a nudist beach.

Ben and Natalia looked at each other and burst out laughing again. But as they looked into each other's eyes, the laughter ebbed away, and they just gazed some more.

'Swim?' said Natalia, trying to diffuse the lust engulfing her. She smiled over her shoulder as she ran down to the water's edge.

'Can't think of anything I'd like better,' said Ben, almost truthfully, as he followed a few paces behind so he could watch her bottom moving.

Natalia swam underneath for some time, feeling a little more compos mentis now. But once she had swum quite a distance from the shore, where it was only just shallow enough for her to stand with her head above water, Ben swam up behind her and put his hand between her legs.

She turned around slowly. Now her hair was wet and all her make-up had been washed off, he could see tiny little freckles on her nose. There were droplets of salt water on her eyelashes. He increased the pressure from his hand between her legs and Natalia groaned.

'Oh, my God, what are you doing to me, Mr Movie Star?' The sun was beating down on their golden heads without remorse.

Ben looked so handsome, with his gorgeous blue eyes and seal-like wet hair and perfectly formed shoulders just visible as they emerged from the sea, that she still couldn't believe what was happening to her, but she closed her mind to any potential repercussions and just went with it. Surely it wasn't possible for a man to be so beautiful, so sexy, so *fucking kind*? She put his behaviour last year out of her head and concentrated instead on the Ben she had come to know over the last couple of days.

Ben played with Natalia under the water a little more, still looking straight into her eyes with his extraordinary blue gaze. But, as she started to breathe more quickly, she noticed some small kids, only about 6 or 7 years old, swimming around close to them.

'This is not right,' she whispered to Ben, nodding in their direction.

'Yup. You're right. Shall we go back to the boat?'

'Uh huh.' She kissed him, full on the mouth, wanting to kiss him more, then swam back to the shore, looking like a mermaid with her long, pale blonde hair streaming out behind her.

When they got back to the speedboat, both still joyously happy and ridiculously turned on by the other's nakedness, Ben opened the cool box. They had bought two bottles of sparkling rosé, and he opened one of them with a flourish, as he inexpertly steered the boat away from the island and further out to sea, away from prying eyes.

When the boat came to rest, the only other craft to be seen were far away, on the horizon.

'What do we do now, then?' Natalia asked, with a mischievous glint in her eyes.

'What you do is lie down, on your back, right there.' Ben kissed her some more. 'Leave the rest to me, and forget about everything.'

Still naked, and feeling the sun hot on every inch of her

body, Natalia did as he said, presenting herself, supine and vulnerable on the boat's gleaming white stern.

Ben started to kiss her nipples, which swelled as soon as his lips touched them.

'You have the most beautiful body I've ever seen.'

'I . . .' Natalia started to say something, but couldn't continue when he was doing such things to her. Instead she clasped his head to her breast, wanting more and more. 'Oh, please . . .'

'How does this feel?' Ben picked up the bottle of fizzy rosé and poured it all over her taut torso. He started to lap it out of her concave belly and her moans got deeper. 'Or maybe this?'

He poured it all over her exposed pussy, which tingled with the bubbles. The blazing sun soon made the bubbles hot, which took her to new, exquisite sensory levels.

'Oh, Ben, oh, God, Mr Movie Star, oh, don't stop, oh . . .'

'Would you like me to drink it out of you?'

'Oh, yes, please, drink me, fuck me, take me.' Natalia was beyond caring now.

Ben looked up at her from under his long, thick lashes, and said, 'One thing at a time. Drinking first, didn't you say?' And he proceeded to lick and suck, and lick and suck, all the while pouring more fizzy rosé wine into her cunt.

Natalia's orgasm was loud, her cries mingling with the sound of the seabirds and the lapping of the sea at the side of the boat. When she came to her senses, she raised herself up on her elbows and looked directly at Ben, challenging him again with her wide-apart, up-slanted eyes.

'I thank you. The drinking was good. Now, maybe the fucking?'

'Oh, Jesus.' The Mediterranean sun was hot on his back, and as he looked at the long, long planes of Natalia's wanton, naked body, he hoped he would be able to control himself. 'Are you sure?' Remembering the state she'd been in the night before, he didn't want to take advantage of her vulnerability, massively turned on though he was.

'Oh, just fuck me, please.'

Ben didn't need asking again. As he thrust into her, she put her slender arms around him, drawing him in for a kiss. Her long, long legs were wrapped around his back. His cock was being sucked into some kind of heavenly vortex. All he knew, as he got ever closer to his climax, was that he loved her. He had to be with this woman for the rest of his life.

# Chapter 10

'. . . and CUT!' shouted Pavel.

'Asshole.' Amy directed her comment at Ben, looking at him meanly, still thoroughly miffed that he appeared immune to her juvenile charms. She had been an attention-seeking nightmare throughout the running-along-the-beach scene, constantly asking what her motivation was and needing Guru Mogadishu, whose real name was Darren, to calm her down in case she had another of her legendary 'panic attacks'. The panic attacks that were known to everybody else as tantrums.

'You too, darling, with bells on.' Ben grinned at her, happy as Larry, his ankles still cool in the frothing surf. He caught the eye of Eloise the make-up artist, who laughed.

Natalia, watching from a safe distance behind a cluster of palm trees, wearing a wide-brimmed hat and an enormous pair of shades, laughed too. Since that amazing day on the island and the speedboat, two weeks earlier, Ben had come back to her yacht every night after filming and they had delighted in one another's bodies, Natalia's years of expertise more than matching Ben's skill in the sack. Again and again they had brought each other to explosive orgasm, never quite satiated, still wanting more and more. Again and again they had cuddled, long limbs entwined, whispering endearments in the dark.

In the daytime, at a loose end, she had bought DVDs of all the TV shows he had starred in back in the UK, and thought that, much as she adored him, his looks were more impressive than his talent. She had felt guilty about this, and wanted to think he had improved since then, which was one of her reasons for asking if she could watch a scene from *Beyond the Sea* being shot. Ben had been more than happy, in fact wanted to introduce her to the rest of the cast and crew with puppyish enthusiasm, but Natalia had insisted on discretion. After throwing caution to the wind about who saw them together those first couple of days, she was starting to feel uneasy.

'Remember, I am being blackmailed,' she had said, kissing the tip of his cock. 'It may not be so good for your public image to be seen with me.' Hence the shades, hat, calf-length kaftan and her current hiding place.

She had been right about the improvement in Ben's acting, thank God. It was almost as though he were too perfect, too larger-than-life, for TV. Movie acting suited him down to the ground, and he stole the show in every scene. Which was another reason, as though she needed one, that Amy Lascelles was so pissed off.

'What the fuck is that old bitch doing behind that tree?' She pointed in Natalia's direction, but Natalia had thrown herself to the ground, commando-style, covering herself in sand for camouflage purposes.

The entire crew looked over, Ben's fists clenched as though he wanted to hit Amy, but all they could see were several coconut palms, swaying in the light breeze.

'Hey, hey, babes, calm down.' Guru Mogadishu sauntered over and put an arm around her uptight little shoulders, reminding himself that anything was better than Basingstoke, where he'd grown up, and he'd be back with his boyfriend in LA soon enough. 'Karma, gorgeous. Beautiful trees, huh?'

Amy looked at him and gave a snort of derision.

'Fucking trees. Seen one palm tree, seen 'em all.' And she stalked back off to her beachside trailer, her little bottom in its frilly red-and-white polka-dot bikini quivering with rage.

Once he was sure that the rest of the crew was concentrating on the last take, on the massive digital video screens, and not taking any notice of him, Ben gave Eloise a brief hug that left her breathless with longing and sauntered over to the trees behind which he knew Natalia had been hiding.

'Nat? Darling, where are you?'

'*Here*,' she whispered, waving a slender foot at him from behind a beach hut. Following the trail in the sand, he saw that she had slithered at least twenty feet, snake-like, on her belly, until she was sure she could sit upright without drawing attention to herself.

Now she was absolutely covered in sand, trying to shake it out of her nose, mouth and long blonde hair. Her eyes were still shut, her shades and hat clutched in her hands.

'Oh, sweetheart.' Ben laughed. 'Look at you!'

'Pffffft.' She spat sand out of her mouth and started moving her hands towards her eyes.

'No, careful of your eyes. Wait till I've got the worst off, then you can open them.' Ben started brushing the fine granules down her cheeks with extreme tenderness.

'It's OK, I am not made of porcelain!' Natalia laughed. 'But I thank you, sweetie. That is better.' She opened her eyes, which drank him in unashamedly, just as they always did now when alighting on his face. 'Have you finished for today?'

'Pretty much. Actually, nearly finished full stop. All of my scenes with Jack Meadows are going to be filmed back in LA, on set. Can't say I'm sorry, really. I'll be glad to see the back of the insufferable Ms Lascelles.'

'Yes, I can understand that. Does that mean you will be going soon?'

'Don't sound so sad, Nat. I can stay another couple of weeks, I'm sure, and then – well, surely you can come back to LA for a bit?' Ben was still on Cloud Nine, full of that bouncy optimism where everything seems possible.

'Yes, I could do that.' Natalia smiled. They hadn't discussed what might happen once filming finished, neither of them wanting to burst their beautiful bubble.

'Actually, I've booked a table tonight at this fabulous place I know, up in the hills of Provence, away from all the paparazzi and stuff. I thought maybe we could have a bit of a chat about what we're going to do after all this. I can't bear to imagine my life without you, to be honest.'

Sitting on the beach, her blonde hair and kaftan caked in sand, Natalia started to relax once more.

\*   \*   \*

165

Under the vine-covered trellis on the *terrasse* of the bustling restaurant, nobody was taking too much notice of Natalia and Ben in the corner, except perhaps to murmur sotto voce what an exquisite couple they made. Ben had instructed the crew on Natalia's yacht to sail to St Maxime, where a driver had been waiting for them. Thence they were taken up winding lanes, past huge trees of vividly yellow and highly scented mimosa, until they reached Plan de la Tour, a little village surrounded by oak and pine forests, all narrow sloping streets, terracotta rooftiles and ancient churches.

On the restaurant's *terrasse* the lights were low, but enhanced by candles on every table and the extraordinary sight of fireflies glowing almost fluorescent in the distance.

'This is beautiful,' said Natalia, smiling and radiant in the candlelight as the cicadas decided as one to up their volume. 'I thank you.'

'So are you.' Ben was aware he was being cheesy but he couldn't help it. He had never been in love before and was now relishing every soppy minute of it.

He wasn't stupid. Given Natalia's age, nationality, extraordinary sexual skills and enormous wealth, he realized it was highly likely that prostitution had featured at some stage in her past. It wasn't rocket science; she was being blackmailed, for fuck's sake. But he couldn't bring himself to hold it against her. In fact, he rather admired her for making the most of herself and hauling herself out of what must have been seriously grim beginnings.

But he was worried about her. Blackmail was no joke.

'So do you really think you could come and spend some time with me in LA?' Ben laid his hand on Natalia's arm.

'I should be able to travel a bit once I've finished filming, but I'm pretty tied up until then.'

'I . . . I don't know, sweetie. I can travel, for sure, but I think maybe it would be wrong for you to be mixed up with me. You don't know much about me. You are about to be international superstar. You still not know why I am being blackmailed, though it is possible you have heard rumours about me, yes?'

'Not really. But I think I can guess. Listen, Nat.' He lowered his voice. 'I don't give a fuck if you were the most notorious hooker in the entire Eastern Bloc. It's something you had to do and you used your best assets . . .'

'*What?*'

'. . . your body *and* your brain. Anybody who has made as much money as you have, from nothing, has to be really fucking clever in my book. And you know how much I *lurve* your body.'

He raised his eyebrows, faux-lasciviously, and Natalia laughed. How did this man manage to disarm her so thoroughly, every single time?

'I thank you. But I will not give you the details, OK?'

'I *so* don't want to know the gory details, darling.' Ben camped it up and Natalia laughed again, leaning forward to kiss him over the table.

'I love you, Mr Movie Star.'

'And I love you, Nat, from the bottom of my heart.'

When they left the restaurant, they were too wrapped up in one another to notice the paparazzo lurking in the bushes.

NEW BRIT ON THE BLOCK SQUIRES BLONDE WITH SHADY PAST ran the headline. Oh, shit. Shit shit shit. Natalia looked in dismay at the gossip rag that Georgiou had placed in front of her, on one of the horrible Formica tables in the seedy bar on the outskirts of Saint-Tropez.

'I think that this interesting new development makes my knowledge of your past all the more valuable. Do you not agree, Talia? I think perhaps it would not be so good for your pretty new boyfriend's career if it came out that he is fucking a former teenage whore, hmmm?'

'I had no alternative and you know it, Georgie.'

He put his head on one side and pretended to consider. 'Hmmm. I don't think the big studios would see it like that. The movie-going public can be quite puritanical, and a scandal like this could ruin him.'

'You are disgusting,' said Natalia.

'Still, you have done well for yourself, I will not deny that.' He started drumming nicotine-stained and heavily ringed fingers on the table. 'Now you have a nice life, a comfortable life. It would be a shame, would it not, to jeopardize what you have now? You can easily afford to keep me happy . . .'

Natalia sighed, resigned to what she had to do.

'OK, you bastard. How much do you want this time?'


She had to write the letter five times as she kept soaking the thick cream paper, her tears mingling with expensive black ink to form rivulets that blurred her carefully chosen words. She had considered telling him it was all one great big lie, that she had never loved him, had just been using him for his beautiful body. But in the end she hadn't been able to bring herself to do so. She knew he'd never buy it; what they'd had together had been too all-consuming. And she didn't want to hurt him unnecessarily, to cast a shadow on what must now remain just a wonderful memory for both of them.

He had his entire life ahead of him, a future glittering with promise. He'd get over her soon enough.

*My Darling Mr Movie Star*
*I have gone away. Please do not try to find me. I thought that maybe I could escape from my past, but I cannot, and it is not good for you to be seen with me. You must focus on your career now – you are going to be big, big star. I thank you with all my heart for the time we have spent together. I have never known such happiness, and I shall never forget you. I hope in time you will be able to remember me with fondness.*
    *Your Nat x*

Ben read the letter with mounting disbelief, then ran faster than he'd ever run in his life towards the *vieux port*. But when he arrived outside Sénéquier, there was an empty space on the waterfront.

Natalia, and her exquisite little boat, had gone.

# PART 2

# Chapter 11

As Sam arched her back, automatically thrusting her boobs out and pouting at the camera, she was running through the answers she had given in her last exam, in which she'd had to compare Nietzsche to Jung. She was pretty sure she'd done well – she had revised thoroughly and her essays were always insightful and well written.

Things had felt a bit flat since term had ended, though. She loved studying, and life had been looking up considerably since Sienna had taken her under her wing, protecting her from evil Josh and his cronies. The Camden scene was proving to be great fun too. But Sienna was now on holiday in her family's newly acquired fourteenth-century palazzo in Tuscany, and Sam was one of the only students staying in halls over the summer.

She missed her family like crazy, but staying in halls made more sense than the long, expensive daily commute to and from Essex while she was still working – her agency had set her up with back-to-back jobs for the next couple of months. Also, reading between the lines, her little brother Ryan was being more of a handful than ever, and the last thing her parents needed was another of their children to worry about under their roof.

Still, she went home most weekends, and at least Marky was back now from his work trip to Saint-Tropez, which had seemed to go on forever. As she thought about him, her eyes softened with love and her nipples stiffened still further in the cold air blasting from the wind machine, lifting her improbably pneumatic tits at least another inch.

The balding photographer, who had a faintly repulsive ginger goatee, thought he might just explode in his pants.

'Oh, God, yeah, Sammi-Jo. Sexeeeeee. Hold it just like that, babe. Oh, yeah. Oh, God, yeah.'

Nikki, the other girl on the shoot, was on all fours. She thrust her bum even higher in the air, hating Sam. In the flesh she looked a lot older than the 21 she claimed to be, with harsh, dyed-black hair framing a hard little face with piggy eyes that she tried in vain to enlarge with smoky black eye shadow and false lashes. The heavy make-up just about worked in photos, but compared to the phenomenally pretty Sam, Nikki was nothing, and she knew it.

Around 6.30 p.m, the shoot was over, and Sam went to get dressed. She stepped into a white denim button-through miniskirt and pulled a red, strappy vest top over her head. It was far tartier than anything she'd wear at college, or even in Camden, but she was meeting Mark for dinner in less than an hour and he liked her looking a bit tarty. Besides, it was 30°C in the shade today and she loved the feeling of the heat on her bare shoulders, arms and legs.

Nikki, who had been flirting in the studio with the

photographer for the past five minutes, pranced in, still topless in her hot-pink thong and stripper shoes, and made a beeline for Sam. Sam wished Nikki would put some clothes on. Even though she took her own off for a living, she found Nikki's piercing-flaunting brazenness a bit disconcerting – almost as though she were challenging everybody with whom she came into contact with her hard little body and even harder little face.

'Babes,' said Nikki, her voice full of faux concern. 'I was so sorry to hear about your fella. How are you bearing up?'

'What? Why? What's happened to him?' asked Sam, with alarm. The glamour-modelling world was small, and Mark, as *Stadium*'s ex-art director, was a fairly big cheese. She was sure Nikki had been jealous of her relationship with him, but maybe she'd been doing her a disservice.

'Oh, my God. You didn't know? Oh, babes . . .' Nikki put a hand on Sam's arm, her long, squared-off nail extensions an acid orange against Sam's smooth skin. Sam shook it off.

'Didn't know what? Nikki, you're scaring me now. Please, just tell me what I don't know about Mark.' Sam tried to stop her voice rising in panic. Had he been in some sort of accident or something?

'Karolina Kristova. Saint-Tropez. On the Linda Lovelace boat.' Nikki could barely keep the glee out of her voice. 'They were at it all night. If it's any consolation, hon, she's a right slapper . . .' *That's rich coming from you, thought Sam numbly.* 'She's hardcore – anal, rimming, roasting, whatever . . .'

'How do you know?'

'Oh, babes.' Nikki looked at her pityingly. '*Everyone* knows.'

175

Sam pushed her away, and, after picking up her handbag, walked out of the studio with all the dignity she could muster.

'Let me know if there's anything I can do,' Nikki shouted after her. 'She spells her name K-R-I-S-T-O-V-A . . .'

Once she had put some distance between herself and the bitch from hell, Sam tried to decide what to do. Should she call Mark, confront him with it? No, she was meeting him shortly anyway, and she wanted to see his face when she asked him if it was true.

The studio was in Hoxton, conveniently close to the bar/restaurant/club they were planning to meet at that evening (Divine Comedy was owned by Bella's brother, Max, and it was *the* place to see and be seen). Sam had time to kill so decided to stop at a greasy spoon for a strong cup of tea to try to get her thoughts together.

Would Marky really cheat on her? She wasn't naïve – her exposure to the seedy glamour world had left her with few illusions about men. But Mark had told her time and time again how much he loved her, and he never seemed to tire of her ripe young body. She had a vivid memory of him lazily kissing her all over, just after they'd both had the most amazing orgasms, and saying, 'Fuck, man, I am the luckiest geezer in the world.'

Then something occurred to her. Taking out her phone, she tapped *Karolina Kristova* – thanks, Nikki, for the spelling – into Google. After a moment she added: *porn star*. At least she could prepare herself by checking out the competition. If what Nikki was saying were true, this KK bitch sounded like a raddled old slapper.

But when the images opened, Sam's heart plummeted.

There, staring sultrily out of the screen at her, were picture upon picture of one of the sexiest-looking women she had ever seen. Fully clothed, topless, naked – it didn't matter. That mischievous, mocking face. That body. That *body*? Oh, God, she was everything Sam wished *she* could be – all lithe, sinuous curves and feline grace, with perfect little boobs. Sam instinctively crossed her arms in front of her own ample chest, feeling like a freak of nature again for the first time since she'd met Mark.

Unwelcome tears came into her eyes, and she pushed them away angrily with the edges of her fingers, trying not to bugger up her mascara. No, she'd wait and see what he had to say for himself. She finished her mug of tea, then walked out of the cafe into the beautiful sunny evening.

Mark was waiting in the restaurant on the first floor of Divine Comedy, a bottle of Veuve Clicquot standing proud on the bare wooden table in front of him. The restaurant was modishly rustic and minimalist, a stark contrast to the insanely over-the-top bar downstairs. After spending a good twelve hours fucking Karolina on the Linda Lovelace boat (during which they had ordered in three times for more coke), he had felt so guilty that he'd checked into a small hotel on his own, until he had felt ready to face Sam again.

He had been so sexually enraptured by Karolina that, had he not caught her, red-handed, trying to pinch all the cards out of his wallet, those twelve hours could have stretched much longer. Now, though, he felt an enormous rush of love for his sweet Sam, and wanted to show her how much he cared. He also had the ineffable rush of having *got away with it*.

As Sam entered the restaurant, looking absolutely gorgeous, all legs, tits and long red hair, Mark rose to his feet, smiling. Until he realized that Sam wasn't smiling.

'Hello, beautiful,' he said nervously. 'Everything OK?'

'I don't know, Mark. Is it?' He'd never heard her sound so cold. And then she did something that made *him* go cold. She held her phone up to his eyes, and – oh, fuck, bollocks and cunt – there was a naked picture of Karolina on it.

'Just tell me you didn't do it.' She looked at him steadily, her enormous dark brown eyes gleaming with intelligence.

'I . . .' He faltered, and realized, at that moment, that the game was up.

Sam's eyes darkened and hardened. Mark was never to know that it was to stop her crying, the only thing she could do to hang on to her last remaining shred of pride.

'Never – *ever* – try to contact me again. You *cunt*.' She was grateful to Sienna for making the word come more easily to her lips than it might have otherwise.

And she walked out of the door with her head held high.

Once she had descended the wrought-iron spiral staircase, though, she allowed herself to cry. Sobbing so hard she could hardly breathe, she stumbled through the downstairs bar until she had made her way outside. The sun was still hot and she just wanted to go home, to have a proper, comforting hug, but she knew she couldn't burden her parents with her trivial problems, when they had so much more on their plate. Not knowing what to do for the best, she just stood there and let herself cry for a bit.

*   *   *

Bella and Andy, enjoying an early evening drink at one of the mismatched tables outside Divine Comedy, both saw Sam at the same time. She cut a woebegone figure, standing against the wall on her own, sobbing her little heart out. Bella jumped to her feet and ran over to her.

'Sam, are you OK? What is it, sweetheart?'

'M . . . M . . . Mark . . . Karolina . . . He's been *fucking* some porn-star bitch called Karolina . . . While I was doing my exams . . .' Sam sobbed some more, and Bella gave her a hug – a big, proper, comforting hug, just like the one she'd been longing for from her mum.

Bella, who remembered all too well the pain and humiliation of being cheated on, turned and raised her eyebrows at Andy, mouthing, 'Shall we get her out of here?' Andy nodded. Their planned night out could wait.

Over Sam's shoulder, Bella could see Mark inside the bar, looming towards the open door, his features contorted in dismay. She shook her head violently at him, then gave him the finger for good measure.

*God, you dick, Mark*, she thought, steering Sam gently away from the door. She had always had a certain *tendresse* for him, and he'd been very kind to her in the past. But seeing this sweet, pretty, clever girl go to pieces over him was a different matter entirely.

'Listen, Sam. Andy and I only came here for a quick drink anyway. Do you want to come back with us for supper at our place? I was going to make some yummy salad-y stuff and we can all bitch about Mark and his ridiculous slapper to our hearts' content, if you want . . .'

Sam laughed a little maniacally.

'Oooh, yeah, I'd like that.'

Realizing that Sam was trying to be cool (cooler than Bella had ever been), and was possibly still a little in shock, Bella guided her towards Andy's car, an old but spacious and very comfortable dark green Renault.

By the time they'd arrived at Portobello Road, Sam had poured out the whole sorry story, displaying some of the grit and courage that had got her out of Romford in the first place.

'My God, Nikki sounds like an evil bitch,' said Bella. 'She has to be soooo jealous of you.'

'Let's not forget Mark,' said Andy.

They climbed the rickety steps to Bella's flat. Inside, it was welcoming and homely, crammed to the rafters with books, paintings, flowers, cushions, mirrors and rugs – all quite clearly Bella's style. In one corner, a laptop sat on an old-fashioned writing desk, messy with papers and reference books. Quite clearly, Andy's workstation.

Bella lit some lamps and a couple of candles before turning off the overhead light.

'That's better, isn't it?' She smiled. 'Much more cosy. Could you put on some music, darling? I'll get us some drinks. What would you like, Sam?'

'Oh, I don't mind. Whatever you're having would be great. Thanks.'

'White wine it is then!'

Bella padded, barefoot, into her tiny kitchen. She was wearing a halterneck maxidress in the palest of pale pink cotton, with *broderie anglaise* trim around the neckline and hem. Her long dark hair fell in tousled waves around her smooth brown shoulders and her tanned cleavage looked maternal and inviting. Neither skinny nor plump, Sam thought that Bella looked like some sort of lovely hippy earth mother, radiating happiness. She felt happier herself already, just being around her.

Andy had put something that sounded like classical Spanish guitar music on the CD player. It suited the hot night air. In fact, it was so hot, even with all the windows open, that he had to unearth an ancient electric fan from a cupboard somewhere. With its intermittent cool wafts, the heat was just about bearable.

Bella returned with a bottle of white wine and three glasses.

'Better drink it quickly, before it gets too warm,' she said, laughing.

'Don't you just love her logic?' Andy said to Sam, laughing too.

'Right, so first things first,' said Bella, once they were settled on cushions on the floor, with their drinks. It really was a tiny flat. But it was lovely, with the candlelight and paintings and books and flowers. 'If it's true – and I'm afraid it does sound like it is – are there any circumstances under which you'd take Mark back?'

Sam shook her head violently. 'No. No way. It makes me feel physically sick to think of them together.'

'Yes, I can understand that,' said Andy, and Bella just knew he was thinking about *her* and Mark together. *God, we're an incestuous bunch.*

'OK, so if no amount of fulsome grovelling is going to change your mind, we have to concentrate on making you feel better,' she said. 'For what it's worth, I think Mark is going to be sorrier than he's ever been to have fucked things up with you. As far as I can see, you're the best thing that's ever happened to him.'

'Hear hear,' said Andy, smiling at Sam through his rectangular specs.

They finished the first bottle of wine in no time. After the second, Bella said, 'Are you ready for the first course yet? I'm absolutely starving!'

'Oooh, that would be lovely – thanks.'

'Belles, surely even you can't have created something delicious out of nothing yet?' Andy laughed. 'You've hardly set foot in the kitchen.'

'Oh, just a little something I knocked up earlier,' said Bella airily, rising to her bare feet.

A minute later, she tottered out of the kitchen, brandishing a huge glass jug of what looked like cold tomato soup in her right hand, while precariously balancing three bowls in the left. Andy jumped up to help her.

'Let me take that, darling. I think I *may* be a steadier pair of hands.' He turned and winked at Sam, who stiffened. Bella had always been so kind to her, there was no way she would let herself be chatted up by her boyfriend. But Bella laughed easily, and she realized that she was way off the mark. They were both just being nice, because that was what she needed. Sam's eyes filled with tears again, and she turned away, unwilling to let them see.

'Oh, Sam, darling, it's OK, you don't have to put on a brave face with us,' said Bella, rushing over to hug her again and nearly tripping over the hem of her maxidress. 'Just cry it all out for a bit, and we'll talk it over a bit more in the kitchen as I make the next course. You must have some gazpacho first, though . . .'

182

Andy hid a smile. No woman likes to be told that she's turning into her mother, but Bella really was getting more and more like Olivia by the day. The easy hospitality, the warmth, the assurance that everything would seem better after a good meal . . . Well, he wasn't complaining; Olivia was a lovely woman.

Bella passed Sam a bowl of the stuff that looked like cold tomato soup, with ice cubes in it. Sam took a tentative spoonful, and relaxed. It *was* cold tomato soup, and absolutely delicious.

'This is gorgeous,' she said in her husky voice. 'How d'you make it?'

'Easiest thing in the world. Just put tomatoes, peppers, garlic and onions into a food processor, whizz it all up with some breadcrumbs, olive oil and water until you've got the right consistency, then shove it in the fridge for at least five hours. I should really have made some croutons and little garnishes of chopped tomatoes and peppers but I thought it was better to keep it simple this evening.'

'Such a domestic goddess.' Andy smiled at her with love and Sam felt tears coming to her eyes again.

'Are you two going to have kids?' she asked, natural curiosity about two people she genuinely liked taking her out of her own misery for a bit.

'Ooooh, don't know about that,' they said in unison. They both laughed. 'Probably, one day.' Again it was in unison, and this time all three of them laughed.

The main course was a salade niçoise.

'Afraid I'm mixing my Mediterranean metaphors a bit,' said Bella. 'And I'm sorry I haven't gone all gastro with fresh tuna, but tinned was all we had in the cupboard.

Anyway, it's far more authentic like this. You hardly ever have it with fresh tuna in the South of France.'

'As Belles seems to have spent her entire childhood frolicking on Mediterranean beaches, I think we'll have to assume she's right on this one,' Andy said to Sam, who laughed.

They had nearly finished eating when Bella managed to drop an entire forkful of tomato, potato and anchovy into her lap.

'Oh, bollocks.' She laughed ruefully, watching the oily stain spreading across the pink cotton. 'Why does this *always* happen when I'm wearing something new and pale?'

'At least it wasn't the gazpacho,' said Sam, remembering how to pronounce it after only having heard it once.

'That's true. Always look on the bright side! Well, I'd better go and soak it. Back in a mo.'

Andy took a pack of Gauloises out of his jeans pocket.

'Do you mind if I smoke?' he asked Sam.

'Course not! It's your flat.' Sam took a sip of her wine and cast around for something to say. 'How's your work going? I remember at Poppy's wedding you were telling us all about some big story you're working on – was it Russian people traffickers?'

'You've got a good memory.' Andy smiled at her through the cigarette smoke. 'Yes, though it turns out it's a much bigger deal than I realized at first. The big boss – who endorses more repulsive cruelty to young girls than I want to burden you with – has been going for nearly thirty years and we think he may be somebody quite high profile.'

Bella walked back into the room with a sarong wrapped around her body. 'Sorry about the lack of proper clothes, Sam, but this heat is almost unbearable.'

'Make the most of it while you can.' Andy laughed. 'You were complaining about the rain last week.'

'So I was. And I wasn't complaining about this weather, not really. Long may it last!'

Sam woke up late, in her small bed in the halls of residence, feeling quite happy, as she'd had a lovely dream, which involved Bella and Andy being her parents, and Dan from the band telling her she was the most gorgeous girl he'd ever met. Then she remembered the Mark situation and started crying.

Masochistically, she reached out for her phone and looked at the pictures of Karolina Kristova. They hardened her resolve. No. She wouldn't allow him to do this to her.

'Fucking wanker!' she shouted at the bare walls. But, with her in-built pedantry, she realized that 'wanker' wasn't quite the right description. 'Fucker' would have been more accurate. She laughed briefly to herself, glad that her own mind kept her entertained, at least.

She squinted to see the time on her phone – it had been a late night, and they'd all got quite drunk. Bella had offered her cushions on the floor for the night, but Sam had said thanks but no thanks, not wanting to encroach on their hospitality any more. Bloody hell, it was 12.30. Hardworking Sam never normally rose later than eight, even as a student.

As she looked at her phone, it started ringing, making her jump. It was Dan.

'Hey, Sambo,' he said in his sexy Northern accent. 'We're having a Leo at the Hawley. Fancy joining us?'

'What's a Leo?'

'Leo Sayer, all-dayer!'

'OK, sounds cool. I'll be there soon.'

Sod the hangover; an all-day drinking session with some cool boys in a band was just what she needed to take her mind off Mark.

Standing at the bar, Sam downed another shot of tequila. Dan, Mikey and Olly were there, in their trilbies and skinny jeans, and loads of girls with radical haircuts were hovering on the sidelines, wanting to be associated with them, but trying to pretend they weren't bothered in the slightest. Ross, the bassist, was out looking at flats with his girlfriend, Katie. They had become inseparable and he was planning to move out of the house the boys all shared in Dalston as soon as he could.

They'd been drinking solidly for about six hours now and Sam was feeling pleasantly dissociated from emotion. It was there, lurking somewhere on the outskirts of her psyche, but not quite able to penetrate the fug of booze.

Mikey's phone beeped.

'Oooh, look, text from Scotty.' He opened it and started laughing. 'She really likes to slum it, doesn't she, our Scotty?' He passed the phone to Sam, who laughed too. Sienna had sent Mikey a photo of herself, reclining next to a vast, mosaic-tiled pool. She was wearing a tiny bikini but protecting her face from the sun with her lace parasol. In the background was the cypress-flanked fourteenth-century palazzo, all marble statues and fountains, and in the distance you could just make out rolling hills, olive trees and vineyards.

'Lucky bugger,' said Sam without rancour. She missed Sienna like mad and could really have done with her company since finding out about Mark and Karolina.

186

'Let's call her,' said Mikey, in that way that pissed people do.

'Oooh, yeah, great idea!'

After five minutes or so of shouting a mixture of filth, sentimentality and gibberish down the phone, Mikey passed it to Sam.

'Hey, Sienna.'

'Hello, darling. Been drinking all day then?'

'How'd you guess?' Sam laughed. 'Don't think I'm quite as drunk as Mikey, but I'm getting there. How are you? That photo you sent was gorgeous.'

'It's heavenly here, but my bloody parents are driving me mad. And Jazz is being a nightmare. She is such a spoilt brat.'

Sam bit her lip to stop laughing at Sienna's reference to her younger sister.

'Also, I feel a total philistine every time I see signs to Siena and realize yet again how appallingly educated my parents were when they gave me the extra "n".' Sam did laugh at this. 'So how are you anyway? Is London terribly dreary without me?'

'I've got lots of stuff to tell you, but not here.' Sam's eyes darted furtively over to the boys.

They chatted for a bit, then Sam handed Mikey back his phone.

'Fancy a fag upstairs?' asked Dan, who was looking incredibly cool in his usual skinny black jeans, blue-and-black-checked lumberjack shirt and a black leather biker's jacket. The brushed-forward dark brown fringe emphasized his high cheekbones and narrowed, watchful eyes. The (almost certainly calculated) air he gave off was one of

187

insolence, arrogance, even menace, thought Sam. Until he looked at you and smiled, that was, making you feel as though you were the only person in the room.

Loyal to Mark, she had purposefully ignored Dan's undisputed hotness, determined to think of him only as a friend. Now she followed him up to the roof terrace, taking in the length of his legs, narrowness of his hips and breadth of his shoulders.

As it was a sunny London Sunday, the roof terrace was rammed with self-consciously trendy locals, which was partly why the boys had chosen to stay inside. It suited their grungy image to be holed up in a dark, grimy pub while the rest of London eagerly lapped up the sunshine. Sam personally would also have chosen to lap up the sunshine but, given the choice of sunshine on her own or the boys' company inside, the boys' company inside won by a long chalk.

There was nowhere to sit, so Sam and Dan went to stand at the edge of the terrace, looking out onto the road and breathing in the traffic fumes. Dan, who had rolled a couple of fags downstairs at the bar, handed one to Sam and lit it for her.

'So, Sambo, you're not looking your usual self today. What's up, love?'

The undivided attention and sympathy were enough to break through the fug of alcohol and open the floodgates. Sam felt the tears she had managed to keep at bay all day start to well up again.

'I . . . I . . . I've split up with Mark. He's been shagging some bloody p-p-porn star. He . . .'

Her bottom lip was quivering, and Dan watched as she

instinctively crossed her arms in front of her chest, in the automatic defensive gesture she'd adopted since puberty. She looked very young and very vulnerable, standing there in her miniskirt and flip-flops, and he realized how much of a brave face she must have been putting on all day.

'Oh, Sam, love, that's just a piece of shite.' He put his arms around her. Slowly, Sam unfolded hers and wound them tentatively around his waist. 'How could anybody cheat on you? You're lovely . . .'

'I'm not good enough for him, Dan.' The words were muffled as she tried not to sniffle onto his shoulder. 'I know I'm not. He travels the world, seeing the most gorgeous women everywhere, and I'm just not good enough . . .'

'Now you're being daft,' said Dan, taking her by the shoulders and standing back so he could look straight into her eyes. 'Nobody is more gorgeous than you, and he's the one who's *just not good enough*.' The way he used her own words, slightly mockingly, was enough to make Sam laugh through her tears.

'Thanks, but that's bollocks really, innit?' she said. 'Can I show you the cow he was shagging on the boat?' And before Dan had time to answer, she had taken her phone out of her handbag and started scrolling through the pictures of Karolina Kristova.

Dan glanced at them briefly, then looked back to her. 'Looks a right old slag, if you ask me.' His tone was dismissive.

'But so am I, Dan. I take my clothes off for the cameras, just like she does.'

'Stop being such a fucking idiot, Sambo. You're a great

kid, and you're not a slag. You're beautiful, and clever, and I really, really like you.'

He was still looking into her eyes, and she hastily wiped them, cursing the tears that had smudged her mascara. His charisma, up close, was hypnotic.

They gazed at one another for a few seconds, hearts beating fast as they stood together on the smoky urban roof terrace. Then Dan bent his head to kiss her and Sam was lost, winding her arms around his neck and responding with delicious abandonment.

'I bet some of these people think we should get a room,' Dan whispered against her hair after a bit, always aware of having to maintain his cool image. 'Fancy coming back to mine?'

They snogged all the way to Dalston in the back of the cab, all Sam's pent-up emotion and longing causing her to kiss Dan back with an urgency that surprised and delighted him. When he put his hand inside her knickers and found her wet already, he groaned, 'Oh, fuck.'

Still snogging, they stumbled into the house he shared with the rest of the band. It was pretty grotty, with no curtains and the bare minimum of furniture. Empty beer cans and overflowing ashtrays littered the floor. But it managed to retain an air of cool. The floorboards were bare, the fridge in the open-plan living area enormous, and musical equipment was strewn casually throughout: a guitar propped up against a wall here, a vast set of headphones chucked onto a shabby old armchair there, a drum kit in the corner over there. The walls were lined with posters advertising Flaming Geysers gigs throughout the country.

'Right then, Sambo. How much do you want to fuck me?' Dan had the hideous ego of any would-be rock star, but Sam didn't care. All she wanted was warm, human contact – anything to make the pain go away. But she wasn't going to beg.

'How much do you want to fuck me?' she countered.

In response, Dan grabbed her by the hand and dragged her into what she assumed was his bedroom. It was pretty much empty save for a large mattress on the floor and a poster of himself on one wall.

They started snogging again, breathlessly tearing at each other's clothes. When Sam pulled her top over her head, revealing her amazing breasts, Dan caught his breath.

'Oh, my God.' He bent his head to suck her nipples, one after the other, until Sam was moaning loudly, head thrown back, long red hair streaming down her back.

But then she realized that tears were streaming down her face, too. It was all starting to remind her of things she had done with Mark. She pulled away.

'I'm sorry, Dan. I'm really sorry. I like you so much, but I can't. I just keep thinking about Marky.'

Dan watched as she picked up the sheet off his bed and wrapped it around herself, suddenly self-conscious, and started crying again.

He was tempted to tell her to piss off – he had enough girls interested in him, after all. But then she said, 'I really didn't mean to be a prick-tease. I'm sorry, Dan. You've been such a good friend to me. I'll go now.' As she started to put her clothes back on, Dan felt a wave of compassion. He wanted to protect her, he realized.

'Don't be silly, Sambo. It's your loss.' He tried to make

a joke of it, and Sam gave a grateful hiccup of laughter. 'And you can stay here for a bit, if you fancy it. How about we just get stoned instead?'

As he started to roll the spliff, he resolved that however much he liked Sam, he would never try it on with her again. They could stay friends, for sure, but he'd never been turned down twice by the same girl before. His ego simply wouldn't stand for it.

# Chapter 12

'Oh, Philippe, I do not want to do ze washing-up,' pouted Rosaline. The ridiculously pretty blonde French au pair that Philip's ex-wife, Lucinda, in a masterstroke of bitchiness, had seen fit to send out to Paxos with their teenage children, was standing at the kitchen sink wearing only a white crochet bikini and an ankle bracelet. She looked like nothing so much as a young Bardot.

'Don't you worry, Rosaline,' Philip smiled, trying not to look at her bouncing young bosom. 'Alison will do it. You go out and enjoy the sun.'

'Oh, merci, merci! You are verrrry kind!' Rosaline leant up to kiss him on the cheek and skipped out into the garden.

Paxos, the smallest and most beautiful of the Ionian islands, lies 11 kilometres from Corfu, a shimmering beacon of peace and tranquillity in a glittering turquoise sea. Philip, Alison, Toby, Imogen and Rosaline were staying for two weeks in a luxurious bougainvillea-covered villa that had

193

been built around an old olive press. It was a short car ride to the nearest unspoilt beach (they were all unspoilt, really – in complete contrast to Philip's children), but there was a large pool in the villa's extensive grounds and plenty of scope for spending day after heavenly day just relaxing in the sunshine.

Not so for Imogen and Toby. Imogen's constant refrain was, 'Daddeeee, I'm bored.' She didn't seem capable of lying in the sun with a book, splashing about in the pool, playing cards or backgammon with her brother, or indeed taking pleasure in anything but constant whingeing. This morning she had been pestering Philip to take her paragliding, on a beach the other side of the island. For once, Philip had refused to pander to his darling daughter's demands, pointing out quite reasonably that, having spent the previous two days water-skiing and windsurfing, it was time to make the most of the expensive villa he had hired for them all.

Toby, in the meantime, was proving to be a sadistic little tyrant. Alison had her suspicions that he might, actually, be a psychopath. The previous evening she had found him dissecting a live frog with his Swiss Army knife, his spotty face contorted with glee as the hapless creature writhed and gribbeted under his merciless hands. Alison had tried to save the frog, but it was too late. Closing her eyes, and holding her breath, she'd killed it as quickly as she could.

Both teenagers were unspeakably vile, too, to Maria, the villa's middle-aged housekeeper, treating her as a serf, calling her 'it' and never saying 'please' or 'thank you'. Their petulance, sarcasm and sense of entitlement knew no bounds. Today was Maria's extremely well-deserved day off, hence the washing-up issue.

'I'm not washing up any bloody dishes,' Alison said angrily. 'If you think it's too much work for Rosaline, then you can do them yourself.'

The following evening, she was sitting in a lively tavern on the waterfront with Philip and the brats. It was Rosaline's night off, and she had sauntered out of the villa wearing white denim hot pants and a tight, faded indigo T-shirt, leaving Philip gazing wistfully in her fragrant wake.

'I hate Greek food,' moaned fat little Imogen. 'Bloody moussaka, bloody fish, bloody salads.'

*Don't eat it then*, thought Alison. *Won't do you any harm to stop stuffing your face for a bit.*

'Oh, darling, I'm so sorry,' said Philip. This comment was directed at his grotesque daughter, rather than at Alison. 'Shall we see if they can get you a steak and chips, instead?'

'They probably won't do it right. Oh, God, I'm sooo bored.'

'Surely there are some bars you and Toby could go to, after dinner?' Alison suggested, just wanting to be shot of the little horrors and wanting Philip to herself for a bit.

'Oh, no, they're full of greasy Greeks.' Imogen wrinkled her podgy nose. 'Why couldn't we have gone to Ibiza, Daddy, or Saint-Tropez, or anywhere all my friends are? You know I don't like to go to places full of council people.'

'You can hardly call this a place full of council people,' said Philip mildly. With no airport, and popular with the international sailing community, Paxos had a reputation as one of the more upmarket Greek islands.

'Oh, shut up, Daddy. Old foreigners then. You don't go on holiday to meet old foreigners. I wish I was hanging out with Clemency and Arabella on the Fulham Road.'

*So do I,* thought Alison vehemently. *Or possibly in the Amazon, being pursued by hungry crocodiles.*

Looking away from Imogen, she noticed that Toby was chucking stones at stray cats under the table, a demonic gleam in his almost lashless eyes. She was starting to think that hooking up with Philip had been the biggest mistake of her life. She had loved Andy – a thoroughly decent man, who, vitally, didn't have repugnant offspring – for nearly thirteen years. She realized that she missed him. What was he doing right now? she wondered.

'I hope Mum and Dad are going to behave themselves today,' said Bella, looking out of the car window at the pretty Oxfordshire landscape. The narrow country lane, flanked by overgrown, honeysuckle-scented hedgerows, had wound its way through golden poppy-strewn rectangles of corn, virulently mustard-coloured rape fields and lush green daisy-dotted meadows teeming with teenage lambs. Now it was approaching Lower Piglet, the ridiculously picturesque village in which she'd grown up. Higgledy-piggledy houses of warm Cotswold stone lined the way to the village centre, which boasted a Norman church, a sweet primary school, a duck pond and two pubs, one of which dated back to the Civil War.

Andy, in the driver's seat, laughed. 'They're usually OK with Bernie around, aren't they? He seems to be a pretty good moderator.'

'True enough.' Bella turned to look at him, tall, dark and handsome in his jeans and navy-blue Guernsey sweater. It was one of those summer days where the puffy meringue-like clouds chose to drift across the sun just as you were starting to get warm; Bella herself had thrown on a vintage biker's jacket over her summer frock, hoping it gave her a bit of street cred, as well as stopping her freezing to death.

Justin was staying with Olivia and Bernie for a few days, as he'd flown over from Mallorca to do a shoot for French *Elle* – provisionally, and unoriginally, entitled *La Style Anglaise* – at nearby Hambledon Hall. Accordingly, Olivia had invited Bella and Andy for Sunday lunch, saying how lovely it would be to have a family get-together (Bella's brother Max was currently travelling around the world with his boyfriend Dave, and was sorely missed by all).

'And don't forget, your mum said that Justin's bringing a guest,' Andy added. 'Presumably, fresh blood will help avert any potential disasters.'

'Hmmm. Depends how young and stupid she is.' Having run the gamut of more of her father's girlfriends over the years than she cared to remember, Bella was sceptical.

'You never know – he may surprise you.' Andy smiled reassuringly as he turned off the road into the slightly ramshackle tree-lined drive that led to Bella's childhood home, a late-seventeenth-century former mill house. 'We'll find out soon enough anyway.'

Andy parked and took their overnight case, and two carrier bags clinking with bottles, out of the boot. He'd booked Monday morning off work, as lunch with Olivia tended to become so boozy that driving back to London was never an option.

They walked past the magnificent horse chestnut tree that concealed the house from the drive, to be confronted by a splendid sight: Bernie, resplendent in a sharp pin-striped suit, open-necked, wide-collared shirt and flash

Gucci shades, his teeth clamped around an enormous cigar, was posing for all he was worth in front of the creaky oak front door. He cut an incongruously Mafioso figure against the ivy-clad stone façade of the lovely old mill house, the climbing roses around the door framing his portly figure.

'Yeah – just like that, mate! Hold it, Bern, hold it – you're a natural!'

Justin was crouching on the lawn, snapping away at his ex-wife's lover with his trusty vintage Leica. He had no truck with digital photography – an attitude that afforded him a certain kudos in the biz (though it quadrupled the work for everyone else involved). As Bella and Andy approached, he leapt to his feet, chucking his beloved equipment onto the grass without a moment's hesitation.

'Angel Face! So groovy to see you, sweetheart! How's my precious little girl, then?'

Bella found herself running into her father's outstretched arms, laughing.

'Hey, Daddy! Lovely to see you.'

'A minute apart from you is a minute too long, baby. And Andrew, great to see you too, Vicar.'

'Likewise, Bishop.' Andy laughed, shaking Justin's hand.

'Just give me a hug, mate.' Slightly awkwardly, the two men hugged.

'Hi, Bernie!' Bella ran across the lawn to hug him too. 'So Daddy's got you posing at last?'

'Yeah. Why not?' Bernie took off his shades and smiled at her, his beady little eyes crinkling up so much they practically disappeared in his big round face. 'He's good at what he does, and I always admire talent.'

Bella smiled back. Anyone could see that Bernie was lapping up the attention.

'Run on in then. Your mother can't wait to see you. Looking prettier than ever, I must say . . .'

'Who? Me or Mum?'

'Both of you, though nobody can eclipse your mother's place in my heart.'

'I know. That's what makes you so great for her.' Bella grinned. 'So what's Dad's latest like?'

Bernie opened his mouth to say something, then shut it again.

'Not my place to say, Princess. Go on in an' see for yourself.'

So Bella hurried through the house, through the sitting room and kitchen and out of the kitchen stable door to the back garden, where she knew her mother and the mysterious guest would be having drinks on the terrace.

She stopped in her tracks.

'*Mark?* What the fuck are *you* doing here?'

'Aw-right, Belles.' Mark grinned awkwardly, getting to his feet.

'Hello, darling,' said Olivia. 'That's not a very nice way to greet our guest, now is it? How was your journey?'

'Hi, Mum.' Bella automatically gave her mother a hug and kiss. 'Journey was fine, thanks. But what's *he* doing here?' She nodded over in Mark's direction.

'Your father asked if he could bring a guest, and I said yes. I must admit, I was expecting somebody more – er . . .'

'. . . female?' Mark laughed sheepishly.

'I don't know how you can stand there so brazenly.' Bella turned to glare at him, hands on her hips. 'Do you know how devastated Sam is by what you've done?'

'You mean I can't get you to put in a good word for me?' Mark gave another nervous laugh.

'So *that's* why you're here?' Bella's voice rose incredulously.

'Please, Belles. I miss her so much; it was a moment of madness . . .'

'And you should have *seen* that girl,' chimed in Justin, who had just walked through the back door, followed by Andy and Bernie. 'Really, you'd 'ave to be made of stone to resist Karolina . . .'

'Justin, I really don't think that's going to help,' said Olivia, rolling her eyes. She was right. Bella rounded on her father, the father that only minutes earlier she had been so delighted to see.

'Oh, for fuck's sake, Daddy, I should have known that *you*'d be involved. You bloody men have no idea how much pain you cause when you can't keep your fucking dicks in your trousers.' Bella was on the verge of tears and everybody fell silent, knowing she was thinking of Ben and Poppy. 'So, no, Mark, I'm not going to put in a good word for you. You should have seen the state Sam was in. Poor little thing said she'd never be able to look at you again without picturing you fucking that slapper on the boat. So maybe you should have thought about that . . .' She turned to her father, her voice rising again. 'However *irresistible* she was, Daddy.'

'OK, darling, I think we get your point,' said Olivia gently.

'Why don't you come into the kitchen and help me get this lunch together. Bernie, darling, make sure everybody's got nice big drinkies, please?'

'Course I will, Princess.'

And Bella followed her mother into the kitchen, leaving Mark gazing forlornly after her, Andy looking at his feet in embarrassment and Bernie busying himself pouring drinks. Justin sat down at the white wrought-iron garden table, looking sad for a few seconds. Then he shrugged and started to roll a joint.

Olivia's kitchen was large and sunny, the heart of the family home. Faded checked curtains in shades of green, yellow and cream framed big sash windows that faced south onto the back garden. A wooden bookshelf crammed with well-thumbed cookery tomes stood next to the old, chipped cream Aga, and a couple of armchairs that used to be overstuffed sagged fatly either side of the fireplace – one upholstered in a shabby cream-and-green Regency stripe, the other a sprigged floral pattern of tiny blue flowers with green leaves on a pale yellow background. The scrubbed pine kitchen table was large enough to seat eight comfortably, and the double ceramic sink made light work of the mountains of washing-up Olivia liked to create with the elaborate meals she prepared (of course she had a dishwasher, but it was terribly old and never really got things as clean as she'd like them). Worn flagstones underfoot and mismatched jugs of flowers from the garden on almost every available surface added to the room's welcoming air of warmth and comfort.

'Sit down and have a drink, darling,' said Olivia, opening

the fridge and taking an open bottle of white wine out of the door. 'And for God's sake, calm down.'

'Calm down? Mum! I don't understand how you can be like this, after the way Dad treated you. Fucking bastards are all the same . . .'

'Just listen to yourself, darling.' Olivia handed Bella a wineglass filled almost to the brim, and Bella took an enormous swig. 'Oh, God, I think I probably indoctrinated you too well when you were little.'

'What do you mean?'

'Oh, Belles.' Olivia shook her head sadly. 'I know I used to say that all men were bastards, because I was so jolly well hurt by your father's behaviour . . .'

'See? That's exactly what I mean . . .'

'Try not to interrupt, darling, it's terribly bad manners.'

'Sorry, Mum.'

'But that was years ago, and I've come to accept that that's the way he is. I think that some men are simply incapable of being faithful to one woman – I'm afraid that Mark's one of them too. The thing is to find one who's a keeper. And you and I are lucky enough, *now*, that we've done so.'

'How can you be so sure, though, Mummy? I mean, I think you're right about Bernie, but how do I know that Andy's never going to fuck around on me? He's been working late so often recently that he could easily be shagging someone in his office . . .'

Witnessing Sam's devastation, just over a week ago now, had burst something of Bella's bubble of joy with Andy. It had brought back all those feelings of pain and suspicion she had felt after the Ben debacle; in fact the distrust of men that she'd had her entire life, really, after observing her father's behaviour over the years.

Olivia hooted with laughter.

'Andy? Having an affair? Now you really are being ridiculous. He's absolutely devoted to you, and you really need to start appreciating what you've got.'

Bella gave her mother a rueful smile. 'I am being silly, aren't I?'

'Yes, you are. And, for the sake of a harmonious lunch, I'd like you to go outside and make it up with Mark . . .'

'Bu—'

'I told you, darling, don't interrupt. Mark is a far older friend of yours than Sam is; he hasn't cheated on *you*; and however sorry you feel for the girl, it's not your position to judge his behaviour.'

'Oh, all right then,' said Bella sulkily, draining her glass in one gulp and reaching for the open bottle on the table in front of them to top it up again.

'And awful though I know Sam must be feeling now, she's very young, and very pretty. I can't imagine she'll be devastated for too long. What she needs is a nice boy of her own age, not a 30-something lothario who gallivants around the fleshpots of Saint-Tropez with your father. Really, it was a disaster waiting to happen.'

Bella laughed.

'Put like that, you're right, Mum. You always are. OK, I'll go outside and make my peace with the buffoon, if I must.'

'You do that, darling. But hurry right back – this lunch isn't going to cook itself, you know.'

\*   \*   \*

'All well?' Olivia looked up from the potatoes she was peeling as Bella re-entered the kitchen five minutes later.

'All fine.' Bella smiled. 'God, that's starting to smell amazing.' She nodded at the Aga. 'Slow-cooked shoulder of lamb?'

Olivia nodded back.

'I can smell the garlic and rosemary. Anchovies too?'

'Of course.' It had been a family favourite since Bella was a teenager, when they'd spent several summer holidays in Provence.

'How long ago did you put it in?'

'About four hours ago,' said Olivia, checking her watch. 'Needs a couple more at least, which will give us a chance to have a jolly old natter.' One rarely sat down to Sunday lunch before five p.m. at Olivia's house. By which time one was generally pretty well oiled.

'OK, chuck me a knife and I'll get started on the shallots.'

Seated at the table, armed with knife and chopping board, an enormous array of vegetables spread out in front of her, wineglass happily within reach of her left hand, Bella looked at her mother over the table.

'You're looking pretty, Mum. I love your top.'

Olivia was barefoot, in rolled-up jeans and a floaty white embroidered tunic top that wouldn't have looked out of place in Ibiza Old Town. She'd tied her very slightly silver-threaded dark brown hair up into a girlish ponytail, and adorned earlobes and wrists with ethnic turquoise jewellery.

'Thanks, darling. I picked it up in a little boutique a couple of days after Poppy's wedding. It's more suited to

204

a Balearic climate than this ghastly English weather though.'
She nodded out of the window, at the lowering clouds and
rapidly darkening sky. 'Looks like we'll be eating around
the kitchen table again. Such a shame – we haven't
managed one alfresco lunch with you and Andy this
summer.'

'Never mind,' Bella smiled. 'We always have a good time
around this table.' She took a sip of her wine and laughed.
'So, how long has Dad been taking pictures of Bernie?'

Olivia groaned. 'I knoooww. Ridiculous, isn't it? Of
course, it's nice that my ex-husband and my . . .' She
paused coyly for a moment.

'Please, don't say lover, Mum.'

'Don't worry, darling. Um . . . it's nice that Justin and
Bernie are friends, but I hadn't anticipated them getting
on *quite* so well. Your father almost seems to hero-worship
Bernie, and Bernie treats *him* with the kind of affectionate
amusement you'd reserve for your favourite naughty child.'

'And which one of us would that be, then?' Bella had
never quite got over her sibling rivalry with Max.

'Don't be silly, Bella. Anyway, I'll be quite glad to have
Bernie to myself again, once your father's buggered back
off to Mallorca.'

'Yeah, I can imagine – he and Bernie had nipped off to
take some more photos by the apple tree when I went out
there just now. You must feel a bit of a spare prick—'

There was a loud clap of thunder and seconds later the
heavy black clouds outside the south-facing windows
disgorged the contents of their swollen bellies. It was really,
seriously, pissing it down.

'Well, they won't be down there for much longer now,'

said Olivia, and on cue a sorry trail of sodden males burst through the kitchen door, dripping and panting like wet dogs.

'Oh, you poor things,' said Olivia, trying not to laugh. 'You'd better go and get into some dry clothes – do help yourselves to hot showers, if you want. There are fresh towels in both bathrooms. And by the time you're down again we'll have got the potatoes on, and then I've got a treat for you all.'

'So what's the treat?' Bella asked her mother as they basted the par-boiled potatoes with sizzling goose fat and slid them into the Aga's pre-heated second chamber. She was expecting homemade Scotch quails' eggs or some such delicacy.

'Poppy's show! It's not meant to be coming on for another month, but there was a preview last night on a really obscure American channel. I thought it would be a nice surprise for you all.'

'I watched it, Mum.'

'Oh.' Olivia's shoulders sagged slightly, the wind taken out of her sails. 'I assumed you and Andy would be out – you know, Saturday night . . .'

'Nope, he was working.' Bella's voice was slightly bitter. 'We don't go out on Saturday nights any more. I stayed in and watched Poppy looking gorgeous in the sunshine instead.'

'And didn't she just?' Olivia beamed. She wasn't stupid, and could hear the resentment in her daughter's voice, but wasn't about to pander to it. 'I've Sky Plus-ed it, but can't work out how to get it to work today. Bloody remote's gone missing again. Please help me, darling. I'm sure everybody else would love to see it.'

So Bella was on her hands and knees, unable to work out, herself, how to get Poppy's show on her mother's telly, when the men, all dry and fluffy now, reappeared from their ablutions.

'Oh, I can't work out how to do it,' she snapped.

'What?' asked Andy.

'Mum recorded Poppy on Sky Plus last night. I've seen it anyway.'

Andy looked at her in bemusement.

'Really? Why didn't you tell me?'

'You weren't in the mood to be told about anything so trivial when you got in last night.'

Andy felt guilty. All he had wanted to do the previous night, after yet another evening steeped in the horrors of people trafficking, was collapse into bed with Bella in his arms.

'Oh, God, I'm sorry, sweetheart. Well, I can't wait to watch it now.' He crouched down next to her and started to sort out the buttons on the machine.

'Poppy's show?' said Mark from the armchair in which he'd ensconced himself. 'Bet it's a stormer.' He was slightly pissed by this stage, but very aware of trying not to offend anybody. Not the most sensitive of souls, he honestly thought that praising Poppy might get him back into Bella's good books.

'Course it will be,' said Justin from the sofa. 'That girl's a knockout. Your best friend for life, isn't she, Angel Face?'

'Yes, Dad.' Bella's teeth were gritted as the opening credits scrolled up, revealing Poppy's beautiful, smiling face framed against the New York skyline.

'Wow,' was her opening comment. Not particularly clever, or eloquent, but as she spread her arms wide to indicate the roof terrace on which she was being filmed, she also exposed her lovely, slender body in its Missoni string bikini, which more than compensated.

'Wow, indeed.' Mark whistled.

*For fuck's sake*! thought Bella. *They'll be rubbing their crotches and panting next.*

'I have to say that I have the best job in the world,' Poppy confided to the camera. 'As an English girl from the sticks . . .'

'Puh-lease . . .' groaned Bella, until she realized that everybody was looking at her weirdly. She shifted uncomfortably on the floor and leant back against the sofa. Andy kissed the top of her head as he sat down beside her.

'. . . who has been lucky enough to do a bit of global travelling, I've seen some amazing places. But I don't think anything can really beat this! I mean – come on! A pool on a roof in the centre of the coolest city in the world? That's what I call glamour. And look at this weather!' She gestured up at the cloudless, almost-navy-blue sky. 'It's as hot as it looks, and – you know what? I can't resist that water. Sorry, Patrick . . .' This was directed at the cameraman. 'But I've always been able to resist everything but temptation.' And, holding her nose, she took a running jump into the bright blue pool, covering the camera's lens with droplets of water.

It was funny, endearing and clearly unscripted.

Poppy hauled herself out of the pool, rubbing the running

mascara away from under her eyes, joking with and apologizing to the rest of the crew. The wet hair and lack of concern about her appearance only served to make her look more gorgeous.

'Sorry about that,' she said, giggling from the screen. 'But if you'd been here too, you'd have done the same. God, this is fab. OK, I'd better get on with being professional now . . .' People were running up to her with towels, and she thanked them all.

'Thanks, Susie – you're an angel.' Poppy took one of them from a plumpish girl in specs, then continued, with an arm around the girl's shoulder, 'This is Susie, my assistant. She's just brilliant, and won't be pandering to the likes of me for much longer, will you, Suze?'

Susie, who was clearly besotted with Poppy, laughed. She was used to bitches and divas.

'And I would like to say, "Hello," to Mrs Arkwright in Wisconsin – or may I call you Elizabeth? Susie's told me so much about you!'

'Hey, Mom!' Susie grinned, waving at the camera.

'Actually, Suze, I'm meant to be reviewing the drinks here, but if it's only me, it's a bit one-sided, isn't it?' Poppy continued, the sun shining off her wet blonde hair. 'How about we try a couple of cocktails together? For a bit of journalistic even-handedness?'

'Wow, yeah – thanks. If that's OK, Marty?' Susie looked over at her boss, who nodded enthusiastically. He loved the way Poppy was with the little people – it just made her all the more likeable.

'Creep,' muttered Bella under her breath.

'You know I'm not Poppy's greatest fan,' said Andy,

putting his hand on Bella's leg and giving it a little squeeze, 'but I have to say, I think she's doing a brilliant job.'

'Yeah, and she looks *amazing*!' Mark laughed.

'Are we going to talk all the way through it?' said Olivia, glancing at her daughter. 'Let's save the comments until the end, shall we?'

So they turned back to the TV and watched the rest of the programme in silence.

'You've excelled yourself again, Princess,' said Bernie, licking his lips and patting his paunch.

They were just finishing off lunch, which had been to die for – the aromatic lamb, so tender it fell off the bone, offset by deeply savoury crispy bits and a variety of summer vegetables. The sweetness of the *petits pois à la français* – peas simmered in stock with shallots and lettuce hearts – had complemented the meat particularly successfully. And nothing beat Olivia's crispy, fluffy roast potatoes.

'It was a joint effort,' said Olivia. 'Credit where it's due.'

'Too right,' said Andy, smiling at Bella. 'To the cooks!' He raised his glass, and Bernie, Justin and Mark followed suit.

'The cooks!'

Bella smiled, feeling all warm and happy again, her earlier resentment towards Poppy all but forgotten. The rest of the show had been equally sparkling, as she drank cocktails on the roof terrace, chatting away happily with Susie, and flirting with random handsome men reclining on sun loungers. But she never lost sight of conveying the important bits, the facts that would be useful to anybody

210

actually wanting to visit this particular hotel. Poppy was destined for TV greatness; that much was apparent to all.

But the show had finished hours ago, much wine had been consumed since, and (largely thanks to Olivia) many more topics discussed. Bella always loved sitting around her mother's kitchen table, eating delicious food and getting happily sloshed.

And it felt especially cosy inside now, as the storm continued to rage fiercely outside the windows. Bernie and Justin had lit a fire in the grate, with much showing off of their manly skills, and Olivia had switched on the many lamps that gave a soft, flattering glow to the family kitchen.

There was another roar of thunder, this one so loud it made them all jump.

'Bloody English summer!' Bella laughed. 'But not for you and Mum for much longer, Bernie. Aren't you off to Miami in a week or two?'

A couple of months into Bernie and Olivia's relationship, Bernie had moved into the mill house, selling his faux-Tudor monstrosity up the road for several millions. But he had kept his two other properties – an ultra-modern villa on Miami Beach and a surprisingly beautiful Art Nouveau apartment in Istanbul – and he and Olivia now led an enviably jet-set lifestyle, dividing their time between the three destinations.

'That's right. Business calls. Places to go, people to see.' Bernie winked and tapped the side of his nose. Nobody really knew what Bernie did for a living, not even Olivia. Bella had once asked her, and her mother had dismissed the question with an airy, 'No idea, darling, and quite frankly, I'd rather not know.'

'Miami Beach!' chortled Justin. 'The stories I could tell you about that gaff in the eighties. I remember shooting Jerry there with Helmut – Newton, you know . . .'

'Jerry Hall?' asked Mark, and Justin nodded, starting to roll another spliff. 'What was she like? Always struck me as a game old bird.'

'Not so old in those days, son, but, yeah, definitely a game bird. Face like an 'orse, mind you, but legs that went on forever. You could see what Mick saw in 'er.'

'Any other stories?' asked Andy, taking a swig of his red wine. He did find Bella's parents entertaining – they were like no one he had encountered in his life before.

'I imagine most of them involve coke and hookers,' said Olivia, and they all laughed. As Justin launched into a scandalous anecdote involving Joan Collins, Jacqueline Bisset and a Puerto Rican rent boy, Bella got to her feet to clear the table and make way for home-made summer pudding. Olivia had knocked it up the previous day, using fruit from her garden and two-day-old home-baked white bread.

Bella put the glistening ruby dome in the centre of the table, with a cold jug of double cream, fresh from the village farm. It was the most delicious cream she had ever tasted. Disgustingly, she could drink it by the spoonful – and probably would, if she wasn't so aware of her increasingly tightening waistband.

'Wow, that looks amazing,' said Andy.

'Do all of you tuck in.' Olivia beamed. 'I've the perfect little tipple to accompany it, too.' She floated into the sitting room, where the fully stocked drinks cabinet lived, and returned triumphantly bearing an almost spherical, gold-labelled bottle with some sort of deep purple liquid sloshing around inside it.

'What on earth's that, Mum?' asked Bella, laughing.

'Chambord. It's made out of black raspberries and is utterly delicious.'

'I bet it is. Looks expensive . . .'

'Oh, it is, darling, it is. It was originally created for Louis the Fourteenth. But worth it, as I'm sure you'll agree when you try it.'

It was. And it went like a dream with the summer pudding. The problem was, it tasted so yummy-ly fruity that it was easy to forget that they were, actually, downing neat spirits.

Soon the bottle was empty, and the mood more raucous than ever.

'I think we need some music,' said Bella, getting unsteadily to her feet. She really was very pissed now. 'Anyone got any requests, or can I be DJ?'

'Oh, you choose, darling, you always do so *so* beautifully,' said Olivia, hiccupping slightly.

So Bella plugged her iPhone into its speakers and opened Spotify. Soon, Ella Fitzgerald was crooning classic Cole Porter hits into the kitchen and everybody around the table had a soppy, drunken smile pasted on to his or her face.

They all sang along to 'Everytime We Say Goodbye', really getting into it when it got to the 'from major to minor' bit, looking sentimentally into one another's eyes, as if it really, really meant something.

The next song was 'I'll Take Manhattan', and the conversation turned, inevitably, to Poppy's show. Well, it was called *Poppy Takes Manhattan*.

Bella cursed herself internally. How could she not have seen this coming?

'I have to say, Angel Face, that that friend of yours is going to be a *huge* success,' said Justin, taking a drag on his spliff.

'She's certainly a very talented young lady,' concurred Bernie.

'And she's looking hot as hell,' leered Mark.

Something snapped inside Bella. It probably wouldn't have, without so much booze inside her, but there was, and it did.

'WILL YOU ALL JUST SHUT THE FUCK UP ABOUT POPPY!' she shouted.

And the room, for the second time that day, fell silent.

# Chapter 13

Marty and Eleanor's clapboard beach house in Westhampton was a monument to understated good taste. White-painted woodwork contrasted with dark floors – slate in the kitchen, polished wooden boards everywhere else – and was complemented by natural linens and cottons in muted shades of cream and taupe throughout. Jaunty blue-and-white-striped cushions and rugs added a nautical flavour, and enormous French windows leading to decks on both floors let in enough light by which to perform microsurgery, if one so chose.

Poppy and Damian were reclining on the lower deck on incredibly comfortable polished teak sun loungers – upholstered, naturally, in cream linen, and piled with cushions in different variations on the blue-and-white-striped theme. The deck looked out onto the white sandy beach, and a cooling breeze wafted in from the glittering cobalt ocean.

Poppy, exquisite in a pale yellow string bikini that matched her surfer-girl hair and showed off her golden tan, was happily immersed in a trashy novel. She'd been working so hard on *Poppy Takes Manhattan* that it had been ages since she'd had a chance to relax properly, and she was practically purring with contentment. Damian, as was his wont these days, was poring over his laptop as he ploughed on with his screenplay.

'Sweetheart, don't you want to take a break?' said Poppy, reaching out to touch his arm. 'You've been slaving away all morning.'

'That's easy for you to say. You've got a job.' Damian didn't look up from the screen and Poppy sighed.

After their Prohibition party, they had both been filled with remorse. Poppy didn't actually think she'd done anything wrong, but she knew that ever since her fling with Ben, trust had been a huge issue for Damian, which she could hardly blame him for. Of course he wasn't going to react kindly to a gorgeous film star trying to snog his wife.

Damian, for his part, felt sheepish at losing his cool, and thought he'd made a bit of a tit of himself. Once the heat of the moment had died down, they were both desperate to make their marriage work, and when Poppy had called Damian the following day, the first thing they'd both said was 'sorry'. In unison. That had broken the ice, and they had both started laughing. The making-up sex had been fast and furious, then languorous and romantic, and for that night at least, everything had been great again between them.

But, much as she loved him, Poppy still felt that she was walking on eggshells around her husband.

'Hey, guys,' trilled Eleanor, approaching them with a silver tray clinking with glasses. Poppy and Damian looked up expectantly. Ellie was wearing a supremely chic Ralph Lauren navy-blue strapless swimsuit underneath a man's white cotton shirt with the sleeves pushed back. Her light brown hair was held back from her face with expensive-looking but logo-free tortoiseshell sunglasses.

'Oooh, I was just thinking it was probably time for a drink,' said Poppy, as it was already two p.m. and normal drinking rules didn't really apply when you were on holiday. Freshly squeezed red grapefruit juice had been the order of the day with brunch, a couple of hours earlier.

'Poppy!' Ellie laughed, faux-reproachfully. 'I have made a selection of iced 'erbal teas. You don't really want to be drinking alcohol before sunset, now do you?'

'Oh, no, of course not.' Poppy caught Damian's eye, and tried not to giggle. 'What I meant was that I'm just really, really thirsty. Gosh, those iced teas look delicious.'

And actually they did. Ellie had gone to the trouble of putting the tall glasses in the freezer, so they had a pleasingly frosty appearance, and decorating each of them with an appropriate garnish: crystallized rose petals and rosehips for the pale pinks; mint and basil leaves for the pale greens; camomile flowers and lemon peel for the pale yellows.

'Yes, they do,' said Damian, smiling at his hostess. 'You really shouldn't have gone to so much trouble, Ellie.'

'Oh, that's OK, I love doing things like this.' Ellie smiled sweetly back. 'It keeps me out of mischief, y'know?'

Poppy and Damian both laughed.

At that moment, Poppy nearly jumped out of her skin as something very cold and very sticky landed – *splat!* – on her flat brown tummy. Looking up, she saw Hammond –

Marty and Ellie's son – grinning evilly from the balcony above, an empty bowl clutched in his sticky little hand. As the dairy-free, sugar-free 'ice cream' melted into her belly button, Poppy realized she couldn't get up without making the most god-awful mess over the pristine decking. She smiled at Ellie through gritted teeth.

'Oh, my God, I'm so sorry, Poppy. Accidents will happen. You just wait there while I go fetch a cloth, then you can go freshen up. Hammy, honey,' she cooed up at the balcony. 'Don't you worry, baby. Mommy will bring you some more ice cream right away.' And she half ran back inside her lovely, airy house.

'Accidents, my arse,' said Damian under his breath, and Poppy smiled at him in a moment of pure complicity. Hammy was an absolute little monster. After suffering so many miscarriages, Ellie could deny her longed-for only child nothing, while Marty's feeble attempts at discipline had resulted in tantrums on such a whopping scale that he had pretty much given up after the third or fourth time.

'How comfortable are you now, on a scale of one to ten?' Damian asked Poppy.

'Erm . . . around one and a half, I'd say,' said Poppy, as the melting fake ice cream made its way down towards her crotch. For something sugar-free, it was quite spectacularly sticky.

'If we were somewhere a bit more private, I'd lick it off you . . .'

'I'd lick it off you! I'd lick it off you!' came an obnoxious, high-pitched chant from above. 'Hahahahahaha!' Hammond started banging his empty bowl on the upper deck in time to his words, laughing like some kind of possessed demon child. 'I'd lick it off you! I'd lick it off you! I'd lick it off you!'

'Shut up!' hissed Damian, at which the little boy's face turned purple as he proceeded to scream the place down. 'Waaaaaaaaaagh! Waaaaaaaaaagh! Waaaaaaaaaagh!'

Ellie, who had been on her way back to give Poppy a cloth, turned her back on her guests and ran upstairs, panic written all over her neat little features.

'Baby! Don't you worry, Mommy's coming!'

'Don't move an inch,' Damian said to Poppy. 'I'll get you a cloth.'

'Nice to have you to myself again,' Poppy said to Damian, who picked up her hand and kissed it.

'Thank fuck for their anniversary,' he said.

They were at the Saltwater Grill, a mere ten-minute walk down the beach from Marty and Eleanor's house, the evening after Hammond had thrown his fake ice cream all over Poppy. The previous night, Ellie had said, winsomely, over dinner, 'I hope you don't mind, you guys, but it's our fifth wedding anniversary tomorrow, and we want to be alone for dinner. I can recommend some awesome places for you two to eat . . .'

'Oh, God, no, that's fine,' Poppy had said, kicking Damian under the table. 'We'll be out of your hair as soon as you want us to be . . .'

Hammond had, despite his tender years, dominated dinner, which had been served at six p.m., and with one bottle of wine between the four of them. Neither Poppy nor Damian could remember having been so bored on holiday. Ever.

219

Now, though, they smiled at one another, already on their second bottle of Zinfandel. The Saltwater Grill enjoyed a superb location, right on the beach. The dunes were so high that they couldn't actually see the sea from where they were sitting, on the wooden deck, but there was a lovely relaxed air to the place. A reggae band was playing just to their left, they could hear the waves crashing against the shore and the smell of ozone filled their nostrils.

It was extraordinarily WASP-y though. Everywhere you looked were preppies dressed in expensive casualwear from Lacoste, J.Crew and L.L.Bean. They all had very straight teeth and exceptionally shiny hair. Just as Damian was reflecting that his was the only dark face for miles around, a couple of young guys – student jocks, by the look of them, both strapping and blond, approached their table, laughing and nudging one another.

'Are you Poppy Wallace?'

Poppy looked at Damian nervously. Oh, for fuck's sake, this wasn't going to help matters tonight. But, as the pro she was, she smiled up at them.

'Yup, that's me.'

'I just wanted to say –' The boys were quite spectacularly drunk, Poppy now realized, but carried on smiling regardless – 'that we all *jerk off* to your show, like EVERY THURSDAY!'

As both boys collapsed in hysterics, Damian jumped to his feet.

'How *dare* you say that to my wife?'

'It's a compliment, dude,' said one of them, setting his friend off into even greater paroxysms of mirth. Poppy bit her lip to stop giggling and making Damian even angrier.

'Well, thank you very much,' she said. 'I hope you all get a lot of sleep on Fridays, and rest your no doubt weary wrists.'

That took the jock-jerks by surprise and, after a beat, faces wreathed in smiles, they started high-fiving both her and Damian, slapping them both on the back for good measure.

'High five! Respect, man! Your wife is one cool chick.'

As Damian high-fived them back, a reluctant smile crept across his face.

'Sorry about that. I love you,' said Poppy, once the jock-jerks had ambled off down the beach, chortling to one another.

'I'm sorry too. In fact, I should probably feel flattered that twats like that want to wank over my wife. Especially as I get to have the real thing.' The previous evening, with nothing else to do, they had shagged one another senseless, giggling as Marty and Eleanor's sex noises drowned theirs out over the salty night air.

Their food arrived – broiled lobster for Damian and clam chowder for Poppy – and they ordered another bottle of wine.

'Sorry I've been a bit of a cunt recently,' said Damian.

'Don't be silly. You could never be as much of a cunt as I was last year. I know it's tough at the moment, but the screenplay is brilliant. You know it and I know it – it's just a matter of time.'

'Yes, you're right. Sorry again, Pops. Let's just enjoy this lovely evening. Oh, my God, *look*!'

Damian pointed over the deck and they both watched as a family of deer strolled by on the beach. Under the clear, starlit sky, the sight was magical.

'You don't get that in Hoxton.'

Damian leant across the table to kiss Poppy and she kissed him back, happy and relieved. When he got up to go to the loo, she picked up a celeb gossip magazine that somebody had left on the bench next to her. Flicking through it, something stopped her in her tracks.

HOLLYWOOD BROMANCE? ran the headline. *Are über-cool Jack Meadows and hot hot HOT new Brit actor Ben Jones the new* Entourage *boys on the LA block? While filming their hotly Oscar-tipped new movie,* Beyond the Sea, *these guys seem to have struck a friendship the like of which has not been seen since Ben Affleck and Matt Damon. Watch this space, movie-lovers!*

And there, in a double-page spread, were photo after photo of Ben and Jack – the lovely Jack who'd been so nice to her at her Prohibition party. God, they looked gorgeous, the photomontage comprising black-tie events, casual coffees on Melrose, hiking in the Hollywood hills, even frolicking in the surf together, both men's chests impressively worked-out. Jack was slightly taller than Ben, and his curly black hair contrasted beautifully with Ben's streaky light brown/dark blond locks. In every photo they were laughing, the rapport between them patently obvious.

*Well, bugger me,* she thought.

Just as she was thinking, dispassionately, but with an understandable degree of vanity, that both these men had wanted to fuck her, Damian returned from his pee.

'What are you reading?'

'Oh, just some tabloid shit . . .'

Poppy tried to hide the magazine, but Damian was too quick for her and grabbed it, laughing. As it clocked, the sudden change in his expression was terrifying.

222

'WHAT? Ben AND that shit Jack Meadows? Oh, for fuck's sake, Poppy, I bet you're loving this. You'd be so much better off with one of them than you are with me, wouldn't you? Fucking loser who hasn't even got a job. I bet you'd *love* a threesome with those vain fucking cunts. Wouldn't you? WOULDN'T YOU?'

And because she couldn't think of anything else to say – they were both quite pissed, and she was deeply tired of Damian's constant jealousy – she stood up, looked him straight in the eye, and said, 'Yes. I would.'

Back in LA, Ben and Jack were sharing a spliff, lying in adjacent hammocks suspended from a large acacia tree whose branches stretched out over one end of Jack's mosaic-tiled pool. His Spanish-style villa was rammed with people he'd known since he was born – veterans of the rock and film worlds, to a man. His father, who went by the improbable name of Filthy Meadows (he'd had it changed by deed poll) was trying to placate his mother, the insanely large-breasted and flashing-eyed ex-groupie Heather Meadows (née Maria Gonzalez); against all odds, they had stayed together, though sometimes Jack wished that they hadn't.

Now she was screaming at him: 'I know you're still screwing that Sandra bitch!'

'And I know you're still screwing José.' José was the 21-year-old Mexican pool boy. 'Just chill, woman.' And Filthy Meadows walked, with his signature languorous gait, over to the pool.

'Hey, guys.'

Ben tried to sit up in his hammock – Filthy Meadows was

a legend, after all – but it was too difficult, and he didn't want to fall into the pool and completely lose his cool.

'Hey, Filthy,' he managed, through a fog of dope.

'Filth to you.' The rock star winked and Ben laughed.

'Filth it is, then.'

Since Natalia's abrupt departure, Ben had found himself heartbroken for the first time in his life. He had used all of the studio's immense powers to try to find her, in all the places he thought she might have hidden: St Barts, Mustique, Necker island, all the major cities in Europe; he'd even tried Kiev. But to no avail. Natalia seemed to have vanished off the surface of the planet.

Thank fuck, he had his work to throw himself into, and, in Jack, a surprisingly good new mate. Although there had been the inevitable locking of horns between two alpha males to start with, Ben and Jack were both classically trained actors, of similar intelligence and with similar senses of humour; they found, grudgingly, that they liked one another enormously. And of course the publicity people encouraged it – the movie-loving saps always loved a good 'bromance'.

'Why do you and Mom keep doing this, Dad?' asked Jack.

'Because we love each other.' Filthy's face, all plumped-up lips and weird facial topiary, went soft. 'When you find the one you love, none of the screwing around means anything. She knows that, and I know that. Sometimes we just like a fight. It means the sex—'

'No, no, no . . .!' Jack put his hands over his ears. 'I've heard it all before and – Dad, *way* too much information, even the first time.'

'I've found the woman I love,' said Ben. The dope and the hammock were giving him a curious sensation of weightlessness, floating on a cloud as the A-list party glittered and twinkled across the way.

'That's awesome, man,' said Filth, with a tear in his eye. 'That's the most important thing you can do in your life. Where is she, then? The one you love should always be by your side. EVEN IF SHE IS SCREWING THE POOL BOY,' he shouted over his shoulder. Then, as if surprised at his momentary lack of nonchalance, he resumed his habitual slouch.

Jack sighed theatrically as he heard his mother screaming a string of Spanish expletives from the kitchen.

'I don't know, Filth,' said Ben sadly. 'I just don't know.'

# Chapter 14

'Full house!' Natalia slapped her cards down and smiled round at her new friends on Bottle Beach, which was on the Thai island of Koh Phangan. Having thought about it carefully, she had decided that the best way for her to disappear was to mingle with backpackers on beaches. Nobody would think of looking for her in such unsophisticated surroundings, and she could wander freely with the constant stream of travellers: gap-year kids, elderly hippies, drifters, party people, earnest, well-meaning couples – and the rest of the hundreds of thousands of people who wanted to take advantage of cheap food and beer on beautiful beaches, while managing to kid themselves that they were having some kind of spiritual awakening.

She was still paying Georgiou through the nose, enough to keep him happy, she hoped. There was no way he'd go to the press when she was such a lucrative source of income, and noncontactable. Every week, she transferred the money from a new Android, on which she had disabled the GPS and downloaded a banking app. The most important thing was that they didn't implicate Ben in her sordid past.

She couldn't believe how much she missed him, and still cried herself to sleep every night. But Natalia was used to pain. And, bizarrely, in this little backpacker haven, she had found a certain degree of comfort. Her beach hut was basic, but it had an electric fan, mosquito net and its own shower and lavatory. It opened directly onto the white sandy beach, and there was a little wooden deck where she could dry her wet towels and lie in a hammock, reading or just gazing out to sea; hardly purgatory when she remembered the dark chill of her Ukrainian upbringing.

She had instructed her crew to take her yacht and designer wardrobe back to Ibiza, and had bought a selection of cheap string bikinis, tie-dye sarongs, faded cotton vest tops and denim cut-offs. She hadn't got over her aversion to denim, but had to look the part. Not wanting to cut her hair, most days she wore it in plaits, and now that the platinum dye was starting to grow out and her mousy roots were becoming streaky in the hot Thai sun, she could easily pass for just another (strikingly good looking) 30–40-something trying to find herself on foreign shores. Deeply tanned and freckled now, her only jewellery was a silver-and-turquoise anklet; she never wore shoes.

Bottle Beach was an extraordinarily picturesque cove, all powdery sand, turquoise sea and gently swaying palm trees, only accessible by boat from Haad Rin, the main village on the island. Natalia remembered Poppy and Damian telling her about it – they had met seven years previously at one of Koh Phangan's notorious Full Moon parties, and spent several days exploring the island together afterwards. They had raved about its beauty and remoteness, and Natalia had thought it sounded absolutely perfect for her requirements. It was the sort of place where, amongst the constant stream of people passing through, some chose to spend an entire season, just chilling out for months on end.

Natalia's story was that she'd just been through a messy divorce, though she didn't give too much away, and nobody pried too much. It was as though life outside the beach didn't count for much when you were there, which suited her just fine. She had attracted quite a devoted following, though. Pretty much all of the male long-termers had a crush on her, from gauche gap-year kids to 40-somethings with long hair and guitars, to a 70-year-old French artist who liked to escape from his home in Provence every winter. Even though she was perfectly friendly and joined in with card games and other communal activities, she had a wounded, vulnerable air that made them want to look after her.

Despite her ongoing heartache, Natalia had come to love the simple way of life on the beach. Every morning, she would rise with the sun and swim out towards the horizon for an hour or so. The beach was particularly lovely at this time of day, and when she swam far out into the ocean, turning back to look at the shore, she felt at one with nature, the sheer beauty and enormity of planet Earth somehow managing to dwarf her own problems. She always swam underwater now, the days of keeping the façade intact long gone.

She would return to a breakfast of mango juice and pancakes with freshly grated coconut and honey, which she ate sitting on a beanbag under a palm tree, alternately looking out to sea and reading. Yoga and meditation on the beach generally followed. These were led by Juho, a Finn around her age who liked to escape his own country as soon as summer was out and the intolerably short days began. It was only mid-September, but Juho had said, seriously, that 'the people in my country, they go mad in wintertime; they drink too much. It is impossible not to, when you have very little daylight for months. For me, beaches and meditation are better. But it is not for me to judge others.'

Juho had a beautifully shaped shaved head, high cheek-bones and an impressively lean and muscular physique, and Natalia liked him. But she wasn't interested in anybody sexually, not when she was haunted by memories of her time with Ben.

The rest of the day would generally comprise a lazy stroll down the beach, some sunbathing, perhaps another swim or two, lunch (even the cheapest Thai food was delicious, she had come to realize), a siesta in the hammock on her deck, a few beers and card games with her fellow travellers in the evening.

And here she was now.

'Gosh, you're so good at cards,' said Fliss (short for Felicity), after Natalia had won yet another poker hand with her full house. 'You probably started playing before I was born!' She gave a dimpled smile and Natalia laughed. She wasn't going to let this bitchy little 20-year-old rile her.

'I probably did, yes.' She realized that her arrival on Bottle Beach had put Fliss's pretty little nose well out of joint; she had been undisputed Queen Bee of the beach until Natalia had turned up, with her endless legs, sexy accent and annoying air of tragedy.

Juho, across the table, caught Natalia's eye and almost imperceptibly winked.

'Good morning, Natalia.'

'Good morning, Juho.'

The pair nodded politely at one another as Natalia arrived for her morning yoga and meditation. Throughout her life, Natalia had, quite understandably, developed more than her fair share of cynicism. Hippy-dippy practices were absolutely not her thing. And yet . . . There was something about doing yoga and meditating on a beach that was calming. Clichéd though it was, the sessions seemed to give her a sense of inner peace, the like of which she had not experienced since before her mother died. She still didn't believe all the mystical rubbish that Juho sometimes spouted; she reckoned that this inner peace was purely a biochemical reaction to contorting yourself into unnatural poses while sweating profusely, then sitting still and silent for twenty minutes. But if it made her feel better, who was she to knock it?

'Is nobody else here this morning?' Natalia gestured around at the empty clearing under the palm trees. Normally, there were at least five or six takers for Juho's classes.

'They've all gone on a fishing boat for the day.'

'Oh . . .' Natalia tried not to feel hurt that she hadn't been asked on the fishing trip; she had thought she was quite popular on Bottle Beach.

Seeing the look in her eyes, Juho said, smiling, 'Fliss suggested it after you went to bed last night . . .'

Natalia smiled back at him. 'Ah. I see. I thank you.'

'So, shall we begin?'

As they embarked on the first series of sun salutations, Natalia tried not to notice how firm and supple Juho's body was; how beautifully it moved. For these sessions, he tended to wear only a pair of white cotton three-quarter-length fisherman's trousers. He wasn't anything like as beautiful as Ben, but in his own way, he was perfectly formed. After years of servicing rich men much older than her, followed by half a decade of celibacy, Natalia's brief romance with Ben had reawakened all kinds of urges inside her. Her loyalty to Ben's memory was too great for anything more – but surely there was nothing to stop her taking pleasure in the sight of Juho?

'Natalia?' Juho was looking at her with a hint of a smile on his face, and she had the feeling that he knew exactly what she was thinking.

'Oh – ah, sorry . . . What did you say?'

'I said, shall we do some floor work now?'

As the day wore on, Bottle Beach became more and more busy, and the air pulsated with excitement. The Full Moon Party was that night, and backpackers were arriving on Koh Phangan in droves; all the accommodation in Haad Rin was full, so people were seeking out the quieter beaches for somewhere to rest their heads. Or more probably just to dump their rucksacks – it was unlikely to be a night of much sleeping.

Natalia couldn't get into the mood for it. The quietness of life on the beach had been balm to her troubled soul, but the idea of an all-night party with thousands of young people, off their heads on various substances, dancing in the sea to thumping techno, was more than she could stomach.

'I think I shall skip the party,' she said to the gang as they sat nursing their usual sunset beers.

'Oh, no, Nat, you must come,' came a chorus of disappointed male voices. Juho's wasn't among them, but he smiled.

'Oh, I think you're right,' said Fliss. 'All that sort of stuff is probably a bit *loud* and *hectic* for you, isn't it?'

'Yes, you are right, Fliss: I am far too old for that sort of thing.' Natalia smiled graciously back at the girl. 'But I am sure you will all have a wonderful time.'

Later, sitting reading on her deck, she luxuriated in the uncustomary silence. Quiet though Bottle Beach was, there was generally a handful of people up and about, sharing beers and spliffs, playing cards or singing along to guitars around makeshift bonfires. Tonight, after the mass exodus (by way of a veritable fleet of longboats), the stillness was unearthly. Natalia put her book down and let her mind drift back to Saint-Tropez – a luxury she rarely allowed herself, as once she returned to the present, the sadness became almost intolerable.

That magical night at Sénéquier, the first time Ben had kissed her; speeding over the waves towards the Île du

Levant, giddy with anticipation; swimming naked in the crystalline waters off the island as the sun beat down on their golden heads; the incredible sex on the *speedboat*; *night after night* of incredible sex on *her boat*, as they whispered and giggled together in the darkness.

So caught up was she in her reverie that Natalia didn't notice the light tread approaching her hut until it was almost upon her. She stifled a scream – surely, Georgiou hadn't managed to find her here?

'Natalia? It is I, Juho. I am sorry if I frightened you.'

'Oh, Juho, oh, thank God.' Natalia laughed, shakily. 'Yes, you did scare me a little. Why aren't you at the party?'

'You know, it really isn't my thing either.' Juho looked at Natalia quizzically, and she smiled.

'No, of course it is not.'

'It is a beautiful night. I wondered if you wanted to take a walk down the beach with me, to watch the full moon?'

'Yes, OK. Why not?' Natalia didn't have to think twice about it. Lying here torturing herself with thoughts of Ben was not helping matters in the slightest.

The sand was silvery and soft between her toes, and the sea glittered under the enormous moon and billions of stars. As they walked along, it felt natural to reach out and take Juho's hand. He was a good man, and there hadn't been many of those in her life. Maybe it was the stillness of the beach, where the only sound was that of the waves against the shore; more probably, it was her desperate loneliness. Juho was a good, decent man, she told herself again, trying to rid her mind of the image of Ben. Juho's bare-chested, nicely muscled body was right next to hers and, as she looked at his fine profile in the moonlight, she was suddenly desperate for something more.

She stopped walking and very slowly turned round to face him, looking straight into his kind hazel eyes.

'Natalia.' Juho ran a finger down her cheek, looking back into her eyes. He was slightly shorter than she was. 'You are a beautiful woman, and I find you very attractive, but I think you are suffering deeply. I want to be your friend, if you want it, but no more than that. Besides . . .' He paused, briefly. 'I am celibate.'

'Oh.' Natalia let it register for a moment, then, out of nowhere, gales of laughter started bubbling up. 'Oh oh oh, I cannot tell you how glad I am! Oh, Juho, oh . . .!' The relief that she wouldn't betray Ben, even though she would never see him again, made her laugh so much that her knees suddenly buckled beneath her, and she collapsed on the sand, slightly hysterical. Juho sat down next to her, smiling benignly. Once she had finished laughing, he took a deep toke on the spliff he had been rolling.

'You want to tell me why you are –' Natalia bit her lip to stop herself spluttering with laughter again – 'celibate?'

'You want some of this?' He offered her the joint and she took it. 'It will not be forever, probably. But everything was getting too much. Back in Helsinki, I worked in advertising, and I was out every night, snorting cocaine, drinking too much vodka, fucking as many beautiful women as I could. Oh, let me tell you, Natalia, I would have been like totally into you in those days.'

Natalia smiled at him. 'I thank you for that.'

'So one day I told myself: enough. This is no good for your karma, man.' Natalia tried not to smile at this. 'So

234

here I am. And I feel more at peace now than I have ever been before. Does that make sense to you?'

Natalia took another drag on the spliff and looked out at the ocean, over which the enormous moon was casting an almost ethereal light.

'Yes. Yes, it does.'

And in that moment, a lifelong friendship was born.

# Chapter 15

Sam stumbled through the wet streets of Soho on her high heels, trying not to cry, but not caring about the rain ruining her hair and make-up. It didn't matter how she looked now anyway – she'd done what she had to do. She'd been so desperate to get out of the basement studio, that she had just slung her neatly folded sweatpants and hoody on over the stockings and suspenders she'd been wearing for the shoot, without bothering to change into her comfortable cotton knickers and underwired bra. In fact, she'd been so flustered that she hadn't even bothered to fish her trainers out of her holdall, just shoving her feet back into the patent black stilettos that looked so sexy in the photos.

Now she stopped underneath a dripping café awning to change her footwear. There was not caring how you looked, and there was wearing stilettos with sweatpants and a hoody. Besides, the five-minute walk to Piccadilly Circus Tube would take more like fifteen minutes in these shoes and she wanted to get out of the rain and back to halls

– her heart sank slightly at the lonely thought – as quickly as possible.

Everything looked seedier in the rain, the multicoloured neon lights proclaiming XXXX, WE SELL POPPERS, VIAGRA, GIRLS GIRLS GIRLS all bouncing in clashing angles off the shiny pavement. She was so sick of all this.

It was bad enough that the other girls on the shoot had been sniggering about Mark and Karolina Kristova. Some of them could be such downright bitches. But the rancid icing on the fetid cake had been the slimy photographer, who thought he had the right to run his hands up and down her body as he told her exactly how he wanted her to pose. Surely there were laws against such things?

As she walked down Berwick Street in the direction of Piccadilly Circus, she found herself bouncing slightly in her trainers. A couple of market traders leered openly at her braless breasts through her hoody, which was getting wetter by the minute.

'Nice tits, love.'

'Oh, just sod off.' Sam, who had been brought up to say please and thank you, was normally polite in the face of catcalls and wolf-whistles, but today she really had had enough. She suddenly wondered what Sienna was doing, and without a second thought reached into her holdall for her phone.

'Hey! Babes!' cried Sienna, in her trying-not-to-be-posh voice. 'How's it going?'

'I've had a crap day,' said Sam bluntly. 'All the girls were being bitches about Mark and Karolina, the photographer was groping me, and . . . and . . . now it's raining, I haven't got an umbrella, and I'm *soaked* . . .' She found herself crying by the end of her sentence, and hated herself for being so pathetic.

'Oh, sweetheart, how utterly disgusting,' said Sienna, sounding more like herself now. She didn't bother to dumb down her accent when she was being sincere about something. 'What are you up to now then? Are you free for the rest of the evening?'

'Well, I've got loads of reading to do for next term . . .'

'Oh, that really is silly. You work far too hard as it is. Just jump in a cab and get yourself to the Crack Den, pronto!' The Crack Den was their name for the boys' house in Dalston. 'We'd all love to see you . . . wouldn't we, boys?' Sam could hear male voices of assent in the background.

'Really?' She hadn't seen the boys since the time she'd turned Dan down after their day at the Hawley, and was still feeling a bit bad about the whole thing. But then again, they'd had such a nice, giggly time getting stoned together afterwards, that maybe it didn't matter.

'Of course, really, you idiot. Just get your arse in a cab and I'll pay for it this end.'

'Thanks, but no need for that.' Sam had her pride. 'I'm nearly at Piccadilly Circus. I'll get the Tube.'

'Piccadilly Circus to Dalston? In the rush hour? You must be . . .' Sam could hear someone shushing Sienna in the background. 'Well, rather you than me, darling. OK, we'll see you when we see you.'

When Sam eventually poked her head around the door, Sienna, Dan, Mikey and Olly were sitting on bare wooden floorboards, smoking joints, drinking beer out of cans and playing Scrabble. Loud rock music blared from the enormous sound system that dominated one corner of the open-plan living room, and the rain still thrashing down outside was clearly audible through the curtainless windows.

'Hello?' she said tentatively, not wanting to make a nuisance of herself.

Sienna, who was wearing a Flaming Geysers T-shirt and black leather hot pants that showed off her long, pale legs, leapt to her feet and ran towards her.

'Sammi-Jo! At last! We thought you were never going to get here. Was the journey absolutely horrendous?'

The journey had involved a Tube so packed that she'd had to let three trains go past before she could squeeze onto one, a bus that lurched with infuriating slowness through the traffic on the Essex Road, and a ten-minute walk in the rain. It had taken nearly an hour and a half in total.

Sam just shrugged and said. 'Had worse. But please don't call me Sammi-Jo.'

Sienna recoiled slightly, looking hurt. 'Sorry, babes, it was only meant to be a joke.'

'Not a very funny one,' said Dan, not looking up from his letters. 'Her name's Sam.'

Sam looked over at him gratefully and smiled, but he was still engrossed in his letters, his dark brown fringe flopping over his face as he looked down.

'Sorry sorry sorry,' said Sienna, giving Sam a huge hug. 'I'm a bit stoned. Didn't mean to be offensive.'

'That's OK. Sorry for being oversensitive. Just had a really bad day, and I don't want to be Sammi-Jo any more.'

'Why? What's happened?' asked Mikey disingenuously, brushing his golden-blond fringe out of his eyes.

Sam looked at Sienna.

'So you didn't tell them?' She knew her friend could never keep her mouth shut.

'Yeah, she told us,' said Dan, still not looking up from his letters. 'Sorry to hear about that shit-head photographer. He needs his face kicked in. Plenty of beers in the fridge, Sambo. Help yourself.'

'Thanks Dan. Just need to go to the toilet.' The stockings and suspenders were starting to feel extremely uncomfortable underneath her damp sweatpants and Sam found her teeth were chattering slightly. Dan looked up.

'You're soaking.' Sam instinctively put her arms around her braless chest in the wet hoody, and he pretended not to notice. 'D'you want to borrow something dry? You can have a look in my room, if you want, but everything I've got will be huge on you.'

'Borrow something of mine, Sam,' said Olly, the drummer, who was shorter and less handsome than the rest of the band, but with a sweet, open face that reflected an endearingly sunny nature. 'First floor, second on the right. Just help yourself to anything you like.'

When Sam returned downstairs, she was wearing a rolled-up pair of baggy Diesel jeans and a fine-knit black V-necked sweater. She'd wrung as much water as she could out of her long red hair and tied it up into a ponytail.

She helped herself to a beer out of the huge fridge and sat down next to Sienna.

'Thanks for the clothes, Olly.' She smiled at him. 'This is much more comfy.'

'Suits you.' Olly smiled back. 'You should wear my clothes more often.'

Sam saw Dan's back stiffen.

'So who's winning?' she asked quickly.

'Dan,' they all said in unison.

'He always does,' added Mikey. 'Don't know why we bother playing him really. Clever bastard.'

'Well, someone's got to write the lyrics,' said Dan, glancing up from his letters. 'You lot were well crap with your "yeah yeah yeahs" before I came along.'

'Worked for the Beatles,' said Sam, taking a swig of her Stella, and accepting the joint Sienna was handing her way. 'Thanks, Sienna.'

'Exactly. It worked for the Beatles, the best band in the world. But we are not a copycat band, or a fucking cover band. We write our own stuff. Original stuff.'

As he finished his sentence, Dan put his letters down. There was a Y free at the bottom of the board, and he used up all seven of his to make RHAPSODY, on a triple-word score.

'Oh, come on, mate . . .!'

'For fuck's sake, Dan . . .!'

'Told you he were a clever bastard!' Mikey grinned. 'No way any of us can catch up now.'

'It's not about the winning, it's about playing the game,' said Sienna, looking and sounding ridiculously posh, despite the band T-shirt and leather hot pants. Sitting cross-legged on the floor, her posture was perfect.

'Oooh, listen to the public schoolgirl,' teased Mikey, leaning over to kiss her. 'Were you a prefect? Or vice captain? I like to think of you as captain of vice.'

'Head girl, actually, until I was expelled.'

The boys looked at her in delight, all their St Trinian's naughty schoolgirl fantasies made flesh.

'What for?' Sam asked, giggling – the dope was strong, and already working its magic.

'Oh, nothing major. I got pissed and shagged the gardener. I've always liked a bit of rough. QED . . .' She stretched her long pale arms out and they all started laughing.

'You're my Marianne Faithfull,' said Mikey fondly.

'I'm so glad you're taller than Mick. Though I probably wouldn't have said no when he was younger – there was something about him, wasn't there?'

'I've always liked Keef,' said Sam, drawing deeply on the joint.

Dan, who was taking seven more tiles out of the green bag, looked over at her.

'Thought you'd be more of a One Direction kind of a girl.'

'Oh, piss off! Just 'cause I'm from Romford, doesn't mean I like boy bands.'

'What do you think we are then?' Dan looked at her again, his gaze challenging.

Sam looked straight back at him, her heart starting to beat a bit faster.

'Well, you're boys, and you're in a band. But you're not a boy band. You're proper rock'n'roll, and when you're older, you'll be legends, like Filthy Meadows.' Her horrible day seemed worlds away now. Despite the grungy surroundings, beer and dope, everything seemed so much more wholesome than the Soho environment she'd just left.

'You've just passed the test, Sambo.' Dan smiled at her, making her feel like the only person in the room, as only he could.

'As if there were ever any doubt,' said Sienna, leaning over to put an affectionate arm around Sam's shoulder. 'Sam's one of us.'

And as incongruous as the 'us' sounded, when it comprised a billionaire's plummy-accented daughter, three wannabe rock stars from Manchester and a student-cum-glamour model from Romford, it was an 'us' that Sam was more than happy to be part of.

Several hours later, surrounded by overflowing ashtrays, empty beer cans and takeaway pizza boxes, they found themselves looking up Disney songs on YouTube. Olly had passed out on the floor, underneath an old checked blanket that Sam (under Dan's watchful gaze) had draped over him. Sienna was snuggled on Mikey's lap in an armchair, Sam curled up at one end of the holey old sofa and Dan perched the other end, as he manned the controls of his thirty-six-inch-screen Mac.

They had already had the best of *The Jungle Book* – 'The Bare Necessities' and 'I'm the King of the Swingers' (Sam's choice, which everyone had applauded), 'Everybody Wants to Be a Cat' from *The Aristocats* (Dan's choice) and 'Once Upon a Dream' from *Sleeping Beauty* (Sienna's choice).

'You're so gay,' had been Mikey's comment on the last. Sienna had responded by telling him it was a Tchaikovsky waltz, calling him a philistine and leaning over for another snog. They looked like a couple of beautiful fallen angels together, thought Sam – Sienna with her white-blonde waves, high cheekbones and bruised dark blue eyes; Mikey with his golden fringe and pretty, pouty, girly face.

Now it was his turn. 'I always liked *Snow White*,' he said, through the dope smoke.

'And you just called *Sienna* gay?' said Dan, and they all erupted in stoned giggles. 'OK, Mr Hard Man, which one do you want?'

'"Whistle While You Work".'

'Oh, the one with all the birds and the animals,' said Sam, smiling dreamily as she accepted the joint from him. 'I always loved that one too.'

'Actually,' said Mikey, 'you look a bit like Snow White, Sam, with your dark hair and enormous eyes . . .'

'Except Snow White had enormous *blue* eyes, shit-for-brains,' said Dan as he scrolled down the YouTube list. Then he started laughing. 'Well, for some reason the only version of "Whistle While You Work" I can find is in *Dutch*, with subtitles. Will that do?'

'Oh, yeah!' They all laughed in agreement, and soon they were singing along to *Snow White*, trying to make the English subtitles sound Dutch, giggling like loons. Sam couldn't remember a time she felt happier.

'Oh, this is so much fun,' she said, when the song came to an end. 'Thanks for making me feel better. It's really lonely in halls at the moment, and after today I don't know how much more I can stand doing modelling.'

'I wish you'd give it up,' said Sienna. 'Surely you can get another student loan? I can easily lend you some dosh to tide you over in the meantime.'

Sienna never tired of offering Sam money, and Sam never tired of refusing.

'Thanks, but you know I can't. It's going to take me years to pay off the student loan I've already taken out, anyway. And I've got to pay next term's hall fees any minute, too. It's going to be even worse there without you next term, Sienna. I'm dreading Josh coming back.'

Sienna had nearly completed on her purchase of a million-pound flat in Notting Hill. She'd have offered Sam a room in an instant, but her canny self-made father, always aware of people taking advantage, had insisted she bought a flat with only one bedroom. His hard-earned filthy lucre was not to be used to support hangers-on.

'I hope you're not going to let Josh be too vile, without me to stick up for you,' Sienna was starting, when Dan interrupted.

'I can't believe how fucking stupid we're all being. Why don't you move in here, Sambo? You can have Ross's old room. It's a tiny shithole, mind, but dirt cheap. Then you can save on next term's rent, stop doing so much of that crap modelling, and concentrate on your studies.'

Sam was staring at him, delight starting to creep over her face.

'It'll be shit, like, having you around.' Dan grinned. 'But you can earn your keep doing a bit of cooking and cleaning . . .'

'Can I? Can I really?' Her head swivelled from Dan to Mikey, both of whom were smiling and nodding. Sienna, from her feline position on Mikey's lap, was giving her a wink and a double thumbs-up.

Sam glanced over at Olly, snoring slightly on the floor. 'You don't think Olly would mind?'

'Sam,' said Mikey. 'When will you realize that we all bloody well like you?'

Sam looked over at Dan again. He was saying nothing. But he was smiling.

In her luxurious home in Eaton Place, Alison frowned as she looked at the evidence. She should be feeling ecstatic: she was home from the holiday from hell, and her evil stepchildren had at long last gone back to boarding school. But even though she should be feeling happy that the little fuckers were incarcerated once more, she couldn't. The case she was working on was just too disgusting. Could she really defend these bastards, when what they were doing – and seemed to have been doing for years – was quite so despicable? Tales of the imprisonment, rape and torture of underage girls, year after year, going back for decades, leapt off the screen at her.

She couldn't ask Philip: he was too much a professional lawyer, and also a man. He would tell her that everybody was entitled to a legal defence, and she couldn't let her emotions get in the way. She had always thought that her professionalism was second to none, but now she found that her emotions *were* getting in the way. She couldn't understand what was wrong with her.

She sighed, and put her face in her hands, completely at a loss for the first time in her life. Then something occurred to her: she could ask Andy. He would know what to do. They had hardly been in friendly contact since he had discovered she was cheating on him in the run-up to their wedding the previous year, but he was one of the only truly decent men she knew. What was more, he had worked on similar cases for his newspaper; if nothing else, it would be good to unburden herself to somebody who understood the depths of filth to which she now found herself exposed.

With a deep breath, she picked up her phone and dialled his number.

# Chapter 16

Bella pottered about her kitchen, chopping onions and garlic, picking rosemary and thyme from her window box and pouring herself a glass of the red wine that she was going to use in the boeuf bourguignon. Andy had worked late every night that week – the bloody people trafficking story seemed to be taking over his life – but he'd promised he'd be home in time for dinner tonight.

Once she'd browned the meat in a separate pan and added it, with some stock, the herbs and the rest of the bottle of wine, to the casserole, she put the whole lot in the oven, which she had preheated to 140°C: for maximum tenderness, the beef needed to be cooked slowly.

It was dark already and pissing down outside, and Bella felt sad that summer really did seem to be over. They'd only had a few weeks' sunshine in London, and she and Andy hadn't been on holiday since Poppy's wedding, right at the beginning of May. Andy had told her, apologetically, that he couldn't go anywhere until he'd got to the bottom of his bloody story. She tried cheering herself up by thinking of all the yummy things she could cook – wild mushrooms, and game, and celeriac – and of how cosy the autumn nights drawing in could be (if only there was somebody to share them with).

With this in mind, she turned the central heating up, the overhead lights down, and lit every lamp in the flat, so that it would be warm and welcoming, as well as full of delicious smells, when Andy got in. Then she opened another bottle of wine, poured herself a glass and settled down with a glossy magazine. She flicked through an interminable piece about 'autumn's exciting new trends', the main gist of which seemed to be that if you didn't spend obscene sums of money on coats, boots and handbags, you were a deeply unfashionable loser.

Even though she was now commanding quite high rates for her canvases, phrases such as 'I'd happily pay double for something decent, rather than a bleurgh, mid-priced nonentity like this' (for a perfectly nice-looking bag costing £250) and, 'I do hope this little beauty [£850 from McQueen] doesn't fall into the perma-tanned, French-manicured hands of the Essex mob' really stuck in her craw. They were in the middle of a fucking recession, for Christ's sake. Where did these moronic fashion chicks get off?

Her phone rang and, as ever, her heart leapt when she saw Andy's name and photo flashing up.

'Hello, darling,' she said warmly. 'Are you on your way home?'

'I'm really sorry, Belles.' Andy sounded slightly nervous. 'But I'm going to be a bit later than I thought.'

'*What?* But Andy, you promised . . .'

'I know, and I'm really sorry,' he said again. 'But I've just had a call from Alison, and she says she's desperate to talk to me about the case she's working on . . . It sounds like she's dealing with similar people to the ones I'm investigating, and—'

'*You're going to meet ALISON?*'

'I'll only stay for one drink, I promise . . .'

'So, let me get this straight –' Bella tried to keep her voice level, but it was rising by the second – 'I've been slaving over a hot stove all evening making our dinner, and now you tell me you're going to meet your bitch of an ex, but I'm not meant to mind, because it's *only for one drink*?'

'Oh, don't be like that, Belles, please. You love cooking, and you're making boeuf bourguignon, right? Surely that improves the longer you cook it? I won't be *that* late – there'll still be time for us to eat together. Alison sounded really distraught – if you knew what these people—'

'I know what these cunts do, you've told me enough times. What if I don't want to wait for you to get back? What if I'm bloody starving now? What if I am SICK TO DEATH OF FUCKING PEOPLE TRAFFICKERS?'

Andy's voice went cold. 'Can you please stop being so childish? There are some things that are more important than your hurt feelings, you know. I'll be home by 9.30 at the latest – is it really such a big deal?'

*If you loved me as much as you say you do, you wouldn't think that my hurt feelings were so trivial.*

But all Bella could say was, 'Oh, just fuck off, you pompous twat.'

'Fine. I will.' Andy sounded angry as he hung up.

Bollocks. Bella hadn't meant to lose it like that, but she had been reminded all of a sudden of similar evenings when she had been waiting around for hours for Ben, while he cavorted with models and, on one particularly memorable occasion, ballerinas. It was shortly after that that she had found him in bed with Poppy; it wasn't surprising she was insecure.

*But Skinny fucking Alison?*

Just as she was debating whether or not to call him back and apologize, her phone rang again.

'Hey, Pops.'

'Belles! How's it going? You OK? You don't sound your usual self.'

Bella hadn't meant to launch into her tale of woe immediately, but she couldn't help herself. 'Andy's gone out for a drink with Skinny fucking Alison. He hasn't been home in time for dinner a single night this week . . . I don't understand why he'd *ever* want to see her again . . .' She stopped, and took a deep breath to stem the incipient flood of tears.

'Well, it can hardly be because he wants to get in her knickers, can it? Come on, Belles, he must have told you why?'

'Well, he came up with some crap about how she sounded really desperate to talk to somebody about some fucking case she's working on . . . but why couldn't she talk to her bloody sugar daddy about it? She's living with him, and he's a *hot-shot fucking lawyer.*'

'I'm sure that if Andy thought it was necessary to talk to her, then it was,' said Poppy patiently. She was used to Bella's outbursts of insecurity. In fact, she felt partly to blame

– Bella walking in on her shagging Ben had probably scarred her for life.

'I'm getting too fat, that's why he doesn't want to spend time with me any more.' Bella morosely squeezed the flesh around her middle and took another huge swig of red wine. She had been getting rather too used to drinking on her own. 'Not a fucking ounce of flesh on Alison, is there? Evil cow has far too much self-control for that.'

'Belles, listen to yourself. You're not fat, and you're being ridiculous.' *How would you know? You haven't seen me for months*, thought Bella mutinously. 'I've never known a happier couple than you and Andy, and I'm sure he's just being nice. Skinny's not exactly his favourite person, remember?'

'Yeah, but he wanted to marry her, and he certainly doesn't want to marry me.'

'Oh, for Christ's sake, you know why he's wary of marriage. It's *because of* her. Belles, you're being ridiculous . . .'

'You've already said that . . .'

'I think you know it too. Come on, lovey, get a grip.'

After a long pause, Bella pulled herself together. She was really starting to annoy herself.

'Sorry, Pops. Can we start again? What are you up to? Any gossip? Everyone's still absolutely raving about *PTM* here . . .'

*Poppy Takes Manhattan* had hit the UK properly a couple of weeks after the episode they'd all watched at Olivia's house, and had been both critically and popularly received. Poppy had had the inevitable offers of nearly naked men's magazine shoots as a result, but had refused all of them. This was partly out of loyalty to Damian, who had been left so badly in the lurch by the men's magazine world for which he had worked so brilliantly. Partly, though, it was because she didn't think that getting her kit off for cameras should be part and parcel of her job; also, cannily, she thought that, even though she'd no doubt look just fine in the shots, her street-cred would be immensely improved by not going down that route. Just because everybody else did it, it didn't mean that she had to.

'Ooooh, yippeeee! Thanks for telling me, Belles! I still can't believe I've got such an amazing job! Actually, at the moment, I'm in LA . . .' *Of course you are*, thought Bella. '. . . *PTM* is up for a Pluto award, so I've got to get all tarted up in a few days' time. I bet they try to put me in some hideous gown with borrowed diamonds, but I'll try to stay a bit me, if I can.'

'Old Converse underneath to scruff it up a bit?'

'Oooh, good idea. Not. A touch Lily Allen circa 2005?'

Bella laughed. 'OK, that was a crap idea. How's Damian?'

'Not great. We've been arguing pretty much nonstop ever since we got to New York. He's so bloody jealous and touchy about everything, I simply don't know what to do about it. It's not exactly how I envisioned married life.' And Poppy told Bella about Jack Meadows and the jocks in the Hamptons jerking off over her show.

'Well, you can hardly blame him for being jealous, can you?' Bella hated herself for not being more supportive, but Poppy seemed so bloody pleased with herself. Film stars trying to snog her? Random strangers telling her that they wanked over her? Jesus H Christ.

'*I KNOW THAT!* But for fuck's sake, Belles, I can't go on apologizing forever, can I?'

Bella looked around at her empty flat, out at the rain

pouring down outside, and pictured Poppy, blonde, aglow and beautiful in the LA sunshine, about to receive an award for something that came so naturally and easily to her, just as everything came so naturally and easily to her. Then she pictured Andy sitting in some cosy pub with that skinny bitch Alison, and squidged the unwelcome flesh around her middle again.

'Oh, I don't know, Pops. Whatever.'

When they hung up, both friends felt sad.

Andy, sitting with his pint of Guinness in the Antelope, just off Eaton Square, was feeling sad too.

He couldn't understand why Bella was being so ridiculously needy. Compared to the disgusting things he was currently immersed in for work, they had such a lovely life together; her mood swings were starting to become pretty tiresome.

He was sad about Bella, sad about people trafficking, and – yes – sad about Alison too.

He remembered the first time he saw her, debating furiously at the Cambridge Law Society. He had been so impressed with the fire in her eyes, her utter determination to make the world a better place, her height, her slim figure, her silky black hair. There was a kind of ice-queen reserve that everybody had wanted to crack, back in those days, when intelligence was valued above all, and Andy had gone out of his way to woo her, to get underneath that slightly stern façade. Finally, eventually, it had happened.

They'd been walking along Trinity Street, arguing passionately about Descartes, when it had started snowing.

Spontaneously, he had taken her cold hands in both of his, intending to warm them up. She had looked up at him, startled, and he had bent his head to kiss her.

Just as he was remembering their first kiss, Alison walked into the pub. She'd kept her figure, and was looking very tall and slim in her impeccably tailored trouser suit. As she got closer, though, Andy saw how pinched and scrawny she really was. There were dark circles under her eyes, and two deep furrows between them.

'Alison, hi.' He stood up to greet her, awkwardly.

'Hi, Andy. Thanks for coming to see me. I – erm – well, it's good of you, anyway.'

This was the closest Alison could get to offering an apology, Andy realized, but he wasn't holding it against her. In fact, he just felt concerned about how haggard she looked.

'What would you like to drink?'

'A glass of red wine, please. As large as they can make it.'

Alison had never been much of a drinker, and Andy, realizing the extent of her turmoil, returned as quickly as he could. Which was easier said than done, as this pub was full of Old Etonian bankers and their hair-flicking girlfriends, who thought nothing of barging their way in front of any other customers waiting to get served.

'Thanks.' Alison smiled briefly as she took the glass from him.

'So what's the problem, and what can I do to help?' Andy was conscious that Bella was waiting for him, and however much she had annoyed him this evening, he didn't want to upset her unnecessarily.

So Alison started to tell him, in as much detail as she was legally allowed. As she spoke, Andy realized that the people she was defending were closely connected to the ones he'd been investigating for his paper. They talked for the best part of an hour, becoming increasingly excited with every new revelation. At last, the final piece of the jigsaw fell into place, and Andy knew, with absolute clarity, the identity of the big guy, the man behind the whole revolting operation.

'Oh, my God,' he said slowly. 'It has to be Alexei Lubanov.' He was referring to a Russian billionaire who had been living in London for the past ten years or so. His constant presence on the charity-ball and fundraising-gala scene, his insanely glamorous wife always at his side, meant that he was practically a household name.

'Oh, my God,' said Alison. 'I think you're right. It has to be. Wow.' She shook her head as the enormity of the realization sank in. 'Well, this is brilliant news for you, Andy – it has to be the scoop of the century!'

'I can hardly believe it. What a disgusting lowlife piece of scum.' Then a huge grin spread across his handsome face. 'But it is going to be a fantastic scoop!'

'I am pleased for you.' Alison's voice was sincere. 'But what am I supposed to do? I really don't think I can continue to defend these sadistic thugs . . .'

'You can always refuse,' Andy pointed out as he drained his pint.

'Hardly good for my career.'

'You never know – it could do your career the world of good. You'll become known as the lawyer with principles, and a QC before you know it!' Andy was feeling so jubilant

256

to have got to the bottom of his lengthy, and at times soul-destroying investigation, that he leant over and gave Alison a hug.

She hugged him back with a lot more enthusiasm than he'd bargained for, and he gently pulled away.

'Erm – would you like another drink? I've got to be home for dinner soon, but you look like you could do with one more . . .'

'Oh, God, yes, I'd love one. Thank you.'

When he returned this time, Alison started telling him about Philip and his repugnant offspring. As she ranted on, Andy was aware of the time racing away, and Bella waiting back at the flat for him.

'They sound spoilt and horrendous, but – let's be honest, Alison . . . You did split up their parents' marriage. You can't expect them to love you immediately.'

'I don't expect them to love me at all – a little civility would be nice, though.' Alison's voice was wobbling slightly. 'I certainly don't love them.' And then her voice broke. 'I'm not even sure that I love Philip, really.' She turned to Andy, unshed tears shining in her pale blue eyes. 'What if I made the biggest mistake in my life? What if it's you I still love?'

She moved towards him, her lips slightly parted, as though expecting a kiss.

Andy jumped back, horrified, thinking immediately of Bella.

'Oh, Alison, no. I'm sorry you're having a difficult time with Philip, but this isn't the answer. I'll walk you home, though, if you want – it's just around the corner, isn't it?'

It took Alison a moment or two to reclaim her dignity.

257

'It's OK, I'll walk myself home. Thanks for the advice though – I think I will refuse to defend the bastards. Nothing wrong with a bit of integrity in the legal profession, for a change.' She smiled bravely. 'You go back to Bella. It's always been Bella for you really, hasn't it?'

'You and I were good together once,' said Andy kindly as he bent down to kiss her on the cheek. 'But I'm with Bella now. I love her, and I always will. Best of luck with everything though. I'm already looking forward to the announcement of the youngest and brightest woman ever to have been appointed Queen's Counsel.'

'Thanks, Andy. You're a good man.'

As Andy let himself into the tiny flat at 9.06 precisely, Bella leapt up off the chaise longue, where she'd been buried in a trashy novel, and ran towards him with her arms outstretched.

'Oh, darling, you're early! I wasn't expecting you till 9.30! Oh, I'm so sorry I've been such a spoilt bitch – I know how important your work is to you. I'm sorry, I'm sorry, I'm sorry! I love you!' She could hardly get the words out in her eagerness for everything to be OK again, and seemed to be laughing and crying at the same time.

Andy looked at her big-eyed, sincere, imploring face for a couple of seconds. Then he took it in one hand, smoothing her hair back from her brow with the other.

'There's nothing to apologize for. I love you too.'

And he proceeded to kiss the life out of her.

# Chapter 17

As it happened, the LA stylists decided not to put Poppy in a floor-length gown.

'Noooo, that would swamp her!' they had said to the designer, who was trying to get publicity for his new collection. 'Don't you have anything shorter? Edgier? This is *Poppy Wallace* you're dealing with. Don't you ever watch TV?'

'Not if I can help it, no,' the designer had sniffed, huffily. But he took their point.

And so it was that Poppy was standing on the red carpet, looking ridiculously cute in a very short white crochet-effect lace minidress. Buttery soft nude suede knee boots emphasized her perfectly proportioned brown legs. She'd had a long fringe cut and her streaky blonde hair swung around her shoulders in a style that her hair designer had described as, 'Nineteen sixty-six to seven, halfway between dolly bird and hippy chick – sooo you.' Privately, Poppy thought that her look was more retro than edgy, but who was she to complain? It suited her.

'Poppy! Poppy Wallace! Over here, beautiful! Look this way, Poppy! Poppy, Poppy, POPPY!'

The lights of the flashbulbs were so bright that she could hardly see, but Poppy turned and twisted and turned and twisted, her smile pasted to her face. Half of her adored the attention; it almost felt as if this was what she'd been born to do. The other half felt a little scared – Jesus, what had she let herself in for?

Just as she was thinking this, she heard some people shouting over the demands of the paparazzi. What was going on? She strained to see in the flashlights, while still trying to maintain a flattering pose: no mean feat.

'Poppy Wallace, I love you!' shouted a fat man who looked as if he needed remedial care. She was just thinking that Bella would enjoy being told that this was the type of fan she attracted, when the nutter managed to break through the velvet rope.

'Poppy! My most beautiful angel, you must be MINE!' He was shouting, and – bloody hell, was that a *knife* in his hand?

It all happened very quickly. The nutter was restrained by the guards, and then everything went dark for Poppy, as somebody threw his dinner jacket over her head and dragged her inside, into safety. Her saviour took her by the hand until they were ensconced in the VIP area, out of harm's way. Only then did he remove her makeshift burka.

Her heart still racing with fear, Poppy looked with amazement at her knight in shining armour.

'Jesus Christ, Ben,' she said. 'What the fuck?'

\* \* \*

'I'm so sorry,' said Ben, for the fifth time in a row. 'I was such a self-centred bastard last year. I don't know what was wrong with me. You're looking great, though.'

They were sitting underneath an enormous crystal chandelier on a purple velvet banquette. Everywhere they looked, film and TV royalty meandered in extraordinarily over-the-top evening dress (Poppy really did stand out in her 1960s-inspired get-up). In the last minute, Owen Wilson, Jennifer Aniston and Reese Witherspoon had wandered past their table. The actual awards were due to start shortly; in the meantime everybody was enjoying the glamorous hospitality.

'Great enough to appeal to religious lunatics with food issues, at any rate.' Poppy giggled. The 'knife' had turned out to be a silver crucifix, and the fat man a harmless enough saddo known locally for his crushes on up-and-coming female stars. 'But come off it, Ben, you've always been a self-centred bastard. What's different now?'

'I *was*. I know that, Pops. Please accept my apology?' Ignoring her question, Ben gave her his beseeching, puppy-dog look and she melted a little.

'Well, we were both self-absorbed twats, weren't we?' said Poppy, draining the dregs of her blackcurrant Martini. 'I don't think Bella's forgiven me, still.'

'Really?' Ben was amazed. He'd always thought that Bella was the ultimate soft touch. 'Wasn't she your bridesmaid?' He'd heard it on the grapevine.

'Yup, and she was lovely in the run-up to the wedding. But – oh, I don't know. She really seems to resent me now.'

They were both silent as they remembered the cause of that resentment.

'So how's married life?' asked Ben, after a bit.

'Just wonderful, thanks!' Poppy couldn't let Ben know how shit things were with Damian – that would be the ultimate betrayal. In fact, she had already decided that Damian must never know at all that she had met Ben here, in LA. It was unlikely to go down well, to put it mildly.

'And you?' Deftly, she changed the subject. 'You're not really having a bromance with Jack Meadows, are you? Believe it or not, he came to one of our parties in NY . . .'

'*What?* Poppy, you're kidding! Jack's here. And even though I cannot abide the word 'bromance' – yes, we're friends. He's a good guy.'

'Yeah, he seemed it . . .'

Poppy's mind drifted for a second. She was still feeling sad, about Damian, and Bella, but more importantly about her father – she had just found out that he couldn't feed himself any more. She struggled to rally round, and found something:

'Anyway, you still haven't told me why you've stopped being such a cunt. Is it just that fame suits your e-NOR-mous ego so fantastically? Or is there a wonderful woman behind the scenes?'

She was being flippant – surely, Ben could never love anybody more than he loved himself? – but as she saw the look in his eyes, she realized she had hit the nail on the head.

'Oh my god, oh my god, oh my god, there is!' she shouted gleefully, gesturing to the waiter for another couple of blackcurrant Martinis. 'Who is it? Please don't say it's Amy

Lascelles. Such a cliché to fall in love with your co-star, and she's always struck me as a horrible little bitch . . .'

'Don't worry, it's not Amy. She is a horrible little bitch. No, it's . . .'

At that moment, Jack Meadows wandered into the VIP area. His eyes lit up at the sight of Poppy.

'Hey.'

'Hey.' Poppy smiled, and got up to give him a hug.

'I was there first, asshole,' Jack said to Ben.

'Actually, I was there first,' said Ben. 'But Pops is married to my erstwhile friend, Damian.'

'Erstwhile? Jeez, you Brits like to milk the old country, dontcha? But hey – small world . . .'

'Indeed,' said Ben in an approximation of 1940s received pronunciation.

Jack laughed. 'I guess somebody has to teach us *ghastly colonials* how to speak the Queen's English?'

'I think Ben had plenty of help being taught how to speak the Queen's English himself,' said Poppy. 'Didn't you, boyo?'

Jack looked momentarily shocked, and Poppy wondered if she'd gone too far, but Ben laughed easily.

'Yup, if it weren't for RADA, I'd still be talking like a boy from the Valleys.'

Poppy looked at him with amazement.

'OK, then, lover boy, tell us who she is, this extraordinary woman who's made you almost human? I don't know her, do I?'

'Actually, you do, it's—'

'*Ladies and Gentlemen, can you please make your way to the auditorium? The awards are about to begin!*'

The three of them looked at one another in excitement,

and Poppy forgot all about Ben's new squeeze as her ego took centre stage once more.

'Man,' said Filthy Meadows, looking at Poppy with undisguised appreciation. 'Are you sure you're not available?'

'Oh, don't be a stupid old dork,' said Heather Meadows (née Maria Gonzalez). 'If she's not interested in Jack and Ben,' – she fluttered thick black eyelashes at Ben – 'you really think this little sex kitten is gonna be interested in an old freak like you? Congratulations on your win, Poppy, hon. We *love* your show.'

Jack rolled his eyes at Ben. He was used to his mother's irrational likes and dislikes when it came to good-looking women. Poppy, it appeared, had rocked his momma's world. Soon, it became apparent why.

'You really showed that Sandra bitch up for the whore she is,' said Heather, taking Poppy by the arm and leading her into the villa. '*It only goes on the wall if I screwed one of the band!* That was just classic, honey. But some of us have more class than that, as I'm sure you can see. Now, let me get you a drink – I make the *meanest* margaritas!'

When Poppy returned with a margarita in her hand, she was slightly glassy-eyed.

'Your mum does make the meanest margaritas,' she said to Jack, who laughed.

'Sorry, babe, should've warned ya. It's her Hispanic roots, y'see.'

He and Ben were lying on adjacent sun loungers. Clambering up the tree towards the hammocks would have proved way too problematic after the amount they'd had to drink tonight.

'Congrats again, Pops,' said Ben, smiling benignly. Poppy had won Best TV Newcomer, and had called Damian in New York as soon as she'd found out. As the TV footage of the awards wasn't going to be shown until the following evening, Damian had been out on the town with Lars.

'Oh, my darling, well done!' he'd shouted, sounding completely shit-faced but endearingly pleased for her. 'I can't believe I'm married to such a clever thing. I LOVE YOU!'

'I love you too, darling,' Poppy had said. 'But I've got to go and mingle now. You don't mind, do you?'

'Course not! Enjoy your success! Can't wait to see you and give you the most enormous hug – and the rest of it!'

Poppy hadn't intended to come back with Ben and Jack, but it had transpired that the ultimate after-party, the really important one, frequented by industry insiders, had for the past couple of years been held at Jack's Spanish-style villa, and Marty had insisted.

'You gotta be seen at all the right places, babe,' he'd said.

Poppy had duly sparkled and twinkled and schmoozed the big cheeses, networking her pretty little feet off. At last, most of the guests had gone, and she, Ben and Jack had retired to his parents' quarters at the back of the house.

So now she found herself swaying slightly in front of the two people her husband would most hate to see her with. As she wasn't planning to do anything untoward with either of them, she excused herself in her own mind and plonked her tiny frame down on the ground between their loungers.

'OK, Ben, I've waited long enough,' she announced dramatically. 'Who is this amazing woman I apparently *know*, who has brought about this transformation in you?'

'Poppy . . .?' Jack looked at her as if to say, *Is this a good idea?*

'It's OK, Jack. I'd like to talk about her to somebody who knows her. It's Natalia, Pops. Natalia Evanovitch.'

'*Natalia?*' Poppy couldn't have been more surprised if he'd said it was Hillary Clinton. 'What the fuck? How on earth do you know her? Oh, tell me, please please please!!!'

'We met in Saint-Tropez . . .' Ben took a long drag on his spliff.

'Good start,' said Poppy approvingly.

'If you're going to interrupt every five seconds, I'm stopping now . . .'

'Oh, sorry, please carry on. I promise I won't say another word.' Poppy did a zipping-up motion across her mouth and Jack laughed, looking at her affectionately.

'As I said, it started in Saint-Tropez . . .' And Ben told them the whole story, from the night he first noticed Natalia's beautiful back outside Bar Sénéquier, to his discovery that she was being blackmailed, to the sad little note that she had left him. When he came to this last bit, he reached into his wallet.

'I carry it everywhere with me,' he said, handing the note over to Poppy, who read it in silence, before passing it on to Jack. Then she got to her feet and gave Ben a hug.

'What a romantic story,' she said. 'Bless you both. But surely you're not just going to give up on her? Haven't you tried to find her?'

'Of course I've tried to find her, Pops, but she's completely disappeared. I've tried all the places she's likely to have gone: Ibiza, London, Paris, Rome, St Barts, Mustique, Necker . . .'

'Oh, Ben, you great lumbering idiot – don't you see she's not going to have gone to any of the places you're likely to look. If she really wanted to disappear, she'd have gone somewhere totally different to her usual haunts . . .'

'She's right,' said Jack, sitting up straight and looking at them both. 'But can we go back a couple stages, please? You forget you both have a head start on me. For example, how do you know Natalia, Poppy?'

'Well, I first met her at my friend Bella's art exhibition last year, and we became friends. She let me and Damian use her amazing villa in Ibiza for the after-party to our wedding.'

'Wow. A yacht *and* an amazing villa. A woman worth blackmailing, huh?'

'Oh, she's absolutely loaded—' Poppy started, when Ben interrupted.

'What's her villa like, Pops?' He was desperate to know as much as he could about the woman he loved.

'Unreal. Five levels of terraces, a tower, a moat around the main house that leads into an infinity pool. And – get this – there's an island in the middle of the pool with full DJ decks on it.'

'God, she's amazing . . .' Ben went all dreamy-eyed for a minute, until Jack clicked his fingers in front of his face.

'Yeah, yeah. If you want us to help you find her, we need you here with us in the present, not drifting off into some romantic dream-world.'

Poppy looked at Jack admiringly, and Ben said, 'Sorry. Thanks, mate. You'll really help me? OK, so what else do you want to know?'

'Well, for a start, what is she being blackmailed for?'

'She used to be a hooker,' said Ben and Poppy simultaneously. They looked at each other and laughed.

'Wow. O-kaaay,' said Jack. 'She told you?'

'It's not really that difficult to guess,' said Poppy. 'No offence, Ben, you know I think she's great, but . . . She's Ukrainian, stunning looking, and has billions and billions of dollars. Rumours have been circulating around her for years.'

'In that case, why would she pay money to somebody who could only really confirm what everybody else was thinking?'

'It would be different to have it confirmed in the press. She's actually quite a private woman, and seeing her past splashed all over the papers would be quite horrendous for her,' said Ben. 'And now she's been linked to me, she thinks that if anything came out, it'd be bad for my career. Lovely, selfless creature she is.' He drifted off into another soppy trance.

'She's probably hiding from the blackmailer too,' said Poppy astutely. 'I can't imagine he's a very nice individual.'

'Then it's even more important for me to find her, and persuade her to go to the police. The sooner the bastard is behind bars, the better.'

'Sounds like a plan,' said Jack, and the three of them shook on it.

Poppy was thinking hard. Something was lurking at the back of her booze-addled brain. It was a conversation she and Damian had had with Natalia, about how they first met, and – yes, it was coming back to her now, in detail.

*'It's so beautiful, Natalia, and so remote,'* she remembered

telling her. '*You could just lose yourself there for weeks on end and forget that the real world ever existed . . .*'

'*It sounds wonderful,*' Natalia had said. '*Maybe I go there one day.*'

'Ben,' she said excitedly, laying a hand on his arm. 'It's just a hunch – in fact, it's a really long shot . . . I'm probably being stupid, but—'

'Come on, spit it out . . .'

'I think I might know where she is.'

'*What?* Where? For the love of God, tell me, Pops!'

Poppy sat back on her heels and smiled at them both.

'Bottle Beach,' she said. 'I reckon she's hiding out at Bottle Beach.'

# Chapter 18

Late the following morning, Poppy was sitting at a white wrought-iron table in the pretty courtyard of her Chateau Marmont bungalow, eating a hearty breakfast of smoked salmon, scrambled eggs and bagels. Hangovers always made her absolutely ravenous. The studio did treat her well, she thought, looking around at the heavenly little whitewashed cottage, with its arched doorway, picture windows and terracotta-tiled, tropical-plant-filled courtyard.

She was feeling very pleased with herself. Not only had she won Best TV Newcomer, but there had also been talk last night of a follow-up series to *Poppy Takes Manhattan*, set in LA. If the last couple of days were anything to go by, she thought she could handle sun-drenched, fawning LA very nicely indeed, thank you. And it would be a perfect place for Damian to concentrate on his screenplay – both writing *and* networking. Marty was setting up several meetings for her, so she was going to be staying on a few more days. *Oooh, twist my arm, why don't you*, she thought to herself gleefully.

She was also thrilled that she'd remembered telling Natalia about Bottle Beach. Ben was going to use the studio spies to find out if she actually was hiding there, and if she was, he planned to fly out there himself and surprise her on the beach. He only had another week's filming and then he was free to travel as he pleased. Poppy reckoned he was looking forward to playing the romantic hero, and she couldn't blame him. It was funny how all her dislike for him had evaporated after he'd 'rescued' her last night. Anyway, she was married now, and Ben was in love, and as far as Poppy was concerned it was all water under the bridge (though she just knew that Damian and Bella, with their thinner, more sensitive skins, wouldn't see it quite like that). It had been easy for her to slip back into the friendship they'd had before all the madness had happened the previous year. She had been genuinely moved by his story about Natalia, and really hoped that the two of them would be able to sort things out.

Her phone rang.

'Morning, Marty, isn't it a beautiful day?' she said cheerfully.

'Sure is, honey. Say – have you seen any newspapers yet today?'

'Not yet, no. Why?'

'You're front-page news, sweet cheeks!'

'Really? Bloody hell, I can't believe it! But why? Best TV Newcomer was hardly the most prestigious award of the night . . .' She laughed, but was actually thinking, *Maybe it's because I looked so different to all the others in my minidress.*

'It's not only about the award, Poppy . . .' Marty took

a breath. 'There was also the stalker guy in the crowd with the "knife" . . .' She could hear him putting the word in inverted commas.

'Oh, my God.' After the knife had turned out to be a crucifix, the incident had rather got lost in the excitement of the rest of the evening. Poppy mentally kicked herself. Of *course* it would make the papers – it had happened right under the noses of the assembled world press, for fuck's sake. And if they'd papped the nutter, presumably they'd also papped her dramatic rescue by . . . Oh, *fuck*.

'OK, Marty, tell me. How bad is it? Pictures of me and Ben? Loads of speculation as we used to be lovers? Oh, Jesus Christ, there's not stuff about me going back to Jack's party with the two of them, is there? Oh, please, Marty, tell me there's not.'

'There's pretty much everything you've just said, sweetie.' Marty sounded sympathetic: he'd witnessed Damian's jealousy first-hand back in New York. 'But try not to worry. I'm sure he'll understand. I'd call him to explain just as soon as you can though.'

'Thanks, boss, I'll do that right now.' Poppy looked at the time on her phone as she hung up: 10.35 a.m. They were three hours ahead in New York. With any luck Damian would just be getting up – he'd sounded completely trashed when she'd spoken to him the previous night, and he liked to lie in. She took a deep breath and clicked on his number.

In the pocket of his rust-coloured velvet jacket, which he'd left hanging over the back of a chair in the penthouse bar of the Gansevoort Hotel, Damian's phone rang and rang and rang. And rang and rang and rang. And rang and rang and rang.

Damian, at home alone in his marital bed, was having a nightmare and pouring with sweat. As he woke with a jolt, he realized why he was so hot and uncomfortable: he was still wearing his jeans, shirt, socks and shoes, though at least he'd had the foresight to take off his velvet jacket before passing out. God, he must have been twatted last night – Lars's insistence on shot after shot of schnapps really was lethal.

He took his clothes off and went to the kitchen for a pint of water, looking for his phone on the way. He and Poppy hadn't bothered installing a landline and he wanted to call her and hear all about her big success again. For all their recent arguing, he really did miss her when they were apart.

It soon became apparent, in their minimalist warehouse apartment, that neither his jacket nor his phone were there. Shit, shit, shit. He had to stop getting so pissed. As he tried to piece together the events of the previous night, he remembered speaking to Poppy just before they headed to the final bar, the late one. That was where his phone and jacket had to be. But what the fuck was the bar called? Was it in a hotel? He had a vague inkling that it might have been on a roof somewhere.

Decisively – or as decisively as he could when he was feeling so rough – he sat down at the kitchen table and opened his laptop. Lars would know.

Hey buddy. Left my bastard phone and jacket some-where last night. Don't suppose you could call the last

273

bar for me and see if they're there, could you, before I have to start cancelling things? (What was the bar called, btw? Were we in a hotel? I seem to have a bit of an – erm – memory lapse). Cheers mate.

Then he emailed Poppy:

Good morning my darling. Congratulations again, you clever thing! You'll never believe it but I seem to have lost my fucking phone (hoping it hasn't been stolen). What a bloody nightmare – I'm dying to talk to you. Maybe we should have gone with the old landline after all. Will let you know how I get on finding it in a bit. Love you, Me xxxxxxx

Then, as there was nothing practical he could do until Lars got back to him, he decided to see what he could find out about Poppy's award online. As he typed *poppy wallace pluto awards* into Google, entry after entry flashed up at him, and a proud smile slowly crossed his face. He clicked on one of them.

Movie and TV fans were left gasping when Best TV Newcomer Poppy Wallace was threatened in the crowd by a crazed stalker brandishing a knife.

What? Damian read on, heart beating furiously – why hadn't Poppy told him?

In a moment of exquisite bathos, the knife turned out to be a crucifix, and the stalker a well-known 'professional fan'

(we all know what that means, don't we kids? LOSER!).
But the real story was Poppy's dramatic rescue by none
other than HOT HOT HOT Brit actor, Ben Jones – who
stars in next year's sure-fire big hit *Beyond the Sea*, with
new best buddy Jack Meadows, fact fans. Poppy, who has
been married to unemployed British journalist Damian Evans
for less than six months, spent the rest of the evening looking
très cosy with Ben and Jack, even accompanying them both
to Jack's villa for his legendary after-party. Sensationally,
Poppy left her then boyfriend Damian (now husband – keep
up, losers) for Ben back in London ONLY LAST YEAR,
before their fling fizzled out. Is history repeating itself, we
wonder? And what of poor Damian? According to friends,
he has become something of a recluse since losing his job
on failed Brit mag *Stadium* earlier this year, and some even
say he is resentful of Poppy's success. We're betting he
won't like this latest development one teensy iota. Watch
this space, gossip fans . . .

The piece was accompanied by far too many photos.
Numbly, automatically, Damian found himself clicking
through them: several of Poppy on the red carpet, looking
utterly gorgeous in her minidress and boots as she posed
for the cameras; a few of Ben looking dashing and manly
as he threw his dinner jacket over her head and swept her
indoors. And then, obviously taken much later in the
evening, and probably through a long lens, grainier footage:
Ben and Jack reclining on sun loungers, with Poppy sitting
on the floor between them, chatting animatedly; all three
of them laughing about something, Jack sitting up straight
this time; Poppy standing up *with her arms around Ben . . .*

'YOU FUCKING BITCH!' Damian shouted at the screen, remembering his conversation with Poppy the previous night. She had probably been with them then, all three of them laughing at him behind his back. Absolutely overcome with pain, humiliation and anger, he threw himself at the bare brick wall, kicking and punching it until his feet and knuckles bled. Then he collapsed in a heap against it, clutching his dark head, sobbing.

After a bit, he picked up some kitchen roll to wipe up his blood, then went back to the computer to torture himself some more. He had two new messages. First, he opened the one from Poppy, every finger joint hurting as he worked his way round the mouse and keyboard.

Oh darling, I've been trying to call you all morning. I've got something to tell you, but you mustn't take it the wrong way . . .

Everything misted over and he couldn't bring himself to read any more. Lying little bitch. He remembered her looking him in the eye and saying, 'Yes, I would,' when he asked her if she'd like a threesome with Ben and Jack. *Fuck her.* He deleted her message and opened the one from Lars instead.

Man is my head heavy. Don't cancel anything – your phone is still at the Gansevoort. You really don't remember? Ha! Are we still meeting tonight to watch your beautiful wife on TV? Maybe we can meet earlier? I need beers and I need them fast. Lars

Damian typed back:

I may need something stronger. Read this:

He attached the link to the webpage and pressed SEND with his little finger, the one that hurt the least. A few minutes later, Lars's reply flashed up:

Meet me at Stone Street in 15 minutes. I'll order drinks. Don't jump to any conclusions. But man, that journalist is one motherfucking BITCH.

Poppy checked her phone again, frantic with worry. Damian hadn't replied to her email and still wasn't answering his phone. Maybe she hadn't explained enough in the first email. She tried again:

Listen darling, whatever you may have seen in the gutter press, there is absolutely NOTHING going on between me and Ben. He is actually IN LOVE, would you believe it? And guess who with? NATALIA, of all people!!! Oh sweetheart, please pick up your phone (if you've managed to find it) so we can have a good old gossip about it. I've got so much to tell you! I'm really, really sorry if you're upset, but really, all Ben did was rescue me when he thought I was in danger, which was quite nice of him really, wasn't it darling? I love you xxxx

Damian and Lars were sitting nursing beers with whiskey chasers on brown leather upholstered chairs at the Stone

Street Tavern, a spit-and-sawdust bar that was, most evenings, packed with secretaries trying to pick up bankers. In the daytime, it was frequented pretty much solely by those made recently unemployed by Wall Street. As Lars had said to Damian, on a jollier occasion, 'It's when you see your former CEO here that you really have to worry for the economy.'

Now he said, seriously, 'Man, you must give her a chance.'

'She's had enough chances: I gave her a chance when I took her back, I gave her a chance when I fucking married her, I gave her a chance when she was canoodling in the toilets with Jack fucking Meadows, I even gave her a chance after she said she'd like to have a fucking threesome with the two vain cunts!'

'I think maybe you put the words in her mouth that time,' said Lars mildly, taking an enormous swig of his beer and trying not to let his belch involve schnapps-flavoured vomit. He had heard a slightly different version of the story from Poppy.

'Makes no fucking difference. You saw the article. She didn't have to go back with the two of them. Why *did* she go back with them, Lars? Why did she do it?' His voice was different all of a sudden, pleading like a little boy's. Then it hardened again. 'Anyway, maybe she *should* be with them. They are both much more her type anyway. How did the article describe me again? An unemployed journalist who lost his job on a failed magazine earlier this year . . . A recluse who resents his wife's success . . . A *loser* . . . Yeah, that pretty much sums me up.' He took a large swig of his whiskey and blinked back the angry tears that had sprung into his eyes.

'Man, you must pay no more attention to that cock-sucking bitch of a journalist.'

Damian laughed drunkenly. It hadn't taken a lot to top up the previous night's alcohol intake.

'It was definitely written by a woman, wasn't it? Fucking cunts, the lot of 'em.'

'That journalist, yes. And my little whore from Romania. Yes, she loved the banker more than the man. That is true of them, and many more of them. But I do not think it is true of your Poppy, Damian. I think she loves you . . .'

'Oh, for fuck's sake, don't tell me even you are taken in by her? Her *big green eyes* . . .' He opened his dark eyes wide and shook his head about, putting on a horrible gooey impersonation of either Poppy herself, or the men who were meant to be falling at her feet, Lars wasn't sure. 'Whose side are you on, mate?'

'If it must be sides, then I am on yours, of course. But surely you should speak to her?'

'No. If I do, I know I'll let myself be fooled – *yet again* – by that angelic fucking face. Or voice. Or whatever.'

'So what are you going to do, my friend?'

'I, my friend –' Damian put his hand on Lars's shoulder – 'am going to take a little holiday. She's not the only one with prospects out West, you know. SKOL!' He raised his whiskey at his enormous friend.

'Skol.'

Lars had never said the word so quietly. Partly because he was so worried about Damian, but partly as his hangover was threatening to kill him. He had pains all around his back (liver and kidneys, he assumed) and would have gladly gone home to lick his wounds had his friend not needed him so badly.

Damian got up to go to the bar again.

'Same again?'

Lars nodded, resigned to his alcoholic fate. His phone rang, and as he picked it up, he saw that it was Poppy. Glancing over at Damian, who was ineptly trying to chat up the barmaid, he walked outside, gesturing that he was going to have a fag.

'Yes?'

'Lars? Are you with Damian? I can't get hold of him, and I think he thinks I've done something awful, but I haven't . . . I haven't . . .' She sounded as if she was crying, and Lars, ever the gentleman, felt his loyalties dividing again.

'He's not happy about the photos, Poppy. Why did you go with that dickhead you broke his heart with last year? Whatever happened, you cannot deny the photos . . .'

'Oh, fuck, I know. Oh, Lars, I can't explain. I thought Ben had saved me from being killed, then I realized it was only a fucking crucifix, and then I won the award, and it was all so exciting, and Marty told me I had to go to the party, and then Ben told me he was in love with a mutual friend of ours, and I-I suppose I just didn't think . . .' Her voice trailed off miserably. 'But I love my husband so much. Pleeeease tell him? I didn't do anything wrong, *I promise* . . .'

'I'll see what I can do.' Lars marched back into the bar, full of goodwill, holding his phone up to Damian. 'It's your wife, and she needs to talk to you.'

Damian – maddened by anger, hurt, jealousy, booze, the idea of being cuckolded, yet again, and pretty much everything else that a man can be maddened by – grabbed Lars's phone and shouted into it.

'Just fuck off, you whore. I never want to see you again.'
Then he smashed the phone onto the bar, smashing and smashing the device to smithereens.

'That was my phone, asshole.'

'Oh, fuck, Lars, mate. Oh, I'm so sorry.' And Damian started weeping copiously once more, sobbing and sobbing against the bar. People around were looking on with some interest, but not as much as one might imagine – after all the recent job losses, scenes like this had become pretty commonplace in these parts.

'Luckily for you, I have a back-up phone, and insurance,' said Lars, steering Damian back towards their table. 'I think we need another drink, yes? For tomorrow is another day, my friend.'

And the good-natured, big-hearted giant steeled himself to feel even worse the following day.

# Chapter 19

'Well, this is a bit more like it.' Bella smiled across the white-linen-clad, ice-bucketed table and raised her wine glass at Andy. 'Cheers, my darling!'

'Cheers, my darling too. In fact, I should probably say, *salut*, *santé* and *bonnes vacances!*'

Andy's brilliant scoop being published had coincided with Bella finishing the painting she had been working on for the last couple of months: a portrait of a very rich socialite's very spoilt cat, sitting on a pink velvet cushion. Bella had loved the cat – an adorable tabby whose parentage had to have been all over the place – and had done justice both to her tawny colours, she'd thought, and to her exceptionally pretty and equally tawny eyes. The socialite (a charming man of a certain age who dabbled in antiques and would have been called a confirmed bachelor in different times) had loved the painting so much that he had given Bella a couple of grand extra, just for 'seeing the real Mimi'.

Never terribly practical when it came to money, Bella

had made a spontaneous decision to blow it on a dirty weekend in Paris to celebrate Andy's scoop. So here they were, sitting outside a bustling bistro on the rue Soufflot, just south of the Panthéon, in the Latin Quarter on the Left Bank. (Left Bank, or *Rive Gauche*, always made Bella think of the perfume her mother used to wear in the seventies.)

Paris was enjoying an Indian summer, so she was able to wear one of her favourite frocks – a sixties-inspired pale pink sleeveless A-line minidress that showed off her legs and skimmed over her tummy. Which was just as well, as she was planning to make the most of all the yummy French food over the next couple of days. The diet could start again on Monday.

'Oh, this weather is so gorgeous,' she said happily, feeling the sun hot on her bare arms. 'I'm sorry I've been such a misery guts all summer – I think this is what I've been missing!'

'You can stop apologizing now.' Andy smiled. 'Yes, you've been a complete pain in the arse, but I did neglect you, so we're probably quits . . .'

'It was certainly worth you neglecting me to expose that repulsive Lubanov character. I'm so proud of you, my darling – you are going to get so many awards for that.'

'Maybe.' Andy smiled. 'But the main thing is that no one else can suffer at his hands now.'

'Yes.' Bella shuddered. 'It's quite horrific to think about what all those girls had to go through.'

'Well, let's not think about it at the moment. I don't want anything to intrude on our romantic weekend. In fact, Belles, how about we both switch our phones off for the next twenty-four hours? No Facebook updates, no emails, no BBC News, just us? In the *city of lovers*.' Bella could hear him putting quotation marks around the last phrase, as he tilted his head to one side and smiled at her through his geeky specs.

'I think that's a brilliant idea. Oh, I love you so much.' She leant across the table to kiss him and at that moment the waiter arrived with their food: duck confit, served on a little wooden board, for Andy, carpaccio for Bella, with a bowl of frites and a green salad to share.

'Oh, *pardon*, *pardon*.' Bella grinned up at the waiter as she sat back down.

'*Non, non*, you are in Paris.' He smiled back at her. 'Enjoy!' Why did they always have to reply in English when you were trying to do your best French?

'God, I love French food,' said Bella, after the waiter had gone. 'Not terribly original, I know, but I just do!'

'Sweet, enthusiastic thing you are,' said Andy, thinking of the cycling holidays he and Alison had taken in Brittany, when she'd had a habit of complaining about pretty much everything.

They finished their lunch, and the ice-cold bottle of Sancerre, at a leisurely pace, then wandered hand-in-hand down to the Jardin du Luxembourg. The trees that lined the graceful paths were just starting to turn golden, and elegant Parisians were sitting on chairs and benches in shirtsleeves and shift dresses, soaking up the sun.

'So different to London,' said Bella. 'In Hyde Park, people would be lying on the grass in bikinis, showing off their horrible pink and white bodies.'

'*Vive la difference!*' said Andy, and Bella laughed.

284

They walked on through the park, past the beautiful Medici fountain, with its deep rectangular basin lined with spectacular bronze-and-marble Italianate statues. They walked along the neat gravel pathways, past colourful formal gardens that reflected the French love of order and harmony; past the magnificent Palais du Luxembourg with its Tricolore waving proudly in the light breeze; past games of boules and exquisite sculptures and the octagonal lake teeming with toy sailing boats – all overlooked by those beautiful green and golden trees.

'Did you know that Hemingway used to shoot pigeons here, when he was a starving writer in the twenties?' said Bella. 'He used to hide their poor, dead bodies in a pram.'

'What a fantastic story. Where on earth did you hear it?'

'I think Mum told me and Max, when we came here as kids.'

'Should have guessed,' Andy said affectionately, kissing the top of her head. 'You and your absurdly spoilt childhood . . .'

'We weren't spoilt.' Bella's tone was mock-cross. 'Half the time, Mum was trying to make up for the fact that Dad wasn't there. We stayed in a really horrible *pension* near Montmartre, and I can still remember being woken up in the middle of the night by a cockroach climbing over my face . . .'

'Oh, my poor love.' Andy knew how squeamish Bella could be about certain things. She was fine with mice, for example, or even snakes, but insects gave her the heebie-jeebies. 'How did you react?'

'I tried to get the revolting creature off, of course, but it was clinging onto my eyelashes, so I screamed.'

'Waking up both your mother and Max?'

'Yup.' Bella was laughing again now. 'Poor Mum. We must have been a bloody nightmare.'

'On the other hand, you could say she brought it on herself, to take two children— how old were you?'

'I was five and Max was seven.'

'OK, then, two *very young* children to some fleapit in Montmartre.'

'It wasn't that bad. Character building. Mum did the best she could, which was bloody brilliant under the circumstances.' Bella was always staunchly loyal to those she loved. 'And she did prise the cockroach off my eyelashes with her fingernails.'

'It was actually hanging off your eyelashes?'

'That's why I screamed, you bugger. I'm not *that* pathetic.'

'I think I'm starting to realize that.'

They walked out of the park, meandering through grand Napoleonic boulevards and kicking up the first fallen leaves. Before long, they hit Saint-Germain-des-Prés, in all its bohemian, Art Nouveau splendour.

'Oooh, *Les Deux Magots*,' said Bella. 'Perfect timing. I was just starting to feel a bit thirsty. Time for a pit stop?'

Andy laughed.

'We're on holiday, we can do whatever we want.'

On such a lovely sunny Saturday, the legendary café was heaving, but luckily for Bella and Andy a couple was just leaving as they approached, so they sat down at a little round table under a green-and-gold umbrella, and ordered another bottle of Sancerre.

All around, people were smoking, sharing carafes of wine or sipping from thimbles of strong black coffee, arguing passionately about things that Bella assumed were terribly intellectual.

'Can't you just feel the spirit of Sartre, and Simone de Beauvoir . . .'

'. . . and Hemingway, with his pram-full of festering dead birds.'

This time the waiter brought their wine not in an ice bucket, but an ice bag – a clear plastic bag the same size and shape as the bags you get for gift-wrapping bottles, but filled with ice and water.

'Oooh, what a great idea,' said Bella. 'We'll have to get some to take home with us – they'd be brilliant for summer picnics. Though it's unlikely to be picnic weather when we get back, of course.'

'They'd still be handy for keeping the wine cold at home.'

'True. It's such a distance from the sitting room to the fridge, after all.'

They both laughed, and Bella gave another happy sigh, looking up at the poplar tree overhead, the cloudless blue sky, and around at all the well-groomed, chattering people surrounding them – though you could spot the tourists a mile off, of course. It was just so – well, so *Parisian*.

The tables were squeezed pretty tightly together on the pavement, and Bella smiled at the woman sitting at the one to their left, reading *Paris Match* on her own. Probably in her mid-forties, slim and very chic in black capri pants, a boat-necked white T-shirt and enormous tortoiseshell shades, she looked utterly content in her own company.

She smiled politely back at Bella, then did a double take, lifting her shades up to inspect her more closely.

'*Mais vous êtes très jolie, mademoiselle. Très, très jolie. Vous comprenez? Belle . . .*'

Bella understood, sure enough, but could barely believe it. Was she really being complimented by a supremely chic Frenchwoman? This was the sort of thing that only happened once in a lifetime.

'*C'est vrai, n'est-ce pas?*' The woman was now talking to Andy, who had a broad smile on his face. '*Très, très jolie.*'

'*Oui, oui, c'est vrai. Je suis un homme très heureux!*'

Bella also had a broad smile on her face. Could life actually get any better?

'*Et je suis très heureuse, aussi! Merci, madame, merci!*' she chimed in, and Andy and the nice woman laughed at her obvious delight in the compliment.

By the time they left *Les Deux Magots*, making their way down to the Seine in the late-afternoon sunshine, they were pleasantly mellow with wine. They had intended to visit the Musée d'Orsay, but realized they'd left it too late to do it proper justice.

'Ooops.' Bella giggled. 'Well, we can always be cultural tomorrow. Let's just wander along the river instead.'

As they ambled in the direction of Notre Dame, they passed a group of young boys and girls, probably students, dressed in jeans, stripy tops and a variety of quirky headwear, playing classic jazz on brass instruments. They were quite brilliant, so Bella and Andy sat down on a bench in the shade of a gold-tinged horse chestnut tree, to watch and listen for a few minutes.

'I'm having such a lovely time,' said Bella, taking Andy's hand and smiling at him. 'Thank you for being you.'

'Thank you for being you, too. I love you.'

And, putting his glasses down on the bench beside them, Andy took Bella in his arms and kissed her. Bella could feel herself melting into his strong frame, one hand entwined in his thick dark brown hair, the other roaming across his broad back, tracing the muscles underneath his navy-blue T-shirt.

She moaned softly into his mouth and Andy reluctantly pulled away from her, laughing slightly.

'Sorry, Belles, I think I got a bit carried away there.'

'You and me both.' Bella was looking into his dark eyes again. 'Do you think we'll have time . . . back at the hotel . . . before dinner?'

'Plenty of time,' said Andy, looking at his watch. 'It's only five o'clock.' They had a reservation at a restaurant the hotel had recommended to them, for eight p.m. 'How about we start heading back, maybe stopping at one more place en route to make the most of Paris in the sunshine . . .'

'. . . and heighten the anticipation.' Bella laughed. 'God, you tease. OK, sounds like a lovely plan.'

So they carried on walking hand-in-hand along the cobbled, tree-lined riverbank, taking in the Bateaux Mouches gliding past them, up and down the glittering sage-green water. There were plenty of other couples doing just the same as them, and occasionally they caught their eyes and smiled complicitly.

'Are we being really, really cheesy?' asked Bella.

'Probably, but I don't care. This is the happiest I've felt for ages.'

'You look it.' The furrow between Andy's eyes had all but disappeared, and he looked carefree, elated, boyish even. 'I know how much of a strain the last few months have been for you. I'm so sorry I haven't been more supportive.'

'I've told you, Belles, you can stop apologizing.' He leant over to kiss her again.

Notre Dame was coming into view now, on the Île de la Cité, in the middle of the river.

'We should really go and have a look,' said Bella. As soon as the words had left her mouth, they both shook their heads, laughing.

'Noooo. Let's leave all the cultural stuff till tomorrow,' said Andy.

'But we could stop there,' said Bella, pointing with delight at an exquisitely pretty, colourfully painted boat, whose flower-strewn deck was dotted with little round wooden tables. Hanging plants trailed down the boat's side, over the rails. 'It's got a bar on it!'

'Now you're talking!'

And with almost indecent haste they raced up the gangplank.

The view from the deck, directly over to Notre Dame on its leafy island, was stunning; in the other direction you could see hordes of people swarming over the bridge that led to it. The sun was just starting to set and the river taking on hues of pinky gold.

The trendy, friendly waitress brought them cocktail menus, and they looked at each other and laughed.

'Cocktails?'

'I suppose it is nearly cocktail hour,' said Andy. 'We should probably have a snack of some sort though, or we'll be absolutely paralytic even before we get to dinner.'

'Plate of charcuterie?'

'Perfect. Margaritas?'

'I think we may be starting to read each other's minds.'

The boat, which, due to its location, could easily be a tourist-trap hellhole, actually seemed to be a hang-out for bohemian, very Left Bank-looking Parisians.

'Looks like we've stumbled on a hidden gem,' said Bella. 'Shame there's nothing like this on the Thames.'

'Yes, it's hardly the Tattershall Castle.' Andy was referring to the huge pub-on-a-boat located between Embankment and Temple Tube stations that became almost unbearably crowded with beer-swilling office workers the very moment the sun shone its weakest light on London.

One of the Bateaux Mouches motored past them and all its passengers waved cheerfully at Bella and Andy. They waved back, raising their drinks at them, beaming from ear to ear.

Bella, mindful of how '*très, très jolie*' she was looking, and not feeling fat for the first time in months, felt as though she were starring in her own romantic movie.

'Right, darling, there's something I've been meaning to talk to you about, and this seems as good a time as any,' said Andy.

'What? What is it?' Bella asked, panicking. Surely this wasn't the time to be breaking some horrible news to her?

'Don't look so worried. I think you may actually be quite pleased, but it will affect us both, so I want to run it past you before I go ahead with it.'

'Right.' Bella took a large gulp of her margarita, her imagination running wild. 'Fire away, then.'

'I want to resign from the paper. After the last few

months, I don't think I can take much more exposure to life's seedy underbelly . . .'

It took a moment or so to register. It had briefly crossed Bella's mind that he might have wanted to propose. But this news was probably second best. 'I . . . I think that's a bloody brilliant idea! What will you do instead though? Have you had any other offers?'

'Yes, actually, a couple, since the Lubanov exposé. But I don't want to take them up. I think I'll freelance for a bit. Without wishing to blow my own trumpet, I think I've probably got a high enough profile now not to be short of work, and I can decide what type of commissions I want to take on . . .'

'Oh, yes, you could do travel writing, or restaurant reviewing, or . . . or . . . or . . .' Bella's head was spinning, somewhat selfishly, with all the fabulous freebies that might come their way.

'Don't get carried away.' Andy laughed. 'That's hardly the kind of writing I'm known for, now is it?'

'Oh, all right, s'pose not.'

Bella smiled up at the waitress as their plate of mixed cold meats, garnished with cornichons and black olives, arrived, along with a basket of sliced baguette.

'*Merci*.' She hated it when people didn't thank waiters and waitresses, and always overtipped too.

'The thing is, it's a bit of a risk,' Andy continued, after also thanking the waitress. 'Many people would say I was a complete idiot to give up the security of a pretty good job in the middle of a recession.'

'I don't think anyone could ever call you an idiot.' Bella was absurdly proud of Andy's intelligence – it was one of the things she loved most about him. 'You'll get loads of commissions, writing about – erm, politics and stuff . . .'

'I hope so. I just wanted to make sure you're OK with it, though.'

'OK with it? I can't think of anything better than you working from home – we'll hardly ever have to be apart again! Bugger the money – we'll be fine.' After a few drinks, Bella's optimism was second to none. 'Jonty was so pleased with the painting of Mimi that he said he'd introduce me to all his other friends with pets, too, so that'll be another source of income . . .'

'Do you really want to be painting spoilt Chihuahuas for the rest of your life?'

'I can think of worse ways to earn a living.' Bella laughed. 'In fact, I've probably done most of them!'

Andy looked at her seriously. 'I'm also thinking about writing a book.'

'What?' Bella was slightly taken aback, though not in a bad way. 'Why haven't you mentioned this before?'

'It's been on my mind for some time, but I've been so busy with the Lubanov stuff that I wasn't sure, and—'

'I know.' Bella shook her head, angry with herself again. 'I've hardly been that receptive recently . . . What sort of book, though?' She started laughing as she finished her margarita. 'Vampire porn for teenagers? A misery memoir? Oooh – the first in a dark, Scandinavian crime trilogy?'

Andy laughed too.

'Have you ever actually read anything I've written? No, I was thinking a history of the Balkans, post-World War Two.'

'OK, yes, that does sound a bit more you. You could

293

probably do it without even having to do much research. You know so much about everything!' Bella was gushing now, waving her tipsy arms about, thrilled at the idea of her beloved being a proper history writer. He might even get an OBE or something.

'Well, almost everything.' Andy laughed again. 'But there *will* be a lot of research involved. I may have to spend some time at the British Library.'

'Oh, nooooo! I thought you'd be working from home, with me? Can't you just Google stuff?'

'Googling stuff is the way that very bad, historically inaccurate books get written. Anyway, you have your Westbourne Studio . . .'

'OK, fair enough. And you never know, we might really wind each other up if we were on top of each other all day in our tiny flat . . .'

Andy looked over the table at her and smiled.

'Can we get the bill now, please?'

'Yeah, course. On me, as I'm the main breadwinner now! But why the urgency? We haven't finished the charcuterie . . .'

'Oh, you silly, gorgeous thing. Sod the charcuterie! Do you realize what you just said? On top of each other all day . . . There is nothing I would like more than to be on top of you right now. I know we said we'd walk back, but I'm willing to blow the last of my meagre earnings on a cab.'

The Hôtel du Panthéon was a gorgeous little boutique hotel overlooking the Panthéon itself, and Andy and Bella's bedroom, on the top floor, was Provençal-inspired, with a wrought-iron balcony, four-poster bed, toile de Jouy curtains and an eighteenth-century armoire with panels upholstered in a checked fabric (underneath wire mesh) that nearly matched the faded blue-and-white eiderdown on the sumptuously inviting bed.

'Oh, it's so pretty!' said Bella, kissing Andy as they stumbled into the room.

'Not as pretty as you. *Vous êtes très jolie, mademoiselle . . . Très, très jolie . . .*'

His words were slightly muffled as he was kissing her neck, which he knew she loved.

'*Merci, monsieur*, but surely we're on '*tu*' terms by now?'

Bella was actually trembling.

'I'm rather enjoying the formality,' said Andy as he ran his hands up her legs, underneath her skirt and stroked her through her wet knickers. 'May I, mademoiselle?'

'*En Français, s'il vous plaît* . . . Oh, fuck it, yes you may.'

Andy stopped for a second, looking directly into her eyes. '*En Français?*'

'*Bien sûr . . . Mais oui, oui, monsieur . . . N'arrêtez pas . . .*' Bella's words were hampered by her breathlessness.

Andy pushed her gently back onto the bed and started to pull down her knickers.

'*Très, très jolie,*' he murmured again as he knelt on the floor, kissing all the way up her legs, from her ankles to her knees, to her inner thighs. He teased her for a few seconds, kissing his way from one hipbone to the next, deliberately avoiding what lay between, before Bella moaned, and pulled away from him.

'This isn't fair,' she said. '*Ce n'est pas* – what's fair in French? Oh, fuck the French!'

And she leant over to him, undoing the belt on his jeans, kissing his torso, every bit of him she could reach, all the while. As soon as she'd pulled the jeans past his hips, his erect cock sprang free.

Bella, still sitting on the bed, took it in her mouth and sucked and stroked and sucked, stroking and sucking and wanting to give as much pleasure as she possibly could to the man she loved more than life itself. Andy, his jeans halfway down his legs, was groaning and pulling at her hair.

Then he stopped her again.

'Please, take off your dress.' He laughed, slightly. 'I'm afraid at this stage of the game, I can't remember how to say that in French . . .'

'Something to do with *deshabiller*?' Bella suggested, looking up at him with flushed cheeks and glittering eyes. 'But yes, *mais oui, bien sûr, monsieur . . .*'

As she pulled the pink A-line shift over her head, Andy just stood there looking at her.

'*Très, très jolie.*'

Oh, God, what was it about compliments – *especially* in French – that was such an enormous turn-on?

'You're not too bad yourself, mister,' she said, trying to sound like Barbara Windsor, and attempting a saucy, *Carry On* giggle as she leant back on the four-poster bed. Andy, laughing, kicked his jeans off and leapt onto the bed beside her, kissing her as he unfastened her bra.

'Oh, *très, très jolie*,' he said again, as he gazed at her full naked breasts, her long dark hair spread out against the blue-and-white eiderdown, her thickly lashed big brown eyes full of love and lust as she looked up at him. He took her left breast in both his hands and gave it his full attention, sucking and sucking until she was clawing at his back in exquisite rapture.

'The other one's feeling a bit left out,' she managed to gasp, after a bit.

'Easily remedied,' muttered Andy as he made his way to it.

Bella's hands were running over Andy's warm body, down his broad back towards his lovely muscular male buttocks.

'Oh, *je t'aime*,' she managed to gasp, as she found his cock and manoeuvred it into her slippery cunt. '*Je t'aime, André, je t'aime.*'

'*Et je t'aime aussi, ma Belle.*' Andy smoothed her hair back from her face and kissed her as his cock started thrusting inside her. Bella wrapped her legs around his back, drawing him in, deeper and deeper, gasping with sheer joy at the length, the breadth of him, filling her up.

And then they were lost, kissing and fucking and kissing and fucking, as though nothing else in the universe meant anything at all. It was just the two of them, together, in their lovely little Paris hotel room, overcome with love and desire, taking and giving pleasure in equal measure.

The release, when it came, was simultaneous and explosive.

Once he had recovered his composure, Andy leant over to kiss her again.

'*Je t'aime, ma Belle.* Forever.'

The following morning, hungover but happy, they breakfasted on chocolate crêpes with chantilly, strong coffee and citron pressés, sitting outside a café in the sun. Considering that dinner the previous night, at the fabulous restaurant the hotel had recommended, had consisted of foie gras on toasted brioche, rare fillet steak in a brandy cream sauce, and a hazelnut praline pudding (all washed down with a couple of bottles of excellent Burgundy), this was definitely erring on the greedy side.

In a vain attempt to work off some of what they'd eaten, they decided to walk to the Musée d'Orsay, where they marvelled at the Degas, Monets and Renoirs. One of the Bateaux Mouches dropped them back at the Île de la Cité, where they did at last venture into Notre Dame.

'OK, I think that's enough culture for one day,' said Andy, once they'd done the full tour of the grand Gothic cathedral. 'Wonderful though it's all been, how about heading back to the hotel for a quickie?'

'You're insatiable.' Bella grinned.

Afterwards, satiated and sweaty in damp, crumpled sheets, they just gazed at each other, smiling.

'You were right,' said Andy. 'This has been a fabulous weekend. It was lovely to get away and spend some proper time with each other again.'

'Mmmm,' Bella agreed happily.

'But we should probably check our phones now, don't you think? There could have been a major terrorist attack on London, for all we know . . .'

'Yes, you're right.' Bella had enjoyed being cut off from the constant stream of information that bombarded them on an hourly basis, but she did think she should check her messages, at least. What if something had happened to one of her loved ones?

As she switched her phone on, she saw she had six missed calls, all of them from Poppy.

'Poppy's been trying to get hold of me,' she said. 'Probably just wants to tell me about the awards in LA, but I'd better call her back.'

Poppy picked up on the first ring.

'Hey, Pops! How were the awards?'

'I won Best TV Newcomer. Oh, Belles, it's all just awful . . .' And Poppy burst into tears.

Bella sat up straight. 'What are you on about? You won? That's great! What's awful? Tell me, lovey . . .'

So Poppy told her.

And as she listened, Bella started to feel very ashamed of herself: ashamed for being so resentful of Poppy's success that she hadn't been able to be sympathetic to her very real problems with Damian; ashamed of her own self-pity about Andy's job, when she was the luckiest woman in the world to have him; ashamed that jealousy and small-mindedness had been eating away at her for absolutely no valid reason whatsoever.

'. . . and now he's gone away, Belles. He's just buggered off, no note, no response to any of my emails, he's still not answering his phone . . .'

'Oh, Pops. Oh, sweetheart, I'm so sorry. Do you have any idea where he might have gone?'

Poppy gave a snort of laughter through her tears at this. 'Yes. Yes, I do. He told Lars that he's going on a road trip across the States on his own. He told him that he needs to *find himself*. When the fuck did the man I married turn into such a ridiculous bloody hippy?'

Bella laughed. That sounded more like the old Poppy.

'So you're just going to wait till he comes to his senses?'

'I can't do that, Belles; he's drinking like a bloody lunatic at the moment, God knows what'll happen to him. No, I'm going after him.'

'How on earth are you going to do that? America is huge . . .'

'I know exactly which route he'll take, silly sod – it's been one of his adolescent dreams for years. We used to plan it when we first started going out.'

An idea was starting to form in Bella's mind.

'How much of a head start on you, do you think he's got?' she asked.

'A day or two, I suppose, though from what Lars told me, I imagine he needed at least a day to recover after their final binge, before setting off.'

'Can you hold off another day?' Bella could hear her own voice rising in excitement.

'It'll take at least another day to sort everything out. Why?'

'Well . . . what would you think about me coming with you?' Bella looked at Andy enquiringly, but he was smiling and nodding, giving her the thumbs-up.

'You'd do that? Really?' Poppy sounded as if she was about to cry again. 'But what about your work?'

'I've literally just finished one commission, with two weeks to go until I need to start the next one. Timing couldn't be better, Pops, really!'

'Really?' Poppy repeated. Bella had seemed so resentful towards her recently that she'd been steeling herself for Bella's reaction to her news. She'd actually thought that Bella might blame her; this response was the last thing she'd anticipated. 'Oh, Belles, it would make everything so much more bearable . . .'

'You never know, it might even be fun. Thelma and Louise, eat your heart out!'

'Well, in that case . . .' Bella could hear Poppy pulling herself together. 'You'd better start looking at flights. Where are you, by the way? Your phone didn't have a UK ring to it . . .'

'Oh, only Paris, darling . . .'

As she hung up, Bella looked over at Andy again. 'Are you sure you don't mind? I know it's totally out of the blue, and spontaneous and silly and everything, but I really think Pops needs me . . .'

'I think it's a fantastic idea. It'll do you good to have an adventure – you've been going a bit stir-crazy, stuck in the flat on your own, with Poppy gallivanting around the States and me working late every night. I'll miss you like mad, though . . .'

'Not as much as I'll miss you . . .'

'You'll be having too much fun to miss me. But as this may be our last night together for a couple of weeks, let's make it one to remember.'

Bella grinned. 'What did you have in mind?'

'Trust me, darling. You'll remember it.'

# Chapter 20

'Oh, Pops, it's absolutely beautiful. I can't believe how generous you've been – this *and* Dorothy. Have I got time to try it on before we go?'

Bella was kissing the beautifully bound *Collected Short Stories of Dorothy Parker* and stroking the peacock silk of the Halston halterneck maxidress that Poppy had bought her in Sandra's vintage store at the beginning of the summer. She had flown into New York late last night and this was the first time Poppy had had the opportunity to give Bella her presents since she'd bought them. They had just finished a disgustingly greedy breakfast of pancakes with bacon and maple syrup, washed down with a huge jug of freshly squeezed orange juice, to set them up for the long journey ahead.

'Yeah, go on,' said Poppy, laughing. 'I'll clear this lot away.' She gestured at the remains of their breakfast. 'But be quick; he's got quite a head start on us already.' When Bella had arrived the previous night, Poppy had shown her the route that she was 'almost a hundred per cent certain' Damian had taken.

'It's the route Kerouac took in *On the Road*,' she'd said. 'Sometimes I wonder if my husband's ever going to grow up.' She'd said it flippantly, but Bella could see the worry in her eyes, and her gamine little face was starting to look gaunt. 'I'm not worried about whether I can persuade him to have me back,' she'd added. 'I know that once I explain about Ben, he'll realize that the whole thing's a bloody idiotic misunderstanding. But I'm shit-scared that he'll do some damage, either to himself or to somebody else. You should see the amount of booze he's been putting away recently, Belles.'

'He doesn't drink and drive, though, does he?'

'Not usually, no. But he's been so angry and depressed, God knows what he's capable of.'

Now, Bella went into Poppy and Damian's bedroom to try the dress on and Poppy started to tidy up the breakfast stuff. Just as she'd finished stacking the dishwasher, her doorbell rang. Impatiently, she walked over to the intercom – it had to be a mistake at this time in the morning.

'IT IS I, LARS,' boomed the huge and familiar voice.

'Oh, hi, Lars, come on up.' What on earth did he want?

Bella emerged from the bedroom, wreathed in smiles. The dress suited her even better than Poppy could have hoped, the empire line emphasizing her long legs and giving her a beautifully slender silhouette (skimming the recent belly podge), while the deep halterneck showed off her impressive cleavage and pretty shoulders.

'I love it, I love it, I love it!' she cried, skipping over to Poppy to give her a hug.

'Well, I just wanted to thank you for being such a good friend . . .'

'I've hardly been a good friend to you this year, Pops. I'm so sorry, I've been so caught up in stupid jealousy and resentment that I seem to have lost track of what's really important. Forgive me?'

'You silly sausage, there's nothing to forgive,' said Poppy, hugging her back. 'And you really do look amazing in that dress.'

'That is very true,' boomed a voice from the doorway. 'Wow! You girls sure know how to dress for a road trip!'

Bella laughed. 'I'm not travelling in this, just trying it on. It's a present from Poppy. I'm Bella, by the way,' she added, wondering what this giant was doing in Poppy's kitchen.

'Lars.' He walked over and kissed her on both cheeks.

'Lars, it's always lovely to see you,' said Poppy. 'But what the fuck are you doing here? You do know that we're heading off this morning?'

'That is why I am here. I am coming with you! I also want to find my good friend Damian, and I think it would be good for you two girls to have some protection.'

'We don't need protection,' Bella and Poppy said in unison.

'Also, Poppy, I can share the driving. You told me that your friend does not drive . . .'

Bella instantly felt stupid, and Lars smiled at her.

'. . . and of course there is nothing wrong with that. But you see that, maybe, I have my uses?' He put his large, square head on one side, imploringly, and both girls laughed.

'Well, it would be good to have a fellow driver, I have to admit,' said Poppy, looking apologetically at Bella. 'And you've been so kind and helpful with Damian's depression, ever since we met you, really. There's more than enough room in the car I've hired . . . What do you think, Belles? It won't quite be Thelma and Louise . . .'

'Are you kidding? I think it's really nice of you to offer, Lars, and we'd love to have you on board.' Poppy had told Bella all about Lars, and she was warming to him already.

'In that case, kiddo, you go put your travelling gear on, then LET'S HIT THE ROAD!'

'LET'S HIT THE ROAD!' repeated Bella and Poppy at the tops of their voices.

'Check.' Sam moved a pawn forward, exposing her queen, which now had an open path to Dan's king. She looked up at him, grinning.

'Shit. Didn't see that coming. You bitch!' He grinned back briefly, then resumed his concentration of the board. After a few minutes, he looked back at her in resignation. 'Actually, Sambo, I think that's checkmate. You got me again. Congratulations.' He held out his hand, and Sam shook it.

A few weeks had passed since Sam had moved into the Crack Den, and so far the arrangement was suiting them all just fine. Sam had made Ross's old room as nice as she could, filling it with her own stuff: her duvet cover and cushions and photos from home, and her black-and-white posters of old movie stars on the walls. And she always had fresh flowers on her bedside table.

She was savvy enough not to attempt a similar makeover

downstairs – it certainly wouldn't suit the boys' grungy image to have fresh flowers on every surface and gingham cushions on the holey old sofa. But she had bought a plain navy-blue throw to cover up most of the damage to the sofa, and a large sheepskin rug that made it a hell of a lot more comfortable when they were all playing Scrabble on the floor. Dan called it their 'Bond villain' rug.

Before she'd moved in, the boys had lived on takeaways, and the fridge had been stocked with little more than cans of Stella, with the inevitable bottle of cheap vodka in the freezer. Now there was always milk, butter, bread, cheese, ham, salad, yoghurts and plenty of fruit. Sam was far from being a domestic goddess, but she did know that it was important to have proper fresh food inside you. She also emptied the ashtrays and cleared away the empties, with the result that the Crack Den, while still retaining the essence of its former self, was a far more pleasant place in which to live.

'So then, clever clogs,' Dan said now, cracking open two cans of Stella and handing one of them to Sam, 'how's the first week of term gone?'

It was Saturday afternoon, and they had the house to themselves. Sienna and Mikey had gone to the cinema, while Olly was shopping for some essential additions to his drum kit. They were all planning to meet at the Hawley later, to celebrate Ross and Katie's engagement.

'It's been fine, thanks. I showed that dickhead Josh up in two seminars, which is always fun . . .' Dan raised his beer at her. 'And I got a first for that dissertation I was working on over the summer.'

'Doesn't surprise me, but well done anyway. You really

are a brainbox, aren't you? What did you get in your A levels?' He was still young enough for this to be a valid question – besides which, he wanted to impress Sam with his own results.

'A stars in Maths, English, Chemistry and Biology.' Sam tried, in vain, to keep the pride out of her voice.

'*No way?*' Dan nearly dropped his beer in astonishment. 'Snap!'

'Really? Same subjects? Same grades?'

He nodded, smiling at her. He really did have an engaging smile.

'We got exactly the same A-level results?' Sam couldn't stop smiling back at him. 'What are the chances of *that*?'

They were looking at one another now in the same way that they had that time on the roof at the Hawley, and Sam could feel her heart starting to beat faster.

'Um, so what made you turn to music then?' she added hurriedly. Moving into the Crack Den had made it a hell of a lot easier to get over her break-up with Mark, but he had been her first proper boyfriend, and she was still a little bruised inside. So she purposefully ignored the sexual chemistry that occasionally flared up between her and Dan, and concentrated on enjoying the very real pleasure of his friendship instead.

'I've always been into music. Learned the piano when I was a kid, but my grammar school shut down, and I had to move to a rough comprehensive for sixth form. Continuing piano lessons was *not* an option.'

'Was that why you took up the guitar?'

'Yeah. Less likely to get me beaten up.'

Sam laughed.

307

'I was studying Chemistry at Leeds when the boys came to play at the Student Union. I joined *them* in a jamming session and they asked *me* to join the band. They weren't much cop without me.' Dan grinned immodestly and Sam laughed again.

'So you just gave up on your studies?' She was genuinely curious: the concept was almost inconceivable to her.

'Yeah.' As he looked at her uncomprehending face, he tried to explain himself. 'I was really bored, Sambo. Realized I didn't want to spend the rest of my life shut up in a lab in a white coat. Reckoned it would be more fun showing off on stage with screaming girls throwing themselves at me.'

'And is it?'

'What do you think, clever clogs?' Dan raised his eyebrows at her.

'I suppose it could be, for a show-off like you anyway. Some of us enjoy using our brains,' said Sam primly, and Dan threw one of the sofa cushions at her, laughing.

She threw it back at him, and soon they found themselves in what was, effectively, a pillow fight, with sofa cushions instead of pillows. They suddenly stopped, and just stood there, gazing into each other's eyes, hearts beating furiously again. Dan's dark-fringed eyes were actually more dark green than brown, Sam noticed.

'Hey, honey, I'm home!' Olly's cheerful voice and the slamming of the front door made them jump apart from one another immediately. When he walked jauntily into the room, laden with carrier bags bearing cool music-shop logos, Dan was getting another beer out of the fridge, and Sam rearranging the sofa cushions. They were studiously ignoring each other.

'Well, that was a successful trip.' Olly started to tell Dan all about his purchases, in intricate technical detail.

'That's great, mate, great,' said Dan distractedly.

'Yeah, well it's important for us to sound our best on Friday. There are rumours that the A&R man from Pistol Records is going to be there . . .'

This was enough to get Dan's attention. His head shot up.

'*What?* Where did you hear that?'

'Hellcat texted me this morning.' Hellcat was one of the barmaids at Barfly, the quintessentially grimy Camden music venue the band was playing the following Friday.

'And you didn't think to tell me till now? Jesus Christ, Olly.' Dan was shaking his dark head in disbelief. 'I know you're a laid-back bastard, but this takes the fucking biscuit. This could be our *big chance*.' His eyes were shining, his excitement palpable. 'Right, I think we need some new material. Something to really make the A&R bloke sit up and notice us.'

'Dan, you're mad – we've got less than a week,' Olly protested, cracking open a beer, switching on the TV and settling down for an afternoon in front of the footy.

'That's six whole days. You can fritter your life away watching twenty-two overpaid losers kicking a ball around a field. I've got choons to write.'

And he strode off in the direction of his bedroom. Halfway down the corridor, he called nonchalantly over his shoulder, 'Thanks for the game, Sam.'

The excitement in the house had been building all week, and was now at fever pitch. Dan had been working flat out writing new songs, only stopping for a couple of hours on Saturday night to congratulate Ross and Katie on their engagement. By Tuesday morning he was pleased enough with three of the new songs to add to the best of the band's existing repertoire, and the Flaming Geysers had been rehearsing nonstop ever since.

Much as Sam had been impressed by the music, it was impossible to concentrate on her work with it going on around her, so she had fallen back on the college library, trying to make herself as unobtrusive as possible. She had been amused to see a couple of posters advertising the Barfly gig on the library noticeboard, and wondered if any of her fellow students would be going. She was pretty sure that none of them was aware of her connection with the band.

Now it was Friday evening, and Sienna had come round to the Crack Den early so they could get tarted up together. The boys were already at Barfly, setting up.

'Oh, God, I'm so excited for them, I could piss myself,' Sienna said in her crude posh-girl manner as she popped the cork on another bottle of Dom Pérignon.

'Charming.' Sam laughed. 'But yeah, it is really exciting. I hope the thing about the A&R man wasn't just a bit of music-biz bluffing.'

'Hmmm. No smoke without fire, I'd say.' Sienna topped up both their glasses and started applying a third layer of mascara.

'Hope you're right. Dan's been working so hard all week, it would be a shame if it was all for nothing,' Sam fretted.

'Well, it wouldn't be all for nothing, anyway – Mikey says they've got some brilliant new material out of it.'

'Yeah, it's awesome.'

'And why the sudden concern for Dan?' Sienna teased. 'Is there something going on between you two? I know he fancied you when we first met, but you were still going out with Mark then. And Mikey said he thought something might have happened when I was in Tuscany, but Dan's always denied it . . .'

Sam felt a wave of enormous gratitude towards Dan. But there was something else too. Something much stronger, which she was only just admitting to herself.

'Well, he's right to deny it, 'cause nothing's ever happened,' she said hotly.

'You've gone bright red!' Sienna said with glee. 'OK, I believe you – I *think* . . . But you'd like something to happen, wouldn't you? Wouldn't you, wouldn't you, *wouldn't you*? Come on, Sam, you can admit it to me – and I could hardly blame you. Dan is *hot*. If I didn't only have eyes for Mikey, I could easily go for him myself . . .'

'Oh, all right then, yes, I think I do like him. Quite a lot actually.' So Sam told Sienna about the pillow fight with the meaningful glances. She didn't tell her about the time they'd nearly shagged though – if Dan had done the honourable thing and denied it, she was going to do the same.

'Hmmm,' Sienna said thoughtfully, once she'd finished. 'Well, it would be awfully convenient, wouldn't it? Me with Mikey and you with Dan. Actually, it would be cool as fuck. But I think you're going to have to give him some more encouragement. In fact, I think *you're* going to have to make a move on *him*, if you ever want anything to happen. Remember, you've turned him down once?' (*You*

311

*don't know the half of it*, thought Sam.) 'Mr Cool's not likely to risk that again . . .'

The queue for Barfly was snaking around the block as Sam and Sienna drew up in a black cab on Chalk Farm Road. Sienna had insisted on paying for a cab, and for once Sam had agreed. As the girls got out of the taxi, half the people in the queue turned to stare.

Sienna was wearing a vintage fox-fur coat over denim hot pants so short that the pocket flaps were visible, black opaque tights and boots. With her white-blonde hair teased madly around her face, she looked every inch the rock-star girlfriend. Sam had gone for a black leather biker's jacket over a short, floaty dark green dress that looked amazing against her long red hair. The ensemble played down her large chest but showed off her pretty legs, a combination she was more than comfortable with.

Knowing they didn't have to wait in line, they walked straight to the front of the queue, where somebody was arguing, in loud, objectionable tones, with the bouncer.

'Look, I've told you, I'll pay whatever you want, just let me in,' the twat was saying, waving a wad of notes into the bouncer's unimpressed face.

'Oh, my God, it's Josh!' whispered Sienna. He had clearly tried to rock up his image a bit, but his jeans were too clean, his leather jacket too expensive-looking and the gel in his light brown hair just plain laughable. He had a Sloaney-looking girl with him he was trying to impress, and they looked woefully out of place.

'Sienna?' Josh turned around at the sound of her voice, relieved to have found an ally (or so he thought). 'God, you look great! Maybe you can explain to this oaf who I am . . .'

'That's it,' said the bouncer. 'You are not coming in, you little twerp, however much you try to bribe me . . . Anyway, make way for these girls, please – they're with the band.'

'What? Sienna? And . . . And . . . Sam? . . . Sammi-Jo? With the *band*?'

The open-mouthed look of astonishment on his arrogant, pink-cheeked face as they sauntered past the velvet rope was worth savouring, so Sam turned and gave him her sweetest smile, with a little wave for good measure.

It was one of those moments that made life worth living.

Barfly was grungy and grotty and grimy and gritty and even still seemed smoky, years after the smoking ban coming in. Drinks were served in plastic glasses, and by the end of the night the floor would be a slimy black mess liable to leave its mark on anybody drunk enough to fall over onto it. There were generally plenty of candidates.

In the upstairs gig area the atmosphere was electric as the 200-odd crowd of loyal fans, random drunks and the odd music-business professional waited excitedly for the band to come on stage. Sam and Sienna, who had chosen not to go backstage to see the boys beforehand, not wanting to distract them, were propping up the bar at the back of the room, trying to look cool but both churning inwardly at what they were about to witness.

'However many times I've seen Mikey perform, it's always the same,' Sienna whispered to Sam. 'Proper, shit-scared fear just before he comes on.'

'Aaah. I think that means you *lurve* him,' Sam teased

her. As the words came out of her mouth, she wondered if the abject terror she was currently feeling said the same about her and Dan. This was going to be the first time she'd seen the boys strutting their stuff on stage (though she'd watched them in rehearsal plenty of times) and her nervousness on Dan's behalf was, at this precise moment, bordering on the maternal – not an adjective she would usually employ to describe her feelings for him.

But now the already dim lights were dimming still further, until the room was in complete darkness. And suddenly – *kerrash!* The spotlight was on Olly and his new, state-of-the-art drum kit.

As soon as he started, Sam and Sienna looked at each other and smiled, squeezing one another's hands, just knowing that it was all going to be OK. Then the spotlight was on Ross, teasing the crowd with the bass line for a good minute or two, which soon had everybody dancing around, spilling their plastic pints on the increasingly slippery floor.

The spotlight turned to Dan, playing the extraordinary melody he had composed in twenty-four hours on his lead guitar, and all the drunken fans were startled into silence. Sam felt the hairs on her arms stand on end. She turned to look at Sienna, who was looking equally gobsmacked.

'Fucking hell,' she mouthed.

But then the spotlight was on Mikey, the lead singer, the pretty boy – the Damon Albarn of the group.

'Awwwright, Camden!' he shouted, and everyone shouted back, 'Awwwright, Mikey!'

'Right. That was just a taster of one of our new ones. This shit-for-brains does have his uses!' He gestured at Dan, back in the spotlight once more, and there was a ripple of laughter through the crowd.

'Love you, Dan!'

'Love you, Mikey!'

'Love you, Ross!'

People were shouting, hollering. Sam could see girls at the front of the stage actually reaching up to try to touch the boys.

'OK, OK, calm down. It's not like we're the Beatles,' Dan drawled, and the crowd erupted in laughter again.

'Yeah, yeah, he thinks he's so funny,' responded Mikey. 'But I'm the singer. I'm the one that everyone fancies . . .' He gave his cheeky grin, and Sienna sighed, 'God, yeah, darling.'

'I fancy all of you! Even Olly!' shouted some girl in the crowd.

'Booo!' There was definitely an Olly contingent here tonight. 'We all fancy Olly!'

'More fool you,' drawled Dan from the back again. 'I have it on good authority that he's a crap shag.'

More laughter.

'Yeah, yeah, these guitarists always have ideas above their station,' was Olly's good-natured riposte.

'And *I*, as the one that everyone fancies, think I should warm you up with an oldie . . .' added Mikey.

As he said it, the other three started, right on cue, to play their greatest hit to date. By the time it got to the chorus, everybody was singing along.

Sam just couldn't stop staring at Dan. He looked so cool, so sexy and, great as the whole band was together, he was by far the most talented musician. God, she'd been stupid.

He'd tried it on with her – *twice* – and she'd turned him down. And he'd been so kind to her, he was clever, he was her *friend*. Sienna was right – if she wanted anything to happen, she had to make it happen herself. She was starting to feel exceptionally excited. She'd do it tonight.

The song came to an end, to rapturous applause. After a bit, Mikey hushed it.

'Thanks, Camden. Thanks. We appreciate it. And now, one of our new ones. It's called "Pawn".'

'Filthy bastards!' shouted one of their male fans.

'No, you're the filthy bastard,' Dan shouted back, walking to the front of the stage. 'It's "Pawn", spelt P-A-W-N, like in the chess game, not the stuff that you have to resort to when you don't get the real thing . . . When you're not a rock star!'

More cheers. God, he was so arrogant, so cocksure. But 'pawn' as in chess? Sam looked at Sienna, who was shaking her head at her in bemusement. Neither of them had heard them rehearse this one.

Olly started the song on one drumbeat, and then Dan was off, taking them all to another planet with his exquisite solo guitar riff.

Sam was utterly transfixed. Had he actually written a song about her? Surely it had to be. She was the only person he'd been playing chess with recently, she was sure of it. When Mikey started to sing, though, nothing was any clearer. The lyrics were deliberately obscure, although there were references to being a 'pawn in your game'.

Well, all she had to do was ask. They'd both waited long enough. Dan had wanted her twice before, and she was sure he still did. She couldn't have imagined the chemistry between them the other day. As she gazed at him, so cool and talented up there on the stage, her heart was beating so fast she was surprised it hadn't burst out of her chest.

It was absolute mayhem backstage, and impossible to get close enough to the boys to speak to them properly; although Sienna, by virtue of her long legs, had managed to squeeze her way through the mob, and was now clinging onto Mikey like a limpet.

Sam was grinning wildly at Dan and giving him double thumbs-up over the heads of the adoring fans. He grinned back, mouthing 'Later' at her and miming swigging from a can of lager. As she watched, a middle-aged man in a black polo-neck sweater appeared out of nowhere at Dan's side. He was speaking urgently into his ear and handing him a business card.

*Oh, God! It had to be the man from Pistol Records. It had to be!*

And from the delighted smile slowly creeping across Dan's handsome face, it was. Sam watched as he shouted over to the other members of the band. One by one they managed to extricate themselves from the mob and get their arses over to where Dan was still talking to the A&R man.

And then Sam saw somebody else approaching the band. Somebody for whom the crowds were parting like the Red Sea, who stood at least a foot above the rest of the female fans. Sam recognized her immediately, of course – and it looked as though everybody else did, too.

With her wild mop of tangled black curls, slanting green eyes and scarlet-painted, bee-stung lips, Carlota da Silva was the coolest new model in London. Fresh off the plane from Brazil, she'd featured on the cover of nearly every glossy magazine in the last few months, as well as in all the gossip pages, as star guest at all the celeb parties. And she was making a beeline for Dan.

Her heart slowly sinking, Sam watched as Carlota da Silva, bold as brass, took Dan's face in her hands and started to kiss him, pushing her phenomenal body, in its skin-tight black leather minidress, up against his. After a second or two of confused hesitation, Dan put his arms around her and started to kiss her back.

When Sam woke up the following morning, she was feeling a little stupid. Maybe she had overreacted, running off the way she had, but she simply hadn't been able to bear to watch Dan running his hands all over that bloody super-model. She should have stayed on to celebrate the band's success, and find out about the man from Pistol Records, though. She realized that now.

Oh, well, she'd just have to go and apologize, pretend she'd suddenly been taken ill or something, and ask them all about it this morning.

She pulled on her dressing gown and padded down the wooden stairs to the bathroom.

The bathroom door opened and Carlota da Silva, her long black hair snaking around her smooth brown shoulders, the tiny towel wrapped around her body, barely covering her arse, walked out. She gave Sam a friendly smile and Sam tried her best to smile back.

Dan's bedroom door opened and Sam started babbling, 'Morning, Dan. Congratulations on last night. You were all

brilliant! Was that the man from Pistol Records? What's . . .?'
Her words were falling over themselves, so hard was she trying to prove she wasn't fazed by Carlota's presence.

'Thanks for staying to celebrate with us, Sam,' said Dan coldly. 'Much appreciated.'

He turned his back on her and smiled at Carlota. 'Morning, sexy. Come back here and help me celebrate some more.'

He grabbed her by the hand and dragged her, giggling, into his bedroom. As the door slammed behind them, Sam found herself shivering violently, her bare feet freezing cold against the wooden floorboards.

Listlessly, she turned on her heel and stumbled back upstairs to bed. She wished she could sleep forever.

# Chapter 21

'And so I told him that he's just like sooo lame not to want to see the rest of the world? I mean, he thought that Bangkok was in Europe?'

The large group of students milling around the departure lounge at LAX was irritating the crap out of Ben.

'When everybody knows it's, like, Africa?'

'Brooke,' said one of the boys, 'we are flying to Thailand, which was, last time I looked, in South East Asia.'

'Oh, you think you're so cool with your world geography, *map-boy*. Man you are such a geek.'

Ben walked over to a newsstand and pretended to browse through a gaming magazine. He wasn't globally famous – yet – but knew that he had to disguise himself to a certain extent in order to get to Natalia without being noticed. He hadn't been able to grow his hair, let alone a beard, for the sake of continuity in the last takes, but he had about a week's worth of stubble, and had asked Eloise to weave in some fake shoulder-length, mouse-brown dreadlocks.

'Method acting for a really exciting new project,' he had told her, smiling his charming smile. 'I want to look like a classic LA stoner going off travelling to find myself.'

Eloise had laughed, and relished all the time she had spent with him, touching his head way more than was necessary, massaging his scalp as she gazed at his beautiful face in the mirror.

So now Ben sported fairly impressive (if disconcertingly ginger) stubble, unpleasantly matted dreads and a pair of aviator shades. He was wearing knee-length combat shorts, a faded black T-shirt, a leather thong around his neck, friendship bracelets all up one arm, and Birkenstocks. He carried an army-issue rucksack, and had even gone to the trouble of getting a fake tattoo inked around one of his biceps.

Plugged into his iPod, from time to time he nodded his head about and swayed a bit, tapping his foot for good measure, even though there was no music actually playing. He thought he was doing the LA stoner thing pretty well.

'Jeez, look at that dude over there,' he now heard the moronic Brooke 'Bangkok is in Africa' say, assuming he couldn't hear her because of the headphones. 'Like, what a loser?'

Excellent. The disguise was working.

On board the plane, ensconced in his hideously uncomfortable economy-class seat, Ben thought back over the events of the past few days. The studio spies had told him that, yes, there was a woman who not only fitted Natalia's description, but also called herself Natalia, on Bottle Beach. *Yes!* He had called Poppy to tell her the exciting news and thank her, and she had been thrilled that she'd been right.

She had sounded fairly subdued though, and when Ben had asked her why, she'd told him about Damian's melo-dramatic departure.

'Let me know if there's anything I can do once you find him, Pops,' he'd said, feeling awful that he had been partly to blame. He had no doubts at all that she *would* find him, just as he had no doubts at all that he'd find Natalia. It struck him as quite funny that while Poppy was heading out west across the States in search of Damian, he was heading even further west in search of Natalia (though it did seem strange to be flying west to get to the Far East).

Ben was incredibly excited that he'd be seeing Natalia in less than twenty-four hours. He had been dreaming about her, night after night, her beautiful long back, her beautiful long legs, the way she looked at him when she said, 'I love you, Mr Movie Star.' But it was her shy smile, which revealed the little gap in her teeth, that stayed in his head always, even when he was awake.

'Sir?' The air stewardess, a pretty Malaysian girl, was looking at him curiously. 'Would you like a drink?'

Ben remembered to stay in character.

'U-huh. Beer would be cool,' he drawled, as though every single word were a massive effort. The girl was looking at him more intently now and Ben started to wonder if he might be overacting a tad.

'Do I know you from somewhere?' she asked.

Shit. He decided to take a chance.

'Maybe we met in a previous life, my little lotus flower.' He put both his hands on both her arms, and stared up at her through his aviator shades.

It did the trick.

'Oh, no, I think probably not, sir. Here is your beer.' And she moved onto the next passenger as swiftly as she could.

Ben downed his tiny beer in one, then pushed his chair back, smiling to himself. He was too excited to sleep, so again he ran over his plan of action. From Bangkok he had to take an internal flight to the island of Koh Samui, and from Koh Samui a boat to Koh Phangan. From the main village, Haad Rin, he then needed to take yet another boat to Bottle Beach, where he planned to sweep Natalia off her feet. The idea of the romantic reunion was thrilling. She would be so overjoyed to see him that she would agree to everything he said – of course it made sense to go to the police about being blackmailed. Then they would swim naked and make love under the stars, and everything would be perfect again. He couldn't wait.

Juho was lying in a hammock under a coconut palm outside Natalia's little hut, slightly worried that she hadn't attended the morning yoga practice. In the months that they had shared on Bottle Beach, Juho and Natalia had become the firmest of friends, and Natalia had blossomed, knowing that Juho was celibate, that he didn't want anything from her except friendship. They had swum together for hours every day, smoked joints, sitting on rocks, played cards late into the night, and talked. God, how they'd talked.

Juho had told Natalia all about the events that had led to his near-breakdown, back in Helsinki, an unoriginal combination of working hard and playing hard (cocaine, vodka and hookers). Natalia, in return, had opened up, telling Juho things she had never told anybody, not even Ben: about the bleakness of her childhood, the grinding poverty; the alcoholic father who had left Natalia and her mother to fend for themselves when she was three years old; her beloved *mamushka*'s death from radiation poisoning after the Chernobyl disaster when Natalia was just 16; the absolute grief and despair that had led her into prostitution – pretty much the only career option open to a beautiful young girl in the lawlessness that engulfed the area at the time; her escape to Moscow, and the early nineties boom years, in which she had quickly thrived; her move to London, and brilliant investments during the property boom of the noughties; and finally, Georgiou's blackmail that had led her here, to Bottle Beach. The only thing she hadn't told him about was Ben.

Juho had experienced a lot of life, and considered himself pretty unshockable. He was, however, enormously impressed by the bravery, determination and resilience that had led Natalia to where she was now, and took every new revelation with his customary Zen-like calm.

So the friendship was solid. But there was a problem. Juho, after all his initial protestations of celibacy, had found himself falling deeply in love with Natalia. She was so sweet and unaffected now, talking about her past with disarming honesty and wry humour, giggling with absolute abandon as they jumped off rocks into the sea or down waterfalls into rippling pools in the island's jungly interior. And no man could be immune to that sensational face and body.

Juho wanted to be a decent man, and thought that he had finally banished his demons, just by living on this beautiful island, practising yoga under the trees, his only intoxicants a gentle smoke every night. He was ready to break his vow of celibacy now. And he hoped Natalia would be the woman with whom to break it.

He looked out to sea, relishing, as he always did, the incredibly calming view, and saw Natalia emerging from the water, looking like a goddess in her cheap string bikini, her long blonde hair dripping down her back. He felt the stirrings of lust that had become all too common this last couple of weeks. He had to tell her.

'Hi, sweetie,' said Natalia as she approached her hut. 'I am sorry I didn't make yoga, but I am having a bad day.' She bent over to kiss his cheek in the hammock, then sat down on the sand with her long arms wrapped around her long legs, gazing out at the ocean.

'Do you want to tell me about it?' asked Juho, and Natalia's eyes filled with tears. She turned to face him, and soon the tears were falling silently down her face as she just looked at him, filling him with both sympathy and fear.

He jumped out of the hammock. 'Oh, my God, what is it, what has happened?'

Natalia continued to stare at him mutely, shaking her head. Juho proffered his hand to her, and she got up, following him, barefoot through the white powdery sand, to the relative privacy of her hut.

'Better in here, huh?' Juho smiled at her, which opened the floodgates. Natalia started sobbing and sobbing, her whole body shaking with the violence of her grief, as she sat on the edge of the ethnic throw that covered her thin mattress, her hands clasping the bed's frame until her knuckles were white. Tentatively, Juho sat down next to her and put his arms around her.

Eventually, Natalia's sobs subsided.

'I thank you, Juho. You are a good man.' She looked at him with gratitude and, spontaneously, kissed him on the cheek again.

'Can I trust you with a secret?' she said suddenly, as though just having come to a decision. 'Of course I can.' She answered her own question. 'You are my best friend, the brother I never had . . .'

Juho's heart sank slightly at this, but he smiled reassuringly and squeezed her hand.

'Of course you can tell me. You can tell me anything.'

Natalia took a deep breath. 'I am in love with a wonderful man, but he is famous actor, and Georgiou was threatening to expose him, for being with *me*. That was the final straw, the one that forced me to come here.'

'I see.' Juho looked at her sadly, wincing at the word 'forced'.

'I ran away from my Ben. I left him a note. I was weak, but I knew I could not do it if I saw his beautiful face. I guess I panicked . . .' Juho squeezed her hand again. 'Sometimes the pain of knowing I will never see him again is unbearable. That's why I was so sad this morning. I am sorry. I feel a little better now, just to have told somebody.'

'Would a drink make you feel better?' asked Juho gently. 'And then you can tell me all about him.'

'A drink? Like a beer?'

'No, a proper, strong drink. Vodka, or Sang Som.' Juho was smiling now. If he was ready to break his vow of celibacy, he could surely allow himself to get smashed for one day, if it would cheer Natalia up. Actually, he was hoping it might make him feel better too. The news that she was in love with another man was a crushing blow.

'Yes, thank you, sweetie.' Natalia smiled at him. 'I believe it would.'

Seven hours later, they were sitting in their special place, a tiny stretch of sand shielded from the rest of the bay by a couple of large rocks, the far end of the beach from where the longboats were moored. The sun had just set, and an enormous moon was starting to rise over the water. It was a full moon, so people were leaving the beach in droves for the monthly party at Haad Rin.

Natalia and Juho were well and truly sloshed. They'd bought a bottle of vodka, two bottles of Sang Som (the local Thai whiskey), and several cans of Coke, lemonade and Fanta from Bottle Beach's one liquor store. All day they'd been giggling as they created different disgusting cocktails from the various ingredients.

'Thank you, Juho, for today,' said Natalia, raising her plastic cup at him. 'You were right, this is just what I needed!'

'It is just what I needed, too.' Juho raised his plastic cup back at her, almost toppling over from his lotus position in the sand as he did so.

'But why?' Natalia's lovely brow was furrowed in concern, and she placed a gentle hand on his forearm. 'What is the matter, sweetie? I didn't realize there was something wrong.'

'Oh, but maybe it isn't wrong!' Juho banged his plastic cup down on the sand. The hard liquor to which he had recently become unaccustomed was making him feel reckless. 'Maybe I am crazy, but . . .'

'But?'

'I think I am in love with you.'

Natalia let out a peal of throaty laughter at this, then stopped, horrified with herself.

'Oh, my God. You mean it.'

'Yes. I mean it.' Juho looked intently into her eyes. 'Natalia, the last few weeks have been so special for me . . .'

'Oh, for me too, me too.' Natalia smiled sadly in the moonlight. 'But are you not celibate? I love you like a brother, I told you that. I am in love with my Ben, my movie star . . .'

'Oh, I am sick and tired of hearing about this goddamn movie star!' Juho rarely got angry, but when he did, it was explosive. 'He seems to me to care more about his career than he cares about you. Why hasn't he come to find you? Huh? You are living in a crazy dream-world, Natalia. I am here, and I love you. And I think you could love me too, if you could only forget about this man.'

Natalia looked at him, so handsome and passionate in the moonlight. He was such a good man, her one true friend, and she did find his lean, yoga-honed body extremely attractive. For a moment she was sorely tempted. But then she remembered that day at the Île du Levant, being with Ben on the speedboat, and she shook her head sadly.

'I am sorry, Juho. But I can never forget about Ben.'

'Then you will have to forget about me.' Juho got angrily to his feet, his hurt pride making him say things he didn't really mean.

'Wh . . . where are you going?'

'To the Full Moon Party. I want to have some fun. And I want to get laid.'

Natalia gazed at his departing body as he marched slightly unsteadily down the beach, and the tears started to trickle down her face again. Was she being ridiculous? If she could never have Ben, could she really never have any other man again? And what was she going to do about Georgiou? She could hardly spend the rest of her life hiding on this beach, beautiful though it was, giving vast sums of money to a thug who had once, briefly, been her pimp.

Her head swirling with vodka, Thai whiskey, unanswered questions and churning emotions, she rose unsteadily to her feet. Maybe a dip in the sea would make her feel better.

So she waded into the still-warm water, her long legs making light work of the shallows. As soon as it was deep enough, she started to swim out towards the full, shining moon.

As Ben stepped off the Thai longboat onto Bottle Beach, he realized why Poppy had recommended it to Natalia, and why Natalia had chosen it as her hideaway. Even in the moonlight he could see that it was utterly stunning, and incredibly peaceful. Now that most people had left the beach for the Full Moon Party, it was quieter than ever.

He did hope Natalia hadn't gone to the party. He couldn't imagine it was her scene really, but if she had, he'd just wait here for her to return in the morning. He'd travelled far enough to wait another night, and it wouldn't be easy to find her among the glow-stick-wielding, face-painted travellers raving in the sea at Haad Rin.

Most of the bars (nothing more than coconut shacks, really) he passed were empty, but at one of them he encountered two very young girls, both wearing denim shorts and bikini tops, drinking bottles of Singha beer on high wicker stools.

'Hey,' he said to one of them, a chocolate-box, pretty freckly, curly haired brunette. 'Great location, huh?'

'Oh, God, yes, we can't believe how lucky we are,' she said, looking up at him from under her eyelashes. However effective Ben's stoner disguise, and however off-putting the matted dreads and ginger stubble, he was still an extraordinarily good-looking man. He noticed her friend give her a not-too-subtle nudge, and sighed internally, realizing what was to come. In the old days he'd have relished turning up on a beach like this, finding a couple of little cuties, and letting the evening take its inevitable course. Now, though, finding Natalia was the only thing on his mind.

Means to an end, though. He sat down on one of the tall, wicker bar stools and said,

'What does a man have to do to get a beer around here?' There was nobody behind the bar; the barman had probably headed to the Full Moon Party, like everybody else.

'S'OK, I can get you one,' said the brunette, walking behind the bar. 'They all know me here.' She was trying to make herself look cool.

'Thanks, babe. You're here for the season, right?'

It was the ultimate backpacker compliment, and he knew it. Being called a 'tourist' was the ultimate insult.

'Oh, yeah,' she said, in her pretty little posh English voice. 'I didn't want to come here like some sort of, you know, tourist . . .' Bingo. 'I wanted to see the real Thailand.'

Resisting the temptation to ask her what she was actually doing to see the 'real' Thailand, Ben instead stuck out his hand and introduced himself.

'Brad.'

'Fliss,' the girl simpered.

'Brad? Actually, you do look a bit like Brad Pitt,' said Fliss's plainer, plumper friend, and Ben cursed himself for not having come up with a better pseudonym. 'I'm Bex, by the way . . .' She also held her hand out, shyly, and Ben shook it, limply.

'So you two not goin' to the party?'

'We'll head off in a bit,' said Fliss, trying to sound cool again. 'No hurry – it goes on all night.'

'Yeah, so I heard. Maybe I'll head over later myself.'

'You could come with us?' said Bex.

'Maybe,' Ben drawled.

'So, what do you do, Brad?' She hastily changed the subject – had she sounded too keen?

'Oh, come on, Bex, that's such a lame question,' said Fliss. 'What do you *do*? That is so, like, capitalist? Brad is a global citizen, just like us. Aren't you, Brad? We don't have to *do* anything! So much better to just *be*.' She giggled as she handed him his beer over the wooden bar.

'Hey, man, you think I never *do* anything?' Fliss was really starting to wind him up, and Ben's imagination went into overdrive, putting him right back into character. 'I made, like, a million dollars writing gaming software . . .'

'Wow,' said Bex, gazing at him with undisguised admiration. He ignored her and, still in character, turned on Fliss.

'Have you ever earned any dollars, or does your daddy just give it ya?' He felt a bit mean as Fliss's pretty blue eyes instantly brimmed with tears. Nobody had *ever* spoken to her like that, let alone taken Bex's side over hers.

'Well, actually,' said Bex. '*I* worked in a pub all summer

to save up enough money to come here. Fliss did get it all from her dad.' She looked over at her friend and giggled nastily. Now Ben didn't know which of them he disliked more.

'Yeah, well, your dad paid for your flight, and all your rent while you were "working" in that scummy pub . . .' She made air quotes and both girls glared at one another. 'It hardly paid for your trip, did it, Bexy?'

Ben thought of Natalia's bleak upbringing, and all he imagined she'd had to do to survive.

'Hey, before I forget.' He directed this at Bex. 'A friend of a friend is staying on this beach at the moment. I've never met her before, but I thought I'd look her up. Her name is . . .' He took a swig of his beer, and paused, as though he were trying to remember. 'Natasha? No, that's not right. Jeez, man, too much weed . . .'

Bex giggled as he fumbled in his rucksack and found the scrap of paper on which he'd written the name in pencil.

'Yeah, Natalia . . .'

'*Natalia?*' squealed Fliss. 'What, is she your mum's friend, or something?'

'No, just someone from back home.' Ben struggled to keep his temper. 'D'ya think she's gone to the party tonight?'

'Oh, no, she never does. Acts like it's beneath her.'

*Yes!*

'So, d'ya know where she might be now?'

'Well, she was getting pissed with her *lover boy* all day. Not very dignified for someone her age.' Fliss's voice was spiteful; she'd quite fancied Juho, but after Natalia had turned up, he'd paid her no attention whatsoever.

'Lover boy?' Now it really was difficult to keep his tone nonchalant.

'Yeah, Juho. He's weird too. They do all this yoga stuff together. He's staying in that hut over there.'

And she pointed over at the second nearest hut to the bar, which had a yoga mat on its deck, and several wind chimes hanging from a branch, tinkling in the breeze, above it.

*God, what a dick*, thought Ben.

'Oh, look, talk of the devil, there he is!'

He was tall, lean and with good muscle definition, Ben noticed. He was trying to stride, but staggering slightly, in their direction, from the far end of the beach. He looked just as his hut had implied he might, all Zen-yoga-bollocks, with a shaved head, bare chest and Thai fisherman's thin cotton trousers dangling above his bare feet and ankles. As he got closer, Ben was glad to see that his rival wasn't anything like as good looking as he was.

*What a cunt.*

'Hey,' he shouted. 'Are you the dude who knows a chick called Natalia?'

'Why do you want to know?' Juho replied angrily.

Ben finally lost his temper, jumping off the bar stool and running over to Juho in the sand. 'Because I've travelled over eight thousand fucking miles to find her!' he exploded in his own voice, losing the stoner façade completely. He couldn't see any reason to carry on keeping up pretences now. 'Just tell me where the fuck she is, you bloody hippy retard!'

Juho looked at him in silence for about half a minute, taking him in. He recognized the face now – Ben's first sitcom, *People Like Us*, had been quite a hit, even back in Helsinki. *Ben Jones*. Underneath the disguise, the man was disgustingly handsome.

'Well, well, you came for her after all,' he said slowly. 'I underestimated you.' His anger was fading now, leaving him deflated. 'I left her right at the far end of the beach, behind those rocks. She will be glad to see you.'

'Thank you,' said Ben, holding out his hand to shake Juho's.

'You're a lucky man. She told me she loved me like a brother.'

'Jesus. You poor bastard.' Ben looked Juho sincerely in the eye, shook his hand again, and started running down the beach, leaving Fliss and Bex gazing after him, bemusement written all over their pretty little faces.

Natalia was swimming out to sea, further and further, feeling calmer as she propelled her body through the smooth, still water, gazing up at the moon, feeling it drawing her towards it.

She was so caught up in her own thoughts that she didn't notice how far she'd swum from the shore, until the sea ceased to be still, and currents were raging madly around her body. She had swum beyond the smooth safety of the bay, and now found herself adrift in the deep, dark ocean.

Shit, I'd better start heading back, she thought. But as she turned and aimed for the shore, she found that she couldn't. However strong a swimmer she was, the ocean's currents were stronger, pulling her back, and worse, in the direction of the jagged rocks to her left.

*I shall not panic. I escaped Kiev. I escaped my old life. I will not let myself be beaten by the sea.*

And she continued to battle against the most dangerous element of them all.

As Ben arrived, panting, at the place Juho had told him about, he looked around in despair. There was no sign of Natalia. But where could she have gone? He'd have seen her if she'd walked back, and she couldn't go any further than the end of the beach. Unless . . .

He looked out to sea, and there, glinting in the moonlight, was a pale blonde head, tiny from this distance, but he would recognize that head anywhere. It was Natalia, and it looked as if she was in trouble.

Without a moment's hesitation, Ben tore off all his clothes as quickly as he could – the combat shorts, with all their pockets, could significantly hinder his progress, and he wasn't wearing anything underneath. Naked, he ran into the still, warm water, and started swimming, his powerful front crawl driving him in Natalia's direction. As he got closer, he was appalled to see how close to the rocks she was. Good God, what had she been thinking?

She was in serious danger now, he saw, her face contorted in fear as she desperately tried to swim against the powerful currents. He watched in horror as her head hit a glistening black boulder, and she started to sink, slowly, underwater. She was still a good ten feet away from him.

Taking an enormous breath, he swam down towards her, the salt water stinging his open eyes. Her blonde hair was floating upwards, streaked with blood from the gash on her head. Summoning every reserve of strength he had, his lungs bursting, he grabbed her under her arms and

335

pulled her to the surface of the water, gasping for air as he hit it.

It was very hard work, swimming against the current with Natalia in his arms, but Ben had been working out a lot recently for his part in *Beyond the Sea*, and was now extremely strong.

At long last they reached the shore, and Ben carried Natalia out of the water, tears streaming down his already wet face, and tenderly laid her out on the sand. He smoothed her wet hair away from her face and checked out the cut on her head. It was no more than a surface wound, he saw, with relief, but that time under the water could have done some serious damage. She was certainly not conscious, and her lips were turning slightly blue.

'Nat? Nat, my darling, please, please speak to me, please don't die. Oh, my love, please live for me, please, my darling. We can live wherever you want, we can do whatever you want; I don't give a fuck about anything except for you.'

Sobbing, and praying to every God he had ever heard of, he bent his head to hers and gave her the kiss of life.

Nothing.

'I'll give up my job, if you want, and we can live in complete obscurity on an island somewhere, if that's what you want. Just please live, my darling. Oh, God, please let her live, please just let her live . . .'

Despairing, he tried the kiss of life again.

Nothing.

And then, just as Ben thought he might have to take his own life if she didn't wake up, Natalia started coughing and spluttering, until, wonderfully, she leant over and vomited a huge deluge of water onto the sand.

Ben sat back on his heels and, weeping with relief, looked up at the star-studded sky.

'Thank you, God, or Ganesh, or Allah, or whoever the fuck you are! Whatever the fuck you are, thank you, thank you, thank you . . .'

'Ben? Is that really you?' Natalia's voice was hoarse, but she was smiling weakly up at him from the silvery sand. 'Have I died and gone to heaven?'

Ben gave a hiccup of laughter through his tears and bent over to kiss her pale forehead, too choked to speak for a moment or two.

Natalia's voice rose.

'Ben? Are you *naked*? My God, I really must have died and gone to heaven.'

She sat up slowly, and, laughing and crying, they hugged and kissed and hugged and kissed, on and on and on, neither of them quite believing that the other was alive, and real.

Eventually, reluctantly, Natalia pulled away. She had so many questions rattling around her drunk, exhausted, very nearly drowned mind.

'How did you find me?'

He put a gentle finger to her lips. 'Shhh, shhh, I'll tell you everything later, once you've had a hot shower and something to eat, and I've got some bloody clothes on.'

Natalia laughed and coughed up some more water. 'No need to put your clothes on for me, sweetie.'

'Maybe not, but I'm fucking freezing.'

Natalia laughed again, then started to shiver violently herself, remembering how terrified she had felt in the sea, how certain she had been that she was going to die. Ben

337

put his arms tightly around her, stroking her hair with one strong hand. 'Shhh, shhh, shhh, it's OK, Nat, it's OK, you're safe now.'

'Thank you.' The words emerged almost as a whisper.

'There is nothing to thank me for,' said Ben simply. 'If you had died, my life wouldn't have been worth living. In the meantime, though, please promise me one thing?'

'Anything.' Natalia pulled back so she could look him straight in the eye.

'Promise me that you'll never run away from me again.'

'Oh, that is easiest promise I have ever made. I promise you, Mr Movie Star. I promise.'

And she started to kiss him again.

# Chapter 22

'We're not in Kansas any more, Toto,' said Poppy, as Lars drove the hired Cadillac across the state line into Texas.

'Thank fuck for that,' said Bella, and Poppy and Lars both laughed. They had left their motel in one of Kansas City's grottier suburbs at around nine o'clock that morning and had been driving for just over nine hours, only stopping for a fairly disgusting lunch of fatty sausages and other cold meats, unadorned by any form of vegetable matter. The miserable grey sky had spat on them all day, and the landscape had been unremittingly dull: miles and miles (and miles) of flat, flat terrain. At one stage they had driven for three hours without seeing a single tree.

'Bloody hell, Lars, you were right about the Midwest,' Bella had said. 'Why would anybody in their right mind choose to drive this way, when you've got the lakes and Rockies in the north, and New Orleans and all that romantic Charleston and Mississippi stuff in the south?' Her grasp of US geography was fairly hazy, but she'd been looking things up on her iPhone to kill the unutterable tedium that was driving through Kansas.

'You mean all that romantic Charleston and Mississippi lynching stuff?' said Poppy. 'It looks to me as if old Jack K was desperate to get back to NY and pretty much drew a straight line across the States . . .'

The day they'd left New York, they had stopped for lunch at a diner on the outskirts of Washington, DC. Over cheeseburgers and fries, Lars had grilled Poppy comprehensively about Damian's route.

'You say Kerouac, huh?'

'Yup. As I said, he has deeply adolescent arrested development.'

'So let's see . . .' He looked at the list that Poppy had written out in her curly turquoise handwriting. 'New York City, Washington, DC, Pittsburgh, Columbus, Indianapolis, St Louis, Kansas City, Dalhart, Albuquerque, Prescott, Los Angeles . . .' He looked up at Poppy.

'Poppy, you are aware that this is the way Kerouac came *back* from LA?'

'What?' Bella looked from Lars to Poppy, not understanding. 'What's going on, Pops?'

'Yeah, yeah, I know. The route he took *to* LA involved Chicago, Des Moines, Denver, Salt Lake City etc., but I just *know* that Damian was much more interested in the whole Midwest thing. I *just know* that that's the way he's gone . . .'

'Oh, come on, Pops, this could be a complete wild-goose chase.' Bella was starting to get angry now. 'You told me you *knew*. It sounds to me like it could be one of two routes

340

(even if he is doing the Kerouac thing, which is sounding increasingly tenuous, I must say), and it's more likely to be the one we're not taking. For fuck's sake . . .'

'Don't *for fuck's sake* me. He's my husband, I *know* him.' Poppy stuck stubbornly to her guns.

'Ladies, ladies,' said Lars, with a twinkle in his humorous blue eyes. 'There is no need for this. I told you that you needed me on this trip, and this is why. May I see your phone, Poppy?'

'Yeah, sure.' Poppy gave Bella a look that seemed to say, *No, I'm none the wiser, either*, delved into her handbag and handed the phone to Lars.

'iPhone, huh?'

'Yup. Oh, come on, Lars, this is hardly the time for a Steve Jobs eulogy.'

Lars laughed. 'No, but I think Damian has an iPhone also, huh?'

Poppy looked up at him, intrigued.

'Yup. Why, you inscrutable Viking?'

'Do you think he will have turned off his GPS?'

'Well, he's turned his phone off, but . . . no, he probably doesn't even know what his GPS is.'

'Him and me both,' said Bella. 'What is GPS, and do I have it?'

'What phone do you have?' Lars asked, smiling.

'An iPhone, of course!' Bella was glad she'd upgraded from her crappy old Nokia a few months ago; she could be one of the cool gang now.

'Well, then you do have it.' Lars smiled at her again and turned to Poppy. 'I know that Damian has not turned off his GPS. How do I know? Because I, also, have an iPhone.

When he told me that he was planning to "find himself" on the road, I – uh – took the opportunity to change the settings on his phone . . .'

'You did what?' Poppy was looking at him in amazement.

'Yes, I took my chance when I went to fetch it from the Gansevoort; I figured it may be useful. Now, whenever he turns his phone on, I can see, on my phone, where he is . . . GoogleMaps . . .'

Poppy and Bella looked at each other, grinning broadly.

Lars continued, 'It is true that most of the time he keeps his phone switched off, but he has been turning it on two or three times every day . . .'

'So you know where he is?' Poppy asked, excitedly.

'I sure do know, kiddo, and it looks like you were right.' Lars smiled at her. 'So far – Washington, DC, Pittsburgh, Columbus – I'd say he was halfway to Indianapolis now . . .'

'*Yessss!*' Poppy slammed her hand triumphantly down onto the sticky plastic-topped table. 'Didn't I *tell you* I knew my husband?' This was directed at Bella.

'Yeah, well, I'm more inclined to believe in the wonders of modern technology than one of your mad hunches, but— bloody hell, Lars, this is absolutely brilliant.'

'My friend Damian has very strange tastes,' mused Lars.

'Oh, cheers,' said Poppy.

'No, no, I did not mean like that. But this route through the Midwest, it is probably the most boring part of the United States. If he had taken the proper route, down through the Great Lakes, *then* we should have seen some spectacular countryside . . .'

'That's hardly the point, is it?' Poppy said mock-sternly, before bursting into peals of laughter. 'Oh, Lars, I could kiss you!' she added, and then promptly did, jumping to her dainty little feet and running round to the other side of the table to fling her arms around Lars and plant a gigantic smacker on his cheek. Was it Bella's imagination, or was Lars blushing?

'Don't you both see?' said Poppy, her eyes shining. 'This means he's alive. As long as he's still moving, it means he hasn't killed himself (or anybody else, touch wood) with his mad wino behaviour. Oh, God, this changes everything!'

And it had. From then on, the mood had lightened considerably: Poppy's face had lost its pinched, drawn look, and all three of them were treating the road trip as far more of a holiday than would otherwise have been possible.

It was just a pity the scenery hadn't been more spectacular, thought Bella as she looked out at the bleak landscape beyond her window. Aside from Washington, DC, the cities they had passed through had been disappointingly homogenous, all gleaming skyscrapers and vast superhighways; or, in the case of the smaller 'cities', four or five shabby-looking skyscrapers in the downtown area that gave them their city status. Admittedly, they hadn't stayed long enough to explore anywhere properly – it was quite possible that each city had its picturesque old quarters, and that she was being deeply offensive by tarring them all with the same brush.

But she had always associated St Louis, for example, with the Judy Garland film *Meet me in St Louis*, Kansas City with *Oklahoma*, and indeed Kansas itself with *The*

*Wizard of Oz* (she had cried at all of them). She knew she was being silly – of course the greatest power in the Western world was hardly going to be trapped in a 1940s Hollywood timewarp – but the skyscrapers and enormous shopping malls that were almost all they'd encountered so far were pretty bloody depressing.

The best bit had been the autumn colours between NY and DC. Bella had gazed out of the back window, utterly enraptured by the extraordinarily vibrant golds, rusts, topazes and corals bringing the countryside alive in a glorious fiery blaze. But it was the reds that had differentiated this autumnal landscape from any she had seen before: proper vermilions, scarlets, crimsons, poppies – she had even seen one tree whose leaves had turned Schiaparelli pink. Bella smiled to herself: she did get carried away when it came to colours. She would definitely be returning to New York State some autumn in the future, with both Andy *and* her easel.

The upside to the relative lack of external stimulus was that there had been little else for the three of them to do but bond. And bond they had. Poppy had poured her heart out about how difficult it was trying to make a success of her new career against a backdrop of constant, unsettling resentment from her husband. Bella had told them how guilty she felt about not being ecstatically happy all the time – after all, she had both the man *and* the profession of her dreams; she had no right to be feeling bored, lonely and restless. Lars, in turn, had wiped away a tear as he described his feelings of complete worthlessness at losing his girlfriend as an immediate consequence of losing his job. Sensitive soul that he was, he had honestly thought that the Romanian stunner had loved him for himself.

And they had all reassured one another that, no, they were not going mad, yes, they were allowed to feel the way they did and, yes, they were very much appreciated by the other two people in the car. Therapy had nothing on it.

So, despite the skyscrapers and shopping malls, and despite Poppy's obvious anxiety about Damian, they had had a pretty good few days. Lars had an apparently inexhaustible supply of road-trip songs on his iPod, which they had played over and over, singing along at the tops of their voices. They had gossiped ('Honestly, Belles, you won't *believe* the change in Ben,' was a recurrent theme), bitched, and laughed till they cried at Poppy's impersonations of some of the characters they'd met en route.

And one of their stopovers had been hilarious. Bella smiled to herself again as she recalled Indianapolis.

'This is where it says he was two nights ago,' said Lars, looking at his iPhone, as they walked into the bar at nearly six in the afternoon. It was, at such an early hour, almost empty, but still, unmistakeably, a . . .

'. . . a gay bar?' Poppy's eyes were wide and horrified. 'OK, I know he's been a bit pissed off with me recently, but I haven't put him off women completely, have I?'

'Oh, no, Pops, don't worry, Damian's just open-minded about stuff, that's all,' said Bella, trying to reassure her, though the same thought had crossed her mind. 'We go to gay bars all the time in London.'

'Yeah, I know. But we go together, or with our gay mates. It looks as if he came in here on his own. He wasn't trying to pick up men, was he? Was he?'

Poppy looked as if she was about to cry.

Lars started to laugh, and pointed at a poster on the bare brick wall, advertising all the events that week. 'No, Poppy, I don't think he was. Check out Wednesday.' Today was Friday.

They all looked at the poster, and saw written, in flamboyant pink and mauve lettering: WEDNESDAY – KARAOKE NIGHT!

'I'm sorry,' chuckled Lars. 'I think I gave him the taste for it.'

'Well, at least you didn't give him the taste for gay sex . . . I hope.' Poppy giggled, relieved.

An enormously fat black man, wearing a woman's business suit, heavy eye make-up, reddish-brown lipstick, a shoulder-length auburn wig and glasses that reminded Bella of Andy's, though with slightly narrower rims, came over to their table.

'Hey!'

'Hey!' they chorused back.

'You not from round here?'

'No, we're from England,' said Bella. 'Well, at least I am, but Lars is from Sweden, and Poppy lives—'

'Oh, just shut up, Belles,' said Poppy impatiently. 'We're trying to find my husband, and we think he might have been here a couple of nights ago.'

She took the photo out of her wallet, and the bizarrely dressed tranny started to laugh.

'Oh, the handsome English dude. Yeah, yeah, he was cool. Difficult to take the mike away from him. He sang—'

'—"Born to be Wild"?' asked Lars.

'How d'ya guess? And "Sweet Home Alabama", and some

old Carpenters hits, and his Elton John was just . . . *beyond compare . . .'*

'Jesus Christ, maybe he has gone gay,' said Poppy. Then, realizing where she was, added, 'Oh, shit, no offence.'

'It's OK, beautiful, your husband hasn't "gone gay". It's not something that just happens overnight, you know.'

'Oh, fuck, God, yes, I'm so sorry,' Poppy repeated, mortified.

'He looked sad, but the singing helped, I think.' The tranny smiled at her, ignoring the last apology. 'Hey, why don't you guys stick around? It should be crazy in here tonight.'

'Why?' asked Bella, intrigued by the nice man, even if he did look decidedly weird (and strangely familiar) in his specs and wig.

'Sarah Palin lookalike night!'

As he said it, around forty men, of vastly differing shapes, sizes and colours, but mostly wearing auburn wigs and glasses pretty similar to the ones the tranny was wearing, started to troop into the cavernous room. Not a single one of them looked like Sarah Palin, but the overall effect was extremely funny.

'Hey, Hockey Mom!' One of them high-fived another, who was wearing a T-shirt over a pair of fake tits, emblazoned with the words OUR ALLIES IN NORTH KOREA.

'It's easy for me to keep an eye on Russia, from Alaska,' somebody else was saying.

'I have many gay friends, but I do think that homosexuality is an *abomination*,' a very camp voice was drawling from another corner of the room.

Poppy, Bella and Lars looked at one another, smiling. This did look as if it could be a fun evening, after all.

'Can we order some drinks? Do you have a menu?' Lars asked the fat black tranny, who was still standing by their table.

'Sure thing, Swedish man. Boy, are you cute.' Lars smiled bravely back. 'But we are only serving one drink tonight, and it is frozen—'

'Do you call it "Alaskan Bitch"?' Poppy giggled.

'Jeez, that is a great name!' He roared with laughter, and shouted over to the bar, 'Hey, double pitchers of Alaskan Bitch on the house for my new friends over here.'

After a couple of pitchers of weird, sweet, icy, and very potent stuff, Bella, Poppy and Lars had started to make some more new friends.

'Heeyyyy,' said one of them, looking at Bella closely. 'Try these on.' He handed her his Sarah Palin specs, and as soon as Bella had donned them, the entire table erupted into laughter.

'Omigod, omigod, omigod, she wins, without even trying,' said one of their new friends. 'Give her your wig, Grant.'

Grant ran behind Bella, twisted her hair up, took off his auburn chignon wig, and plonked it on top of her head.

'Oh, fuck, fuck, fuck, I can't believe it,' spluttered Poppy. 'You are the spitting bloody image! All you need is some heavy lip-liner and your own mothers couldn't tell you apart!'

'I am nothing like Sarah Palin,' said Bella, with as much dignity as she could muster after the quantity of Alaskan Bitch she'd just consumed.

'There is only a passing resemblance,' said Lars, trying to be chivalrous, as ever, but giggling madly. 'You, of course, are younger, and much more beautiful, but I think that maybe you share something in the eyes and the cheekbones . . .'

'Oh, just give me a mirror, somebody, please?'

One of the local Sarah Palins (small, blond and not very convincing) took a compact out of his neat little handbag and showed Bella her reflection.

'Noooooo!' she wailed, instantly whipping the wig and glasses off. 'Nooooo!'

'Don't worry, Belles, it's not your face, it's more your innate bigotry, xenophobia and stupidity that I think are the real comparison.' Poppy was almost beside herself with mirth now. 'You should show Andy what you look like in his glasses. You could do Democrat/Republican role-play sex games.'

'I am never showing Andy what I look like in his glasses.' Bella was laughing too now. 'And if anything ever goes wrong with my eyes, it'll be contacts all the way.'

After much persuasion (and another pitcher of Alaskan Bitch), Bella put the wig and glasses back on, and let Poppy make her face up, for the judging of the competition. She won hands down. As she received her prize – a sweatshirt with HOCKEY MOM written across the front, she saw that Poppy was taking photo after photo on her phone.

'If you ever show those to anybody, I'll kill you.'

'They're all going on Facebook tomorrow.'

'Don't you bloody dare! Pleeeease, Pops? Can you imagine the piss-taking I'd get from Mark? Or just about everybody we know, for that matter!'

'Oh, all right then. Just as you've been the best friend ever, coming over here for me, I'll delete them all. But can we just have one more look?'

'And I, also?' Lars enquired mildly.

They looked at all the photos again, laughing their tits off, until Poppy, true to her word, pressed delete.

'I'll have you know that a woman in Paris told me I was *très, très jolie*,' said Bella haughtily.

'You obviously weren't wearing your glasses then. Or maybe she wasn't!' Poppy giggled.

'You are such a fucking bitch.' Bella laughed.

'I know. But you know you love me really.'

So that had been a good night. But then there was the interminable drive through Kansas.

'It says here that Dalhart, in the panhandle of Texas, was the centre of the dustbowl of the Great Recession of the 1930s, and still suffers from both poverty and dust storms,' said Poppy from the passenger seat.

'Oh, fabulous, another uplifting location,' said Bella.

'Hey, hey, we made it through Kansas without encountering a tornado.' Lars laughed. 'You should count yourselves lucky, ladies.'

'D'you mind if I have a look at your phone, to see if Damian's moved again?' Poppy asked Lars for the second time that hour. Lars caught Bella's eye in the rear-view mirror.

'Sure, help yourself.'

According to Lars's phone tracker, Damian had now been in Albuquerque, New Mexico, for two days. The tracker was proving absolutely invaluable. (Of course, it only showed the places where he had actually switched his phone on, which had read, pretty much consistently: road, motel, bar, motel, road, bar. The reason he had been switching it on had been to update Simon Snell, his best man, about his road trip; there was no love lost between Simon and Poppy, so he knew he was on safe ground there.)

There had been some movement around Albuquerque, so Poppy was reassured that he was still alive, but he didn't appear to be in any hurry to get back on the road, which was great as far as she was concerned. Even though they had been gaining ground on him daily, he still remained that one elusive step ahead of them. Traffic permitting, Albuquerque was only a four-hour drive from Dalhart – if he'd only stay put, they could be with him by tomorrow lunchtime.

'Oooh, he switched his phone on twenty-seven minutes ago, and he's still there,' Poppy said a minute or so later. 'Yippee!'

'Same bar?' asked Bella.

'Yup, looks like it – silly drunken sod.'

'So he will not be going anywhere tonight. I do not blame him for staying in Albuquerque,' said Lars. 'It's a helluva lot nicer than anywhere we've passed through the last few days . . .'

'How on earth do you know these things? Is there anywhere you haven't been?' Bella laughed. 'Whatever – I'm all for experiencing some nicer places!'

'But first, my friend, there is Dalhart.'

The reason Damian hadn't yet left Albuquerque was that he was having too much fun being drunk and maudlin every waking hour to want to hit the road again. He'd found a bar, imaginatively called La Hacienda, with a particularly chatty and accommodating barman, and had made several new friends in the other old soaks who frequented the place.

He had to admit that he had probably got it wrong, route-wise – the only two stretches of open road that had fired his imagination had been New York to Washington, DC, and Dalhart to Albuquerque – but he had drowned his sorrows pretty much every night in a new bar, in a new town, before hitting the road again the following morning, feeling like shit. It had then occurred to him that there was nothing stopping him from staying in Albuquerque for a few more days. It was a pleasant enough, New Agey kind of place, with a relaxed vibe and mild climate, even at the beginning of November. Apart from anything else, he was nearly at the end of his journey, and wasn't sure what he was going to do once it had finished.

He was a stubborn bugger, as Poppy put it, and didn't relish going back to New York with his tail between his legs, but he was starting to think that maybe he'd acted a little rashly, storming off the way he had. The hours of driving along monotonous Midwestern roads had given him rather more time for introspection than he'd have liked – which was ironic, considering the purpose of the journey had been to 'find himself'.

Far more pleasant to hang out in this friendly, accommodating bar, with its friendly, accommodating barman, a little while longer.

La Hacienda was what might kindly be termed a dive. But as dives went it was pretty jolly, with a mixed Hispanic and Irish clientele, plastic cacti lined up on the windowsills, sawdust on the floor and a slightly unnerving combination of jaunty mariachi music and equally jaunty Irish jigs playing from an ancient CD player behind the bar. It also boasted an impressive array of bourbons and tequilas (through which Damian was steadily working his way). It was open twenty-four hours a day, but all the windows were blacked out, so unwelcome daylight never intruded.

A couple of local drunks staggered through the door, letting their eyes become accustomed to the gloom. One of them, a Hispanic chap called Pablo, had a fearsome black moustache and a serious tequila problem; the other, whom everybody called Paddy (he'd forgotten his real name years ago), had three missing teeth and a penchant for flowery whimsy.

'Sheet, man,' whispered Pablo as he spotted Damian still propping up the bar. 'The Eenglishman is steel here. If I have to leesten to him talk about his broken heart again, I weel keel myself!'

'Duck!' Paddy whispered back, with impressive presence of mind, considering how few brain cells he had left.

But too late; just as they were attempting to duck behind a couple of chairs that afforded them no cover whatsoever, Damian looked up from his conversation with – no, make that *monologue at* – the barman. With enormous relief, the barman went to serve another (imaginary) customer.

'My friends,' Damian shouted, slurring and opening his arms. 'What are you doing down there? Come and have a drink! Whiskey and tequila, yeah?'

Never ones to refuse a free drink, Paddy and Pablo answered in the affirmative.

After several toasts, Damian, inevitably, went all misty eyed.

'Guys, guys, you are the best friends I've ever had. Have I told you about my wife?'

'Eeees she blonde and beautiful and successful?' asked Pablo, grinning. He was happier to indulge the loser, now that he was being bought tequila.

'Wow! How did you guess?' said Damian, gesturing to the barman for more drinks.

'A floating little faerie from the Emerald Isle, a leprechaun looking for the pot of gold at the end of the rainbow,' said Paddy. 'She dances with flowers, that's what she does. A faerie queen indeed.'

Damian wasn't sure if Paddy was actually referring to Poppy, but he smiled soppily nonetheless. He hadn't shaved for over a week, and the effect, combined with the soppy smile and seriously bloodshot eyes, was faintly disturbing. Even in this company.

Poppy, Bella and Lars, 270 miles away in a bar called the Texas Tavern, weren't quite as drunk as Damian, but they were giving it their best shot.

After the tedium of Kansas, they had all needed to let their hair down a bit, and Poppy had started to panic, now that they were, apparently, so close to her husband.

'I mean, what if I'm completely wrong and he really doesn't ever want to see me again?' she had asked, through a mouthful of incredibly hot chili con carne. It was served by the bowl, pint, quart or gallon. Both girls had gone for the bowl, while Lars, bravely, had attempted a quart. But even he had been unable to finish it, though it had been delicious, in a revolting kind of way.

'Really, what level of lunatic would you have to be to eat a gallon of it?' Poppy had asked, sotto voce.

Their stomachs had been too full to finish the beers they'd initially ordered, so Bella, in a moment of divine inspiration, had said with glee, 'Margaritas! That's what we need!'

'YESSS! MARGARITAS!' Lars had shouted, and they had all laughed with a certain degree of manic anticipation.

And so it was that, four margaritas each later, they were all talking much more loudly than they'd intended.

Somebody approached their table, and the room fell silent.

*Fuck*, thought Bella, looking up at the Hell's Angel looming over them (he was even bigger than Lars, if that were possible). His black leather trousers squeaked and his Guns 'N Roses T-shirt rode up over his vast, hairy belly. Tattoos covered every last inch of flesh, from fingertip to throat, and his long, bushy beard still bore traces of the chili he'd consumed earlier.

'Did you just say, *Damian*?'

'Uh – yeah,' babbled Poppy, who was looking cute as ever in skinny jeans and a blue-and-white-checked shirt, in a nod to the cowboy territory in which they found themselves, her hair hanging just above her delicate shoulders in silky blonde pigtails. 'We're not talking about the devil or anything like that . . .' (Did Hell's Angels believe in the devil?) she panicked '. . . it's just that he's my husband . . . I mean, Damian's my husband, not that the devil is my husband . . . and we're looking for him – Damian, I mean, not the devil . . .' she trailed off, flushed.

The Hell's Angel smiled slowly, giving her the once-over. He held out his hand.

'You must be Poppy. Yeah, he described you well enough.'

'What? You mean he was here? In this bar?' The tracker hadn't picked that up – Damian clearly hadn't switched his phone on in the Texas Tavern.

'Hell, yeah! Your husband won the annual Roadkill and Rolaids Chili Cook-Off just a couple days ago . . .'

'What?' Poppy repeated, her usual eloquence deserting her completely now. *'Roadkill?'* How fucking insane had Damian actually become since she'd last seen him?

The Hell's Angel laughed. 'It's only a name, honey bunch. Us Americans can do "irony" too, you know.' He settled his huge frame into the last chair left at their table. 'Your Damian . . .' he drawled the word out . . . 'sat here, right at this very table. And man, did he talk about you. He was so goddamn boring that we asked him to take part in our annual chili cook-off, just to shut him up. Man, his spices were good . . . We didn't think you English guys knew how to cook . . .'

Poppy, Bella and Lars looked at one another for a few seconds before collapsing in hysterical giggles. Poppy and Bella were holding their sides, gasping and spluttering; Lars was thumping the table.

'That's because he's half Indian,' Bella spluttered eventually, wiping her eyes, and Poppy and Lars both cracked up again.

'Roadkill Chili Cook-Off,' Lars gasped. 'Oh, Damian – oh, man . . .'

'So what did he say about me?' asked Poppy, once she could get her breath back, her heart overflowing with love at the idea of Damian beating all these chili-obsessed freaks at their own game with his wonderful spices.

'It would make your ears burn, beautiful. He loves you. Man, does he love you. But *we, the whole Dalhart community*, we love that guy. Tell me you didn't do it with his old friend Ben?'

Suddenly the Hell's Angel looked at Lars, menacingly. 'You ain't Ben, are ya? Don't look much like him, from what my friend Damian say-ed.'

'No, no, my name is Lars. Damian is my good friend. I am from Sweden.' Lars got out of his seat, drawing himself up to his full 6 foot 7, and proffered his hand.

'Sweden? My wife is from Sweden,' said the Hell's Angel, shaking Lars's hand in his equally enormous, but somewhat more calloused one. 'Hey, Gunilla,' he shouted over his shoulder. 'Got one of your countrymen round front here.'

A ridiculously pretty blonde woman, also in full leathers, appeared from behind the bar. Smiling, she started to talk to Lars in Swedish. Poppy and Bella stared at them, trying (with unsurprisingly minimal success) to follow what they were saying.

Eventually, the gorgeous Swedish Hell's Angel smiled sweetly at them and said, in the deepest US hick accent that one could possibly imagine:

'Sorry 'bout that, ladies. I don't have many opportunities to talk to people from the ol' country. How's about I get some schnapps for y'all?'

Riding along in their automobile, the three Musketeers sang along to Chuck Berry at the tops of their voices. Despite their schnapps hangovers, they were enjoying the route to Albuquerque from Dalhart more than they had enjoyed any of the roads so far. Truth be told, they were probably all still pissed, but Poppy and Bella had absolute confidence in Lars to drive them safely to their destination.

'Look!' Poppy squawked, pointing at Lars's phone. 'He's still there! Still in that bar! I love the fact that my husband's such a bloody drunk!'

'Can't blame him for staying there,' Bella shouted over the music, cracking open the third beer of the afternoon. 'This is a bit more bloody like it!'

And it was.

The Texas-to-New Mexico highway was proving an awful lot more satisfactory than the Midwest one, road trip-wise. All around them was scrubby desert dotted with proper, multi-pronged cacti, some of them even taller than Lars. Bella half expected Clint Eastwood to leap out from behind one and start shooting at them. In a good way. The rugged Sandia Mountains glowed terracotta in the distance as the sun started to set.

Ah, yes, the sunset. They had ended up getting so drunk with the Hell's Angel and his Swedish wife that none of them had surfaced until midday. Poppy had been furious with herself, until she'd seen that Damian was still in his motel room in Albuquerque.

'Oooh, we're on his tail, we're gonna get him,' she now shouted with glee.

'You do realize, Pops,' said Bella, 'that there's absolutely no fucking way we'd have found him without Lars's brilliant phone-tracking thing?'

Poppy turned around in the passenger seat and stuck her tongue out.

'Piss off, Palin.' Then she slumped back against the seat.

'Yeah, I know. Even though I *knew* what route he'd take – *I did know that, Belles*, you've got to give me that? – it might have been a bit "needle, let me introduce you to haystack".'

Bella laughed and stretched out her arm to squeeze Poppy's shoulder.

'No worries, lovey, that's all hypothetical now, isn't it? We're nearly there now.'

Lars looked at Bella again from his rear-view mirror and smiled.

It had been touch and go at times, but it seemed like the girls' friendship was back on track.

'I cannot stand talking to him a moment longer,' said the formerly chatty barman. 'Jeez, I feel like I know his beautiful blonde wife better than I know my own.'

'No worries.' Pablo grinned from behind his enormous moustache. 'I have brought in a distraction. If my little niece Juanita does not distract him, then the man is beyond hope.' He staggered slightly and wheedled, 'Tequila, please, amigo?'

On cue, Juanita slinked into La Hacienda, turning every male head in the joint. At the grand old age of 19, she had been fully aware of her effect on the opposite sex for at least three years, and dressed to accentuate her youthful attributes in tiny denim miniskirts and strappy vest tops that showed off her slender dusky limbs and bouncing bosom. Shiny black hair snaked all the way down to her waist and large dark eyes sparkled with mischief in a heart-shaped face.

Following her uncle's instructions, she danced over to

where Damian was sitting, and slumped against the bar. Giggling and talking incessantly, she climbed up onto his lap, as he tried to work out what the fuck she was on about.

'Ayayayayayayayy!' she finished, tossing back her black shiny mane and laughing up into his face.

'Ayayayayayyayay, to you too!' he eventually managed, laughing back at her. *Fucking hell, she's gorgeous*, he thought, as she snuggled up to him like a playful little kitten, practically purring as she writhed about on his lap.

Thanks (partly) to his dark good looks, Damian hadn't been short of female attention during the course of his road trip, but he had been too caught up in his self-pitying melancholy to take any of the various hookers and good-time girls up on their offers. Besides, he'd have lost the moral high ground. Even if Poppy never knew, he knew that *he* would know, and that would pretty much nullify his enormously high dudgeon.

But he was starting to get just a teensy bit bored with high dudgeon.

'*Cómo te llamas?* What is your name, handsome man? Your skin, it is the same colour like mine . . .'

The gorgeous little thing put her arm against Damian's, and he realized, with a moment of what felt like clarity, but was probably just lust, that she was right. He had always liked the contrast of his skin against Poppy's, but maybe that was stupid; maybe it was time for him to be with somebody whose skin resembled his own . . .

As they drove downhill into Albuquerque, Poppy, Bella and Lars belted out the words to 'Route 66'. What they lacked in harmony, they made up for in enthusiasm and volume.

In the last couple of hours they had passed canyons and mountains, Native American pueblos, strange roadside sculptures and cactus after cactus after cactus, all bathed in a rich golden light. The excitement in the car now was at an all-time high as they approached the city, which glittered with promise in the early evening dusk.

'We're going to follow GoogleMaps straight to the bar, right?' said Bella. 'I must say I'm intrigued to see this place where Damian's been spending so much time.' *Shit, I hope it's not a brothel*, she thought suddenly, then banished the thought as quickly as it had entered her head. No, Damian wasn't like that.

They drove on until they reached the Old Town – a charming, bustling area full of pueblo-style buildings housing cafés, shops and galleries with window displays of Native American jewellery, rugs, pottery and sand paintings.

'Oooh, I like it,' said Poppy. 'Bit of a hippy-Ibiza vibe.'

'Yeah, me too,' said Bella, smiling. 'No wonder Damian seems to have taken up residence. It would be nice to stay on a few days once we've found him – though of course, we'll give you both a bit of privacy, Pops. Promise not to dog your every move . . .'

'Don't be silly. I'm so grateful to you – both . . .' Poppy looked around at her companions, her eyes shining with unshed tears. 'I'm not going to abandon my partners in crime just because I've found my stupid bloody husband . . .'

'Let's play it by ear, huh?' said Lars mildly.

They continued to follow the map on Lars's phone, leaving the charming Old Town and entering a significantly grottier area.

'Might have guessed,' muttered Poppy.

At last, they drew up outside La Hacienda, a building for whom the word 'unprepossessing' would have been outrageous flattery. All of its windows were blacked out and its sign was hanging at what might have been a rakish angle, had it not been obvious that this was due to neglect, rather than design.

'OK, here we go,' said Poppy, visibly steeling herself for what she might find within.

'We're right behind you, Pops,' said Bella, giving her a brief squeeze from behind and kissing the top of her head.

They entered the bar, and everything went quiet.

'Shit, that's her!' whispered the barman to Pablo. 'I bet you ten dollars that's his beautiful blonde wife.'

The only man in the whole bar who hadn't looked up at their entrance was Damian, who was indulging in an incredibly enjoyable snogging marathon with little Juanita in a corner. As Poppy clocked them, an extraordinary sound came out of her mouth and she ran over to them as fast as her feet would carry her.

'Get your hands off my husband, you fucking tart!' she screamed, prising them apart with her surprisingly strong small hands.

'You owe me ten dollars,' said the barman to Pablo.

'Qué?' asked Juanita, bemused.

'What the fuck . . .' said Damian. '*Poppy*?' He looked at her through bloodshot and crossed eyes and Poppy burst into tears.

'You bloody idiot drunk,' she sobbed. 'Do you have any *idea* how worried I've been about you?'

Juanita, looking quickly at them both, realized it would be in everybody's best interests for her to bugger off.

'Adios!' She gave a little wave, then jumped off Damian's lap and ran, nimbly, out of the bar. Tio Pablo owed her one. Big time.

'I did nothing with Ben,' said Poppy, standing with her hands on her hips, tears streaming down her face. 'Or Jack bloody Meadows. Why didn't you listen to my messages, you dickhead? I could have explained everything. But no, you had to go running off like some bloody prima-donna drama queen, switching your phone off, scaring us all shit-less. If it wasn't for Lars, we'd never have been able to find you . . .'

*Lars?* Hazily, Damian saw that his enormous Swedish friend was standing near the entrance of the bar. And was that *Bella* with him?

'Poppy . . .' he started, trying not to slur.

'When are you going to get it into your thick head that I love you?'

'Ahhh,' said the assembled drunks. Poppy glared at them over her shoulder.

Looking at her angry, tearful face, and realizing how much he had missed her, Damian stretched out his arms.

'I love you too.'

'God, bloody bad timing,' Bella muttered to Lars. 'Poor Pops, to have seen him snogging that girl, quite so – um – enthusiastically.' She grimaced. 'Pretty cool of her not even to have mentioned it though. I'd have been absolutely distraught. Livid too,' she added, as an afterthought.

'Yes, she is a clever girl, not to show she is bothered by the indiscretion.' Lars was smiling slightly. 'But I think that from now on, this marriage will be conducted on more of an equal footing.'

Bella laughed.

'You really are a wise old sage, aren't you? Thanks for everything this last week, Lars, you've been wonderful. Love you loads!'

Lars embraced her in an enormous, manly hug.

'Love you loads too.' He was feeling a little sad that their adventure was over. It had been nice to feel wanted and appreciated once more – even if it had only been for his phone. And he had come to love these two girls – though only in the most honourable of ways, of course. He pulled himself together. Poppy had found Damian – that was the most important thing.

'And after all that, kiddo . . .' He smiled at Bella. 'I think we deserve a drink.'

# Chapter 23

Sam was happy to be home. Yesterday, she had helped her mum do the Christmas tree, as they listened to Bing Crosby and Nat King Cole and Slade. Little Ryan had made it difficult, of course, but he had been so sweet, proffering his homemade decorations and clapping with glee every time Sam had hung one of them onto a branch, that nobody had had the heart to be cross with him. Even when he'd had one of his 'episodes' and hurled himself at the tree, screaming, trying to bring it down to the ground.

Resigned, Sam and her mum had started picking up the decorations that had fallen onto the pine needles the tree had already shed, as her dad had taken Ryan upstairs for his medication.

'It's great to have you back, love.'

'Oh, Mum, I can't tell you how great it is to be home.' Sam meant it.

After the Flaming Geysers had been signed by Pistol

Records, they had been dispatched on tour almost immediately, so Sam had been rattling around the house in Dalston on her own for most of the term. Of course she'd had nights out with Sienna, and spent several evenings at her luxurious new flat in Notting Hill, but Notting Hill was a long way from Dalston, and it had been pretty lonely, really. She had only ventured into college for lectures, seminars and tutorials, steering clear of the Student Union, canteen and bar. Still, she had taken advantage of the solitude at the Crack Den to throw herself into her work, and as a result was getting better grades than ever, and more and more enthusiastic praise from her tutors.

The Flaming Geysers were gaining in fame and popularity by the day, and Dan and Carlota da Silva were rarely out of the tabloids and gossip columns. They made a ridiculously glamorous couple – the rock star and the supermodel – and Sam tried to ignore the pain she felt whenever she saw a picture of them together. She knew it was her fault for blowing it with Dan – she had turned him down twice, after all. Anyway, it was far better for his image to be seen with a supermodel than with her.

Mark had called her earlier that day, and she had been surprised by how little pain she had felt in hearing *his* voice.

'Um. I want to say sorry,' he had said hesitantly. 'I was an idiot, I know that now. I miss you, Sam. I miss you like hell. Will you please give me another chance?'

Sam, lonely and sad about Dan, wavered for a second. But then she recalled the photos of Karolina Kristova that had made her feel so crap about herself.

'No, Marky, I'm sorry, I can't.' She could hear the steel in her own voice and it spurred her on. 'I can never trust you again. That girl . . . that . . . porn star tart could have been one of hundreds. Even if she was the first, she certainly wouldn't be the last. There are too many temptations in your job, and I can't live like that. I've got to get on with my own life, I've got to concentrate on my studies and get my degree. I can't be constantly wondering what you're getting up to. I don't want there to be any hard feelings, and I hope you have a nice life, but your life isn't the one for me. Happy Christmas!'

She had done a little dance as she hung up on him, knowing, without a shadow of a doubt, that she'd done the right thing.

Now she looked at the familiar view out of her old bedroom window and smiled. It was starting to snow, and she was starting to feel all warm and festive, despite the constant dull ache in her heart about Dan and Carlota. At a quarter to four, it was nearly dark and she could see the trees in people's windows twinkling merrily all the way down the suburban street.

As she gazed out, watching the snow falling faster now, the flakes fat and fluffy in the street lights, she saw somebody, a man in leathers, roaring down the road on a motorbike. It definitely wasn't a pizza delivery, or anything like that – this was an extremely expensive and cool-looking vehicle. It drew up in front of her house, and its tall, leather-clad rider dismounted. As he removed his helmet, Sam realized, with a shock of excitement, that it was Dan.

A couple of seconds later, the doorbell rang, and Sam's mum called up the stairs, 'Sam, love, you've got a visitor.'

'I'll be right down!' she shouted. She quickly checked her appearance in the mirror attached to her old Barbie pink dressing table. She was dressed comfortably in jeans, Ugg boots and a white zip-up fleece, with her dark red hair tied back in a ponytail. She looked incredibly pretty and fresh-faced, though she didn't see it quite like that herself. Oh, well, she was no competition for a supermodel, anyway. She wondered what Dan wanted.

He was standing at the bottom of the stairs, tall and dark and gorgeous in his leathers, holding his motorbike helmet in his right hand.

'Hi, Sambo.' He smiled into her eyes and her heart started to beat quickly, the way it always did when he smiled at her like that. She couldn't believe how sexy he looked, and made her feel.

'Hi, Dan. Um – why are you here?'

In response, Dan walked towards her, took her face in his hands, and started to kiss her. Oh, God, it felt so good, so right. She responded enthusiastically, her hands stroking the back of his neck, as if of their own accord.

After a few seconds, he pulled back from her, gazing into her eyes with his intense, dark green ones.

'Please don't turn me down again, Sambo. I'm a proper rock star now, you know. I've even got a motorbike.'

Sam laughed shakily at this.

'Some people would think I'm a pretty good catch.'

'But . . . but . . . What about Carlota?'

'Oh, Carlota's a great girl. She's been fun, and it was bloody brilliant for my image to be seen with her . . .'

'Yeah, I know.' Sam hadn't intended the words to sound quite so bitter.

'But it's over. It wasn't fair on her. I wasn't really that into it, and she deserves better.'

'Why?' Sam's heart was beating faster again.

'Because I couldn't get this pretty little clever clogs out of my head.'

Sam thought her heart might burst.

'Me?'

'Yes, of course you, you idiot!'

They stood there, gazing at each other for a few more seconds, in her parents' hallway, just by the front door.

'Listen, Sambo. I've got to head back up North tomorrow, for family Christmas stuff, but I don't want to leave you like this. Any chance you can come back to Dalston with me tonight?'

Sam thought for a second. She'd done all her Christmas shopping, and already wrapped the presents, which were sitting under the tree in all their shiny paper and bows.

'Try keeping me away,' she said, smiling up at him.

The ride on the motorbike through the snow had been both exhilarating, and an enormous turn-on, as she felt the throb of the engine between her legs.

Now, though, they were back in Dan's bedroom in the Crack Den. They had shed their clothes as soon as they got in, and were standing naked, kissing and groping, happy and excited beyond belief.

'I've missed you, Sambo,' said Dan, between kisses. 'God, how I've missed you.'

'I've missed you too.' Sam kissed him back with puppy-like enthusiasm. 'Are you sure you really want me, over a *supermodel*?'

'As I said, Carlota was great.' Sam didn't particularly enjoy hearing this. 'But she wasn't you.' She did enjoy hearing this.

Dan lay down on his back on the mattress on the floor, pulling Sam on top of him. Naked, he was pale and lean, but strong, with a broad chest and shoulders and those long, long legs. His cock was rock hard as she lowered herself onto it.

As Sam felt it filling her up, she gasped. Then she rode it and rode it, rocking her hips and leaning backwards, supporting herself with the tips of her fingers on his flat belly. Dan reached out to touch her pussy and she started to shake, violently.

'Oh, my God, you're beautiful,' said Dan, gazing up at her lovely young face, her back arched in ecstasy, those incredible tits; at her tiny waist and slim thighs astride his cock.

As he felt the first of her spasms, with an almighty groan, Dan came too.

'Happy Christmas Eve Eve,' said Sam after a bit.

'Ditto, you.' Dan squeezed his arms more tightly around her.

Sam thought that she was probably the luckiest girl in the world.

After a bit, Dan said, 'One thing, though. Can you please stop that bloody glamour modelling? I can look after you, and I hate to think of those disgusting photographers leching over you, all those horrible girls bitching about you.'

'I—' Sam started.

'Besides, it's a bit of a cliché for a rock star to be going out with a glamour model.' Dan leant back on the bed, his head resting on his arms.

'What, and a rock star going out with a supermodel isn't?' Sam laughed.

'Oh, all right, touché!' Dan laughed too.

'Anyway, you needn't worry. I've stopped already. Sienna finally made me realize how stubborn I was being, not to accept a loan from her. We drew up a proper contract, and I'm going to pay her back properly, in instalments and with interest, as soon as I've got a job. I've already been offered an internship over next year's summer holidays, and it would just be stupid to miss out on that because of bloody modelling.'

Dan leant over and kissed her again. 'Would you think it was really uncool if I said I loved you?'

'I'd think it was really uncool if you didn't.'

Poppy gazed at Damian's dark sleeping head, displayed to good effect against the plump pillows and crisp white sheets of their quirky little Shoreditch House bedroom. They were staying in London for a few days before going to spend Christmas with Damian's large, rowdy family in Wales. They planned to pick up Poppy's mother on Christmas Eve, after the three of them had had 'Christmas lunch' with Poppy's father in his dementia care home. It was better this way: leaving the home these days rendered him incoherent with fear, and they would make it as festive as they could, with presents and crackers and King's College Cambridge on the CD player in his room. The little details that reminded her and her mother (and to a tiny extent, they hoped, her father) of past

Christmases were probably the most heartbreaking, Poppy thought.

The Shoreditch House rooms, with cool and commendable honesty, were classed as 'Tiny', 'Small' and 'Small +', and they had gone for a 'Small+', which had a little balcony looking out over the rooftops of East London, wooden shutters and Scandinavian-inspired tongue-and-groove panelling on the walls. Everything was white, except for a raspberry-pink cashmere blanket that had fallen onto the floor as they'd slept. Feeling suddenly chilly as she saw the snow falling outside, Poppy picked it up and wrapped it around both herself and her sleeping husband.

Her heart tightened as she thought how close she'd come to losing him. She was never going to take him for granted again, that was for sure.

Poppy had been far more shaken than she'd let on about catching him snogging little Juanita. She had never had cause to be jealous of anybody or anything in her charmed life, and it wasn't an experience she relished. Finally, she'd understood how Damian must have felt when he'd had his suspicions about both Ben *and* Jack Meadows.

After finding Damian at La Hacienda, Lars and Bella had stayed on in Albuquerque for a couple of days, until Bella, missing Andy enormously, had managed to get a flight back to London. Lars was happy to drive the Cadillac back to New York, but this time was going to take the scenic route, he'd said, laughing. Poppy hoped he hadn't found it too lonely. She loved Lars to bits, and knew that she owed him one, massively.

Deciding she needed to take her wifely duties seriously,

Poppy had declared that she and Damian were going to take advantage of the New Agey nature of New Mexico, to dry out for a bit, eat healthily (God, did she need it after their revolting diet during the road trip), embark on a journey of yoga, meditation and whatever other hippy practices they could lay their hands on, and get to know one another all over again. Sober. It had worked. They had driven out into the desert, gazed at spectacular sunsets and actually talked properly for probably the first time since they'd moved to the States – Poppy having been so all-consumed with her new career, and Damian with both resentment and booze.

During one of their trips into the desert, Ben had called Poppy to tell her what had happened with Natalia. Even Damian had been impressed.

'Can I call him back?' he'd asked, once Poppy had told him about Ben's unlikely heroics, and Poppy had handed him her phone, hoping against hope that everything would be OK.

'Ben? It's Damian. I was your best friend, if you remember, before you decided to shag my wife . . .'

Oh, fuck, Poppy had thought.

'Yeah, yeah, I know she wasn't my wife at the time . . .' Pretty crass thing for Ben to be pedantic about, Poppy had thought. Clearly, Ben had realized this too, as Damian had started to smile, looking as if he was feeling a bit better about himself. 'OK, enough with the apologies. I still think you're a cunt. But I do think I should give you credit for saving Natalia's life. She's an extraordinary woman. Er – well done, mate.'

Having hung up, Damian had said to Poppy, 'You know

what? I think I want to see him now. Him, and Jack Meadows, if that can be arranged . . .?'

'Um, yes, I'm sure it can,' Poppy had said. 'Are you going to tell me why?'

'Because if everything you say is true, I want to see you with both the vain cunts, just to put my mind at rest. See what they're like around you. Surely, you can give me that, Pops?'

Of course she could give him that (she had nothing to hide, after all), and together they had driven all the way to LA – the originally intended final destination.

And they'd all got on just fine. It was obvious to Damian that Ben was completely besotted with Natalia. And now that he wasn't blinded by jealousy, he could see that Jack was a thoroughly decent sort of chap, too. If he'd fancied Poppy to start with (and who could blame him, really?), he now did seem to respect the fact that she was off-limits as a married woman. And Filthy and Heather, Jack's parents, had welcomed him with open arms, which had been bloody brilliant, he'd had to admit. Filthy Meadows was a legend, after all.

Now Poppy's phone rang from the white-painted wicker bedside table.

JACK MEADOWS came up on the screen. She didn't know any other Jacks, but it was pretty fucking cool to have a film star stored in her contacts list. Surely anybody, given half the chance, would have stored him under his full name?

'Hey, Poppy,' he started.

'Hey, Jack. Um . . . does this mean you've read it?' She looked at the time on her phone: 9.35 a.m. It was half-past one in the morning in LA.

'I've read it, and I love it! In fact, I couldn't put it down, which is why I'm calling you at this ungodly hour.' Poppy could hear him smiling down the phone. 'Can I speak to Damian now?'

'Oh, my God, that's amazing! Yes, wait a sec, I'll just wake him up . . .'

At the other end of the phone, Jack laughed as he heard Poppy trying to rouse her husband.

'Darling, darling, sweetheart, darling, wake up, wake up, wake up, you've got a phone call . . .'

'Urgh . . .?' Damian opened his eyes groggily.

'Just take the call!' Impatiently, Poppy shoved her phone at him.

Unbeknownst to her husband, she'd given Jack a photocopy of Damian's screenplay, under the condition that if he thought it was rubbish it must never be mentioned again. She had just known that Damian wouldn't have agreed to her helping like that, but thought that he might, just about, accept it as a *fait accompli*.

'What?' Damian said, sitting up naked in the pink-and-white bed. 'She did *what*?'

Poppy decided not to look at him until he'd heard Jack out. She got out of bed and stared out at the snow, falling even more thickly now, giving Damian a good view of her perfect little bottom.

After hanging up, Damian walked over to Poppy and put his arms around her from behind, resting his chin on her shiny blonde head.

'You went behind my back and showed my screenplay to Jack Meadows . . .' he started slowly.

'Oh, don't be cross; please, don't be cross,' Poppy babbled,

375

turning round to face him. But as she did she saw that his face was wreathed in smiles.

'He loves it, Pops! He loves it! He wants to turn it into a major motion picture! He has huge clout with the studios – everything he touches turns to gold. Just think . . . Jack Meadows starring in *my* movie!'

Poppy thought that now wasn't the time to remind him that he'd once referred to Jack as a 'gobshite son-of-a-rock-star twat'. Instead, she jumped up and down, clapping and laughing. 'Yippee, yippee, yippee!'

'Does this mean I'm forgiven?' she asked, after a bit.

'You've got a bloody nerve, young lady; but, yes, this time I'd say you're forgiven.'

And Damian took his wife by the hand and led her back to bed.

In another hotel room the other side of town, Ben and Natalia were just stirring.

Ben had booked the ridiculously decadent and romantic Round Bed room in the Portobello Hotel, the one where Johnny Depp had shared a champagne bath with Kate Moss. The muslin-draped bed was indeed round, and an antique Victorian bathing machine, equipped with all manner of intriguing-looking hosing devices, took pride of place in the open-plan en suite bathroom.

'Hello, Mr Movie Star,' said Natalia, smiling lazily.

'Hello, Ms Beautiful.'

Ben leant over and started to kiss her. Her lips parted and soon they were writhing about together, each lost in the other's warm, human, sexual self. Natalia ran her hand through Ben's silky hair, then let it drift down his beautifully muscled body until she found his cock. Already, there was a tiny droplet of semen on the end of it.

'Oh, God,' she whispered, using it to moisten her finger-tips and run them up and down the shaft. 'Oh, my God.' She still couldn't believe that this beautiful, beautiful man was all hers.

Ben moaned, pushing her back onto the bed so he could play with her breasts and kiss her nipples, which were now stiff and sensitive to even the merest whisper of wind. He nipped one with his teeth and she gasped again.

'Oh, Ben . . .' Natalia tried to reach for his cock again, but he drew away from her, smiling into her eyes.

'Wait, my darling. Just wait. It'll be worth it.'

And very slowly he leant over and kissed her again. Soon they were kissing and kissing, rolling around in the expensive sheets, their hands roaming over one another's bodies until they'd both reached fever pitch. Natalia was so wet that when Ben slid his fingers inside her he stopped for a second.

Raising himself up on his arms to look her straight in the eye, he said, 'Do you want me as much as I think you do, Nat? Do you want me as much as I taste you do?' He raised his right hand, keeping himself propped up on his left arm, and licked his fingers with relish.

Natalia looked him straight back in the eye with her clear grey-blue gaze.

'Oh, yes.'

'Do you want to taste how much you want me?'

'Oh, yes.'

So Ben put his slippery fingers into her mouth, and she

sucked and sucked and sucked. Her cunt was throbbing, desperate for release.

'My God, you're beautiful,' said Ben. Her features were more feline than ever, eyes half closed, high cheekbones emphasized by the fact that she was sucking his fingers with such abandon.

Gently, he removed his fingers from her mouth and walked over to the roll-top bathing machine.

'I think it's about time this was put to good use,' he said, turning on the taps and pouring in some of the wonderful smelly stuff that the Portobello Hotel had so thoughtfully provided. Soon the room was steamy and hot with jasmine, ylang ylang and honeysuckle.

Natalia, lying dishevelled on the round bed, looked at Ben's perfectly put-together body and laughed. He could have been sculpted by Michelangelo.

'What's so funny? This was meant to be romantic.' Ben was half joking. 'Have I done something wrong?'

'Oh, no no no, my darling. Everything is right. I am laughing because I cannot believe how happy I am.'

He walked back to the bed and picked her up. Her long, slender limbs were dangling over his and she laughed again.

'Oh, Mr Movie Star, you treat me like princess.'

'That's because you are my princess,' said Ben as he lowered her into the steamy, scented water. He kissed her again for added emphasis.

'Please, you must get in with me.'

'No, I thought I'd just stand here and look at you,' said Ben, climbing in to join her.

Natalia laughed again. She couldn't believe how much

laughter there was in her life, now. After Ben had saved her from drowning on Bottle Beach, they had returned to London, and reported Georgiou for his blackmail. He had been arrested, and a super-injunction imposed by the courts.

Now, Ben poured some more of the expensive gel into his palm and lathered it up against her shoulders, until they were covered in smooth, silky bubbles. He was looking at her face all the while.

'You are everything I've ever wanted,' he said.

Tears came into Natalia's eyes. 'You are more than I ever could have dreamed possible,' she replied.

They kissed for a long time in the steamy, scented water, until Natalia pulled away. She had a mischievous look about her.

'So what shall we do with these?' She picked up one of the intriguing-looking hosing devices.

By the time they had finished, half the water in the bath was on the floor and they were both flushed, panting and utterly spent. The words 'post-coital bliss' would have done their state of being an injustice.

Ben got out of the bath and held out a large, fluffy towel for Natalia to wrap herself up in.

'Hmmm, you look after me so well,' she said, kissing him again as he gently rubbed her down. 'But what is the time? I do not want to be late for your friends.'

'They're your friends as much as mine,' said Ben, kissing her again. 'Probably more so now, considering.'

They had arranged to meet Poppy, Damian, Bella and Andy at the Cow, a lovely, cosy pub just around the corner from their hotel, for pre-Christmas drinks and lunch before they all went back home to their respective families. Ben was taking Natalia to meet the folks in Wales, and was looking forward enormously to showing off his Hitchcock blonde. Besotted as he was, it hadn't occurred to him that his mother might not take too kindly to this older woman with a definitely suspect past getting her claws into her beautiful, beloved boy; but thereby hangs another tale.

Within half an hour, Natalia had got herself ready. After her brief flirtation with hippy-chic on Bottle Beach, she had reverted to the look with which she was most comfortable: über glamour. Not many women, Ben thought, could carry off white suede cigarette pants. She had teamed them with sky-high Louboutin ankle boots, an ice-blue cashmere polo-necked sweater and a chignon that wouldn't have looked out of place on Grace Kelly.

Ben himself was successfully rocking the clean-cut preppy look in immaculately faded jeans under a navy-blue knee-length cashmere coat with a cashmere scarf draped around his neck.

'Oh, my God!' said Natalia as she turned around from perfecting her *maquillage*. 'You look just like Robert Redford in that movie –' She drew from her vast internal movie Rolodex – '*Barefoot in the Park*.'

'Not such a hideous comparison.' Ben smiled. 'I'm happy with old Bob Redford. How do you feel about Grace Kelly?'

'Grace Kelly?' Natalia smiled at him in the mirror. 'Yes, I think I am happy with that too.'

Bella and Andy were walking hand-in-hand down Portobello Road, both smiling from frozen ear to frozen ear. Bella was wearing a short white coat over a short caramel-coloured skirt over chocolate brown woolly tights underneath darker brown suede boots. Her long dark hair was flecked with snowflakes and her cheeks were flushed pink, glowing in the cold. The appealing coffee-and-cream effect was not lost on the Santa-hat-wearing stall-holders, who shouted out to her: 'Happy Christmas, beautiful!' and, 'You're a lucky man, sir,' to Andy.

'You don't know just how lucky!' he shouted back, tightening his arm around Bella's waist and kissing her freshly washed brown hair.

They walked past Christmas trees of vastly differing shapes and sizes, standing for sale on the street, snow quickly settling on their outstretched branches. Other stalls were selling mulled wine, mistletoe, holly, ivy and festive wreaths, and the snow seemed to have affected everybody with seasonal bonhomie.

'Merry Christmas!'

'Happy Christmas, darlin', have a good one!'

Everywhere they looked, people were being nice to each other (which made a wonderful change from all the stuff they were reading in the papers or seeing on the news on a daily basis).

A lone woman with a steel drum had started to sing about chestnuts roasting, and her voice was so exceptionally beautiful that she'd already drawn quite a crowd.

'Oh, isn't this just lovely?' Bella looked up at Andy, her face aglow.

'I can't think of anything lovelier,' said Andy, kissing her again. Then he stopped, right in the middle of

Portobello Road, took off his glasses and really, properly, kissed her.

'I love you so much. Thank you for making my life complete.'

The only thing Bella could do was kiss him back.

The snow was falling more heavily as they turned onto Westbourne Park Road, chatting excitedly about things. As they got a bit nearer to the Cow, Andy said, pointing at a couple about to enter the pub,

'Isn't that Natalia? And . . . Ben?'

He wondered how Bella was going to feel about seeing the man who had broken her heart by shagging her best friend. He also slightly wondered how *he* would feel about seeing the bastard again, though he did have more respect for him now. The fact that he had saved Natalia's life was pretty impressive, even by his standards.

Bella laughed. So many more important things had happened since she had been with Ben, and she was hugely intrigued to see how he and Natalia interacted with one another, after everything Poppy had told her.

'Yeah, definitely looks like them. What a glamorous couple they make.' Though it was hard to tell from this distance, it looked as though Natalia was wearing a floor-length silver fur coat (fox? mink?) over cripplingly high heels on which she manoeuvred her way through the snow with absolute confidence.

A cab pulled up beside them, and one of its passengers jumped out.

'Belles!' cried Poppy, flinging her arms around her. 'Happy Christmas!' Clad in a bright red duffle coat over skinny jeans, with a matching scarlet woolly pompom hat pulled down low over her silky blonde hair, she looked about 12. 'We've got some wonderful news!'

Damian, getting out of the cab behind her, laughed and said, 'Hi, Bella, hi, Andy. She does get overexcited, doesn't she?'

'It's actually quite endearing,' said Andy, smiling. He felt he might smile forever.

'I know. Lucky for her she's so pretty,' said Damian, and Andy laughed, feeling none of the usual resentment from his erstwhile professional rival.

'Shhh, you boys, I want to hear Poppy's wonderful news,' said Bella, looking at Andy out of the corner of her eye.

'Actually, it's not my news, it's Damian's,' said Poppy. 'Jack Meadows wants to use his screenplay and turn it into a MAJOR MOTION PICTURE!'

'*What?*' Whatever Bella had been expecting, it wasn't this. 'Oh, my God, you're going to be so rich!' A couple passing them on the street looked at her oddly, and it crossed her mind that her comment didn't quite chime with the spirit of Christmas. It was what they were all thinking, though. 'Oh, Damian, well done, I'm so pleased for you.' There were more hugs all round. 'So will you be moving to LA?'

'Well, yeah, I've got to go there anyway for *Poppy Takes LA*,' interrupted Poppy, chattering away like a magpie, while the two men raised eyebrows at one another, laughing. 'It's all worked out brilliantly.'

And they all carried on towards the pub, the two girls in front talking nineteen to the dozen.

'You must be over the moon,' said Andy, shaking Damian's hand. 'Well done.'

'Thanks, mate. Yes, I am,' said Damian, shaking back. 'Only just heard this morning and it hasn't quite sunk in yet.'

'I can imagine.'

'And congratulations to *you* on breaking that story about the people traffickers. That has to have been the scoop of the century!' Now that Damian was on the verge of proper success, he could allow himself to be gracious about other writers' triumphs.

'Thank you.' Andy smiled. 'I'm just really glad that we managed to stop him before he could ruin any more lives.'

They had reached the pub now, its tiny old-fashioned exterior festooned with Christmas garlands and foliage, its warm, welcoming interior glowing through the windows.

Poppy pushed open the door, and they all followed her in.

Ben and Natalia had managed to bag the table closest to the door, the large, square one that was big enough to seat them all comfortably. Ben and Natalia's very presence made the cool little pub look like a movie set.

They jumped up and there ensued another flurry of hugs, greetings and Christmas wishes.

When Bella moved round to greet Ben they both paused slightly, as neither of them knew quite how to react to the other. Then Bella opened her arms and, smiling, said,

'Happy Christmas, you treacherous bastard.'

Ben laughed and gave her a hug.

'Happy Christmas to you too. Does this mean bygones can be bygones?'

Bella nodded. 'Thank you,' he whispered in her ear. 'And sorry for everything. I have to say you're looking *great*!'

Bella smiled. Some things never changed.

'OK, so who wants champagne?' asked Poppy. 'We're celebrating!'

'Why?' asked Ben and Natalia in unison.

'Your buddy Jack wants to make a movie out of my screenplay!' Damian grinned at Ben.

'Oh, mate, that's brilliant!' Ben's delight was genuine and he enveloped his former best friend in a huge man hug. Poppy and Bella smiled soppily at each other. 'Hmmm, I wonder if he needs a supporting actor?'

'Oy, don't push your luck,' said Damian, and everybody laughed.

Once they were all sitting down with their drinks, Poppy noticed that Bella was drinking mineral water.

'*What?*' She looked from Bella to Andy, her eyes sparkling. 'Belles, I don't think I've known you order a non-alcoholic drink in a pub since . . . well, since we started going to pubs! Does this mean what I think it might mean?'

Bella laughed, ignoring the feeling of pure joy bubbling up inside her.

'What? That I've joined AA and about time too?' Everybody laughed at this, a bit more than Bella found necessary, as it happened.

'Come on, you know what I mean . . .' Poppy's head was tilted to one side as she gazed up at her friend expectantly.

'God, you do jump to conclusions, Pops. I'm on antibiotics. Pain in the arse just before Christmas, but I want to get rid of this bloody cold before going home. I need to be feeling better than I do now to cope with my family over "the holiday season", as they insist on calling it in the

States. Mum and Bernie, Dad and his latest (whoever she may be), Max and Dave, mad Auntie Charlotte and her motorbike . . .'

'Yes, last year's was unlike any Christmas I've ever known.' Andy laughed. 'You need crazy stamina to keep up.'

'And Mum and Dad are bound to end up bickering about *something*,' added Bella, downing her mineral water and wishing it was champagne. 'You'd think they could manage to stay civil in each other's company at least *once* a year . . .'

'Oh, bugger, silly me with my wishful thinking.' Poppy laughed. 'Poor you, not being able to drink today though.' She looked at Bella beadily and Bella looked away from her. 'Oh, well. Let's just toast all of us again, and the fact that we're all together again.' She raised her glass and looked around at the happy, smiling faces.

'To love and friendship!'

'Love and friendship!'

'And enormous commercial success!' added Damian.

Back in her flat later that day, Bella was lying on the chaise longue with her feet propped up on Andy's lap, looking and feeling like the cat that got the cream.

'Why did you change your mind about telling them?' asked Andy, who was massaging her feet.

'A couple of reasons. Partly the tempting fate thing – excited though I am, I'm starting to think that it would be better to wait till we've got the twelve-week all-clear.'

Andy laughed. 'God knows how you'll be able to pull

it off around Poppy, bloody little bloodhound. You can't be on antibiotics for another whole month.'

'Oh, I'll probably tell Pops anyway. The whole public announcement thing just suddenly seemed a bit premature, I suppose.'

'Yes, I agree,' said Andy, and they were both silent for a moment, offering up an internal prayer that their baby was going to be fine. 'OK, so what was your other reason?'

'Didn't want to take the limelight away from Damian. This screenplay is a huge deal for him . . .'

'You sweet girl.' Andy leant over and kissed her tummy. 'I hope our baby has your lovely nature.'

'God, I don't! Self-pitying, jealous, insecure . . . Wouldn't wish that on the poor little bugger. I hope he or she is exactly like you.'

'What, pompous and a slave to its tiresome principles?'

'Well it wouldn't be such a bad thing if those particular traits skipped a generation or two . . .'

Andy laughed and again leant over to kiss her.

'Another cup of tea?'

'Thanks, darling. I've got a feeling I'm going to get extremely bored with herbal tea over the next seven months . . .'

Andy went into the kitchen and Bella hugged her knees up to her chest.

A baby. Their very own baby. She still could hardly believe it. How grown up. How incredibly exciting. And how unutterably wonderful it was going to be to create a new person that they would love forever, out of their love for one another (it looked as though the conception had probably been in Paris).

Bella's head was full of distinctly impractical dreams of eco-friendly terry-towelling nappies and embroidered smocks and hanging fresh washing out on a line somewhere it would dry beautifully in the sun, when her phone beeped with a text.

It was Poppy.

*I know you're up the duff, Belles! Antibiotics never stop you drinking. I promise not to tell anyone, but congratulations! I'm so so happy for you! Namewise I suggest Poppy if she's a girl or Paris (just a guess) if he's a boy. Love you!*
*xxxxxxxxx*

'God that woman's got a nerve,' said Andy, reading over Bella's shoulder. 'Can we veto those two names immediately? One Poppy in our life is more than enough. And Paris? Does she think we're the Beckhams or something?'

Bella laughed.

'But do tell her that she and Damian can be godparents, if they want . . .'

'Oh, they'd love that! Thanks, darling . . .'

'It would set Junior up for life if Damian starts to earn as much as I think Hollywood screenwriters earn.'

Bella looked at him, smiling. 'You know what, I think that is possibly the least noble thing you've ever said in your life.'

Andy smiled back at her.

'I've never had a child before. I can quite honestly say,

my love, that when it comes to our baby, *bugger my tiresome principles!*'

'Bugger your tiresome principles.' Bella laughed, overwhelmed by happiness.

Andy kissed her. And then he kissed her tummy again.

# Acknowledgments

To my fantastic agent, Annabel Merullo at PFD, for enabling me to do what I've always wanted to do, and the amazing Laura Williams, for your constant support and dedication beyond the call of duty (I didn't really expect you to respond to that Sunday night email immediately!).

Sarah Ritherdon, my brilliant editor, for being right – yet again! – the blood, sweat and tears behind the enormous rewrite were definitely worth it in the end; Kate, Elinor, Hannah, Alice and the rest of the team at HarperCollins for all your hard work behind the scenes.

My wonderful friends and family (especially the Mafioso team of cousins!), for being such fabulous promoters of *Revelry*. At times I've felt overwhelmed by all your love and support.

And, as always, to Andy. For having the patience of a saint combined with the culinary ability of Michel Roux; for making me laugh, keeping me sane, and just for being you.

# Coming in
# November
# 2013

# TREACHERY

## By
# Lucy Lord

Find out where it all began ...

# Revelry

## One crazy summer changes everything.

Can you ever have too much of a good thing?
And what happens when a friend breaks the
one rule that should never be broken?

Poppy, Bella and their friends live life to the full,
spending the summer having as much fun as
they possibly can – from the hedonistic escapades
of Ibiza to doing Glastonbury in style.

But living life to the max can push friendships to the
limit and amongst the laughter come tears, betrayal
and backstabbing. When one devastating decision
threatens to bring it all crashing down, Bella is forced
to question whether her lifelong friendship has been
broken beyond repair ...